AMBER
&
CLAY

AMBER

&

CLAY

LAURA AMY SCHLITZ

WITH ILLUSTRATIONS BY
JULIA IREDALE

THORNDIKE PRESS
A part of Gale, a Cengage Company

**LIBRARY OF CONGRESS CIP DATA ON FILE.
CATALOGUING IN PUBLICATION FOR THIS BOOK
IS AVAILABLE FROM THE LIBRARY OF CONGRESS.**

ISBN-13: 978-1-4328-8827-5 (hardcover alk. paper)

Published in 2021 by arrangement with Candlewick Press

Printed in Mexico
Print Number: 01   Print Year: 2022

For Stephen Barbara
LAS

For Ryan
JI

CAST OF CHARACTERS

⊓⅂⅂⊓⅂⅂⊓⅂⅂⊓⅂⅂⊓⅂⅂

THESSALY

Alexidemus's Household

ALEXIDEMUS a rich man

GALENE wife of Alexidemus

MENON elder son of Alexidemus

LYKOS second son of Alexidemus

THUCYDIDES younger brother of Alexidemus

TYCHO son of Thucydides

TIMAEUS son of Thucydides

RHASKOS THE THRACIAN, later known as THRAX, later known as PYRRHOS an enslaved boy

MEDA, later known as THRATTA an enslaved woman; a nurse; mother of Rhaskos

7

GEORGIOS an enslaved man; a stable master

DEMETRIOS an enslaved man; in charge of the storeroom

ATHENS

Arkadios's Household

ARKADIOS a rich man; a citizen

LYSANDRA wife of Arkadios

MELISTO daughter of Arkadios

SOSIAS an enslaved man; head of the household slaves

THRATTA, previously known as MEDA an enslaved woman; a nurse

TAKIS son of Arkadios

Phaistus's Household

PHAISTUS a potter; a freedman

ZOSIMA wife of Phaistus

KRANAOS an enslaved man; a master potter

PYRRHOS, previously known as THRAX, previously known as RHASKOS an enslaved boy

GRAU, later called PHOIBE a donkey

8

MARKOS a citizen; protector of Phaistus

ANYTUS a friend of Menon

SOKRATES a philosopher
ALKIBIADES a friend of Sokrates
SIMON a cobbler; friend of Sokrates
ARISTOKLES, nicknamed PLATO a friend of Sokrates
KRITO a friend of Sokrates
APOLLODORUS a friend of Sokrates

BRAURON

KORINNA a priestess of Artemis
ELPIS a Little Bear

MOUNT OLYMPUS

HERMES bringer of dreams and king of schemes; crafter of lyres and sometimes of lies; protector of travelers, tricksters, and thieves; the luck bringer; god of the golden wand

ARTEMIS goddess of childbirth; protector of youth

9

HEPHAISTOS maker of beautiful things; god of fire

ATHENA goddess of wisdom, war, and craft; defender of cities; the she-dragon; the victory giver

10

ΡΑΣΚΟΣ Ο ΘΡΑΞ
ΓΡΑΦΕΙΝ ΔΙΔΑΣΧΩ
ΕΣΠΟΤΗΣ ΕΜΟΥ
ΧΙΤΩΝ ΡΑΓΕΙΣΑΝ
ΤΑ ΓΡΑΜΜΑΤΑ ΔΙΔΑΣΚ
ΑΛΦΑ ΒΗΤΑ ΓΑΜΜΑ ΔΕΛΤΑ
ΣΩΚΡΑΤΗΣ ΜΙΜΝΗΣΚΟΜΑΙ
ΗΝ ΦΙΛΟΣ ΕΜΟΣ ΕΦΗ
ΕΙ ΣΥ ΤΟΝ ΒΙΟΝ ΜΗ ΦΡΟΝΤΙΖΗΣ
ΤΟΥΤΟ ΟΥΚ ΑΝ ΕΣΤΙΝ ΩΣ ΑΝΗΡ ΖΟΤΗ
ΕΓΩ ΜΑΙ ΠΟΤΕ ΑΝΗΡ
ΟΥΚΕΤΙ ΔΟΥΛΟΣ
ΕΛΕΥΘΕΡΟΣ
ΤΙΜΗΣ
ΓΡΑΦ
ΦΡΟΝΤΙΔΕΣ ΕΜΟΥ ΟΥΚΕΠ
ΑΦΑΝΗ
ΕΙΜΙ ΡΑΣΚΟΣ Ο ΘΡ
ΓΡΑΦΕΙΝ ΔΙΔΑΣΚ
ΣΩΚΡΑΤΗΝ ΜΙΜΝΗΣ
ΤΟΥΣ ΙΠΠΟΥΣ ΓΡΑΦΕΙΝ ΔΥΝΑΜΑΙ
ΕΙΔΩΛΟΝ ΕΟΡΑΚΑ
ΑΡΚΤΩ ΣΥΝΕΧΟΡΕΥΣΑ
ΕΝ ΤΟΙΣ ΟΡΕΣΙ ΥΜΕΤΤΟΥ

EXHIBIT 1

Ostracon, or fragment of a broken pot, circa 400 BCE,
found in the marketplace of Athens.

The letters scratched on the clay are unevenly formed, suggesting that the writer was learning to write. Though many words are missing, what remains is remarkable. Some scholars have interpreted lines 10 –11 to mean "I will be a free man someday. I will no longer be a slave." If this is so, the inscription gives us a unique example of a Greek enslaved person expressing himself in writing.

Still more extraordinary is the writer's assertion that he knew Sokrates and the reference to Sokrates's famous saying "The unexamined life is not worth living." A few art historians have been tempted to identify Rhaskos the Thracian as the "Horse Painter" responsible for the famous red-figure vases in the British Museum. While this is an appealing theory, there is little evidence to support it.

Translation .....*Rhaskos the Thracian.*
I am learning to write

My master...............broken pot
...............learn my letters:
alpha, beta, gamma, delta...
I remember Sokrates.
He was my friend. He said
if you don't think about your
    life
that's no life for a man.
I.......be a.....man someday.
......no longer....slave.
.........free.
...will remember........
....write.......
My thoughts....no longer...
    invisible.

I am Rhaskos the Th......
....learning to write
................ember Sokrates.
I can draw horses.
I have seen a ghost.
.....danced with a bear in the
    mountains of Hymettus.

HERMES SPEAKS

Hermes here. The Greek god —
No. Don't put down the book —
    I'm talking to you. If the lines look
    like poetry,
        relax. This book is shorter than it looks.

I am Hermes,
    a Greek god,
        young, fleet-footed, good-looking:
Note my winged sandals,
    my cloak, my crooked hat —
I'm the Jack that slays the giant,
        Bringer of dreams and king of schemes,
        The crafter of lyres and sometimes of
    lies.

15

Protector of travelers, tricksters, and
thieves.
Also, communication:
poetry, picture books, opera, the
internet,
television, smoke signals,
whispers in the night.
It's all my territory. I hear it *all*.

—What am I doing here?
I assure you, I go everywhere —
I can soar above Olympus
or dive to the deeps of the
underworld,
talk to the dead and come out quick —
that's a pun. *Quick* means *alive*,
or used to. Which reminds me:
I bring you a story that tells
of the quick and the dead:
the tale of a girl as precious as
amber,
the tale of a boy as common as clay.
The meaning, the moral,
is up to you. We gods swap stories,
but you are the ones

who divine what they mean.
I think because you suffer. We gods don't.
We think pain
 is overrated. We watch you
 the way you watch television. If you
   make us laugh —
 and believe me,
   you *do* —
   we adore that.
If you make us cry, so much the better.
That's a good show. But we don't lose
 sleep over your suffering,
   or puzzle over what it means.
   You poor mortals, you want to
     know *why*.
   We gods don't suffer, so we don't
     care *why*.

Where was I? This story: two children. A
 boy, Rhaskos, and a girl, Melisto,
   plus a bully, a wise man, and a bear.
   Wait!
I've thought of something else:
   A tale I stole from a playwright!
   It may shed light on our story:

17

Long ago.
In the beginning.
Every person was two people,
    gummed together like a globe. Belly
      to belly!
        Four legs, four arms,
        twenty fingers, twenty toes!
They could flip and turn cartwheels,
    a riot to watch:
They could curl like waves,
    creep like spiders,
    and climb like monkeys,
    double-quick, and so wise . . .
    (two heads are better than one!)

—Wait. Did I mention the sex thing?
    Most of them
        were male *and* female:
        hermaphrodite
        (the word comes from Aphrodite,
        my sister,
        and also from Hermes — that's
        me).
    but some were two men or two
    women . . .

Either way, they were priceless,
 those fabulous, two-for-one
 twins!
The only thing was, they were bound to
 make trouble —
 plucky and puckish and proud to
 boot.
And Zeus, my father, doesn't like trouble,

 so *he* decided
to chop them in two.

(That's another thing. We Greek gods
 are not known for our tender hearts.)

So! He sliced up the twins as you'd cut up
 an apple,
 cutting their power in half.
And ever since,
 people have been lonely:
"Where's my twin? What happened to my
 old self,
 my other half?"
The men who'd been fastened to women,
 chased women.

19

The men who'd been fastened to men,
   chased men . . .
      and so forth. We watched. It was
      amusing.

It's *still* amusing. All that panting and
   longing,
      and loving and losing. Dear child,
      somewhere in the world is your
         missing piece,
      and you're going to spend your life
         trying to find her
      or him, as the case may be. I wish
         you good hunting.
      I wish you good luck.

The children I spoke of before were like that.
      They weren't alike, but they fit
         together,
      like lock and key. The boy, Rhaskos,
         was a slave boy. Unlucky at first.
         A Thracian boy — (Thrace is
            north of Greece)
         — redheaded, nervy, neglected.
         A clever boy who was taught he
            was stupid.

A beautiful boy whose mother
   scarred him with a knife.

The girl, Melisto, started life lucky.
      A rich man's daughter, and a
         proper Greek.
      Owl-eyed Melisto: a born fighter,
         prone to tantrums, hating the
            loom.
      A wild girl, chosen by Artemis,
      and lucky, as I said before —
         except for one thing: she died
            young.

This is their story. When it's over, if you
   like,
      you can tell me what it means.

Rhaskos in Thessaly

1. Honey

I wonder if I speak aloud —
    can my words reach you?
It's been over a year since you spoke to
  me —
You and Sokrates: I lost you both
    the same month. I think of him, too;
        but you're the one I want to tell.
I want you to hear me remember.

Sokrates taught me:
    if you don't think about your life,
    that's no life for a man.
I've tried to write my story,
    but writing's slow,

and Sokrates said
    written words can't be trusted.
    When you read,
you can't ask questions. You have to
    ask questions.
Those are the most important things:
    to remember;
    to ask questions.

My memories are like my drawings.
Some are no good. I mean —
    when I used to draw in the dirt,
    the line was fat and blurred,
    and you couldn't tell what the picture
    was.
Now I draw on clay with a knife,
    and my lines are sharp. Clear. Detailed.
Some of my memories are like that.
The early ones are blurred.

I was born in Thessaly,
    a land known for witchcraft,
        horses,
    and meadows rich with grain.

23

I belonged to Alexidemus,
  a rich man. He had wide pastures,
  and swift-stepping horses,
  but no witches, as far as I know.
My mother was his slave.

My mother watched the children of the
 household.
   She was their nurse.
   There was a whole flock of us.
We played in the courtyard:
  an olive tree, good for climbing,
  a grapevine, an altar, a flock of geese.

Lykos was the oldest of us,
His cousin Timaeus was the baby.
I wasn't allowed in the house,
  and I ate what the others didn't want:
   the rind of the cheese,
   the crust of the bread,
   radishes. Lykos never ate his
    radishes —
  but I liked radishes. I never went
   hungry.
My mother gave me food off her plate.

This was before my mother left.
I was three, four, five years old.

I was a warlike child.
My mother was a Thracian woman,
    and the Thracians are warriors.
Lykos and I wrestled every day.
He was older and taller,
    but I was strong for my age.
My mother let us fight it out.

My mother had red hair, like mine,
    Thracian hair.
She was a slave, so her hair was cropped
    short,
    but I found her beautiful.
She was tall, not meek.
She was born free. The Thracian women
    are free
        until they marry. My mother used to
        walk
        on the shore of the Black Sea,
            free
        but one day raiders came. They
        kidnapped her.

They wronged her
    and made her a slave.
Once I asked if we could go back to
  Thrace,
    and she said no. She was ashamed.
She said we could never go home.

But she told me about Thrace.
Her father owned horses, precious horses.
    Once he dined at the banquet of a king
    and drank from a golden cup.

She told me those stories at night.
We shared a stall in the horse-barn.
    That part I remember: the sounds in
      the dark:
      the straw rustling; a long snort,
      the thud of a hoof.
    My mother taught me Thracian words,
      tales of the gods,
    and how to count. She was proud of
      me.
In the summer, she took water from the
  horse-trough
    and made me wash.

In the courtyard, she favored the others.
  She held Timaeus in her arms
    and bounced him till I burned
      with jealousy.
  When she took the others into the house
    and put them to bed,
  I stayed in the courtyard, staring up
    at the windows.
  She sang lullabies to them.
  I picked up the heaviest rocks I could
    find
      and threw them as hard as I could.
She was *my* mother. Not theirs. *Mine.*

But as soon as the others slept,
  she came back outside.
She swept me up on her shoulders
    and I rode her like a horse. I dug my
      heels into her
    and clicked my tongue —
    she gripped my ankles
    and we galloped.

Once we were in the barn, she held me in
  her lap.

27

She squeezed my feet.
I kissed her. Sometimes I bit her.
She said I was her warrior-boy, her little
    Thracian,
        better than all the others.
We slept curled up together.

There was one night —
        I don't know how she knew —
        but the storeroom was left
            unguarded.
It was a moonlit night: I remember that.
        The sky was pale, and the stars were
            dim.
        We stole over the grass without a sound,
            and opened the door by inches.
There was no one but us.
She took a loaf, split it, and poured oil
    over the bread.
She opened a jar of crystallized honey.
She showed me how to dig into it
        and take out a great knob,
            which I sucked off my fingers
        slowly, making it last.
My time with my mother was like that,

golden and secret
and over too soon.

2. Horse

This I remember clearly: we were playing
   a game:
  Lykos's game: he called it
  Do-What-I-Do.
He circled the courtyard,
  arms like wings.
  We panted to keep up.
  He grabbed a branch of the olive tree —
  Some boys couldn't reach that branch,
   but I could. We swung, kicking
    our feet,
   jumped down, took off:
    whirling like leaves, darting and
     scampering,
    following Lykos the leader,
    hopping on one foot, crossing
     the courtyard —
   into the shadowy house.

I don't know where my mother was that
   day.

She would have stopped us.

It was cool inside, the shutters drawn.
I wasn't allowed in there.
Even Lykos, the master's son,
      wasn't allowed in the *andron*.
That was the best room in the house.
It was for the men, for drinking parties.
There were couches along the walls,
      Lykos scrambled up on one:
      "Do what I do!" Then he leapt
         from couch to couch —
      they were strung with rope, those
      couches,
         cushioned with sheepskins,
         loose and springy.
         He slipped
         skidded
         onto his bottom. That meant
      we all had to slip.
      We were
         bouncing
         and falling,
         leaping,

30

shrieking with laughter,
trespassing,
asking for trouble.
That just shows how little we were.
We didn't know when to shut up.

Then I caught my breath
struck dumb.

A wonder before my eyes: a horse on the
wall.
A whole horse, large enough to ride,
and it was flying.
You could see the wind ruffle its mane,
the sinewy legs pranced, the
nostrils flared;
and it had wings,
luminous
spread like the wings of a
swan.

The beauty of that horse was supernatural,
and all around it was the sky,
dazzling blue, with winds and
clouds.

31

The horse kept galloping,
  galloping,
  soundless
  staying in one place.

You're thinking I was stupid.
  But I wasn't. I'd lived all my life in
    the barn.
    I'd never seen a *picture*.
  And the man who painted that horse
    must have been like a god.
  He knew how to draw legs, and set
    them in motion,
      how to make wings that fanned
        the blue air,
      how to paint the moist glint
      in a horse's eye.

I had to get up close —
    this impossible thing.
I had to touch it.
I stood on the couch
    and pressed my hands against the
    horse.
I thought it would be warm. I thought I'd
  feel the muscles

32

under the shining skin.
But the wall was cool and rough.

There was a cry. Galene —
　　the master's wife, mistress of the house
　　　　—

stood in the doorway. She screamed at us.
　　The others scattered.
　　　　She seized me by the arm,
　　　　yanked me off the couch,
　　　　　　and slapped me so hard
　　　　　　my head swam.

　　　　　　　　　　"I've told Alexi —
I won't have that slave brat in the house!"

Slave brat.
I fled. I raced for the courtyard, the olive
　　tree;
　　　　I scurried up like a squirrel.
　　　　My mind was cut in half.
One half echoed: *Slave brat. Slave brat.*

The other half-mind was fixed on that
　　horse.
I wanted to see it again.

33

3. Knife

This memory is blurred,
    painted with a dark glaze.

My mother: standing in the doorway of
    the barn —
        the light behind her. Twilight.
            The air smelled of thunder. She was
            holding a knife
        and a bowl of ashes.
There was dread in her face. She told me
    she was going to cut
        marks on my arms. Tattoos. The
        Thracians wear tattoos.
She warned me: it would hurt —

I was afraid of the knife.
    I said so. I said *no*.
She moved quickly. Next thing I
    remember
        I was flat on my back
            struggling —
                She was pinning me down,
                her knee on my chest

gripping my wrist,
holding my arm   so she could cut.
　　I screamed. She was rough. Her
　　　hand shook. She hissed
hold still! She was doing a thing
　　　　she feared to do
　　　and she wanted to get it done.
Even in the dim,
　　　I could see the cuts:
　　　　my blood: fat drops oozing
　　　　then red ribbons
I screamed *stop!* but she wouldn't stop —
　　My throat ached.
Something flared in my mind
　　　like a torch catching fire:
　　　　I don't know what I did,
　　　　or how I did it,
　　but I, Rhaskos, turned to smoke
　　　　or dissolved like salt in water —
　　　after that
　　　　someone else was wailing
　　　and the pain
　　　　and the blood

                    and the cries came from
                        someone else
only
        time
                stretched out
                                immeasurable.

When my mother set aside the knife
        I came back to myself.
        I thought it was over,
        but it wasn't. She took ashes
            from the bowl
                and rubbed them
                into the cuts.
It stung. I begged her to stop,
            but she wouldn't. Not till she was
            done.
            She let me get up.

I ran at her.
        I punched her with all my strength,
        I kicked her shins.
She sank down on her knees
            and covered her head. She stayed
            like that

36

while I hit her
over and over
her whole body drawn together
like a closed fist.

When I stopped hitting her
I wept. It sounded like a baby
crying —
I remember the shame of that.
She held out her arms
her hands were fouled with ashes
and blood.

I remember her rocking me to sleep.
There was thunder in the night
glaring white
but the rain never came.

The next morning, they took my mother
away.
They put her on a grain ship, headed for
Athens.
I never saw her after that.

EXHIBIT 2

Necklace of twelve gold palm leaves with amber head of sphinx (?) or goddess, circa 450–400 BCE.

This unusually fine necklace was found on the Athenian Akropolis, near the ruins of the Sanctuary of Artemis Brauronia. Since the palm tree was sacred to Artemis, the necklace may have been a gift to the goddess. The sphinx head and the twelve palmettes were threaded together on a linen cord, which fell apart when the necklace was removed from the site. The necklace measures thirty centimeters, or twelve and a half inches, an average size for a Greek necklace of this period.

The sphinx pendant is of an earlier date, perhaps 500 BCE, and may be of Etruscan workmanship. The facial features show signs of rubbing and wear. Amber was sometimes worn as an amulet, especially by pregnant women; it was thought to ensure a safe childbirth. Amber is also found in the tombs of women and young girls, perhaps as a magic charm to ease the passage into the underworld.

MELISTO IN ATHENS

"The gods sent that child to punish me!"

Melisto, who had just been soundly slapped, stopped bellowing, her mouth wide open. Her short life had taught her that slaves and children were often beaten; the idea that the gods might punish her mother attracted her strongly. She wiped her nose on the back of her hand and spoke directly to Lysandra. "What bad thing did you do?"

Lysandra clapped her hands to her ears. "Didn't I tell you to be silent?" she demanded. "Do I have to smack you again?"

"No," said Melisto, answering the second question. She bottom-scuttled across the floor, ducking under the loom, setting the loom weights clanking. Once safe, she peered around the frame. "What bad thing did you do?" she persisted. "Why did the gods —"

Lysandra lost her temper. She darted forward and caught her daughter by the elbow, almost upsetting the loom. Melisto felt her feet leave the floor. She reached out blindly, her fingers crooked like claws. Her hand closed over the necklace around her mother's throat.

The cord snapped. Gold palm leaves fell with a sharp tinkle; the amber pendant dropped with a solid thud and rolled across the floor. Lysandra released her daughter and knelt to scoop up the pieces. Melisto retreated, her teeth bared.

Lysandra passed from fury to bafflement. She looked at the amber sphinx head in her palm; she touched the sore place on her neck, where the cord had broken. Two slave women stepped forward to calm her. They gathered the gold palmettes, showing Lysandra that none were damaged. Another cord, and the necklace would be as good as new. Melisto retreated behind the largest loom and shut her eyes to make herself invisible.

The weaving room where the women spent their days was a large space, crowded with oversized baskets, four looms, and three chairs. The windows faced south, and the light was strong. To Melisto, the yellow room was a prison. She hated the smell of new-dyed cloth, of lanolin and women's sweat. The work she was taught there — picking through the wool for burrs, rolling it against her thigh — was the same thing over and over again. She could not bear it.

Someone was coming upstairs. Melisto pricked up her ears. Sosias, the head slave of the household, appeared in the doorway. Behind him was a tall woman with cropped hair: a slave.

Melisto stepped around the loom to see the slave woman. Under her head wrap, her hair was orange. Her pale eyes were red-rimmed, and her face was a blank.

Sosias addressed Lysandra. "I've found you the woman you wanted. One hundred and eighty drachmas." He opened his fingers to convey that this was a bargain. "She's used to looking after children; she has a firm hand. The trader assured me she's skillful with wool work."

Lysandra had regained her dignity. She stood gracefully, and spoke in a soft voice. "Bring her forward. I want to look at her."

Sosias stepped aside. The slave woman was a full head taller than Lysandra, and broader in the shoulders. Lysandra pursed her delicate lips. "What is she, Sosias? Thracian? Skythian? I don't want a barbarian. Does she speak Greek?"

"She's Thracian. There's a slight accent, but she speaks Greek."

"She doesn't look well."

"She comes from Thessaly; she was seasick on the boat." Sosias shrugged. "Maybe she hasn't eaten. She comes from a good household; her master was son to Menon of Pharsalos. She's never been sick a day. The trader swore by the gods."

Lysandra's eyes narrowed; she scrutinized the slave woman closely. Then she whirled round and caught Melisto by the arm. "This is the child you'll have to tend. My daughter. She's four years old and she's a wild animal. As you can see, her hair is matted — it's all cowlicks. I can't get her to stand still so that I can comb it. Just now she tore my necklace off my neck — you see the

44

mark on my throat! Do you think you can manage her?"

"I can manage her."

"Good." Lysandra clapped her hands lightly. "We'll have the ceremony. After it's over, you'll take charge of Melisto. See if you can comb her hair." She made a fluid and commanding gesture. Sosias stepped back to allow her to pass. Lysandra headed down the stairs, followed by the slaves.

Melisto knew how a new slave was made part of the household. She edged past her mother and arrived at the altar of Hestia before the adults did. The Thracian woman knelt before the altar while a bowl of dried fruit and nuts was poured over her head. This act would please Hestia, goddess of the hearth, who would make the new servant fruitful in her service.

Melisto kept her eyes on the dried fruit. She was especially fond of figs. These belonged to the goddess, but she could palm one or two and eat them when no one was looking.

"We will call you Thratta," Lysandra told the slave woman, "because you are a Thracian woman."

The slave woman said nothing.

"You'll go to the fountain house in the morning and fetch water. You'll help with the wool work and take charge of the child." Lysandra nodded toward Melisto. "Her father makes a pet of her, and she's been badly spoiled."

At the mention of her father, Melisto glowed. She adored her father. Arkadios was a busy man, a citizen and a soldier; he was away during the day and went to banquets in the evening. Melisto seldom saw him. But when she did, he tossed her in the air and swung her in circles; he let her climb on him and listened when she chattered. Melisto knew, because her mother complained of it, that few men loved their daughters as Arkadios doted on her.

"You'll sleep upstairs," Lysandra told the slave woman. "Come. I'll show you."

She led the way up the stairs. The other two slaves turned to watch them go. Melisto snatched up two fistfuls of dried fruit, darted to the open door, and trotted out into the courtyard. Freedom! She loved the courtyard, where there were animals to watch: birds and insects and a tortoise as big as her father's bronze helmet. In one shady corner

46

of the courtyard, she was digging a hole. When it was deep enough, she would fill it with water and make a pool.

In an instant she was down on her knees, grubbing in the dirt. She worked energetically, patting the excavated earth into a mound and pounding it hard. The hole was wide and deep: a little more work, and she would be able to sit in it. When the slave woman emerged from the house, Melisto scowled and shrank back into the shadows.

The slave woman saw her. She was carrying a comb, a sponge, and a large water jar. But to Melisto's surprise, she made no approach. She sat down on a block of stone and lifted the water jug to her mouth. It was a pitcher made for pouring, not drinking, and as the woman drank, the water splashed down her face, wetting her neck and the front of her gown.

Melisto watched intently. She had never seen anyone drink so much. It struck her that the woman must be very thirsty. She remembered that Sosias had said she hadn't eaten. Melisto picked up her last fig. It was coated with dirt from the hole, but she would not have hesitated to eat it herself.

The woman poured water on the sponge and washed her face. She squeezed the sponge so that water squirted down her arms. Once she had dried her hands on her dress, she turned her eyes on Melisto.

Prompted by an impulse she didn't understand, Melisto went forward and held out the fig.

The woman accepted it mechanically. She brushed off the dirt and put it in her mouth. She chewed slowly; Melisto could hear the grit against her teeth. After she swallowed, the woman picked up the comb.

Melisto shifted her weight to her back foot, poised to flee. But she was not quick enough. The woman caught her hands.

"I'm going to comb the knots out of your hair. I'm going to hold your hair in clumps, very tight, and comb out the ends. That way, it won't hurt. Do you understand?"

"No," said Melisto. She lowered her head like a bull about to charge.

"Now," said the woman. She swung Melisto around, pinning her between her knees. She took a handful of Melisto's matted hair.

Melisto flinched. She thought of shrieking — she could scream loud enough
to make everyone in the house put their
hands over their ears — but something in
the woman's silence dumbfounded her. She
submitted, shifting her weight from foot to
foot as the woman eased the mats out of
her hair. The slave woman's hands were deft
and sure, lifting the damp locks away from
her hot neck. Melisto hunched one shoulder
in pleasure. When the braids were finished,
she allowed Thratta to turn her around and
wipe her face with the sponge.

Melisto spoke boldly. "I want to sit in
your lap."

The slave woman moved her head: *No.*

Melisto paid no attention. She crawled
up on the woman's knees, leaned back, and
stuck her thumb in her mouth.

The Thracian woman smelled bad.
There were the ordinary smells of sweat
and wool, but beyond that was another
odor that the animal in Melisto found dis-
turbing. She shifted, wrinkling her nose.
Her eyes fell to the woman's arms. "What's
that?" she asked, rubbing the row of Vs
with one finger. "How did you get them on
your arm?"

The slave woman shuddered. Her mouth opened in an ugly grimace, releasing a cry of agony. She wept, her tears striking Melisto's face.

Melisto trembled. That terrible smell was suffering. She squirmed, but now the woman's arms were clutching her, rocking her back and forth. Melisto hid her face against the woman's breast and cried along with her. She was as frightened as if she were out in a thunderstorm.

The storm subsided. The slave woman gulped and sniffed. Melisto could feel her pulling the grief back inside. In a moment, she found herself pushed out of the lap. The woman took the dirty sponge out of the water jar and lifted the jug to her lips. Once again she drank as if she were dying of thirst.

Melisto stuck out her hand. "I want some, too."

Thratta's eyes met Melisto's. She handed over the jug of dirty water and let Melisto drink.

Turn and Counterturn
Lysandra and Artemis

TURN: LYSANDRA

Of all the children!
That bad-tempered, owl-eyed, snot-nosed
Brat of a child!
Rough and rude and disobedient!

What did I do to deserve her?
Even before she was born
 she was a curse. Day after day
 I vomited; I could eat nothing.
 She sickened me, even then.
I had one comfort: I said to myself,
 It must be a boy. I know it's a boy.
It has to be a boy.

51

Only a boy could be so robust,
        could kick so hard, like a hammer
        striking my womb.
I promised my husband: *I'll give you a son.*
I was in love. I boasted:
        It's a boy. I can feel it. A woman knows.

I was fourteen.

She tore me when I gave birth to her;
        I labored a night and a day,
        yet one more endless night
I screamed till my throat was raw —
        only to hear: "It's a girl!"
My mother-in-law — she laughed at me.
And so did the slaves.
I ought to have had them beaten.

But even after all I suffered,
        I might have loved her,
        if only she had slept, or bloomed with
        beauty.
A child like a flower, clinging to my skirts . . .
I could have loved a child like that.

Instead I'm stuck with Melisto!
She pierces me with those black eyes,
　　　glaring like Medusa.
And she defies me!

She won't spin, she won't work wool.
She's plain and squat and savage.
She's a child who asks *why*.
She's a child who says *no*.
I fear that some day
　　　I'll hurt her, really hurt her.
Not a pinch or a slap —
　　　or a whipping . . .
I'm afraid I'll crack her skull,
　　　or black her eye, or shake her
　　　　　so hard I break her neck. I am
　　　　　　ashamed.
I lose control.

I cry to the gods,
Why have I no son?
Why am I stuck with this curse, Melisto?

COUNTERTURN: ARTEMIS

I gave you that child.
I, Artemis, goddess of childbirth,
gave you that child.
Strong and wild and disobedient!

What did you do to deserve her?
You have neglected my shrine
since you were born. Where were my gifts?
You owed me the toys of your
childhood —
miserly child — you kept them!
When you were pregnant, your husband
gave you
the necklace you wear: gleaming,
resplendent,
a wonder to behold:
Twelve gold palmettes — my favorite plant

and carved with marvelous cunning:
the amber sphinx.
A trinket even a goddess could desire.
You prayed to me, Lysandra:

*Let me live, and I'll give you the amber
sphinx.*

Remember that?

Oh, how you hedged your bets, Lysandra!
Goddess, grant me a healthy child.
If I survive the birth,
I'll give you the amber sphinx;
I swear by the deathless gods.
A woman who loves and fears the gods
would give the gift first
and save the requests for later.

You never worshipped me, Lysandra.
You broke your promise.
You prefer Hera, the goddess of marriage,
or laughing Aphrodite, the man-pleaser.
You are too tame to worship me
and so I give you Melisto!
A child as wild as you are tame —
and if you don't like her
that's your misfortune!

I like her. She's a bear cub,
born to follow the goddess.
I will make her ask *why*.
I will make her say *no*.
One day, Lysandra,
she'll make you keep your promise.

She will stir you, sting you
until you do.
She will judge you with her eyes
and she will find you wanting.
She will never love you. Aren't you
ashamed?
That is my curse.

Don't cry to the gods!
If you want a son,
thank the gods for your firstborn, Melisto!

And give me the amber sphinx!

EXHIBIT 3

Horse bits made of iron, found near Kolonos Hippios (Horse Hill).

The ancient Greeks revered horses and gloried in their strength and beauty. Horses symbolized power, nobility, and wealth, and as such they were greatly cherished. Horses were sacred to Poseidon, and the goddess Athena was credited with the invention of the bridle.

The Greek horseman and historian Xenophon stressed the importance of gentle handling for horses. At the same time, Xenophon recommended the use of two bits: a "smooth bit," which was similar to a modern snaffle, and a rough "hedgehog" bit, which was used for training and may have been barbed or spiked. The smooth bit could be used once the horse had learned to submit to the painful influence of the hedgehog bit.

EXHIBIT 3

Horse bite made of iron, found near Koraus, Hittite (horse zith).

The ancient Greeks revered horses and gloried in their strength and beauty. Horses symbolized power, nobility, and wealth, and as such they were greatly cherished. Horses were sacred to Poseidon, and the goddess Athena was credited with the invention of the bridle.

The Greek horseman and historian Xenophon stressed the importance of gentle handling for horses. At the same time, Xenophon recommended the use of two bits: a "smooth bit," which was similar to a modern snaffle, and a rough "hedgehog" bit, which was used for training and may have been barbed or spiked. The smooth bit could be used once the horse had learned to submit to the painful influence of the hedgehog bit.

RHASKOS IN THESSALY

Thrax

After my mother was sold,

    I was sent away from the courtyard.

So was Lykos. We were too old to play all
the time.

He was seven, old enough to be educated.

I was five, old enough to work, Georgios
said.

    Georgios was the slave in charge of
the stables.

After my mother went, he told me what to
do.

I was too small to be much use,

    but I was big enough to pick up turds.

61

The pitchfork was taller than I was,
>> so Georgios gave me a leather bucket
>> and I picked up turds with my hands.
At first, I was squeamish —
>> they were wet and they stank.
>>> Flies buzzed around my head
>>> and sucked my eyelids.
I sulked. I cried. I wasn't thorough.
Georgios gave me a good beating.

I heard a fable once:
>> An eagle from out of the sky
>>> caught a nightingale in his talons.
>> She cried and fluttered in pain.
>> The eagle said, "What's wrong with
>>> you?
>>> Only a fool fights against a
>>> stronger force."
And that's the way it is.

Georgios said a boy
>> is like a warped plank.
>> You have to pound it until it's
>>> straight.

He taught me not to talk back,
    or ask questions.
He said when anyone gave me an order
    I should jump to do it,
        scurry,
            as if I couldn't wait to obey.
He taught me to bow my head,
    and not look up
    at people who were better than me —
    which was everyone.

I had a new name: *Thrax*. It means
    Thracian boy.
I said I wanted my old name, Rhaskos.
He gave me a clip on the ear.
I decided it didn't matter what people
    called me.
Nobody spoke to me much.
He was a horseman, Georgios was.
He told me: A horse is only as good as his
    feet.
        A horse's hooves can get soft and sick
            if he stands in his own muck.
        The stalls and paddocks had to be
            kept clean.

63

Our master, Alexidemus,
    was proud of his horses. Horses
    are precious.
There wasn't a horse in the stable
    that wasn't worth more than I was.
Even their turds were precious.

So I picked up turds:
    Squat and stoop,
    till the bucket is full,
    lug it to the dung heap. Dump it.
That's what I did all day.
In summer, the blinding light,
    the stink and the flies.
When winter came, I was cold.
I outgrew the tunic my mother wove,
    and no one gave me a new one.
The turds froze to the ground.
I was glad to find a fresh one
    to warm my hands.
Rainy days were best. You can't scoop
    turds out of the mud.
Sometimes I hid in the barn.
    I burrowed into the straw and slept.

64

If I was lucky, no one found me.
I was always starved for sleep.

Sokrates once asked me,
    how do I know I'm awake when I'm
      awake?
    how do I know when I'm dreaming?

It's strange. In those days
    I felt more awake when I slept.
      My dreams were full of color
      and surprises
        sometimes terror — my mother
        holding the knife —
    but also action: wrestling in the
    courtyard,
        riding on my mother's back.

I'd wake up
    and the dreams drained away.
I'd go back to work.
My hands moved, but my mind stood still:
      a pool of rotten water.
I felt like a shade, like one of the dead,
    as if no one could see me.

As I recall these things,
   I imagine you sitting across from me.
   I see your face,
      and it makes me laugh,
      because when I talk about
         turds,
            you screw up your mouth:
            disgusted.
Look; I got used to the turds.
They weren't the bad part. Horses are
   cleaner than pigs,
      or men. The bad part was
      if you do the same thing over and
         over,
      and nobody talks to you,
      you see your life stretching ahead
      endless and dull and lonesome —
         You think the gods have forsaken
            you,
               because you're just a *thing*
                  that picks up turds,
               a nothing.

Two years went by like that. I think it was
   two.

I got bigger. I groomed the horses
 and picked the mud from their feet.
I walked them out
 after the master rode them.
Their lives weren't easy, either.
 The bits in their bridles were spiked,
 like burrs,
 and the master rode them hard.
They came back lathered with sweat;
 their mouths wet with foam and
 blood.
Some were sent to fight in the wars.

It's strange
 how those days blur together.
But here is one memory
 bright and clear as water:

I was in the high pasture,
 where no one could see me.
There was a horse on the ridge,
 a stallion; a fiery chestnut
 blood-red against the sky.
His head was up, ears pricked. He was
 sniffing the air.

Something had spooked him.
      —There was the line of his neck,
    the arc of his withers,
    the saddle-scoop of his back.
    Then his rump, almost round,
        like a ripe apple.
    His tail streamed like a waterfall
        teased by the wind.

There was a sharp stone in front of me:
    and a bare patch: the puckery dust
    of a dried-up puddle.
I dragged the stone over the dust
    and made that horse:
        the spear-sharp ears,
        the crest,
        the flanks, the rippling muscles —
Point and line and curve and scoop —
Alive in the hollow of my hand —

I glanced back at the horse. He'd dropped
    his head to graze.
        Whatever had spooked him was
        gone.

I looked down. A shock of joy:
There was the horse
    small but real
    dug in the dust.

I'd made the horse.
I'd curved his rump.
I made the wind
    that combed his tail.

Have you ever done that — ?
    Tried to do the impossible,
        without thinking?
        and you did it?

I remembered the horse I'd seen
    long ago, on the *andron* wall.
I'd wondered how that horse came to be.

Now I understood:
    Another man had seen a horse,
        and picked up a tool,
        and made that horse.

I, Rhaskos, was like that man.

HERMES SPEAKS

Me again. I forgot to tell you two things.
   One: about the land. This boy
   Rhaskos —
      who's just found beauty
      in a horse's behind —
      lives in a radiant land.

Ελλαδα. Don't call it *Greece*.
   That's a word like a sneer:
      hissy
      greasy
      unmelodic
      and worst of all, Roman.
         The Greeks call their land
         Ελλαδα. That's *E*,

70

which more or less
rhymes with *play*,
and λλα is *la*, as in *tra-la*,
and the thing that looks like a *d*
is more like a *th. Eh-LA-tha.*
Ελλαδα.
Isn't that better?

Now close your eyes a second —
Not yet. Wait till I tell you —
Close your eyes and imagine *blue*,
a startling, bracing, breathtaking blue:
the sun on a kingfisher's back
— *Now!*
. . . Open your eyes. Take that blue
and brush the dome of the sky.
Look up! There's the sun, a burning
chariot
drawn by shell-white horses
plunging through the clouds.

That's Ελλαδα:
a land of wind and sunlight,
rimmed by a restless sea.

71

A land of rough volcanic rock
    and forests, dense and fragrant:
        alive with bearded centaurs,
        stags and wolves,
        and nymphs with delicate feet.
And underfoot, cold with dew:
        sweet clover and violets,
        parsley, mint, oregano,
        poppies, wild garlic, and thyme.

                        Though
    to be perfectly frank
it's not a land
    that feels that it owes you a living.
    The soil
    is laced with acid and iron. The
    country
has always been poor.
There's the constant threat of hunger. As a
  god,
    I don't have to worry about that.
    On Mount Olympus,
        there are endless banquets,
        nectar poured from gold . . .
What else? Oh, yes,

the other thing I forgot to mention:
The country is always at war.
Civil war. Roughly, it's Athens versus
    Sparta.
        It's been waged
        for twenty-some years
        and will likely keep on going.
Rhaskos knows nothing about it. Who
    talks politics
            to a slave? He only knows
            that the horses are sent off
            and few of them return.
        The battlefields are far away.

Melisto's city, Athens,
        is bleeding. Money, bronze, horses,
            lives,
        all lost in the war.
It's a war that Melisto
        is too young to understand
            (and I have to admit, it's
                complicated),
        but she's not too young
            to have nightmares about the
                Spartans,

73

those long-haired warriors
in their red cloaks. Personally, I
find them picturesque,
albeit deadly. Melisto hates and
fears them.
I wonder: does she know
if the city walls tumble
and the Spartans take the city,
what could happen to her?
The women and children enslaved,
the men (her beloved father)
put to the sword?
It could happen tomorrow.

And does she know
that on other islands,
it's the Athenians, men like her
father
helmeted in bronze,
who wage war,
and besiege the cities?
They say at Potidaea
the people inside the city walls
were so hungry

        they ate the dead before they
           surrendered.
I don't know for sure. I'm a bit
  squeamish.
I didn't watch that part.

And then there's plague.
      If there's a war,
        there are armies on the move,
        and that means disease. If you crowd
          too many people
            inside the city walls,
        there's bound to be sickness. There
          was plague in Athens,
        twenty-some years ago. A filthy
          business.
I didn't watch that, either.
Plague is disgusting
      and tedious, too.
          It's the same thing over and over.
One-fourth of the people died.

My point is, this miraculous city, Athens,
      exists in the middle of war,
      and Melisto knows that.

She still has all her baby teeth,
but she knows about war. She's a
    warlike child,
    always waging battles
    against the greatest tyrant she
knows: her mother.

Rhaskos is a year older,
    his mother is gone,
    and his life is hard. He knows that.
    He searches for horses in the dust.

Are they luckless children, these two little
  Greeks?

Perhaps.
But neither is in any hurry to die.
It's good to be alive, even in wartime,
    even in slavery,
    even long ago,
      in Ελλαδα . . .

RHASKOS IN THESSALY

Thief

After I made the first horse,
  I wanted to make horses.
That's all I wanted to do.

I cleared dirt patches. I yanked up
 weeds,
   and plowed the soil with a rock.
   I ground the dirt, loose and
    soft.
When no one was looking,
   I'd set down my bucket,
   pick up a stick,
   and try to make a horse.

Whenever I cleaned the stalls,
    I'd watch the horses
    and feel my fingers twitch.
Wherever I went with my bucket,
    I saw horses
        afloat in the shimmering air.

When I drew them,
    I couldn't get the lines right. They
      were lopsided,
        misshapen.
  I muttered and scratched
    scraped away the bad lines
    and forgot to fill my bucket.

Georgios caught me at it one day.
    He whacked the back of my head.
He called me slavish,
    and said I was a thief,
    playing mud pies like a baby
    instead of working for the master.

If my eyes hadn't filled with salt water,
    I might have laughed.

He was a slave himself,
    and all of us stole.
We stole because we needed things.
      We stole to get back.
      We prayed to Hermes, god of thieves,
        so we wouldn't get caught.

Demetrios — he was the slave who
  guarded the storeroom —
      Demetrios was favored by the god.
      The master trusted him.
      Who wouldn't? Demetrios was
        frugal,
          thin and grave, and his hands
          were always clean.
He was respectful, too, never raising his
  eyes.

But he was loyal to us, not the master.
There were nights when the master was
  away,
      when he'd unlock the storeroom door.
Those nights, if we wanted a lump of
  cheese,
    or a handful of olives,

or a little wine,
we could help ourselves.
By dawn the next morning,
  Demetrios would have swept the
    storeroom
  and rearranged the goods.
Demetrios could read and write,
  and he knew how to keep
    a straight face
    and a false tally
  better than any man alive.
Every other month or so,
  he'd steal a water jug of ruddy
    wine,
  and bring it to the stables
  to share with Georgios.

Those were the nights when Georgios
  smiled.

Years later, I told Sokrates that I stole —
  I mean, that I used to steal.
I was ashamed to tell him,
  because everyone knew how virtuous
    he was.

80

He wouldn't have stolen a crust if he were
starving.

He said, "Did you know it was wrong
to steal?"

I was tempted to lie, but he was my
friend.
"I knew it was wrong," I said.

He said, "Good."
He said it was better to do wrong
knowing that it's wrong
than to do wrong in ignorance,
by accident.

I thought that was crazy.

I talk to him sometimes,
not the way I talk to you,
but in my head. I ask him questions,
and I argue with him. He'd like
that.
Sometimes I want to say,
Look, I know it was wrong to steal,
but have you ever thought about what
was stolen from me?

81

He didn't know how bitter it is to be a slave.
He couldn't see that it was wrong
that *I* was a slave. He was the wisest
man in Athens,
but he couldn't see that I'd been
wronged.
He always said:
"To suffer a wrong is nothing.
To do wrong harms the soul."

It's not always nothing to suffer a wrong.
As for doing wrong —
I guess I harmed my soul, those
days,
because I stole. After my mother's
tunic fell apart,
winter came, and I'd have frozen
to death
if I hadn't stolen a cloak from
Georgios.
He beat me, but he let me keep it.

I don't steal now.
Even then, I didn't steal much. But there
was one thing I stole
over and over,

and I'm proud of it.
It wasn't a *thing*,
     so maybe it didn't damage my soul.
I think it was good for my soul.

On moonlit nights,
     I would visit the *andron*
     and look at the painted horse.
     I went six or seven times.
It was a risk. It was a thrill.
My heart would jump in my chest,
     like a colt leaping. I'd hide in the
          courtyard
     and listen till I knew
     the whole house slept.
Then I'd climb into a window
     and creep down the hall to the room
     where the horse still pranced on the
          wall.

The full-moon nights were best, of
     course.
But the man who made that horse —
     I remember how excited I was when I
          found this out —

83

had dug into the plaster with
    something sharp,
to make the horse's outline.
Even when the moon was down,
    I could find that horse in the dark.
    I could stand on the couch
    and trace the shape with my fingers.

One night
    when the master was away
    I decided to take a lamp.
There was always a light in the kitchen,
    at the altar of Hestia.
I would borrow the lamp
    and see the horse by lamplight.

I was risking a beating;
I was doing a thing
    no one would imagine a slave would
    do.
If I were caught stealing a loaf, Georgios
  would understand.
He'd have me whipped, but he'd
  understand.
    But to steal in at night,

to the best room in the house,
to see a horse?
He'd never understand that.
That made it even better.

Then came the night I was caught.

HEPHAISTOS SPEAKS

I am Hephaistos, the lame god:
    foot twisted,
    hip wrenched out of joint.
I am the ugly god,
      cast out of Olympus,
      rejected,
      the maker of beautiful things.

I see this boy who has no one:
    his father indifferent,
    his mother sold.
I see this boy as he stoops and labors,
      sweats and survives. I am the god
      who does not turn his back on
        ugliness.

Beware, all you
    who cast out children,
    who use them as tools
        for your shameful needs.
    I tell you, these children are
        not alone:
    A god stands beside them,
        a Fury, a Nemesis,
        who will avenge them.

I will shape this boy's fate
    like a tool at the forge;
    through fire and hammer
    I will shape it.

Look at him! Silver-crowned in the
    moonlight,
        hoisting himself over the windowsill!
        He risks his skin
            to visit a forbidden room
            and worship a painted wonder.
            How he desires it!
    Not the horse only, but beauty:
        that is the thing he seeks.

I will give him
    the best consolation a mortal can
    know:
        not love, which is fickle
        as faithless Aphrodite,
        nor power, which makes a man
        first drunk,
        then thirsty.
I will give him the power to create.
I will make him like myself:
        a maker of beautiful things.

Rhaskos in Thessaly

I slipped into the house on silent feet.
I went to Hestia's altar;
>I prayed:
>*Help me, O Goddess,*
>*and I will remember you.*

I filled a lamp with oil and lit the
wick.
I sheltered the flame with my hand;
>my fingers glowed red.
I passed through the shadows step by
step,
>listening,
>holding my breath:
Everyone slept.

There was the horse in the *andron*.
Each time I saw it
I ached to make a horse like that:
vigorous, mettlesome, his muscles
rippling like water,
I stood on the couch
wonderstruck.

How long did I stand looking? I heard
someone behind me.
I turned so fast I almost slipped —
I should have blown out the lamp.

Instead I lifted it high.

He stood in the doorway.
Not a grown-up: a boy.
The master's second son: Lykos.
How many years since we played in
the courtyard?
Often he came to the stable to ride.
I'd bring his horse in from the pasture.
He never looked at me.
I'd hand him the rope and slink off.
When someone doesn't see you,
you want to get away.

"Rhaskos?"

He remembered my name.

"Is that you? What are you doing here?"

I stepped down from the couch.
To be caught in the *andron*
in the middle of the night —
There wasn't a lie I could tell.
I hung my head.

"I heard a noise. I thought it was a thief.
Then I saw the light.
For a moment, I thought the house was on
fire!"

I stole a glance, sideways. He was older,
thinner,
but that look of mischief —
the corners of his mouth puckered,
his eyebrows lifted —

"Whew, you stink! I can smell you from
here!
Sometimes Father says the *andron*
stinks like the stable.

91

Is that because of you?
Have you come here before?"

My mouth was dry.

"You're supposed to answer when I
speak to you.
I'm your master, you know."
He sat down on the couch,
and pulled up his feet, sitting
cross-legged.
He rubbed the sole of his foot with his
thumb,
as if he had a callus there,
and spoke without lifting his head.

"I think about you sometimes."

When he said that, I stared at the floor:
Rows of flat pebbles, black and white,
cunningly arranged,
but that wasn't why I stared.
I didn't know anyone thought about me.

"We used to have good times together,
didn't we?
All we had to do was play. And fight.

You were the best one to fight with."

"You were stronger."

His head came up.
He grinned at me.
"I was, wasn't I? Even then! But you put
up a fight.
I'm learning wrestling now. I bet you'd be
good at it.
But I guess you don't learn wrestling."

"I don't learn anything."

"You should thank the gods for
your good luck!
All they ever *do* is teach me things,
and half the time, I can't learn them.
Sometimes I think I'd rather be you,
working with the horses.
You were always crazy about horses.
Remember how
we used to take sticks,
and switch our legs,
and gallop?
You could whinny just like a horse.
I remember your mother made you a
little horse out of clay,

and I broke it.
Do you remember that?"

I'd forgotten.
The memory came back to me: a rough
  little figure,
    sun-dried, short-necked;
    more like a dog than a horse.
It was my only toy.

                    "*I* remember,
because your mother smacked my bottom
                    so hard,
          I howled like a wolf.
      That seemed like a regular whipping,
                    back then.
    We used to have good times, didn't we?"

He sounded like Georgios and
  Demetrios.
Whenever they were drunk, they liked to
  talk
    about how good things were
    when they were young.

                "Then your mother was sold
          and I got to be seven years old.

After that, we never spoke."

"I'm not supposed to talk unless someone
talks to me first."

He nodded briskly.
"I've got a slave of my own now, old
Zotikos.
He takes me to school every day.
If I don't learn fast enough, he beats me."

"A *slave*? A slave beats *you*?"

He threw up his hands.
"All boys have slaves to make us learn.
Zotikos is old, but he uses a cane, and he
can hit hard.
He says I'm bone-lazy and good for
nothing. It's not fair,
because I'm not so bad at wrestling,
and I win all the footraces.
I just hate memorizing all that Homer.
Hesiod and Homer, they're poets,
and I have to learn them by heart.
Homer tells stories, so he's interesting
once in a while —
but Hesiod's boring.
Then I have to play the lyre.

95

Zotikos is always yelling at me
because he says the lyre's out of tune.
I don't see how he can tell. It sounds all
right to me.
Does old Georgios beat you?"

"Sometimes."

"It's worse for you.
When I grow up, I'll be a soldier,
and nobody will dare lay a hand on me,
but you'll always be whipped.
At least no one makes you learn poetry.
You ought to be grateful for that."

I didn't argue with him.
I didn't know what poetry was,
and it had been so long since anyone
spoke to me —
not giving orders, but talking.
And he was a boy. Like me.
I hadn't talked to another boy in years.

He heaved a sigh. He sounded like a
horse:
a long breath and a brief snort.

"Sometimes it seems to me that nobody
ever gets out of anything.
I mean, you've got to be a slave,
and I've got to go to
school,
and be a soldier, like my big brother,
Menon —
only I won't be like Menon, because
he's awful.
But you know what I mean.
You have to work for old Georgios,
and I have to learn to play the
stupid lyre."

He frowned.
"But why are you here in the
middle of the night?"

I had been standing that whole time.
I went to him and knelt down, setting the
lamp on the floor.
It was the pose of a suppliant. If I
had to,
I would kneel up,
and cup my hand around his chin,
and beg for mercy.

97

"Don't tell on me, Lykos!
I came to look at the horse on the
wall.
I always liked that horse. Remember
that day — ?
We were playing Do-What-I-Do,
and you led us in here?
I saw that horse, and I couldn't see how
anyone could do that:
make a horse out of paint.
That man must have been like a god."

"Like a god!
He was just a workman,
dirtying his hands to make a living!
His name was Parrhasius,
and he charged a pretty penny, Father
says.
Is that really why you're here?
You'd risk a beating to look at that horse?"

"Yes. But the beating's up to you.
Are you going to tell on me?"

"No. I'm not a sneak!
But you're lucky it was me that found

you.
What do you want to do now?"

"Do?"

"Oh, come on, Rhaskos!
We're both awake, and there aren't any
grown-ups.
We could sneak out of the house and go
swimming.
No one would know!
There's a bend in the river where the
water's deep.
Menon goes there with his friends —
We'd have fun."

He was offering me his friendship,
treating me as an equal, almost.
I leapt to my feet. I was afraid he'd change
his mind.
"I can't swim, but I know the place."

I blew out the lamp.
We rushed out of the *andron*
and into the courtyard.
We'd forgotten to whisper. All at once, I
heard her voice:

99

Galene, his mother,
and mistress of the house,
Galene, who'd slapped me
and called me slave brat.
Her voice was a croak; she was
half asleep.

"Lykos! What are you doing out of bed?
Come back to the house!"

I backed into the shadows.

Lykos shrugged, giving in.
He whispered: "Tomorrow?"

I nodded in the dark. I don't know if
he saw.
I went back to the courtyard the
next night
and the next.
The third night, I didn't go.
I don't know whether Lykos changed
his mind
or fell asleep.
I never spoke to him again.

A week later, the master was back.
There was fearful news: Apollo was angry,
    and was shooting his arrows of
      plague
    at the city of Larissa.

In a few days, Lykos was struck down.
He was buried by a nearby shrine.
Sometimes at dawn, I saw Galene,
    bowed with grief,
      coming from his grave.
Alexidemus was left with only one son:
    Menon.

EXHIBIT 4

Red-figure oil jar (lekythos) found near Phar-
salos, Thessaly, circa 400 BCE. Lekythoi are
commonly found in graves and were often
given as gifts to the dead.

The scene shown is Hermes leading a boy toward a boat. Hermes wears his characteristic traveler's cloak and winged sandals. The youth behind him was originally labeled, but the inscription has been rubbed away; only the final two letters, ος (os), remain. Because Hermes was Guide of Souls, the scene may depict a voyage to the underworld. The man holding the oar is probably Charon, who ferries the dead over the river Styx.

TURN AND COUNTERTURN
LYKOS AND HERMES

᚜ᚒᚔᚒᚔᚒᚔᚒᚔᚒᚔᚒᚔᚒᚔᚒ᚜

TURN: LYKOS

I thought I had more time.
I thought I'd grow up
    and be an athlete
      crowned with olive leaves.
I wanted to grow strong
      so I could pound Menon;
I wanted to go swimming with Rhaskos.

Instead I've come here —
    this steep and crooked canyon,
    darkening
    forcing me forward
    closing in.

It reminds me of something.

A sound in the dark:
    the splash of rushing water.
There's the boat for the dead
    and that monster of nightmare:
        Charon
    the boatman — so hideous
        with his red and feverish eyes,
        I want to run. My feet
    are rooted to the ground.

Music? Someone is whistling:
    a god, boyish and radiant,
    light-footed as a goat.
His skin sheds fragrance
    and flakes of dazzling light.

I'm afraid of them both.
I've come to the land of gods and
  ghosts
    and I don't like either one.
I'm afraid of where they're taking me.

And I'm afraid of the dark.

COUNTERTURN: HERMES

This is the fate of man:
to run out of time,
to pass from the earth
to the House of Death.
It's time to say farewell
to everything you've known.
Now Rhaskos must go swimming by
himself.

Keep on straight ahead;
follow the vanishing path,
narrowing,
squeezing you onward:
birth passage
into Persephone's realm.

Listen! the river!
white water chattering —
Here's your boat! The pilot
is that sour gondolier,
Charon.
I admit he's not pretty —
rotten teeth and halitosis.
No style. And no manners.
And no conversation.

Buck up! I'm coming with you.
I am Hermes, the luck bringer,
giant killer, jaunty,
your friend and companion,
god of the golden wand!

I've come to show the way.
I'll introduce you to gods and ghosts,
and keep you from getting lost.
There is no night that does not end.

And I can see in the dark.

EXHIBIT 5

Terra-cotta doll found in Kerameikos district of Athens, late fourth century BCE.

This finely crafted doll may have been part of a child's grave goods. Unlike dolls from earlier periods, the doll is unclothed, and the legs are jointed at the knee instead of the thigh. The movable arms attach to the shoulders with twine. Traces of pigment show that the doll was brightly painted. One foot is missing and was not recovered during the excavation.

Though many toys were created in the home, Greek potters also made children's playthings: dolls, tops, yo-yos, rattles, and pull-toys. The beauty of this doll suggests that it must have been a special gift for a much-cherished child.

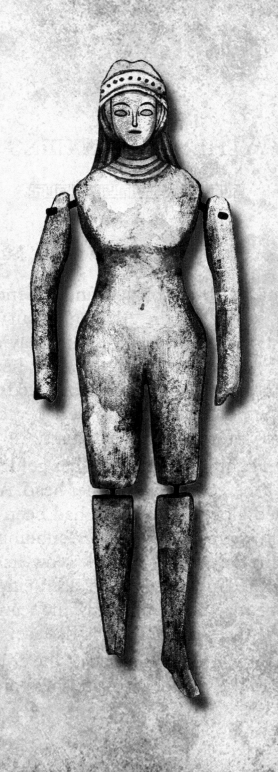

ATHENA IN ATHENS

Athena, goddess of war and defender of cities, stood on the Akropolis, surveying the city below. It was the third day of the month, a time set aside to honor her, and the smoke of sacrificial fire billowed in the air. The people of Athens were beseeching her for victory over the Spartans.

Sunlight flashed against her golden helmet as the goddess shook her head. Athena relished glory, and Athens had been glorious: an aggressive sea power, sublime in its arts, unmatched in genius. Now its glory was in decline. Athena had seen cities fall, and she recognized the signs: the scarcity of fighting men, the dread, the disease.

Her sea-grey eyes followed the city walls down to the harbor. Spartan ships prowled back and forth across the narrow bay, depriving the people of timber and grain. The Spartans had achieved a navy, funded by Greece's old enemies, the Persians. Without wood, the Athenians could not replace the ships they had lost; without bread, they would starve.

For an instant, the goddess's face was shadowed by an expression of regret. Then she launched herself into the wind like a bird of prey, wheeling north to Mount Olympus.

MELISTO IN ATHENS

꧁꧂

Melisto was drunk. The taste of wine was sour in her mouth, and her bandaged head pounded. The world was no longer spinning, but she felt sick and hot. She kicked off the blanket Thratta had spread over her and glared at the raftered ceiling.

There was something she couldn't remember. She knew she had tumbled down the stairs and cut her head; she recalled that vividly. There had been so much blood that she had panicked, and her mother cried. Only Thratta remained calm, wrestling Melisto to the floor as she staunched the wound and bandaged her head.

One of the slaves was sent for a doctor. Another ran to the storeroom for a cup of wine to ease the pain. The doctor said that the upper bone in Melisto's arm was broken. At that, Melisto became frantic. To her, *broken* meant that part of her arm was about to fall off. As the doctor set the bone, she became half-crazed. She tried to bite him until Thratta held her down. The doctor encased her arm in bandages, stiffening them with a mixture of lard and wax.

Once the bandage was finished, Melisto stopped screaming. It dawned on her that the bandage was meant to hold her arm together. She submitted to having a sling tied around her neck and drank the last of the wine. The room spun. She closed her eyes and slept.

Now she was awake, and it was late afternoon. Melisto shifted onto her left side. Thratta stood by the window, spinning. The slave woman put down her distaff and came to the bed.

A glowing figure appeared in the doorway: Lysandra in her yellow gown. "Is she awake? Is she better?"

"She has a fever," Thratta answered. "Her arm's swollen. The doctor said it would swell."

"I sent Sosias to the market to buy her a present." Lysandra held up the doll in her arms. "Look, Melisto! Have you ever seen a more beautiful doll?"

Melisto stretched out her hand. She loved dolls, but she was hard on them, battering them to bits. Her mother had threatened never to give her another one.

The new doll was made of hard clay. Her painted face was serene, with chalk-white skin and lips as red as apples. The arms and knees were jointed. It would be possible to pose her and make her dance.

"You can weave her a little dress when your arm heals," Lysandra suggested.

Melisto made a sour face. She was six years old now; her wool work was improving, but she had yet to develop a taste for it. She averted her head as Lysandra felt her forehead.

Lysandra spoke to Thratta. "I don't think she's very feverish. It's hot this afternoon." All at once she spoke sharply. "You saw what happened, Thratta! She stepped on the hem of my gown and tripped! It was an accident — it happened so fast, I couldn't catch her! I nearly fell myself!"

The ugly thing was back in Melisto's head again: the thing she didn't want to remember. She had followed her mother up the stairs. The hem of her mother's gown brushed the top of each step, rippling, almost floating, tempting her to step on it. The gown was new, the product of skillful and painstaking work. She remembered the sound it made when it tore: *skritch!*

"You *saw* what happened!" Lysandra insisted.

Thratta echoed, "I saw what happened."

Melisto shifted onto her back and sat the doll on her chest so she could look into its face. If she thought about the doll and only about the doll, the other thing would go away. She fingered the doll's foot, which was sharply pointed; the doll would be an uncomfortable companion in bed. Nevertheless, Melisto would sleep with her. If she didn't, the doll's feelings might be hurt. She wondered if she could tie the doll to the tortoise in the garden. That would be funny, if she could make the doll ride the tortoise.

She smiled at the thought and shut her eyes. She slept.

When she woke again, the room was dark. Outside, birds were singing the dawn chorus. Melisto's mouth was dry. Anxiously she sucked her tongue and licked the roof of her mouth. She croaked, "Thratta?" but the room was empty. Thratta must have gone to the fountain house for water. Usually Melisto went with her: it was her favorite time of the day.

Melisto shifted to see if her arm had stopped hurting. It hadn't. The bandage around her head itched, and her very bones were sore, as if they had been shaken inside her skin. Her stomach growled.

Something sharp dug into her side. She fished the doll out from under her and gazed through the dim light at the painted face. The doll was as lovely as she remembered. She held it to her breast and started to get out of bed. Her foot knocked against something hard: there was a *clink*, and the floor was wet. Thratta must have left a cup of water beside her bed. She had knocked it over.

The thought of water increased her thirst. She would go down to the kitchen and tell one of the slaves to give her something to drink.

She adjusted her arm inside its sling and passed through the room where the women kept their looms. When she came to the stairs, she stopped. She remembered hurtling down them. All at once, she felt dizzy. She sat on the top step, hugging her doll. She did not cry, but panted, breathing in short gasps.

A murmur of voices came from below. One was her father's. Melisto leapt to her feet. Her bandaged arm upset her balance and she swayed, almost dropping the doll. She imagined the poor doll falling head over heels down the stairs and tightened her grip on it. "Father!" she cried.

Her father's shape appeared below, thickset and powerful. In an instant he mounted the stairs and stood beside her. "Melisto, what are you doing out of bed?"

"I was thirsty and there was no one to wait on me. Thratta's at the fountain house." She lifted her elbow, showing the bandaged arm. "I fell down the steps this morning. No, yesterday. My arm broke, but it didn't come off. And I bled," she added proudly. Now that her father was there, she was not frightened. "I bled a lot."

Arkadios laid his fingers against her cheek. "Your mother told me. I spoke to her last night, before I went out. I looked in on you, but you were asleep."

Melisto leaned toward him, sniffing. "Were you at a drinking party?" She always sniffed him when he came home late. It was their joke, the way she could detect the slightest trace of alcohol on his breath.

"Yes, but the wine was mostly water. My friends and I had politics to discuss."

"The Spartans," Melisto said, hoping to impress him with her grasp of state affairs. "Have you thought of a way to kill them and sink their ships?"

"Not yet. That's a nasty bruise on your face. Does your arm hurt much?"

"Yes, but not as bad as before. When the doctor bandaged it, it hurt." Melisto rolled her eyes at the memory. "And when I fell down. Mother said, 'I've killed her!' because I bled so much. And she cried."

"You tripped over her gown," Arkadios prompted her.

"Yes, I ripped it. And I fell. Now I'm thirsty and I want something to eat."

"Come to the kitchen then."

Melisto hesitated, cowed by the stairs.

"Do you want me to carry you down?"

"No. I'm not a baby," Melisto said scornfully, and wished she could take the words back. It would have been a great treat to be carried downstairs by her father. "I can go by myself."

She squeezed the doll against her left side and started the descent, two-footing each stair. When she reached the bottom, she exhaled.

Arkadios laid his hand on the crown of her head. "That's my brave girl."

Melisto glowed. She followed her father into the kitchen and stood like a good child, without speaking. Her father told the cook to prepare a meal for her: a bunch of grapes, a cup of water, a chunk of bread and a pool of honey to dip it in. He carried her cup and bowl out into the courtyard and sat next to her on the wooden bench.

She drank first, gulping the whole cup of water. The grapes were easy to eat one-handed, but the bread was more difficult; she could not tear it into small pieces and ended up with honey smeared all over her face. She stretched her tongue to its limits, licking her chin and lips.

Once her appetite was satisfied, she turned to watch her father. Arkadios sat with his head thrown back, his eye on the brightening sky. Even with the doll across his knees, he did not look foolish. He was dark, well muscled, and battle-scarred: a warrior and a citizen. Melisto imagined that Zeus must look exactly like him.

She touched his hand to get his attention. "I have a new doll."

Smiling, he passed it to her. "So I see. I told your mother she was foolish to spend money on a toy in times like these, but she insisted you needed a new doll. She was very frightened when you fell."

"She cried," Melisto repeated. "When there was all that blood."

"Your mother is good to you," said Arkadios, but Melisto scowled. How could her father know so little? She thought of Lysandra's hands, with their sharp nails and pinching fingers. She thought of the sore patches on her scalp from the times her mother twisted and yanked her hair. All at once, the world darkened. The thing she had forgotten swam to the surface of her mind. She heard the sound of the tearing dress and the ugly snarl on her mother's face as she whirled around, hand upraised. Lysandra had struck hard and on purpose, knocking Melisto backward into the empty air. None of it had been an accident. Her mother had meant to hurt her.

Melisto bared her teeth. "She's not!" she fumed. "She's not good to me, she's *bad* to me, she doesn't even *like* me, because I hurt her when I was born —"

Her father's face was startled. He didn't understand, and she couldn't tell him. Some demon had tempted Melisto to step on her mother's dress: that, also, was true. In a spasm of wordless rage, she snatched the doll and swung it upward, smashing it down on the edge of the bench.

Crack! The doll's foot flew into the air and fell to earth. It landed on the grass: pure white and perfect. Melisto gasped. She had broken her beautiful doll. She was bad even to herself. She crooked her elbow over her face and sobbed. Arkadios had never whipped her; that was Thratta's job. But he had seen her break her new doll. He would have to whip her now, and he was strong. She began to shake all over.

Arkadios moved deliberately. He slid one arm under her knees and eased her into his lap. The movement jarred Melisto's arm, but she scarcely felt the pain. Her father loved her. Burrowing, she tasted his smell: sweat, wool, masculinity. She gulped back her sobs, determined to show that she would be good, if he would just go on holding her.

"Melisto, I want to tell you about the night you were born."

Melisto lifted her head. She had heard the story of her birth countless times. It was a bad story. "I know all that," she objected. "Mother tells me. The pains went on for two nights and a day, and I hurt her because I have a big ugly head like an owl. And after all that trouble, I was a girl."

"That's your mother's story. Not mine." Arkadios eased his arm under her sling so that her broken arm was held securely. "The night you were born, I had the worst headache of my life. You've had headaches, haven't you?"

"Yes. You get them from the sun."

"Sometimes. But I think my head hurt because your mother was in labor. Her screams rang through the house. There was nothing I could do to ease her pain. I left the house hoping that by the time I got back, you would be born. But every time I came back, your mother was still in agony. My head went on aching."

"Did *I* hurt your head?" Melisto asked apprehensively.

"No. You must listen when I talk and not talk back, Melisto. Be still."

"I will," Melisto promised. She raised her hand to stopper her mouth and remembered in the nick of time that thumb-sucking was babyish.

"You weren't born until the second night. By that time, the whole household was waiting, listening and praying. At last I heard the sound of a baby crying. I gave thanks to the gods. The midwife brought you to me."

"And I wasn't a boy."

"No. But I took you in my arms — you were wet and wrinkled and screaming your head off, and here's the strange thing:

my headache went away. I remember the moon was full that night, and I carried you to the window. I looked at you in that strange blue light, and you stopped crying and looked me full in the face. I was filled with joy."

Melisto said wonderingly, "You were happy?"

"Yes. I hadn't known how happy I would be. It made me think of Zeus, the father of the gods. There was a time when Zeus had a headache, too. He suffered so much that Hephaistos had to split open his head with an axe. And when he did, out sprang Athena, the goddess of wisdom, and the patroness of our city."

"Athena," whispered Melisto.

"Yes. I believe Zeus loves Athena more than all his sons. More than Hermes, or Apollo, or Herakles. I believe the poet Homer thinks so, too. I remember what I said to myself: *This child will be my Athena.*"

Melisto waited transfixed, until she was sure Arkadios had finished. Then she wriggled closer. "Tell it again."

EXHIBIT 6

Bronze strigil, fifth or fourth century BCE.

The bow shape of this bronze strigil is characteristic; so is the groove inside the curved blade. The strigil, or scraper, was used to clean the body after exercise. Greek athletes anointed themselves with olive oil at the gymnasium. After their workout, they applied more olive oil and used the strigil to scrape the skin clean. Dead skin, dirt, oil, and sweat accumulated inside the groove and could be dislodged by running the blade through the thumb and forefinger.

Aristocratic athletes were often scraped down by an enslaved person.

Rhaskos in Thessaly

᠌᠌᠌᠌

1. Water/Moonlight

The summer Lykos died was very hot.
    The horses stood in the shade,
        tortured by the flies.
Sometimes Georgios gave me a bucket
  and sponge
        and told me to rinse them off.
They came to me willingly,
    shuddering with happiness
        as water streamed over their coats.
    The water made a sheen on their
    skins
        and light ran down the water.
I wondered: was there a man alive

who could draw *that*?
Light on water,
water on skin . . . ?
Even a god couldn't draw that.

That long hot summer
I went on drawing horses.
I remember how dry the dust was
when I rubbed them out with my
hands.
The horses were proof of my idleness —
dangerous:
so I had to rub them out.
I was getting better at making horses.

I once told Sokrates about the beauty of
horses.
One horse can be better than another,
not because it's faster, or stronger,
but because of the way it's shaped.
Haunches and crest, angle and arc —
I couldn't find the words. I sounded
stupid.
But Sokrates,
he knew what I was talking about.

He said

    maybe there's another world,

    where there's a *real* horse,

    a perfect horse,

        and all the horses in our world

        are copies of that perfect horse.

    All *our* horses

        come from that pattern —

        except a copy

        is never as good

        as the real thing.

The best horses are the ones that stick close

        to the *real* horse.

That's why some horses are more beautiful

  than others.

I asked him where that other world was.

He said he didn't know.

He was the wisest man I ever met,

    but he was always saying that: he

    didn't know.

The summer Lykos died,

    I wondered about other worlds. I

    wondered where Lykos was.

The underworld, I knew that much,
  but what's it like there?
At night I couldn't sleep.
  I thought about how Lykos said:
  Nobody ever gets out of anything.
He couldn't get out of dying,
  and that scared me stiff,
  because I might die, too.
I was afraid Lykos might be a ghost.
  The ones who die young,
  they're likely to be ghosts,
    because they're not satisfied.
    I felt sorry for Lykos,
    but I didn't want to see
    his ghost.
At night, I'd squeeze my eyes shut
  so I wouldn't see him. But then I
  heard things,
  the straw rustling, or a horse snorting
    out dust,
  and that was worse.

Those were long nights,
  when it was too hot to sleep,
  and I thought about ghosts.

131

One night I got up and went to the river.
Under the moon,
    the river was moving,
    white where the water caught on the
      rocks
        and curled into froth.
I went to the shallowest place.
I walked into the wet. And farther in
    till my knees tingled with cold.
The pebbles were hard under the arches of
  my feet,
    the mud soft on my toes.
I walked deeper
      till the water was up to my chest.
There was one place close to the bank
    where the river curved,
    and a tree root snagged into the water.
    I clutched it, lifted my feet,
    felt the river pull against my skin —
    I held on to the root,
    swayed,
    rocked myself in the cold current.
I knew if water covered my face,
    I could drown. So I held on tight.

I went back the next night and the next.
Each night I tried to swim.

 I gripped that root, and bobbed, and
  thrashed;
I didn't like the water on my face,

 or up my nose. It made me snort and
  choke.

 I pawed the water, scooping it
  back —
  Then there was one night, one
   moment
   I felt the water hold me up.
   It could bear my weight.
    I could rest on it!
  I wouldn't sink.
  I wouldn't drown.

After that it was easy.

By the next full moon, I could float on my
 back,

  stroke through the water, kick myself
  forward.
I stared straight up at the face of the moon,

  and my mind went blank.

133

Most of the time, during the day,
    my mind was full of struggling things:
        anger at the heat,
        fear of Georgios,
    missing Lykos,
    drawing horses.
But when I floated, it was clear
    like clean water,
        white as the moon with her single eye.

I'd been afraid Lykos might haunt the river.
I'd been afraid of drowning.
What I hadn't been afraid of
    was getting *clean*.

I hadn't thought about that.
But night after night, that hot summer,
    I swam in the river. And it made me
        clean.

And that's what sealed my fate.

2. Water/Daylight

Every slave knows his master.
No master knows his slaves.

Our master: Alexidemus. We knew he
   was vain,
      quick-tempered,
      and unjust.
He was generous with food, and a
   glutton.
He was pious and feared the gods.
On sacrifice days, even the slaves
      got a gobbet or two of meat.
He hated stinginess
      and was proud of his horses.

He was the son of that Menon of
   Pharsalos,
      who fought in the Persian Wars.
Everyone said the master
      wasn't the man his father was.
He knew that, and it gnawed at him.
      We knew all his tender points.
If there was a slave woman he wanted,
      we knew of his desire
         before he did. If he ate too much,
         and his bowels ran loose and
            black,
         we knew that, too.

He was *kyrios*, lord of the household,
    and our master.
He could have been worse.

His younger brother, Thucydides,
    and *his* sons,
        Tycho and Timaeus,
    shared the house.
There were also some girls.
We didn't know them.
They stayed indoors.

I don't mean to bore you,
    telling you all these names,
    but what I'm trying to make
      you see
    is that we needed knowledge,
      and we gathered it,
      and when we found it,
      we passed it on.
Menon was the master's son,
    and I ought to have known —
    even Lykos warned me.

One morning he came down to the stable
with his cousin Tycho. Georgios
saddled their horses
and off they went.
Menon was a bruising rider,
fearless,
destined for the cavalry.

They galloped back at noon, the horses
lathered white.
Menon yelled for someone to
hot-walk his horse.
That was often my job.
See, when a horse has been worked hard,
you can't just let him rest,
you have to walk him out,
keep him moving
till he's breathing soft and steady
and the fleshy pad between his
front legs is cool.

So Menon called for someone — he just
called "Boy!"
which could be anyone: Georgios was
a boy,
old Orestes, who was toothless, was a boy.

I was the closest boy,
    so I came forward. In those days
    nobody looked at me much. They
        just handed me things,
    a pitchfork, a bucket, the reins,
    so it was a shock
    when Tycho whistled and said:

"Look at that hair! Like firethorn berries!"
            Then his voice changed.
        "Menon, he looks like you!"

Menon said, "What? With that hair and
    that skin?"
        — because Menon was dark.

                "Don't look at his hair!
            I'm talking about his face!
        Look at his brow and his nose and his
                            chin!"

I ducked my head. Before my mother left,
        she used to wash me,
        and people noticed my red hair. After
        she went,
    I never washed,
        and I guess the red

was hidden under filth:
      sweat and oil and dust.
That summer, I'd gone swimming,
      and the filth got washed away;
            my face was still dirty
            because I swim on my back.

Menon frowned at me,
      eyes narrowing. He had a gaze like a
         hawk's.
Arm and scruff, he seized me,
      and dragged me to the water
         trough.
      I struggled and yelped.
He was strong as iron,
      supple as a python,
      and Tycho came to help him.

Then I was spluttering,
      coughing, held fast
         facedown in the trough
      while they scrubbed me.
      Hands in my hair, their fingers
         poking my eyes,
      I thought I would drown.

Menon's fingers were twined in my hair;
    he lifted my head —
    I could breathe.
My lashes streamed water,
    and snot ran out of my nose.
There was the world, seen through water:
    sun and sky and grass
    and Georgios walking the horses.
He must have seen everything
    but Menon was the master
    — so —

Menon said, "He's not like me."
He wasn't laughing anymore.

"He's like Lykos."

The two of them looked at me
    as if I were a ghost —
I'd heard how Menon bullied his
  brother
    and wept for him after he died.
I could see it in his eyes:
    his grief.

Tycho let out his breath.

"He's probably your father's brat. Or my
father's brat.

There was that Thracian woman,
remember?

With the red hair? She must have been the
mother.

The two of you together!
with those matching faces — "

He didn't finish. Menon wasn't listening.

He smiled at me

and it was the first time.

Later on I loved his smile

and courted it, shameless as a girl.

"Little brother!"

After that day, he never called me
that —

"Little brother, I want a boy to wait on me,

to be my personal slave. I choose
you.

You'll like waiting on me.

It's got to be better than what you're
used to!

141

You'll sleep by my bed,
>   and go to the gym —
You'll watch me work out and rub me
  down after.
What do you think?"

He asked as if I had a choice.
I was dazzled and half drowned —
>   but I wasn't stupid: I knew I had no
>   choice.
If Menon wanted me,
>   I would be his slave.
>   I wouldn't have to pick up turds,
>   but there would be other things.
>   Nobody ever gets out of anything.

>   Tycho warned him:
"Your mother won't like it. She hated that
>   Thracian woman.
>   She won't want him in the house."

Menon shrugged. "It's nothing to do with
  her.
>   I'm a man now. Mother has to see
>   that.
>   If I want my own slave, I'll have one."

That's how my life changed.

I followed Menon like a dog.

I slept beside his bed that night.

The floor was harder than my bed in the
barn —

no straw —

and I couldn't run off to the
river.

I couldn't sleep. I missed the horses
snorting

and the smell of the stable.

I thought of Menon calling me *little
brother*.

He'd given me a new tunic to wear,

with no holes in it.

If he was my brother,

I was son to the master,

and brother to Menon

— or his cousin.

I hoped he was my brother.

3. Gymnasion

It's hard to tell you about Menon.

I know I was stupid
         — you'll see that —
      but you have to see how it was for me.
      One moment, I was a stable boy,
            a ghost with a bucket,
            a human tool.
Then there was Menon.

 At first, I was a plaything;
      we roughhoused together
      and he teased me. He taught me to
         laugh.
I never laughed so much in my life.
      Half the time, I had no idea
         why I was laughing. Menon
            would say something
            — he used big words —
      and the way he spoke
         told me it was funny. I
            remember
         the creases in his cheeks
         deepening —
         the white of his teeth —
         the spark in his eyes.

He was like a horse, Menon.
He made me want to look at him.
His eyebrows double-slant
    like the wings of a pelican,
        his dark hair
        falling in waves,
        which were beautiful.
He knew that and wore his hair long.

Sometimes he'd stick out his hand, not to
   hurt me
    but to rest his palm on my head.
    I'd stand proud
      still
        as if I'd been crowned with laurel.
Then he would push me away. We'd
   roughhouse
    as if he were my brother.

He called me his wild Thracian.
    He told his friends he meant to tame
    me.
Some of them said I was beautiful. A
   beautiful boy. I never knew that.
    I stared into water, trying to see
      if it were true. I couldn't tell.

Menon taught me to stand straight,
    only bowing my head.
He wouldn't let me fidget or scratch
  myself.
He slapped me if I picked my nose.
He gave me a sponge
    and made me wash myself. Every
      morning:
    first my face,
    arms and hands,
    chest and legs,
    groin and feet.

I followed him to places I'd never seen:
    taverns and temples,
    and the market.
He gave me his coins to carry in my
  mouth.
Once I swallowed one. It was an obol,
    the size of a pea. I thought he'd
      beat me —
    you can buy two loaves of bread
      for that —
    but he only laughed.

Almost every day, we went to the
　　gymnasion.
　　　　I carried his weights, his oil flask,
　　　　　　his lucky discus. Slaves weren't
　　　　　　　　allowed to work out there,
　　　　　　to mingle with boys who were free.
But Menon wanted me to wait on him,
　　　　　　to scrape him clean,
　　　　　　to watch him win.
He made the gymnasiarch let me in.

We passed through the groves of
　　sycamore trees,
　　　　the leaves yellow-green or brown as
　　　　　　leather.
　　　　We walked past the track, which was
　　　　　　pounded hard
　　　　　　by rapid-running feet.
At the entrance there was a shrine with
　　three gods;
Menon told me who they were:
　　　　Herakles for strength,
　　　　Hermes for swiftness,
　　　　and Eros, god of love.

Inside was a punching bag
    and wrestling pits,
    everywhere the smell
      of sweat
      and olive oil
      and naked boys.
There was a din of flutes playing —
    the boys exercised to music —
    and the voices of men and boys
      laughing and jeering,
      panting and grunting.
The older men were teachers,
    citizens and warriors,
    scholars and poets.
They watched the boys at sport and chose
  their favorites,
    predicted the winners;
    I saw how they watched Menon.

He stood out. There were athletes
    as strong and some were beautiful,
    but they weren't like Menon. They
      shifted from foot to foot,
    awkward and bashful.

But Menon stood like a god,
>   almost posing, tossing back his head;
>   he knew the men were choosing him.

I took off his tunic and folded it,
>   anointed him with oil,
>   and watched him stretch:
>>   muscles working under the glossy
>>   skin.
I watched him sprint, his fists tight,
>   his head up, his stride boundless.
>   No one else ran like that —
>>   as if it were pure joy.
I sprinkled him with sand for the wrestling
pit.
He gripped his opponent by the arms,
>   and they stood forehead to forehead.
Like rams, like stags battling,
>   their sinews straining, their breath
>   loud and hoarse.
Menon was often the shorter man,
>   but the stronger man: when he
>   threw the other,
>>   I shouted his name:

149

"Menon, Menon, Menon!"
He liked that.

When he cast the javelin,
 the black spear arced,
 splitting the blue of the sky.
 I shuttled back and forth,
 setting sticks in the earth
 to mark his distance.
What I liked best was to watch him throw
 the discus:
  Crafted of shining bronze, smooth as
   an apple peel:
   moon-round, pressed flat, heavier
   than it looked;
He clasped it with his knuckles,
 steadied it with his thumb,
Rocked and swung back his arm —
 then! he wheeled around,
 that swift-circling spin,
 the arm upthrust —
  and the discus leaping
  flashing with sun-fire!
I wanted to grab a stick
 and try to draw

that spiral in the air
but it happened too fast
 and besides, I had to run
 and mark the ground
 and bring the discus back.

Afterward I scraped him clean.
 The strigil scooped against his
 skin.
He stank worse than a horse. The inner
 curve of the blade
 gathered brine and silt,
 dark, gritty, reeking;
 his scraped skin gleamed like
 honey.
Like a horse, he trusted my touch,
 and liked the grooming. After I
 scraped him,
 he sponged himself with water,
and I rubbed him with oil again.

Sometimes, in the evening, there were
 banquets
 or drinking parties. He liked to see
 me tipsy
 and forced me to drink.

He'd take a morsel of meat from his plate,
> lamb with the fatty edge burnt crisp.
He'd smile at me,
> and my mouth would water. Then —
> "Catch!"
> and he tossed it. He'd show me a ripe fig,
> lift his hand, elbow angled, ready to
> throw;
I'd ready myself, hands cupped for the
> catch —
> Then he'd eat it himself.

I remember the first time
> he beat me hard. He was drunk;
I held out his wine cup
> full to the brim. His hand jostled
> mine.
The wine lapped over the edge
> and his arm lashed out
> the cup cracked
> the wine splattered —
He gripped my shoulder, twisted me
> round,
> punched my back,
> knocked the wind out of me.

He seized me by the hair
    and slapped my cheeks.
I felt my face twist;
        I was going to cry —
        I couldn't help it —
        I don't know
            what god put it in my head,
            or if Lykos was there,
            I mean, his ghost —
I saw *him*. Lykos. I remembered
        the way *he* cried
            when he was little and skinned his
            knee.
I aped that look:
I grimaced —
        I grimaced like Lykos.

Menon's face changed.
    He swayed on his feet.
        He saw Lykos in my face,
    and the drunkenness, the cruelty,
    emptied out like spilt wine.
I learned to do that —
    make another boy's face.

I don't know how I did it.
More than once it saved my skin.

When Menon was drunk,
    I tried to keep out of his way. But he
      needed me then.
      I held the pot for him to piss in.
      I cleaned up his vomit.
    I guided him home on moonless
      nights.
He said I could see in the dark like a cat.
I could dodge like a cat, when he hit me.

Sokrates said it's shameful
    not to speak the truth,
So here's the truth, though it shames me.
At first,
    I loved him. I was proud of him. I
      was Menon's boy,
    and Menon was like a god to me,
      beautiful.
If sometimes he was cruel,
    sometimes he wasn't. And he
      talked to me.
    saw me. Noticed me.

154

Taught me things, and told me stories.
　　If sometimes he was cruel,
　　　　so are the gods.

And the man who questions the gods does
　not live long.

HERMES SPEAKS

Don't listen to that boy!
*The man who questions the gods does
not live long —*
What does he know? Everyone questions
the gods!
Not a day goes by
without some mortal shaking his fist
and bawling to the sky:
Why is there suffering in the world?
Why is there death?
and — my personal favorite —
Why me?
Yes, there's pain in the world, but don't
blame the gods —
we're pussycats!

. . . Maybe not Hera.
Being married to Zeus is hard on the
heart.

My uncle Poseidon
is moody: too much salt,
those dreary barnacles,
and all those storms at sea. Hades
lives in hell,
so he's bound to be dismal.
And Ares is worse.

. . . But then there's laughter-loving
Aphrodite!
with her sea-splashed legs
and shapely buttocks —

and look at *me*!
The kindly god, the bringer of good
fortune,
guiding you through this story!

—That reminds me: Remember I told
you
about the war?
Athens versus Sparta?

(It wasn't just Athens versus
       Sparta, actually:
   both sides had allies,
   but the allies, like Thessaly,
   kept changing sides.
   I'm not going to confuse you
       with that.)
The point is, after twenty-seven years,
   the war's over. Let's talk about who won:
Athens was beloved by my sister Athena,
   the she-dragon, the victory giver,
   goddess of wisdom, war, and craft.
She's a perfectionist, my sister;
   she cherished her pet city
   and gave it genius. The Athenians are
       good at
       architecture,
       sculpture,
       philosophy,
       democracy,
       vase painting,
       theatre,
       history,
       and law.

The Spartans are good at war. Guess who
won?

Exactly. It took a long time,
    but the Spartans had the backing
        of bloodthirsty Ares, father of tears.
        (Plus cash from the Persians.)
The Spartans bled Athens
    of money, men, and ships.
            . . . Oh, those ships,
            those naval battles!
            The rowers
        crammed below decks,
        tier upon tier
        sweating, doubled over,
        working as one
        to ram the hulls of the enemy ships,
            the splintering wood, and the
            slaughter.
The ocean seething with blood:
    O, the wine-dark sea!

I'm getting away from my point. But those
    naval battles
        were tremendous,
        spectacular. The land battles?

Even gorier. The Spartans excelled
on land.
>They're not stupid, the
>>Spartans:
>Good soldiers, and good
>>dancers.
>Not all of their poetry's bad.

— I've wandered off topic again. The next
time I go off like that,
>just stop me.

Here's my point:
>when Athena saw Athens was losing,
>>she left: cast off, jumped ship.
>Who can blame her?
>Who wants to captain the losing
>>team?
Once she was gone,
>man-slaughtering Ares
>ran amok. His sons
>>Panic and Fear
>>>circled like vultures
and Athens surrendered. The great Greek
experiment,

democracy,
whereby men cast votes
and rule themselves —
gone. Now Thirty Tyrants,
friends of the Spartans,
rule over the city.
Athens the valorous, Athens the free,
is now the home of torture and
terror,
and trumped-up charges. Hundreds
of citizens
arrested,
questioned,
put to death.
Hundreds more killed in secret.

And Melisto? What does she make of her
city in ruins?
What does the child of Arkadios know?

Nothing. She's stuck in the weaving
room.
Wool is the business of women.
War is the business of men.

Whether there are Spartans at the gate
    or Athenians killing Athenians,
    the wool must be washed and
      picked
      and carded and spun;
      the web on the loom
        must be strung.
Melisto strums her loom,
    her arms above her head
    aching —
    she counts the patterns under her
      breath
    and beats the weft threads upward.
When the city was besieged, she did not
    hunger.
Now murder's afoot, and she doesn't
    know.

Except, of course, that she does know.
    When something's deeply wrong,
      children know.
As fog creeps into a shuttered room,
    so does the poison of terror. Melisto
      smells it.
No one tells her what it is.

Melisto has nightmares. Sometimes she
    dreams
        of the Spartans, her old enemies,
        killing her father.
More often she dreams of the weaving
    room
        where the yellow walls are
            shrinking —
                there's the smell of wool,
                and women's sweat,
                and her mother's voice
                sharp with dislike.
Every day, all day,
        they spend together.
They are enemies still.

Melisto's nightmares
        come and go. Far worse
        are the nights
        when she can't sleep. She lies awake
        and frets about dying. Melisto knows
            what death is.
She's seen animals sacrificed.
Now she breathes in poison
        and imagines death.

The horror of it,
    having to be still,
    forever
    having to lie in the dark
    with the damp earth pressing her
      down
    unable to scream.

In her room at night,
    she clenches her teeth
    and jerks her legs,
    kicking away death.

EXHIBIT 7

*Fragment of red-figure hydria (water jar)
bearing the inscription* POLYGNOTOS
EGRAPSEN *("Polygnotos painted it").*

Polygnotos was among the greatest of
Greek vase painters and most active in Athens between the years 450 and 420 BCE. He
seems to have preferred working on large

vessels, such as water jars. His paintings are large in scale: the figures are formal, rhythmic, and dynamic.

Only a few pieces of this water jar survive. The artist's signature is on one of the larger fragments. Two other fragments show the legs of horses and warriors, suggesting that the original painting was a battle scene.

MELISTO IN ATHENS

Melisto stood at the foot of the stairs, listening. It was not yet dawn, and the house was dark. She had been awakened by the clink of water jars in the storeroom. Until recently, she had been in the habit of going with Thratta to the fountain house. A month ago, her mother had forbidden it.

Melisto missed the daily outing. Before daybreak, the fountain house was crowded with women: young and old, rich and poor, slave and free. Melisto eavesdropped as they filled their jars and chattered together. She liked the noise of the splashing water and marveled at the lions' heads on the stone walls: how did the water get into the lions' mouths, and what made it gush out? She pestered Thratta with questions, but Thratta said that plumbing was the work of men and gods, beyond the understanding of women.

Now Melisto crept to the silent kitchen, brushing the walls with her fingers. Forbidden or not, she would shadow Thratta and visit the fountain house. She swung around the door frame and groped for the three-handled shape of a water jar. Snatching one up, she headed for the courtyard. She shoved open the gate and took to her heels.

When she stopped, she was panting, but her lips stretched in a grin of triumph. She was free, all by herself, out in the city. The birds of Athens were singing the dawn chorus. Melisto wanted to sing with them. She skipped and pranced. The world around her was fresh and vast.

She hooked a right-hand turn, passing between houses so crowded that she had to hug the water jug to her chest. One prosperous-looking house had been daubed with red paint, black in the dimness. Melisto knew the markings were letters, but she could not read. It crossed her mind that there was something angry about the way the paint had been laid on, but the ugly message in the graffiti was hidden from her. She zigzagged into another street.

There was something white and small blowing over the ground — no, running: a Maltese dog. Melisto raced after him. She would have given everything she owned for a dog like that. She pursued him for ten minutes before he squeezed under the gate of his own yard.

She looked up to the Akropolis to get her bearings. Even in the semidarkness, she could see the opaque shape of the high city, and the sight of it thrilled her. Arkadios had told her that there was no more beautiful city in the world than Athens, and no buildings lovelier than the temples on the Akropolis. Melisto believed him. Captive and female though she was, the city was in her blood: the worship of the goddess, the gray guardian mountains, the steep profile of the rock against the sky.

A crossroads lay before her. Melisto paused. A fluttering ribbon caught her eye, and she turned left. If she had turned right, she would have come across a man lying faceup with his throat cut.

Instead she went left and came to a roadside shrine.

The statue was only a little smaller than she was: a maiden holding a bow, black-haired, red-lipped and smiling. Melisto recognized her: it was Artemis, the only Olympian goddess who had ever been a little girl. Melisto set down her jug by the goddess's feet and went in search of wild-flowers. As the sky brightened, she gathered a fistful: some were weedy, and many were closed, but Melisto was pleased with them. She bound them with a thread from her belt and left them at the goddess's feet. Halfway down the street, she remembered the water jug, and ran back for it.

The sun was almost up. Between the tallest slopes of the mountains, the sky was pearl, tinged with orange and rose-color. Men were coming out into the streets now, slaves sent on errands and horsemen exercising their mounts. The city gates were open, and farmers passed through, taking their wares to the market. The last of the women hurried home, their faces veiled.

Melisto followed the flow of the crowd. In one narrow street, she found herself an arm's length from a red-haired boy who was carrying two snared hares to market. The hares hung limp, their legs dangling. Melisto edged closer so that she could stroke the soft fur. The boy turned, startled. When he saw her, he smiled shyly and Melisto smiled back.

In the marketplace, the shopkeepers were putting up their tattered awnings, preparing for the fierce heat of the day. Melisto gazed around the stalls with delight. The richness of the Agora was overwhelming. There were clay pots and chickens, sandals and spices, trinkets and weapons and new-dyed wool. There were smells, too: the sulfurous wind from the metalworkers' quarter, the stink of dung and leather and pigs. Melisto loved smells. She liked best the smell of roasting meat, but rank smells did not disgust her. She inhaled deeply, drawing in the life of the city.

Still hugging her jar, she passed from stall to stall. She wished she had a coin to spend; she would have liked to buy a ribbon or a toy, something to remind her of her adventure. If she had known more about money, she might have observed that food was scarce and luxuries were selling cheap; if she had looked at the adults around her, she might have noticed the strain in their faces. But Melisto had little interest in people. She

173

preferred watching the animals: the foraging goats, the wandering pigs, the rare and costly horses.

As the morning wore on, the day grew warmer and the sun reddened her cheeks. She circled the crowded space, determined to extract every drop of amusement the city had to offer. A bronze helmet at a metalworker's stall caught her eye. It was child-sized: made for a boy, Melisto knew, but she reached for it to try it on.

"There you are!" Thratta seized her from behind. "I've been searching for you for hours! What are you doing out of the house?"

Melisto's heart plummeted. Thratta's grip was rough. A fierce beating lay in store for her, though not a public one; Thratta never shamed her by punishing her in front of other people. "I'm sick of staying in the house! You used to let me come and get the water. You said I was a help. Why can't I come with you anymore?"

"You must not say *why*." The words were tinged with weariness: Thratta spoke them several times a day. "You know you're supposed to stay indoors. You're sunburned, did you know that? Your mother will be furious.

I'm going to switch you hard when we get home." Her eyes lit on the jug in Melisto's arms. "Why did you take that jar? That's your father's best water jar, the one he uses when he has guests."

Melisto held the jar away from herself to look at it. She had meant to pick up a plain jar, but this one had a picture on it: armored men and spears and cantering horses. Even to Melisto's ignorant eyes, it was beautiful. She quailed when she recalled how she'd left it by the shrine. "I didn't know it was good. I took it in the dark."

"Give it to me. You'll smash it. We'll fill it on our way home."

Melisto brightened. The trip to the fountain house would postpone her punishment a little longer.

The fountain house was empty of women. While Thratta filled the jar, Melisto scooped up handfuls of water and drank. Thratta adjusted her head wrap, making a pad for the jar to rest upon. "Come," she said shortly.

On the way home, Melisto dragged her feet. Just outside the marketplace, she stopped, her eye caught by a flash of copper. "There's that red-haired boy!" she exclaimed. "I saw him a little while ago, and he smiled at me! He must have sold his hares — "

Thratta spun around so abruptly that the jar pitched sideways and smashed to the rocky ground. The clay shattered. Thratta ran toward the boy. When she reached him, she caught hold of his arm and fell to her knees.

The boy was startled. He tried to escape, but Thratta's grip was strong. She grabbed his other hand and spoke to him urgently. He shook his head. She drew him closer, gazing down at his left arm. When she released him, he stumbled, regained his footing, and ran.

Thratta bowed her head. Still kneeling, she lifted her hands as if to mask her face. Shakily she got to her feet. She came back to where Melisto stood and stared in shock at the broken jar and the wet earth.

Melisto shifted uneasily. "You can say I broke it," she offered. She could not have said why she made so rash an offer. "I won't tell."

Thratta's eyes were blank, like the eyes of the dead hares. "I must get you home."

Melisto fell in step behind her. They walked in silence until they came to a cluster of sycamore trees. Thratta turned aside, leading a surprised Melisto into the grove.

It was a different world among the trees. The sounds of the city were muted. There were tufts of green grass between the rocks, and a woodpecker flew to a high branch, flashing his scarlet crown. Thratta sank down on the grass. Melisto followed suit, sitting with her arms clasped around her knees.

"Listen to me." Thratta's voice was low and fierce. "You're eight years old, and I'm going to tell you the truth, though your father told me not to. The city's dangerous. There've been child snatchings — people stealing children and taking them away from their homes. That's why you can't help with the water anymore."

Melisto puzzled over the words. "But why —" She bit back the word, remembering Thratta's dislike of it. "I mean, who does it? Who steals the children?"

"I don't know." Thratta pulled up a blade of grass and tore it down the midrib. "I only know what the other slaves tell me, and they only know what they overhear. There are thirty men in charge of Athens now, men who were friendly with the Spartans. They want to get rid of their enemies. So there have been deaths —"

"Children?" interrupted Melisto.

"No. It's mostly men who've died. Citizens — some of them rich men, like your father. They've been arrested and put to death."

"Men like my father?" echoed Melisto.

Thratta put out her hand, silencing her. "There's a list of men the Thirty have agreed not to harm. Your father's on that list. At least, that's what Sosias says. But other men have been killed by the Thirty. Hundreds of them. Perhaps more."

"How do they kill them?"

Thratta averted her eyes. "Your father wouldn't want me to say."

Melisto jabbed her fingers against Thratta's knee. "I want to know."

"The Thirty give them hemlock to drink. That's poison. It's not an easy death, but it's easier than the other. Sometimes they'll strap a man to a board with an iron collar around his neck, and choke him to death.

Some men are never arrested or charged; they're killed at night, murdered with a club or a sword." Thratta dug her fingers into the earth and ripped up a handful of grass. "Are you satisfied? You like the answer to your *why*? The city's still at war. The Thirty are on one side, and the rest of the people on the other. Everyone knows how much your father loves you. Don't give his enemies the chance to hurt him."

Melisto nodded slowly. She imagined an iron collar around her neck and touched her throat. "What happens to the children?"

"Nobody knows. Maybe they're sold as slaves. Whatever happens to them, your father doesn't want it to happen to you. That's why you must stay indoors where it's safe. Your father will be safe, too, as long as he doesn't go against the Thirty." She paused to let the words sink in. "So for once in your life, you're going to do as you're told and stay indoors. If you run away again, I'll beat you black and blue, and tell your father that you're bad. Do you understand?"

"Yes, but —" Melisto stopped. The silence was so fraught with questions that Thratta snapped, "But what?"

"But why did you run after that boy?"

Thratta tensed. She answered in a voice so low that Melisto scarcely caught the words. "I thought he was my son."

Melisto's mouth opened in a silent O. A wave of emotion swept over her: astonishment, pity, jealousy. "Was he?"

"No."

"Where is he? Your son."

"Thessaly."

"Where's Thessaly?"

"North. Over the mountains. By sea it took three days."

"What's his name?"

"Rhaskos."

"Why didn't you bring him with you?"

"My old master wouldn't allow it. Rhaskos is his son, too."

Melisto worked this out in her head. First and foremost she was her father's daughter; she knew that. It was the male parent who gave life; she belonged to Lysandra in a lesser way. She supposed it must be the same way for Rhaskos.

"What was he like?"

180

Thratta was silent. Overhead, the leaves shifted, and the woodpecker attacked the tree trunk: a brittle staccato in the stillness. Melisto shifted, peeling her bottom away from the damp grass. She hoped this would not be one of those times when Thratta didn't answer.

When Thratta spoke, her voice was full of longing.

"He was quick. I named him well. *Rhaskos* means *quick*, brisk as a bird. He was quick like that — like a bird or a little colt, or like a flame — his hair was so red . . . But then he could be still, when there was something he wanted to look at. I've never seen anyone *look* the way my son did. He'd see a bird crossing the sky; he'd lean back his head and follow it with his eyes as if he could fly . . . He was fierce and brave; he fought with boys bigger than he was. He was a warrior, my little Thracian." A long shiver ran through the slave woman. "I hurt him when I left. He was too little to understand. He fought me. He was a little older than you, and different from you, but . . . he was beautiful, all lightness, and you're heavy; he was bright and you're dark, but both of you — you fight. You don't give in."

Melisto was silent, willing Thratta to say more. The image of a boy took shape in her mind, a boy who shone like a flame, who gazed into the sky as if he could take flight. She wished she were like him: bright and swift and beautiful. The wave of jealousy crested and broke. "You love him more than you love me."

Thratta turned her head, incredulous. "He's my *son*." Her tone left no doubt in Melisto's mind. Compared to Rhaskos, Melisto was nothing.

Melisto scowled. She hugged her knees to her chest and bent her head to hide her face. Next to her father, she loved Thratta. "I don't care," she said, between clenched teeth. Then the words did a somersault inside of her. She spoke them again in a soft voice. "I don't care. If you want to love him best, you may. I'll still love you."

Thratta picked up a twig and broke it in half. "You won't always."

"Why won't I?"

Thratta rose and shook out her dress. "You just won't. You'll grow up." She held out her hand to Melisto. "It's time to go back."

Melisto took Thratta's hand. "Are you going to beat me when we get home?"

Thratta sighed. There was indecision in her sigh: Melisto pressed her advantage. "If you don't beat me, I'll say I broke the jar. You can say you found me in the market, and the jar was already broken, and you beat me then."

"That's a lie. A citizen's daughter shouldn't tell lies."

"You're not a citizen's daughter," Melisto pointed out.

"Aren't you ashamed to tell a lie?"

Melisto shrugged: she was not.

"Very well. We'll lie. I'll tell your mother you've already been punished. You always have plenty of bruises to show. Keep your head down, as if you're sulking. And don't tell anyone about my son. That's my business. Do you understand me?"

"Yes," conceded Melisto. "I won't tell."

"And from now on, you'll stay indoors."

Melisto cast one last look at the trees: the peeling bark, the curling leaves, the radiant sky between the branches. She looked for the woodpecker, but he had gone. "From now on, I'll stay indoors," she agreed sadly, and followed Thratta out of the grove.

HEPHAISTOS SPEAKS

Forgotten me?
>I, Hephaistos,
>>crooked-foot,
>>foreign,
>>am often forgotten.
I'm not as chatty as my cousin Hermes.
>No one is.

Do you think I've forgotten the boy? I
haven't.
>Anyone who works with fire,
>>as I do,
>>learns concentration.
>I steady that boy like a pot on the
>wheel.

He spins inside my hands. He's still a
    child,
        hot with hero worship,
        unlucky, unwise.
            He's liquid bronze,
                malleable. Like iron beneath the
                hammer,
                    he glows scarlet,
                        throwing out sparks. Nothing
                        takes shape without struggle:
        Clay resists.
            Bronze fumes.
                Iron fights.
The craftsman keeps his eye on his work.

As for Menon —
    whom I dislike —
    he's gone to war. His first battle:
        There's a civil war raging.
        Some tyrant named Lycophron —
            I think that's the name.
    I'm not interested in war.
Battles are all the same,
    brawn and blood and chaos,

186

the cruel maiming
of that most intricate beauty: the
    male body. Now, *armor* . . .
I like armor. There's skill in armor. I can
    appreciate
            the flex
            and bite
                of a good sword. I value
            the carving of a fine sarcophagus.
    But the bloodbath between
                the sword and the coffin?
I can't get interested in that.

When Menon goes off to battle,
        the boy's sent back to the barn.
He's bored. He scratches with a burnt
    stick
        on the stable wall, trying to capture:
                Grace
                Speed
                    Menon throwing the discus —
The stick breaks. The boy has forgotten
        most of his Thracian,
        but he still knows how to curse.

I'm not going to leave him like that.
He's too good for Thessaly. What's this
    country famous for?
        Horse races, gluttony, drunkards,
        witches who call down the moon —
Look at the temples! Mud brick!
No one honors me here!
                    but in Athens —

In Athens, I am worshipped;
        the Athenians spring from my seed.
They honor me with sacrifice,
        torchlight, and festival.
In Athens, there are temples
        to rival the work of the gods:
        forests of fluted marble,
            a wonder to behold!

I will send my boy to Athens
        and wrest him away from Menon.

RHASKOS IN THESSALY

1. Patroklos

When Menon went to fight
> I wanted to go with him. I said I
> could carry his shield.
> He said I'd slow him down.

He had to go to war.
> What else could he do? A rich man's
> son?
He couldn't dirty his hands, like a
farmer.
He couldn't twist rope or sell sausages.
He was born to rule other men,
> or to fight them.

189

So Menon went off to fight battles,
   and I went back to the barn.
I'd forgotten how picking up turds
   makes your back ache and your
      hands stink.
I'd forgotten how it was:
   the same task,
   the unbroken silence,
   day after day.
Was I a fool if I missed him?
He'd taught me things. Told me hero
   stories,
I remembered those stories, over and
   over;
They were all I had to think about.

There was this man named Akhilleus
   — he's been dead a long time —
   but he lived in Pharsalos,
   right down the road. There was a
      shrine
      where he used to live
      with statues of him and
         Patroklos,
      his friend.

One day
        on the way to the market, we passed
            them.
        I asked who they were.

                                        Menon said:
            "You never heard of Akhilleus,
            the greatest warrior who ever lived?"

I never had. So here's the story:
Akhilleus was beautiful,
        swift-footed and proud.
        He was the son of a sea-nymph,
        almost a god,
        but there was a doom on him.
If he fought, he would win
        undying fame —
        but he would die young.

The way I saw it, he couldn't win.

Patroklos was his friend. And here's the
    thing:
Patroklos was shorter — at least, his statue
    was —
        so I thought of him as a boy.

In my mind, there was Akhilleus, who was
  like Menon,
        and Patroklos, who was like me.
They went off to battle together.

For a long time, Akhilleus didn't fight.
Not because he was a coward,
        but because one of the other men
          had shamed him.
Everyone wanted him to fight,
        because then the Greeks would win,
        and these other people, called the
          Trojans,
            would lose.
But lion-heart Akhilleus was too angry to
  fight.
He stood on the sidelines
        while the Greeks were butchered.

Patroklos couldn't stand it.
He wasn't a great warrior himself,
        but he cried like a girl
        when his friends were slain.
So then Patroklos fought.
And he was killed.

And his death broke the heart of swift-
  fated Akhilleus.

Then Akhilleus fought, and Akhilleus was
  killed,
    but the Greeks won the war.

I felt bad for Akhilleus, because:
First, he was shamed in front of
  everyone;
    so his pride was broken.
Then he lost his friend.
Then he died. And the story was *true*.
They used to live just down the road.

When Menon told me that story,
I was so caught up, I said,
    "I know how he felt."

    I saw the mocking light in Menon's eyes.
                                    "You?
                You crumb, you mouse,
                    you compare yourself
                        to godlike Akhilleus?"

"I didn't say I was *like* him.
I said I know how he felt."

And I did. And I do. Because Akhilleus —
  he couldn't win.
He couldn't have both life and glory,
      and he had to lose his friend.
That's what I understood,
      and Menon didn't,
      because he always won everything. In
        the gymnasion
      or when we play-wrestled,
      he had to win. Every single time.
If he couldn't win,
      he was like a drunkard without drink.

I didn't think about that, after he went to
  war.
I didn't think how he mocked me,
      or called me *andrapodon*,
      which is a word for *slave*
      that means *thing with human feet*.
I missed him. I remembered how he made
  me laugh.
I thought about how proud I was
      when he won a race or a wrestling
        match. And after a while,

194

I made up a new Menon. I was
  Patroklos,
    and I made him like Akhilleus. I
      remembered him
    different from the way he was. It
      was stupid,
  but after Menon left
    I had nothing to do inside my
      mind
    but make up crazy stories.

Sometimes you *have* to lie to other people.
But you don't have to lie to yourself.
It's like what Sokrates said:
  When I lied to Georgios —
    about whether or not
    I'd picked up turds in the far
      field —
  I knew I was lying. I lied *on purpose*.
When I made up stories about Menon,
    it was worse, because after a while
    I didn't know I was lying.

Then Menon came back from the war.

2. Warfare

The minute I laid eyes on him, I knew he
   wasn't Akhilleus.
      And I wasn't Patroklos.
If I died, his heart wouldn't break.

He was changed.
He'd always been lean, but now his bones
   were sharp.
He put me in mind of a bow strung tight
      just at the point of breaking.
No less beautiful, but —

Three days Menon was home
     before he came to the barn to find me.
He snorted like a horse with his nose full
   of dust. He said I needed licking into
   shape.
He said he could tell
     I'd gone back to my own ways,
     my old stink.
I'd like to see *him* pick up turds all day and
   not stink.

196

I went back to serving him;
>he went back to teaching me things.

He taught me about war:
>the blows he'd dealt, the deaths he
>>dodged.

He showed me dents and scrapes in his
shield.

He had a new sword, the blade inlaid
with iron;
>he taught me how to oil it.

He was wolf-hungry, those first days
back.
>>He drank too much. He took me to
>>drinking parties
>>so I could lead him home. I carried
>>the torch
>>and steadied his footsteps when he
>>stumbled.

I helped him into bed. I filled a water
jug,
>emptied the piss-pot,
>placed them on the floor where he
>>could reach.

Then I crawled under his bed. He
   wanted me nearby
      and it was safe under there. When he
         slept,
            he was prey to the winged god,
               the frightful one,
                  Ikelos,
                     bringer of black dreams:
I'd hear the bed frame creak,
      the bed ropes straining. He'd twitch
         in his sleep
      and mutter. Then there came a
         night —
      he wasn't yelling —
         he was whimpering
         high and thin,
and I pitied him. I crawled out
      from under the bed
      knelt beside him snatched his arm
      tried to shake him awake —

I hit the ground.
                        I saw stars.
      my eye and my nose

198

blood gushing

warm

blinding me

slicking my chin

my blood on his
hands
he shrieked like
an owl
inhuman

There were footsteps,
his mother,
a slave with a light.
They managed to wake him and calm
him.

That was the first time he broke
my nose.

3. Mycalessus

When dawn came
I went to Georgios. My eye was
swollen shut.
I was afraid I'd go blind.

Georgios said it was nothing: my eye
would mend,
  but my nose might be crooked.

  "—Which wouldn't be the worst that
                could happen.
    Good looks are bad luck for a slave.
  You'd never have caught the master's eye
    if you hadn't been so good-looking.
          And what's it got you?"

I thought of saying,
    A black eye
    and a crooked nose,
    but it hurt to talk.

When Menon saw me next, he looked away.
He said it was a pity about my nose,
    but I'd already been *disfigured*
    — that was his word —
  because of the scars on my arms.
      They were *barbaric*.
I remember learning those words that
  morning:
    Disfigured: made ugly.
    Barbaric: not Greek.

Thracians, Menon said later,
    were barbarians. Brutes, not men. He
      said they were brave
  but hotheaded,
      stupid like me, with my thick
      Thracian skull.

I remembered my mother's stories.
I said to Menon,
      "My grandfather was a Thracian
      soldier. He feasted with kings
        and drank from a golden cup."
And Menon laughed. When he laughed —
  his eyebrows lifting
  and his head thrown back —
  my heart took wing like a gull,
      because I'd made that joy in him —
  but then his eyes narrowed
    and I braced myself.

He asked me if I knew what the Thracians
  were,
    what they'd done
    at Mycalessus.
      I didn't. He told me.

Mycalessus is small. Just a village,
> so out of the way
> that the wall had tumbled down
> and nobody bothered to fix it. The
> Thracians came.
> They were hired soldiers,
> fighting against the Spartans.
> They'd fought their battles
> and were heading back to Thrace.

But there was Mycalessus,
> right on their way home,
> and the gates stood open.
There was no one to fight.
There was nothing to steal.
The people who lived there
> defenseless.

The Thracians thirsted for blood. They
> attacked without warning.
They slaughtered
> men, even the old men, women
> and children —
> even livestock. There was a school
> full of children

young as me —
they hacked them to bits with
their swords.

Menon snapped his fingers in my face.
"How do you like being a Thracian now?"

I didn't have a word. To kill old and young,
male and female,
beast and human,
where's the glory in that?
What courage was shown? What god was
served?
If the story was true —
then the Thracians were cowards,
monsters, barbarians,
brutes.
And I was one of them.

That's what Menon taught me about
being a Thracian.

Turn and Counterturn
Menon and Rhaskos

⌇⌇⌇⌇⌇⌇⌇⌇⌇⌇⌇

TURN: MENON

At the feast of Poseidon Petraios
    we honored the God of the Sea, the
      Horse God.
Black-haired Poseidon, who shattered the
rock with his trident
    and gave us the plains
    and the river Peneios.
We honored the god with verse,
    and the slaughter of bulls,
      races with chariots,
      swift-footed horses
      and hard-muscled men.

204

After the games, the feast

where the world is turned upside
down and shaken.

Just as Poseidon

combs out the waves with his trident
and makes the earth tremble —

so the banquet reverses

the natural order: Slaves
command their masters.

They lie at their ease,

guzzling and gobbling,

while masters wait on their
slaves.

I took the boy Thrax. I spoiled him —

right from the start. Some trick in his
face

that recalled to my mind

Lykos, my brother —

As if a barbarian boy,

a man-footed *thing*,

could replace or resemble

the brother I lost . . .

The day of the feast shone blue;
    the ground was hard with frost.
As the hungry wolf scatters the sheep,
    the wind gave chase to the clouds in
      the sky.
When I toed the line for the footrace,
    the boy stood on the sidelines, shrilling:
"Menon! Menon! Menon!"

Then some god came into my breast
  — Herakles
    or fleet-footed Hermes —
I won, and they cheered me, and crowned
  me
    with a fillet of pine and wild celery.
The boy scraped me clean,
    and we went to witness the sacrifice.

Twelve fat bullocks, my father's wealth —

No man gave more that day. They passed
  in parade,
    their horns gilded, their heavy necks
    collared in pine.
      First the procession

and then the slaughter. The priests
    stunned them with clubs
    and sliced open their throats.
The blood was dashed on the altar,
    the victims flayed, and the fires
      kindled,
    the smell of fresh blood and the smell
      of smoke,
    the fragrance of roasting meat . . .

No one on earth
    had the right to insult me.
I gave my strength and my wealth to the
  god.

Then the banquet began. I'd given the boy
    a tunic that matched his hair. I led
      him to one of the benches
    and told him to lie down. What slave
    knows how to recline and eat?
      He lay there, stiff and awkward,
    sucking the meat from his fingers,
    slurping and spilling the wine —
        I waited on him,
        I watered his wine.

In between courses, I drank —
 Since the war
 I've suffered a thirst
 no cup of wine can quench.

I drank. And I drank. The banquet wore on.
 It grew dark and the night was a
 blur —
At some point — I don't know when —
 I decided to mimic the boy.
He was altogether too sure of himself,
 lounging and giving orders:
 He was flushed and excited,
 licking his fingers,
 drawing all eyes to himself —

I wanted to hold up a mirror
 and show him who he was.

Bowing and blinking, cringing and
 fawning,
 Rushing to refill his cup —
Some of the others laughed at me —
 the boy was blind to the joke.

I picked up a stick — the boy was
  always
      scribbling in the dust.
I poked at the ground. He blushed like a
  girl.
He shouted my name, and I ran to his
  side:
      Lifting his cup, he dashed the
        wine —
      Disgraceful! — into my face.
I knelt there dripping — this boy that I'd
  pampered and favored
      defied me.

Silence. Then laughter.
      I would have killed him —
      beaten him senseless —
Who would have blamed me?
I would have taken the skin from his
  back,
      but the rules of the feast forbade it.
He was saved by the power of custom
  and law
      at the feast of Poseidon Petraios.

At the feast of Poseidon Petraios
we worshipped Poseidon, father of
horses,
Hothead Poseidon, who stirred up the
earth with his pitchfork,
split open the rock,
and freed the first stallion.
We honored the god with games,
so Menon could compete.
He'd been drunk every night
seven nights running.
I prayed he would win.

After the games, the feast —
which I dreaded. I knew there would be
trouble.
Just as Poseidon
tosses the bottomless ocean
and makes the earth queasy —
the banquet turns upside down
the way of the world. The masters act like
servants:
pretend to be meek

stupid and clumsy
make fools of themselves, and us.

I was hoping he'd leave me behind.
He tipped up my face between his hands;
He wanted to see if
my bruises were gone.
He didn't want people to know
he'd broken my nose.
He'd been proud when they called me
a beautiful boy.

The day of the feast dawned fair.
Menon was hung over.
I rode behind him, clutching his waist,
his sweat and his breath fermented with
wine.
He met with his friends, and they cheered
him.
I stood beside them at the sidelines
shouting "Menon, Menon!"

When I saw him running, his long locks
streaming,
swift as Akhilleus,
my pride in him swelled. I was

211

spellbound
in spite of myself. When the race was
over,
I scraped his skin clean,
and we went to witness the sacrifice.

Twelve fat bullocks, his father's wealth,
a gift to please the god. They passed in
parade;
their horns were golden, curved like the
arms of a lyre.
I wanted to draw
their blackness against the sky:
their bulk, their strength,
and those lyre-shaped horns.
I felt a terrible pity —
but there was no time. They were stunned
with clubs;
their throats cut, the blood dashed on the
altar.
. . . The sweet aroma of meat . . .

Everyone there
looked on Menon with favor.
He gave the sacrifice. He wore the crown.

Then the banquet began. I had to lie down
as if I were the master. He'd given me a
tunic to wear,
rust red and soft, bordered with leaves,
the work of skillful women.
I leaned on my left elbow,
and tried not to look like a fool,
He brought me food, and I ate:
Meat on a skewer,
dripping with richness
— Warm grease ran down my fingers —
salty cheese;
figs dipped in honey;
later on, cups of wine.

I drank. I was thirsty. All that rich food —
the skin on my belly felt tight.
The world spun round like a top,
and whenever I snapped my fingers
Menon came running. He knelt before my
couch
and filled my cup to the brim.
I was tempted to giggle —

213

I got the hiccups —
some of the other slaves laughed.

We were tasting not wine, but freedom,
which was sweeter than wine.

Then I looked up. I saw him mocking me.
Squatting down, stick in hand —
I didn't know he knew I drew.
He grinned an idiot grin.
He jabbed at the earth and batted his
eyes,
mocking my drawing —
I didn't know what he meant. Then I did.
I saw red. Like fog. I was blind with rage.
I shouted his name and he came.
I threw my wine in his face.
He flinched. I disgraced him; I shamed
him; I swear by the gods
I was glad.

Silence. Then laughter.
I knew he'd beat me.
Maybe not then,

but he'd bide his time.
Both of us could have done murder that
night —
but the rules of the feast forbade it.
We were bound to obey the decrees of
the god
at the feast of Poseidon Petraios.

Rhaskos in Thessaly

Aftermath

The worst thing Menon taught me was
  this:
> When you're beaten, surrender.
> Cry out loud to the pitiless gods.
There's no point trying to be brave. You
  can't win.
When a man beats you, he wants to break
  your spirit;
> he'll keep on hurting you
>> until you knuckle under.
If you start crying right away,
> you'll rob him of something he
>   wants —
> a secret:

the exact moment when he breaks
you.
Afterward he'll taunt you:
Coward!
Slavish!
Womanish!
and you'll be sick with
shame.
But there isn't a master alive
who's going to say: *Well, boy, you're
brave,*
and that's manly, so I'll spare you.
No. If you try to hold out,
he'll just keep beating you
till you beg him to stop,
so you might as well beg first
thing:
abase yourself.
Say whatever you need to say.

Then he'll stop,
because he's proved it: you're a
coward,
slavish,
and womanish. *All slaves are like that —*

217

which warms the cockles of his
heart.

You'll hate yourself for crying,
but you'll have fewer
stripes
and smaller bruises,
and maybe you'll have
time to heal
before he beats you again.

That's what I learned from Menon.

EXHIBIT 8

early fifth century BCE

This fragment from a black-figured *krateriskos* was found near the spring at the Sanctuary of Artemis in Brauron, where young Athenian girls served the goddess as "Little Bears." This mysterious practice is mentioned, though not described, in Aristophanes's play *Lysistrata*.

Two girls dance around an altar decorated with scrolls. The girl on the left wears a short chiton, which balloons around her legs as she leaps into the air. The girl on the right, whose head is missing, stands on one foot and kicks with the other. Though the painting is primitive, the general effect is one of joy and spontaneity.

HERMES SPEAKS

Me again: Narrator. Next scene: Brauron.
Imagine a bit of broken pot
    shaped like a crooked square: a faded
      background,
    and two little figures in black: girls
        leaping in midair
        knees bent
          exuberant
        one girl wears a whirling
          dress —
        the other one's missing a
          head.

The pot came from Brauron
    and it never looked like much,

even before it was broken. These pots
were small,
    the size of juice glasses,
    and crudely made.
They're called κρατερισκοι:
    that's *kra* — as in *crawfish*
    ter — as in rip and *tear*
    ree — as in *repeat* (roll the *r* if you
    can)
    and *ski* — as in *skis. Krateriskoi.*
You'll find them near shrines to my half-
sister Artemis.
    Brauron was one of her shrines
    — and it's where we're headed next.
(The *B* in Greek
    is more like a *V*.) *Vrauron*:
    a wild place; sea-girdled,
    watered by a sacred spring. My sister
    Artemis likes marshes,
    the way I like doorways, gates, and
    gyms.

At Brauron, little girls lived as bears
    and served the goddess Artemis.

223

Why bears? The story goes
    long ago
    Artemis had a tame bear,
    and a girl child played with it;
      she teased it.
The bear, being a bear, killed her.
The girl's brothers killed the bear.
    My sister Artemis
        — who's a crackerjack archer —
    let loose her arrows of plague
    and started killing *everyone*. I'm fond
      of Artemis,
      really, I am; I adore her. Who
      wouldn't?
      Goddess of sweet garlands,
      guardian of young girls —
    but let's face it: she and Apollo
    are a little too quick with their
      bows.
If you irritate them — and they're
    touchy —
      you've got plague on your hands,
      and I've told you before,
I'm not wild about plague. I could do
    without it.

224

All those bodies,
    all that misery;
    and always, there's a *smell* . . .

But I'll say one thing for plague:
    it gets everyone's attention.
When people have plague,
        they pray. Everyone prayed to
        Artemis,
        and she relented. All she desired
    were some little girls
    to come to her shrine
    and act like bears.
What could be more reasonable?

So the girls came to Brauron,
    and acted like bears. How, you ask me?
I don't know. Nobody knows.
A lot of that stuff happened at night,
        and an active, mettlesome god like me
        needs his sleep. It was women's
        business;
            I wasn't supposed to know about it,
            which isn't to say
            I didn't peep.

The bear game was a mystery —
　　　no one wrote anything down.
All we have are pots like these,
　　　the *krateriskoi*,
　　　and the guesses of scholars.
　　　　　— Oh, those scholars!
　　　　　　what little ducks they are!
　　　　Dabbling into history:
　　　　　truth-seekers,
　　　　　archaeologists,
　　　　　dippers and diggers.
　　　　　They pore over bits of
　　　　　　broken clay
　　　and wonder what went on.
They drive themselves crazy:
　　　What age are the girls on the pots?
　　　Why do some have short hair
　　　　and others have long hair?
　　　Why do some wear their hair in a bun?
Does it *mean* something if you wear your
　　hair in a bun? And if it does —
　　　what does it mean?
　　　　What's the ritual
　　　　　symbolic
　　　　　　reason

226

for wearing your hair in a bun?
According to a written source,
    the bears wore crocus-colored robes —
      that is, saffron yellow —
but on the pots
no one ever wears a yellow robe. It
  drives the scholars nuts!
     What does it mean?
       Was the yellow robe a bridal veil?
       Or the pelt of a bear?

Here's what the scholars have agreed on:
Every highborn Athenian girl
    — or maybe just a few —
  went to Brauron every year,
  unless it was every four years.
They stayed at the shrine a few weeks —
    maybe a year,
    maybe four —
      and they served the goddess.
They were five to ten years old,
    unless
      they were ten to fifteen years old,
      (they might have been seven to
        eleven years old)

— but here's what you can tell
from the pots:
they raced each other,
or they chased each other;
they carried garlands. They
burned incense.
We're sure about that, because
the pots have traces of ash inside.
The girls danced. With them were people
in bear masks —
or maybe they weren't masks. Maybe
they were people
changing into bears!
And sometimes the girls went
naked.

. . . You know,
scholars
spend a lot of time sitting still:
working in libraries,
reading, taking notes,
so naturally
the idea of people
running around naked
is very exciting to them.

You can't blame them if they want to
    know more.

> *Why* were the little girls naked?
>
> *When* were they naked?
>
> Was there a ritual? Did they take off
>   their clothes
>
> > at the beginning of the ritual?
> >
> > Or at the end? Here's what one
> >   woman writes:

The convergence between on the one hand
>   *the profile of the rite,*
>   *and on the other*
>   *what on my hypothesis*
>   *would be the representation of a part*
>   *of the rite,*
>   *provides some confirmation*
>   *for that hypothesis.**

> > > Dear gods!

* Unlikely as it might seem, this quote is proof
that Hermes has read Christiane Sourvinou-
Inwood's *Studies in Girls' Transitions: Aspects of
the Arkteia and Age Representation in Attic Iconography.* He characterized it as "no place to go
for a laugh."

My point is: little is known.
    What was meant to be a mystery
        is still a mystery.
Except we're going to lift the veil a little,
        and peek. We'll see Brauron
        through Melisto's eyes —
Melisto's going to Brauron,
        to serve as a Little Bear.

EXHIBIT 9

Fragment from the Poet Sappho

Πλήρησ μὲν ἐφαίνετ' ἀ σελάννα
αἰ δ' ὠσ περὶ βῶμον ἐστάθηοαν.

full appeared the moon
and when they around the
    altar took their places . . .

(translation by Anne Carson)

The moon shone full
And when the maidens
    stood around the altar . . .

(translation by Julia Dubnoff)

The moon rose late,
and the breathless girls,
each taking her place
around the altar.

(translation by Sherod
Santos)

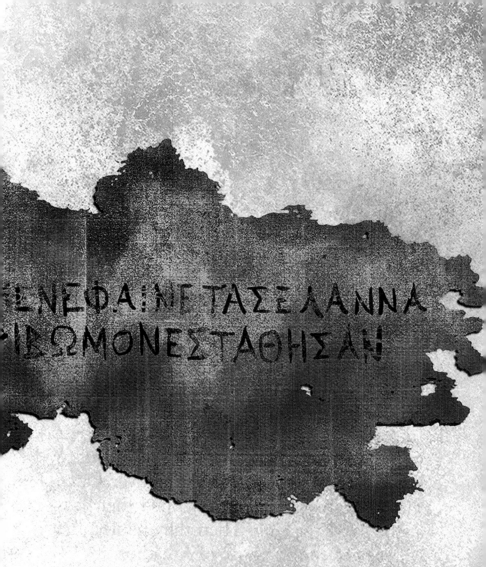

ΕΝΕΦΑΙΝΕΤΑΣΕΛΑΝΝΑ
ΙΒΩΜΟΝΕΣΤΑΘΗΣΑΝ

This fragment may be the beginning of a
poem. Like many fragments from
Sappho, it teases the mind with
questions: Who are these nocturnal girls,
and why are they gathered around the
altar?

MELISTO IN BRAURON

᚛ᚒᚒᚒᚒᚒᚒᚒᚒᚒ᚜

1. The Yellow Chiton

On the day Melisto left for Brauron, the
women of the household rose before dawn.
In a sleepy procession they carried their
water jars, not to the fountain house, but to
the southeast bank of the Ilissos River. Once
the city gates opened, they filled their jars
at the sacred spring. Then they hauled the
water back to the house of Arkadios.

Home again, the women dragged out
the terra-cotta tub from the storeroom.
They emptied their jars. Lysandra
supervised as Melisto crouched in the
icy water and sponged herself. Two of the
slave women, Chresthes and Evnike,
dipped cups into the water and poured it

over Melisto's head. Thratta knelt beside the tub, scrubbing the girl's scalp with her fingertips.

Once purified, Melisto stepped out of the bath. Her teeth chattered as the slave women rubbed her dry. Droplets of water ran down her back as Thratta massaged scented oil into her hair. Evnike, the youngest of the slaves, brought fresh clothes down from the weaving room.

Melisto regarded her new tunic with interest: a pale-yellow chiton with a violet-colored sash. Artemis's colors were purple and gold. There was also a saffron-colored himation, a cloak-like garment that symbolized the pelt of a bear. It was too heavy to wear on a spring day; it would be rolled into a pad and carried on her back.

Melisto was still shivering when Thratta plaited her hair, shaping a braid that circled her head like a crown. Sprigs of myrtle, violets, and willow leaves meandered between the sections of hair. Thratta's skillful fingers smoothed and twisted, tugged and poked. Melisto stopped shaking, but from time to time she twitched.

She tried to imagine the world that lay ahead. She was going away to Brauron, which was near the sea: she had never looked upon the sea. She would serve the goddess Artemis: how, or for how long, she did not know. At least a year would pass before she came back home. Every four years, the priestess of Artemis Brauronia was blindfolded so that she could select her bear-servants from the daughters of distinguished men. The potsherd that bore Arkadios's name had been picked. He was proud to offer his daughter to the goddess.

Melisto fastened upon that thought. Artemis had chosen her; it was an honor. No one had told Melisto that it would be shameful to weep when she left home. She had known without being told. She hadn't cried last night, when she said goodbye to her father, though she clutched him tightly, hiding her face against his chest. Leaving her mother would be easier.

"Hold up your arms," said Lysandra, easing the yellow tunic over her head. The slave women murmured approval. The short chiton was the work of Lysandra's hands: expertly woven and bordered with stags' heads. Lysandra had wet-folded it to set the pleats and pressed it under stones.

Now she bent to tie Melisto's sash. When she straightened up, she looked at her daughter with surprise. "You are very passable," she said, and consulted the slaves. "The goddess's colors flatter her, don't you think? And flowers are always becoming." She held up a bronze mirror so that Melisto could see herself.

Melisto barely glanced at her reflection. She knew she was ugly when she was with her mother, and beautiful when she was with her father. The rest of the time, it didn't matter: she was just herself. She studied her mother's face. If Lysandra were beginning to like her, it was a pity to leave home.

"Put on your sandals, and we'll see the whole effect."

Melisto grumbled, "I wanted new sandals." She was glad to have something to complain about; it made the world familiar. It was Thratta who had argued against the purchase of new ones, reminding Lysandra that Melisto had a two-day walk ahead of her. Thratta had oiled the old sandals and wiped them free of dust.

Lysandra circled her daughter, checking every detail of her appearance. "You are perfectly presentable. There will be prettier girls, I'm sure, but you need not be ashamed to stand with them. One more thing —" She reached behind her neck with both hands, unclasping the necklace from her throat. "Take this with you."

Melisto's eyes widened. She gazed with disbelief at the gold beads, the glowing amber of the sphinx's head. "For me?" she said. Her fingers uncurled like poppies opening to the sun. The necklace, still warm from her mother's flesh, fell into her hands.

Lysandra's voice broke the spell. "No, not for you! What would a child do with such a treasure? You must take it to Brauron and give it to the goddess as an offering. Don't you understand? I need Artemis to bless me."

Blood rushed under Melisto's skin. She shook herself as if another jar of water had been poured over her head.

"I'm pregnant," Lysandra said bluntly. "The whole household knows. Are you so backward that you haven't guessed? Doesn't it occur to you, when I'm sick morning after morning, that I'm going to have a child?"

"I've heard you throwing up. I don't think about it."

"Of course not; you think only of yourself. Can't you understand what a source of shame it's been, to have only one child, and that child a daughter? What about your precious father! Haven't you seen how he longs for a son?"

Melisto lifted her eyes. It was the accusing, owl-eyed look that Lysandra most detested.

"Don't scowl at me like that! How many times have I told you: a girl of good family keeps her eyes lowered! What will the priestesses at Brauron think if you glare at them like a wild animal?"

A retort flashed through Melisto's mind. "Maybe they'll think I'm a bear."

Unexpectedly Lysandra laughed. "Maybe they will. Perhaps they'll tame you; I never have. I pity them, all the same." The smile died on her lips. "Remember your father, Melisto. Have pity on him, if you have none on me. He's wanted a son since before you were born. If the goddess favors us, he'll have one at midwinter. Take the necklace to the priestess at Brauron. And pray for me. Another birth like yours could kill me. I could *die*." Her voice sharpened. "Does that mean nothing to you?"

Melisto wasn't listening. Before her mind's eye rose an image: her father with a son in his arms. Jealousy leapt and burned inside her. Then her mother's words sank in. Lysandra could die. Melisto didn't want that. She wondered if there was any point in saying so. She gnawed her lower lip, searching for words.

"It's light outside," observed Thratta.

The four women turned as one to the storeroom window. Dawn had given way to bright morning. The procession was to begin on the Akropolis before noon. Melisto's heart beat double time.

"We mustn't be late." Lysandra's voice was calm. "Put on the necklace, Melisto. That way, you won't lose it. Remember what I've told you and kiss me goodbye."

Melisto kissed her mother's cheek. The two of them embraced ceremoniously and separated in perfect unison. Melisto held out her hand to the slave women. She was not fond of Chresthes or Evnike, and she thought it was good of her to take their hands.

"Goodbye, Chresthes. Goodbye, Evnike."

Her face paled when she saw Thratta standing before her. The Thracian woman stood with the rolled bear-cloak in her arms. Melisto had not prepared herself to part with Thratta. All at once it was as if some god possessed her, pulling her face into a tragic mask. In a moment her mouth would grimace, spilling forth grief like lava.

Rough hands clamped down on her shoulders. "Turn around," Thratta ordered. Melisto felt the wadded bear-cloak press against her back. Thratta was lashing it into place: crisscross over her chest, crisscross between her shoulder blades. The cord was too tight, and the irritation was distracting.

Thratta leaned forward, speaking into Melisto's ear. "Do you know what I think? I think you will be a good Bear. I think some god has made you strong."

Melisto blinked. Thratta tied the final knot, yanking the two ends of the cord so sharply that Melisto rocked on her feet. Then she whirled about, flinging her arms around the slave woman. She tensed her eyelids to seal the tears inside.

A moment passed, then another. Melisto stepped back: she wanted to be the first to pull away. She set her chin, screwing her mouth into a fierce line that was meant for a smile. Some god had made her strong. She would go to Artemis and serve as a Bear.

2. Sacrifice, Butterfly, Fire

On the crown of the Akropolis, the sun blazed, and the wind breathed in gusts. Melisto stood before the Temple of Artemis, conscious that the crowd was watching her. She had known there would be a ceremony and a sacrifice, but she hadn't known so many people would come to watch. As a Bear, she was a celebrity, destined to serve both Artemis and Athens.

The Athenians had reason to be grateful to Artemis. When the citizens fought against the Thirty Tyrants, the goddess appeared on the battlefield, bearing a torch. It was Artemis who granted the warriors inspiration and victory. The Tyrants were overthrown, and democracy was restored. A new temple dedicated to Artemis the Torchbearer was being built down at the harbor.

Melisto tried not to fidget. She kept her eyes downcast and obeyed the four strong-looking women in charge of the Bears. They herded the girls away from their mothers and discouraged them from tearful goodbyes. One frizzy-haired child of six or seven defied them, waving to her mother, calling out, and sobbing. Melisto darted a scornful glance in her direction.

The temple doors opened. There was a murmur from the crowd as the priestess of Artemis emerged. Melisto glanced sideways and then stared. The priestess from Brauron was the most beautiful creature she had ever seen.

She was seventeen years old and dressed like the goddess herself in a deep violet robe with a fluted hem. The cloth was tissue thin, with pleats that rippled open and shut with every stride. The priestess wore a fawn skin over one shoulder and a quiver on her back. Two large hunting dogs followed at her heels: Melisto had never seen dogs so magnificently obedient. They walked with their heads up, stately and alert. When the priestess paused in mid-stride, they stood like statues, ears pricked.

Melisto's skin tingled with gooseflesh. She felt she was in the presence of the goddess herself. She knew her mother was an attractive woman, but there was something feral about Lysandra's grace, something that reminded her of a weasel she had once watched kill a snake. The young priestess was flowerlike in her beauty. Her cheeks were flushed, not painted, and her dark hair was unbound. In the wind, her tresses were borne upward; they seemed to move of their own free will.

The crowd fell silent as a priest approached the altar. Libations were poured: milk and honey and wine. A young girl led a goat with gilded horns toward the priest. Like the Bears, the goat had been washed and groomed for the occasion. Its coat shone like silver in the sun. The girl holding the lead carried a basket of grain. From time to time she fed the goat, who nuzzled her, asking for more. The priest sprinkled water on the animal and the goat tossed its head, agreeing to the sacrifice. Deftly the priest reached into the basket. He drew out the sacrificial knife. The goat, suspecting nothing, licked the young girl's hands.

The knife flashed, cutting the animal's throat in one swift movement. Melisto joined in as the women in the crowd gave a great cry of mourning and shock. The goat's knees buckled, and the blood began to flow.

What followed was familiar: the blood splashed over the altar and the swift butchering of the dead animal. Melisto did not watch. The small girl who had waved to her mother was sobbing afresh, undone by the death of the goat.

But the mood of the crowd was relaxed. The mothers of the Bears exchanged greetings, taking advantage of the holiday that allowed them to leave their homes. The goat was cooked, and the meat shared among the people. Melisto was given a mouthful on a spit. She leaned over to eat it so that she wouldn't drop grease on her tunic. The four women — were they priestesses or only handmaids? — divided the girls into groups of fifteen. A dark-skinned Syrian girl began to play the double flute. The procession took shape: the priestess first, then the dogs, the girls in their four lines, and the handmaids bringing up the rear.

The priestess headed toward the great gate. She did not look back to see if the girls were following her. She trusted her presence to draw them. Melisto fell into step, head high. She was keenly aware of the picture the girls were making, with their yellow tunics, purple ribbons, and crowns of flowers. Like water, they flowed through the great marble columns.

Once they reached the bottom of the Akropolis, the four women collected a pack donkey each. The procession wound its way through the Agora and down to the Sacred Gate. Melisto looked from side to side. Athens was her city, and she wanted to remember everything: tombstones and boundary stones, shops and shrines, forge and kiln.

By the time they reached the Sacred Gate, the crowd had dispersed. The flute girl stopped playing and stepped aside. The Bears passed out of the city, heading northeast to Brauron, a journey of twenty-four miles.

Away from the city, the terrain changed. The road was less marked, and the ground was rough, with rocks breaking out of the thin soil: the bones of the earth cutting through. The air was fragrant with thyme and spring onion. Wildflowers dotted the path: scarlet poppies and gleaming butter-cups, cranesbill and windflowers. Melisto snatched up handfuls and tucked them under her belt.

The girls no longer kept to their lines. They formed small clusters and whispered to one another, glancing warily at the women in charge. Names were exchanged: the first seeds of friendship. As the hours passed, the children began to limp, but they did not dare complain. One of the hand-maids scooped up a weeping five-year-old and set her on the donkey's back.

As the sun sank in the blue sky, the mountains loomed ahead. They looked daunting: the slopes so thickly furred with greenery that the shadows appeared black. Melisto had been told that the world out-side her city was a wilderness, peopled by wolves and satyrs and centaurs. Now she saw that it must be true. She quickened her pace until she caught up with the dogs.

The path was steeper now. The girls climbed it, crushing stems of myrtle and oregano underfoot. When they faltered, the women urged them onward. Sometimes they stopped to point out a clump of weeds. "Girls, look closely. This is fennel. You can eat every part of it: bulb, stalks, seeds." "This is cat's-ear: you can boil the roots and eat them." At the thought of food, Melisto's stomach growled. She eyed the wild plants warily, hoping she wasn't going to have to eat them for supper.

By sunset, many of the children had bleeding feet, and the smallest ones were in tears. Melisto looked down at her well-worn sandals and felt a surge of gratitude to Thratta. During the long hike, she had pulled ahead of the others. She had expected to be as inferior in strength as she was in beauty, but she was not. Once the Thirty had been defeated, Melisto had resumed her trips to the fountain house. Keeping up with Thratta, lugging the heavy water jars, had made her strong.

Her arm prickled. A butterfly had come to taste the salt on her skin. Melisto held still, transfixed. Its wings were dull gray, spotted with black. All at once the creature opened its wings, showing a flash of pure and glistening blue. Melisto opened her mouth to cry *Oh, look!* but the butterfly had flown away. She followed its flight and saw that the priestess of Artemis was watching it, too. Their eyes met. Melisto's lips spread in a dazzled grin. Then she was overcome with shyness and hung her head.

The priestess let them onward. The dogs and the girls followed. In a few minutes, Melisto heard the sound of trickling water. She was thirsty.

They had come to a spring in the foothills of Hymettus. The priestess bent and scooped up the water, dashing the drops at the children. She was purifying them so that the nymph of the spring would let them play in the water. She spread her slender hands and announced that they would camp for the night.

The girls took off their sandals. The promise of rest and the sight of bubbling water refreshed them. They stepped in gingerly, cooling their aching feet. Then they waded deeper, up to the knees. Silence gave way to squeals and splashing. The little girl who had cried so hard on the Akropolis caught sight of a frog and began to chase after it, laughing.

Melisto waded in with the others. High up on the bank, the priestess of Artemis was kneeling, uprooting tufts of grass.

Melisto left the water so she could watch her. She flattered herself she was inconspicuous, but the girl's dark head came up. She looked directly into Melisto's face.

"If you want to ask a question, ask it."

Melisto's mouth fell open. Swiftly she gathered her wits and spoke before the priestess could change her mind. "What's your name?"

The priestess smiled. "Korinna," she answered. She reached into the quiver at her back and took out a digging tool.

Melisto risked a second question. "What are you doing?"

"Digging a pit for the fire."

An idea flashed into Melisto's head. She could find no fault in it, but she hesitated, afraid to risk the friendliness Korinna had shown her. "I could dig, if you want. That way your dress —" She indicated the pleated masterpiece that was Korinna's peplos.

"I don't fuss over my dress," Korinna retorted. Her smile was the smile of a goddess: tender and radiant. She held out the digging tool as if it were a scepter. Melisto snatched it and dug for all she was worth.

Once the pit was dug and lined with stones, she looked up. Two of the other women had dug firepits, and the girls had been set to gathering sticks. Most of them had never seen a fire kindled. The hearths in their homes were kept burning in honor of Hestia; if the fire went out, a slave went to the Temple of Hestia to fetch live coals. Here there was no temple. Civilization had been left behind.

Korinna knelt by the firepit. She reached into her quiver and took out two stones; Melisto was close enough to see that the larger stone had a deep cleft in it. The priestess opened a leather pouch and withdrew what looked like a dried mushroom. She held the grooved stone tightly, on top of the mushroom, and struck the larger stone with the smaller. There was a scraping noise. After some moments, a wisp of smoke crept up from between Korinna's hands.

The priestess bent forward and blew on it. A flame the size of a teardrop rose from the pitted surface of the mushroom. The children pressed forward. This was magic.

With a sharp knife, Korinna sliced off the smoking part of the mushroom, setting it in the firepit. She fed the flame with pine needles and twigs. Once the flames grew strong, the oldest woman came with a dried branch and carried it to the other pits.

The women unpacked the donkeys. To Melisto's relief, they brought forth loaves of barley bread — there was a little round loaf for every child — dried figs, hard cheese, and honey cakes made with sesame seeds. When one of the children complained of thirst, the older woman waved her toward the spring.

Melisto stood by the donkeys until she was given her share of food. Some of the girls sat in clumps, chattering as they ate. Melisto climbed up the bank and sat between two pine trees. She ate slowly, relishing the food. When she had licked her fingers clean, she unbraided her hair and shook her head, like a horse freed from the bridle.

The air was cooling. The handmaids had tethered their donkeys. Now they prepared the children to sleep. They led them to a space some distance from the water, where they could relieve themselves without fouling the spring and offending the nymphs. The girls turned their backs to each other so they could unknot the cords that fastened the cloaks to their shoulders. The cloaks would serve as blankets for the night.

Melisto watched as they laid out beds around the fires. She reached behind her back and tugged at Thratta's knots, working her own cloak free. The himation was saffron yellow and thickly napped, like an animal's pelt. When she spread it out, it was twice as long as she was tall. She was later to learn that a girl like herself had woven it, and that she would have to make one for a Bear who would come after her.

Some of the girls draped their himations over tree branches to make tents. Melisto chose a hollow for her bed and gathered armfuls of pine needles to make it soft. The pine boughs were thick above her head, but she used her belt to lash them together, making a roof. As she spread her cloak over the pine needles, a faint whimper reached her ears.

It was the child who had cried that morning — the same child who had laughed so merrily as she chased the frog in the stream. In the firelight, her face was shiny with tears. Like a moth she flitted from bed to bed, looking for someone to pay attention to her.

Melisto got off her knees. She brushed the pine needles off her dress and stumbled down the steep bank, setting her feet sideways because of the slope. She held out her hand to the child.

"It's time for you to stop crying." Her voice was brusque, with a hint of Thracian accent.

The little girl scampered up to grab her hand. Her eyes were half drowned in tears.

"Come and bring your cloak. You can sleep with me. If we have two cloaks, we'll be twice as warm."

The little girl wiped her nose on her palm and handed her cloak to Melisto. Melisto showed her the sheltered place under the pine trees. The little girl spoke respectfully. "Did you make that? It's good."

Melisto nodded, happy to have this confirmed. "We'll have two blankets," she pointed out, "and we can pile pine needles between them."

"I can sleep with you?"

"I said you could, didn't I?" Melisto squatted down and smoothed out a wrinkle in her cloak. "Lie down. I'll cover you."

She covered the child with half her cloak and heaped pine needles on top. Over the pine needles, she draped the second cloak, folded in two. "Now, let me in." She squirmed under the blankets and curled up on her side, knees bent.

"What's your name?"

"Melisto, daughter of Arkadios." Melisto spoke proudly, as befitted the child of a distinguished man.

"Mine is Elpis." The girl wiggled closer, fitting her body into the curve of Melisto's. "I saw you when we were on the Akropolis. You've got a necklace, too." She pointed to a circlet of beads around her neck. "Mine is new."

Melisto had forgotten the amber sphinx. She cupped her fingers around the carved sphinx head.

"Did your mother give you yours? Mine gave me mine."

Melisto frowned. "In a way."

"My mother gave me mine, because she's going to miss me. She cried, and I

255

cried. I didn't want to leave home. But she says I'll like it. She was a Bear when she was a little girl."

Melisto raised herself up on her elbow. "Did she tell you what it's like?"

Elpis shifted onto her back. She propped her legs on top of Melisto's knees. The warmth of her childish body was surprisingly sweet. "She told me everything, but I'm not supposed to tell. It's a secret, what it's like being a Bear."

"But what *is* it like?"

"We get to play outdoors all the time. The priestesses don't care about us getting dirty or sunburned, because we're Bears. Except, when we stop being Bears, and go home again, we have to stay indoors. Till our skins get pale. Then we can get married. But as long as we're Bears, we can play outside. And we can have pets. I want a frog and a little rabbit. All the animals around the sanctuary are tame, because nobody dares hunt them. Artemis would punish them. Some girls like hunting, and they go out with bows and arrows, but they can't hunt close to the sanctuary. Mother says the priestesses like wild girls, so they aren't strict during the day, but at night we have to do everything they say, as soon as they tell us, and the best we can —"

"At night?"

"Yes, because at night we play the games and say our prayers and do the dances for Artemis. If we don't do them right, we're disobeying Artemis. That's bad."

"What happens if we're bad?"

"If we're really bad, we get sent home. And we have to find the way back ourselves, and we might get lost. Or eaten by wolves. And even if we found our way home again, it'd be shameful for our families, and no man would want to marry us. No man wants a girl who wasn't a good Bear." Elpis gave a great yawn. "And even if we did get married, we might not be able to have babies, because Artemis won't help. My mother was a good Bear, but I was hard to birth. She prayed, and Artemis saved her life, but she *almost* died. She said she loved me all the more, because she had to fight so hard for me." Her voice was drowsy.

"She didn't say that," Melisto said accusingly.

"Yes, she did," insisted Elpis. Sleepy she might be, but she was definite on that point.

257

"She says it all the time." She snuggled closer to Melisto and gave a little sigh. All at once she was asleep.

Melisto's mind sifted through the day. Thratta was braiding her hair; Lysandra was giving her the amber sphinx . . . By midwinter, her father might have a son. She shut her eyes at the thought and seemed to be back on the Akropolis: she heard the women cry out as the goat's blood spattered the dust. Then she was walking by the grave markers outside the city, the butterfly perched on her arm . . . The butterfly's wings were blue as rosemary flowers, and Korinna was smiling, that godlike, roguish smile . . . "Korinna," murmured Melisto, and then: "Elpis." These were the two new people in her world, and she must not forget their names. She repeated them to herself until she fell asleep.

3. Cave, Grove, Bridge

On the second day of the journey, there was thunder and downpour. The rain fell in veils that blinded the children and blurred the green of the trees. The four handmaids gathered the Bears and divided them into groups, locking their hands together. Korinna led her group to a steep hillside. Like a shuttle finding its way through warp threads, she tugged the girls between overlapping rocks.

The girls shivered. Inside the cave, the air was dim, but Melisto's owl eyes adjusted quickly. Korinna was counting the girls, touching each one on the crown of her head. There was a firepit surrounded by black stones. A rough niche held a clay figure of Pan, the god of caves.

Korinna finished her head count. She untied a flask that hung from her belt and went to the clay image. She poured a few drops of liquid in front of it, her lips moving in praise to Pan.

Melisto picked at the knot that fastened her himation to her back. She undid the cord and draped the bear pelt around her like a cloak. Wool grease had prevented the rain from soaking in. The inner folds were not even damp.

Elpis tugged at her. "Do me, too."

Melisto snorted: an exasperated sound she had learned from Lysandra. She untied the cord that bound Elpis's himation, shook out the cloth, and began to towel-dry the younger girl. Elpis's skin was goose-pimpled; her body was as fine-boned as a fawn's. Melisto had never been delicate like that.

"This is the first cave you have seen." Korinna's voice echoed against the stone. "There are many in these mountains. As a Bear, you must learn to provide yourself with shelter and food. Before the battle of Salamis, the women and children fled the city. My grandmother told me how it was. The women who'd been Bears were able to help the others. They knew which plants were safe to eat. They knew the caves. If there's a war — and there is always war — the wisdom you learn as a Bear could save lives.

"The knowledge we give you is a gift. But it is secret knowledge, and you must not boast of it. When you leave Brauron, you will speak only of what all women know: wool work and cookery and the care of children. Once you marry, you will no longer be a wild bear. Marriage will tame you. But you will remember what you learn from us. In times of hardship, you will share what you know."

The girls listened gravely. Already Melisto's imagination was at work, envisioning a city besieged by Spartans. She would be a heroine, stealthy and wise; she would lead her mother and Thratta to a cave like this one.

There was a cache of firewood in the driest corner of the cave. Melisto followed Korinna and helped her carry the logs to the firepit. The priestess kindled a fire and told the girls to wrap themselves in their himations. Then she left them. She returned some time later with an armful of roots, ferns, and green plants.

Melisto gazed at her worshipfully. Korinna was drenched, but she seemed refreshed, even exhilarated. Her skin gleamed with water, and she quivered like an animal, without seeming to notice that she was cold. She pulled her rope of hair around one shoulder and twisted it, squeezing out a small waterfall. Then she hunkered down and separated the plants into piles: one for each child and one for herself.

Melisto saw herself performing the same action: dividing food for herself, Thratta, and Lysandra. She would give Thratta and Lysandra the same portion, not shortchanging the slave. She was eager to sample the plants, but found them sharp and tough. Some of the wild herbs stung the inside of her mouth, cutting her tongue, but leaving a clean aftertaste. Other plants oozed sap so bitter she was tempted to spit them out. She liked the dandelion flowers the best: they tasted like food, not grass. Elpis wrinkled her nose over the plants and ate little, complaining of hunger. In her heart, Melisto sympathized.

The children prepared for sleep. The floor of the cave was sharp and uneven. The fire provided light and smoke, but little heat. Melisto wrapped herself and Elpis in a tight cocoon. The younger girl's skin was icy. Melisto held her close, chafing her bare arms. At last the child grew warm, and she fell asleep.

Melisto remembered Thratta's words: *I think some god has made you strong.* She was proud of herself. She had eaten wild plants, and she was sleeping in a cave. She had never been afraid of the dark, and Korinna had smiled when she helped with the firewood.

The following day dawned chilly and clear. The children rose at first light and shoved their sore feet into their sandals.

They draped their cloaks over their wet chitons and resumed their journey, limping. Elpis was pale. She walked hanging on to Melisto's hand, sagging against her, almost tripping her. Melisto wanted to shake her off, but something held her back.

The fiery sun climbed the arc of the sky, opening the poppies and hardening the mud underfoot. Wind dried the girls' tunics. As the day grew warmer, they shed their himations. They began to whisper and chatter; they picked up speed. Midmorning the procession passed through a village, and the villagers left their houses to honor the Bears.

They fed the bedraggled children bowls of barley porridge sweetened with honey. Melisto savored every grain, licking her forefinger and scraping the bowl. Some of the village women gave offerings to the children. These were not gifts, but objects to be passed on to the goddess at the sanctuary. The most beautiful girls were adorned with ribbons: Elpis received three. The women made a pet of her, stroking her frizzy curls and praising her. They decorated her: a yellow ribbon around her right wrist, a scarlet one around the left.

A sea-green ribbon hung in loops from the shoulders of her tunic. Elpis spun in circles, watching the ribbons float around her. Color bloomed in her cheeks.

Melisto received no ribbons and understood why. She sat in the shade of a juniper bush and watched the younger girl twirl. It hadn't occurred to her that Elpis was so pretty. She felt hoodwinked.

After a brief rest, the handmaids gathered the girls, reminding them that they had lost a half day because of the rain. If they were to reach Brauron while the moon was still full, they must travel quickly, following the river Erasinos.

The landscape was changing. Forest and foothills gave way to marshland. All her life, Melisto had looked up to the breathtaking height of the Akropolis, the Rock of Ares, and the Hill of the Wolves. Now the horizon was low and soft; the hills curved like the haunches of a sleeping woman. The sky was full of seabirds: shearwaters, pelicans, and herons. Melisto was aware of the wind, not because it blew hard, but because it stirred the leaves and the reeds along the river. There was a constant murmur in the air, not conversational, but secretive, intensely private.

When the sun began to go down, the handmaids removed the bridles from the donkeys. The freed animals shook their heads, drawing together into a herd. The leader broke into a trot, and the others followed suit. In a few minutes, they were out of sight. A rumor made its way through the flock of girls: the donkeys were bound for the stables at Brauron, where they would receive their evening fodder. The sanctuary was near at hand.

Korinna led the girls to the riverbank. The river curled, swift-flowing, but wide and shallow. Korinna told the Bears to strip naked, wade in, and wash themselves from head to foot. Melisto dragged her tunic over her head. She kick-splashed her way into the river.

Once the girls had bathed, Korinna guided them to a grove of trees: olive, pine, pistachio, and willow. She ordered them to spread out their himations and go to sleep. As soon as her back was turned, there was a murmur of discontent: if the sanctuary was nearby, why not finish the journey? The girls were hungry: they wanted to see where they would live; they wanted to sleep in beds, with a roof over their heads.

If Korinna heard their protests, she gave no sign of it. She stalked away from the grove with the dogs at her heels.

Elpis came to Melisto and held out her wrists. She had neglected to untie her ribbons before entering the river, and there was a rose-colored ring around one wrist. The yellow ribbon had left a mark like a bruise. "Do you want to wear one of my ribbons?"

Melisto's eye strayed to the scarlet ribbon. It was her favorite color, but she wasn't going to say so. "They're not your ribbons. They're for Artemis."

"They're mine for now. I'll let you wear one."

"They're wet. You can keep them." Melisto pointed to one of the willow trees. "Let's spread our blankets under that tree. Nobody'll be able to see us."

She parted the willow branches and ducked between, knowing Elpis would follow. Inside the trailing branches, the world shimmered. The young leaves were yellow-green on one side, silver on the other. Melisto squatted down and spread out the two himations. "Melisto," Elpis said in a coaxing voice that Melisto was getting to know, "would you let me see your necklace? Up close?"

Melisto hesitated. Over the past days, she'd grown aware of how heavy the necklace was. She wanted to take it off. "You can try it on, but you'd better give it back."

"I will." Elpis knelt up to kiss her cheek. "You're good to me."

Melisto didn't know what to say. She dug her fingers into the grass and watched Elpis play with Lysandra's necklace. The little girl crowned herself, tried the necklace around her neck, and tossed it lightly up and down. "It's heavy, isn't it? I like the way it jingles. Your mother must love you a whole lot." She nuzzled the amber head. "I like the face part best. Is the lady Artemis?"

"No. It's a sphinx head."

"What's a sphinx?"

Melisto paused. She knew a sphinx when she saw it, but she didn't know how to define one. "It's a winged monster, only beautiful. They protect graves and ask riddles."

"What's a riddle?"

"A riddle's like a question, but the answer's a trick." Melisto smiled as she remembered a riddle Arkadios once taught her. "Here's one. *I'm the dark child of a golden mother. I fly in the sky without wings.* What is it?"

Elpis shrugged. "I don't know. What?"

"You're supposed to guess," Melisto rebuked her. "The riddle's about something that's *like* a dark child, and comes from a golden mother. It can fly, but it doesn't have wings. You have to guess what it is."

Elpis wrinkled her nose. "Is it your mother? Does your mother have golden hair like Demeter?"

"No, she's dark, like me. The riddle's not about mothers, silly. It's about a thing. What kind of thing floats upward, but doesn't have wings? What rises up in the sky?"

Elpis clapped her hands. "A bird!"

"Birds have wings. So that's wrong."

Elpis frowned in concentration. Then her face lit up. "A bat!"

"Bats have wings," Melisto reminded her. Elpis's failure to find the right answer was balm to her soul. "The answer's *smoke.* A dark *child* — you know how smoke is darker than air? And fire makes smoke, so fire's like the smoke's mother. The golden mother, see? And smoke rises up to the sky without wings."

She watched Elpis's face as the child thought through the riddle. "Let's tell the others!"

"No." Elpis was a nuisance; Melisto had accepted that, but she wasn't about to share her. "What's the point of a riddle everyone knows? From now on, this'll be our riddle. I'll only tell it to you. That way, we'll be the only ones who know the answer."

"Tell me another one."

"Tomorrow." Melisto couldn't remember another riddle. She stretched out on the bear pelt. "Now give me back my necklace."

Elpis handed it over. Melisto curled her fingers around the amber sphinx head, fitting it inside the hollow of her palm. As her mind fished for riddles, she sank into sleep.

Darkness fell. It was Melisto's third night sleeping with Elpis, and by now they had the knack of it. Their bodies shifted and balanced, nestled and flopped; they slept like puppies from the same litter. Melisto dreamed of caves and a fluttering ribbon, a sea-green flame. She dreamed of Arkadios holding his infant son.

Then her dreams were fractured like eggshells. The night was full of voices, rustlings and flares of light. Melisto sat up, alert.

"What is it?" Elpis clutched her arm. Melisto shook herself free. The curtain of willow boughs stirred; the face of Korinna, lit by torchlight, hung like a mask in midair.

"Come! Get up! At once!"

Melisto grabbed her himation and rolled it into a ball.

"Is she angry?" Elpis was half asleep. She sounded as if she might cry.

Melisto shook her head. "No, but we have to get up. There's a rush. Get off the blanket and give me your belt. I'll help you."

She snatched Elpis's himation, rolling it tightly. She lashed it to the little girl's back, yanking the rope into place. "Come *on!*" she urged Elpis. All around them, the girls were putting on sandals, tying their cloaks to their backs.

The handmaids shuttled between them, their torches ablaze. One of Korinna's dogs howled. The moon was high overhead; dappling the grass with light like frost. Yellow fire from the torches, streaming: white light cast from above. Melisto shivered.

Korinna threw back her head and cried out like a wolf howling: *"Ololyzo!"* The word held no meaning, but called the gods to attention. *"Ololyzo!"* She whirled away from the pack, sprinting ahead. The dogs lunged forward, barking. The girls dashed after them, out of the grove and into an open meadow. Dew moistened their feet and their naked legs. Melisto fell and was up in an instant; Elpis kicked off her sandals. Breathless and damp and moonstruck they ran, trailing the priestess's torch.

There before them they saw it: the wide bridge, the foaming spring, the sacred cave and the temple. This breathless, headlong flight was their entry into Brauron. Just at the edge of the bridge, Korinna spread out her arms like wings. The girls stopped in their tracks, obedient as the dogs.

"Ololyzo!" Korinna tossed her torch in the spring. It hissed like a snake. The

priestess raised her arms to the sky and began to spin in circles.

Melisto found herself spinning. Her unbelted tunic ballooned around her. She spun until she was dizzy. There was a tumult of sound: the liquid noise of the water, footfalls on soft earth, Elpis's laughter. Korinna was singing a tune that surged and broke as she panted for breath. The ragged song reached an open space deep inside Melisto. It was a praise song for Artemis, Artemis the fierce and bright, the tall and chaste; Artemis the deer slayer, the strong-voiced; the protector of maidens, of stags and wolves and bears.

Melisto staggered in circles. Her head was tipped back, her arms flung wide. Her heart pounded. She loved the night and the round moon; she loved Korinna; she loved the goddess Artemis with all her heart.

The song reached its end. Korinna scooped up handfuls of water from the spring and dashed it into the girls' faces, laughing as they flinched and squealed. She pivoted and crossed the stone bridge, the dogs leaping after her. The girls followed in a rush.

Elpis caught up with Melisto and grabbed her hand. Melisto squeezed hard. They tumbled forward, toward the sanctuary. Old women with oil lamps poured out of the building. They greeted the children with kisses and smiles, and ushered them inside.

Inside were more lamps, and rooms lined with dining couches. The rooms were like Arkadios's *andron*, which puzzled the girls: banqueting halls were for guests and men, important men. Still the women urged the children forward, settling them onto the couches. There was a mouthwatering aroma of food: not wild plants, not porridge, but bread and cheese and roasted fish. For that night, the girls would feast as men did, half reclining.

Melisto climbed onto one of the couches; Elpis scrambled up beside her. The table in front of their couch held deep cups of water. Melisto gulped hers and found it laced with wine.

Hungry and thirsty, she ate and drank. The wine lulled her and made Elpis tipsy. After the first pangs of hunger had been satisfied, Melisto untied their himations. She covered Elpis with one, and the little girl curled up next to her, falling asleep at once.

Melisto stayed awake. With her thumb, she smeared goat cheese and honey on bread, craving the salt and the sweet. She saw the other girls stretching out and covering themselves, accepting the dining couches as beds for the night. The older women passed back and forth, gathering up bowls and cups. They blew out the lamps. The rooms were still bright; moonlight spilled between the columns, painting white stripes on the floor.

Melisto unfolded her own himation. She pulled it over her shoulders, grunting with satisfaction as she snuggled down, warm and fed. She was almost asleep when she brought her half-closed hand up to her throat.

Her neck was bare. The amber sphinx had been left behind, on the opposite side of the bridge.

4. Sanctuary

She left it there.

Her life at the sanctuary was a new world. It was as if Artemis had plucked her from her native soil and shaken the earth off her roots. At Brauron, Melisto was transplanted, watered, and refreshed. She was not homesick at all. Her world had not been turned upside down, but right side up; Brauron agreed with her, and she thrived.

There was little supervision during the day. Though the priestesses and their handmaids had the power to correct the girls' behavior, they seldom bothered. Melisto rose late; she liked lying in bed, tangle-haired and lazy; she liked watching the sunlight glow against the dormitory wall. When at last she got up, she went in search of bread — some of the girls, for reasons Melisto could not imagine, liked baking and cooked for the others. Melisto would snatch a loaf and go to eat on the stone bridge.

Often she sat for hours with her feet in the bubbling spring. She dropped crumbs for the fish, caged them between her fingers, and let them swim out again. Leaning back, she squinted against the blue sky; flopping over, she was spellbound by the play of light on water. One morning she was moved to strip off her chiton and bathe. No one criticized her, and she made a habit of ducking into the water and splashing herself. She kept on good terms with the nymphs of the spring, honoring them with cleanliness and prayer.

Her skin blistered, peeled off in flakes, and darkened to a ruddy brown. No one objected. When her hair grew too matted to comb, she persuaded Elpis to cut it. She began to understand that at Brauron, the ordinary rules of life were suspended. As long as she kept inside the boundaries of the sanctuary, she was like Artemis, a free child of the woods and marshlands. No one threatened her or shamed her. No one put a distaff into her hands.

As spring turned to summer, she explored the woods. She shinnied up the trees, and ventured out on the flexible branches, daring them to break. Korinna provided flint and iron, and Melisto spent hours striking sparks onto tinder, building small fires and extinguishing them with earth. She gathered food plants and gnawed them determinedly. She wove garlands for the wooden statue of Artemis and scattered seed and salt for the animals that visited the sanctuary.

The construction of a rough shelter absorbed her for weeks. She dragged fallen trees into a lean-to, lashing them together with vines and willow boughs. By the time she finished, her arms and legs were crosshatched with scratches, but she was proud of her work. The girls were encouraged to make such shelters. There were festival days when elders and priests came to banquet at Brauron, and on such occasions the dining couches belonged to the men. The little girls took their bearcloaks and camped outdoors. During a squall, Melisto's shelter proved surprisingly weather-worthy. She had built it on a knob of rising ground, and it did not flood; it rocked a little when the wind gusted, but it kept her and Elpis dry.

For some weeks, Melisto avoided the open-air spaces where the girls pitched their looms. She knew that at some point, she would have to weave one of the bearcloaks for another Bear, but no one ordered her to begin work, and she put it off. When she snagged her yellow chiton on a tree limb, it ripped from hem to neck, and she knew she would have to make another one.

Grudgingly she set up her loom under the stoa. She strung the warp threads, bundled them, and tied clay weights to the ends.

She had woven four inches when Klotho, the handmaid in charge of wool work, called the girls over to admire the even tension of her weft. Melisto listened with her mouth ajar. Neither Thratta nor Lysandra had ever praised her: they were perfectionists. Now she saw that their strictness had served her well. Her pattern was good, and her hands were deft. Melisto took up her beating pin with a light heart. If she was going to be good at weaving, she might not hate it so much. With a thrill of insight, she understood that what she had really hated was the confinement of the weaving room. She had been too close to her mother.

Now she was free of Lysandra. She could wield her shuttle without having to brace herself to duck or dodge. No matter what she did at Brauron, no one yanked her hair, or shook her breathless, or stung her with poisonous words. If sometimes she missed Thratta, there was Korinna, who could be adored from a safe distance. If she grew lonely, Elpis was always underfoot, sometimes a joy, more often a nuisance, but never a danger.

Such happiness could not last. At the age of ten, Melisto was one of the oldest Bears. She would not serve Artemis for long. Once she began to turn into a woman, she would be sent back home, and Arkadios would find her a husband. The rest of her life would be spent indoors. There would be endless wool work, slaves to command, and children to bear. She was the daughter of a wealthy man, and this was the life to which she was entitled. All the same, she did not want it. She peered under her arms for the first shadowing of hair, and pinched her small nipples, dreading the day when her breasts would begin to swell. So far, so good: her round and sturdy body was still a child's.

She almost forgot about the amber sphinx. At the back of her mind was the knowledge that she would have to go in search of it, though it lay outside the boundaries of the sanctuary. The necklace belonged to Artemis. It was Melisto's duty to deliver it. Her mother must not die in childbirth, and her father wanted a son. The last thought hurt like biting her tongue or touching a sore place in her mouth. If Lysandra gave birth to a son, Arkadios's affection would be divided. She, Melisto, would be eclipsed.

There was yet time. Lysandra's child was not due until midwinter.

The nights at Brauron were different from the days. On moonlit nights, the Little Bears went to bed knowing that their sleep would be interrupted. One of the priestesses would enter the dormitories with a torch, summoning them to worship. No disobedience, no delay, was tolerated; the girls rose in a rush, stifling their yawns, knotting the belts around their tunics, finger-combing their hair.

Melisto never knew what to expect on those nights. It seemed to her that there was no pattern. She knew only that disobedience was unthinkable. She, who had been the most wayward of girl children, never opened her lips to ask a question.

The children gathered around the altar outside the Temple of Artemis. Some nights there was a sacrifice, usually a goat. One night it was Melisto who was chosen to distract the animal with handfuls of grain so that its throat could be cut. The goat was affectionate, nibbling Melisto's fingers. Its innocence pierced her heart, and she clenched her teeth to keep from crying. All her life, she had seen animals sacrificed. It was a woman's job to shriek when the priest wielded the knife and the blood began to flow. Now she learned to catch the blood in a bowl, to cut up the carcass, to impale chunks of raw meat onto skewers for the feast. She did not like it, but she willed herself not to flinch. The sacrifice was for Artemis. It was an honor for the animal to be sacrificed, and an honor for her to stand by.

On other nights, the altar was used as a finish line for races by torchlight. Strong though she was, Melisto was not built for speed, but running with fire excited her, and she jumped up and down and screamed with the other girls.

The races strengthened the girls for one of the most vital of their duties. As Bears of Artemis, they marked the boundaries of the sanctuary with their naked feet. They were wild and pure, and Brauron was the borderland of civilized Athens: if the frontier remained holy, the core would hold.

By circumscribing the boundaries of the sanctuary, the Bears safeguarded the city.

So they ran, following Korinna's torch: beginning at the altar and spiraling around the sanctuary buildings. They crossed the stone bridge and beat a trail through the wetland, filling the air with their moist breath, flattening the dew-soaked grass. They carved a path through the trees, sometimes circling the low akropolis or passing down to the bay where the ships were anchored. In their early days at Brauron, the girls ran in short sprints, stumbling, wheezing, halting. By the next full moon, their pace had quickened; they had grown sure-footed and hardy. Even Melisto thudded along steadily, her fists clenched, her eyes fixed on Korinna's torch. Somehow, she managed to keep up.

More difficult for her were the dancing nights. The girls sang hymns and paraded toward the altar, bearing wreaths and palm leaves tied with ribbons. Their movements, stately at first, grew wilder; they spun like tops and leapt into the air, arms outstretched. Melisto was self-conscious when she danced. She could not lose herself. She felt as if her feet were caught in a net.

The most difficult dance was the Bear Dance, the oldest and most sacred dance of all. It was composed of subtle gestures and circling steps, and the sequence was baffling. A girl who mastered the Bear Dance would find favor with the goddess; Artemis would protect her during childbirth. Melisto knew that her survival might someday hinge on how she danced the Bear Dance, but that only kept her from learning it. She watched jealously as the other girls practiced, holding their hands like claws. Sometimes a girl was possessed by the spirit of the bear and threw off her tunic to dance naked, no longer a child, but a wild animal, one of Artemis's own. Melisto averted her eyes from the ecstatic girls. She could not imagine dancing like that.

She was happiest on the nights when Korinna led the girls down to the bay so they could bathe in the water. The children raced across the narrow beach, breathless and damp from running. Melisto splashed and squealed with the rest, but as soon as she could, she broke away from them, going deeper into the bay. She knelt down until the water lapped her chin, and let the small waves lift her, so that she was half afloat. She stared. The sky was flecked with stars, and the moon scattered white light over the water. When the black waves crested, there was glitter and foam and a noise like breathing. Melisto fell into a trance. She spread her arms and bobbed up and down, weightless. Something frantic and trapped inside her was laid to rest. She became invisible to herself. She knew only the rhythm of the rising waves, and the taste of salt on her lips.

5. The Bear

"What has sharp claws and feet like a baby?"

Melisto sat on the curving branch of her favorite olive tree. Elpis reached up and tickled her feet. "What has sharp claws and feet like a baby?"

Melisto sighed. She wished she had never taught the younger girl about riddles.

"What has feet like a baby's, but sharp —"

"I heard you the first time." Melisto swung down from the tree. She reviewed her knowledge of animal feet. Most tame animals had hooves, not claws; hawks and owls had talons; foxes and dogs had round paws. She remembered Elpis's love for rabbits and tossed out, "A rabbit."

"Rabbit feet are tiny. The animal I'm talking about has big feet." Elpis's eyes gleamed: there was nothing she liked better than baffling Melisto. She held her hands apart. "Wide and fat."

Melisto eyed the space between her hands. "A goose."

"Geese don't have claws."

Geese did not have claws. "A tortoise, then." Melisto recalled the tortoise that lived in Arkadios's courtyard. Its feet were round, tipped with horny nails. "That's what it is! A tortoise."

"It's not a tortoise. Do you give up?" Elpis waited; Melisto did not concede. "It's a bear! I've seen it! It's a baby bear, and it sits on its bottom like a baby, and its feet are wide and fat, but the claws are like needles. Korinna has scratch marks. She made the men take the muzzle off. She says we girls have to keep away from it, because in the Brauron story, a bear killed that girl and —"

"Where is it?" interrupted Melisto. She had once seen a painted bear on a jar. It was something like a wild cat with a pig snout.

"It's chained up in the stable. A pair of hunters brought it. For sacrifice. In honor of Artemis. They killed the mother and chased the cubs into a net. They brought them in a sack, but one of them died. We can look in the stall, but we can't go in."

Melisto broke into a run. She expected Elpis to dash past her; Elpis was light on her feet and could easily outrun her. But once they had cleared the strip of woods, Elpis spotted two other girls and veered off to share her news with them. Melisto doubled her pace. She wanted to look at the bear by herself.

The stables at Brauron were not elaborate. There was an open shed where the goats were milked and a three-sided shelter for the donkeys. There was also a barn with four stalls, reserved for the mounts of honored priests or patrons. Melisto leaned over the top rail of the largest stall. The contrast between the brilliant sunlight and the dimness of the stall baffled her eyes. Her first idea was that Elpis had gotten it wrong: the prisoner in the barn was not a bear, but a child. A shadowy, shaggy-haired boy stood with his head bent and his arms curled inward. Her mind flashed to Arkadios and the brother whose birth she feared. In an instant, she conceived that in some unseen world there was a brother she might be able to love.

She blinked. The naked boy took a step and fell backward, landing on his bottom. He uttered a cry of discontent, a raven-like screech from the back of his throat. The noise was animal, not human, and all at once Melisto realized that she was seeing the bear. It was not at all like a cat or a pig. It was and was not human. It sat on its rump with its back legs splayed. The back paws had five toes and leathery soles that tapered into heels.

The bear lifted its snout. Melisto caught the liquid spark in its eyes. The bear's face was not human, but it was indisputably a face. It wore an expression she could not decipher. They stared at each other.

As Melisto's eyes adjusted, she saw the cub wore a rope harness, looped tight around the neck, crossed between the front legs, and knotted over the shoulder hump. A chain through the knot connected the harness to a post. The stable floor was littered with a broken bowl and a sack of rough wool. A bucket of water had been knocked over.

The bear rolled its eyes at her. Melisto swung her legs over the top rail of the stall door and jumped down. The bear rose up, snuffling. It studied her with intense curiosity, but without fear or rancor. Then it dropped on all fours and circled her. Melisto squatted, stretching out her hands. Reason warned her that the bear might attack, but she was ruled by desire, not reason. She felt the bear's rough fur and inhaled the ripe, gourd-like smell of its body.

The bear's reaction was immediate and forthright. It let out a noise that Melisto chose to interpret as friendly. She watched its nostrils flare as it tasted her scent. A long tongue swept out of its mouth and found a patch on her dress where she had spilled a bowl of porridge that morning.

"You're hungry," Melisto murmured. Her mind went ahead to the bread she would steal from the kitchen, the cheese curds, the roots she could dig in the woods. The bear set one paw on her thigh — she winced as the claws sank in — and began to lick the stain. Its tongue looked too big to fit inside its mouth. Melisto stuck out her own tongue and examined it cross-eyed. Her tongue was the same color as the bear's.

The bear leaned in, determined to extract every atom of flavor from the wool of her tunic. The weight from the paw was painful. Melisto set both hands on the bear's shoulder and rocked it away from her. The bear lost its balance and skidded sideways. It rolled over and bounced back. Melisto gave it a tentative shove. The bear raised a paw and smacked it against her forearm. They were playing. Both of them understood this at once.

The bear played rough. Melisto was too fascinated to mind. She wrestled and tumbled, shoving the bear onto its back. The cub was far smaller than she was, but its strength more than matched her own. The babyish roundness of its body was deceptive. The bear was swift and agile and tireless. It climbed on top of her, mouthing her, rooting at her dress and pawing at her hair. One claw left parallel scratches across her collarbone. Melisto gave a cry and sprang to her feet, claiming the advantage of height. The bear wheeled around, springing from its muscular hindquarters. It squealed: one back paw was caught in the chain. At once Melisto was on her knees. She pushed the bear sideways to gain slack and lifted the paw free. The bear whuffed, plopped down on its rump, and regarded her intently.

"Melisto!" Korinna's voice was sharp. "Come out at once!"

Melisto obeyed. The bear cub started to follow, but the chain yanked it back. Melisto felt a pang, but she climbed over the rail. She stood before Korinna with her head bowed in submission.

"Did no one tell you it was forbidden to go into the stall?"

Korinna had never spoken to her like that. Melisto confessed in one word. "Elpis."

"Why did you disobey?"

Melisto faltered: "Some god put it in my heart to go inside." She dared not look up. Never in her life had she defended herself by suggesting that her behavior had been inspired by a god. If it were true, no one could blame her. If she were lying — and she didn't know whether she was or not — it was blasphemy, and the gods would punish her.

Korinna did not answer right away. Melisto stared at her feet. The silence was so protracted that she was able to study every one of her dirty toes.

"It isn't safe," Korinna said at last. "Perhaps now, when the cub is young — but it won't stay safe. I don't know much about bears — I've never seen one before today — but the hunters claim they're the strongest of all animals, and they can't be tamed. It's a dangerous gift. I gave my orders, and you ought to have followed them."

"I know."

Korinna seemed to have forgotten Melisto. She gazed past her into the darkness of the barn. "The bear belongs to Artemis. There are places where they sacrifice bear cubs — wolf cubs, too. They drive them into a pen and burn them alive. But we've never done that here. Brauron has always been a sanctuary. We've never sacrificed a bear — only stags and goats. I don't know what's meant."

"Why must the bear be sacrificed?" The words burst from Melisto. Her head shot up and she challenged Korinna with the accusing owl gaze that her mother loathed. "Artemis is the goddess of children and sucklings! The bear's a suckling — or would be, if its mother hadn't been killed. In the Brauron story, Artemis sent the plague when her bear was killed. What if we sacrifice the bear and she's angry?"

"It's a risk," Korinna admitted. Melisto was surprised; she had expected to be punished for her outburst, not taken seriously. "And yet — the hunters traveled a long way to bring us the bear. It's their offering to the goddess. If we don't sacrifice it, what then? It can't be trained. It will have to be fed. After a few months, it will be strong enough to kill."

A loud clank interrupted her. The bear cub was playing with the bucket. It had one paw inside and was knocking it against the wall of the stable.

"It doesn't have any water," Melisto said defensively.

"Then go and get some," Korinna retorted. She smiled at the surprise in Melisto's face. It was Artemis's own smile: sweet-lipped and enigmatic. "Did you think I would forbid it? I dislike being disobeyed, Melisto. If I have to change my orders, I will. Get the water bucket from the stall and take it to the spring. When you come back, hold the bucket while the bear drinks. It's bound to knock it over a second time."

Melisto paused for a moment, hypnotized by Korinna's smile. Then she hurried back to the bear's stall.

That night, the moon was waxing, and the sky was clear. Melisto was not surprised when the priestesses came to summon the Little Bears to the altar. The children burned incense in small clay pots and sang prayers to the goddess. After they learned a new hymn, they were told to circle the sanctuary.

Melisto's limbs felt heavy. Even after the singing, she was half asleep. Gradually her muscles stretched and warmed. She found her stride and ran steadily. By the time the altar came in sight again, she had hatched a plan.

She made sure that Desma, the priestess in charge, counted her as she passed the altar. On her way back to the dormitory, she ducked behind a juniper bush. Once the other girls were gone, she set off for the stable.

She noticed that the two rails that served as a stable door had been reinforced with boards. Someone had decided that the bear's prison was not secure enough. She whispered, "Bear?"

She heard a rustle and smiled in the direction of the sound. The bear was listening. Perhaps it could smell her, too. Something opaque moved in the shadows. Melisto swung herself over the stall door. She hunkered down on the hard earth.

The bear came to her. Melisto's heart swelled. It was lonely, or it liked her; she thought it must be glad that she was there. It sniffed at her tunic, searching for the spilled porridge. Melisto patted it cautiously. It wiggled against her hand, and all at once they were playing again. The bear kicked and batted the air; Melisto tried to grab its paws; they rolled and jostled and shoved. The bear nuzzled her and tried to climb on top of her. Its paws clamped down on her shoulders. She felt its warm breath against her throat and then its tongue. It suckled at her neck, pulling the blood inside her skin.

Melisto tensed. The suction was painfully strong. At the same time, she understood. The bear was alone and wanted its mother. "I don't have any milk," Melisto protested, but the bear made a low humming sound, like a prolonged chuckle or a hive of bees. It sounded happy. Melisto abandoned all thought of pushing it away.

She took a deep breath, bracing herself against the discomfort. The bear continued to suckle, murmuring contentment. Tentatively, Melisto put her arms around the furry body. She did not squeeze. It was enough to encircle the bear loosely, to know that she was making it happy. From time to time, she reached up and slid her thumb between the skin of her neck and the bear's mouth. It broke the suction, easing the pain.

She touched the bear's shoulder hump. Her fingers felt the intertwined cords of the knot. It seemed to her that the harness must be uncomfortable. It was snug. She wondered what would happen as the bear grew.

The bear was suckling more gently now. At last it flopped down beside her, half in and half out of her lap. Melisto shivered with joy. The bear was going to sleep beside her. She leaned against the stable wall and closed her eyes, relishing the warmth and the bear's weight.

She dozed. When she woke, she was shivering. She reached across the stable floor for the woolen sack she had noticed earlier in the day. She touched it —

— and the bear was awake. It uttered a close-mouthed shriek of rage; it leapt to its feet and scrambled up the post inside the stall. Melisto got up, baffled. She had not known that bears could climb; she had no idea what had enraged the animal. It had happened so quickly, and she was still half asleep.

The bear was huffing, digging into the weathered post with its needle claws. It climbed until its head touched the barn roof. Melisto stared at it stupidly. Then she looked down at the sack in her hand.

"Are you afraid of the sack?" she asked incredulously. Then she thought. The bear had been imprisoned in the sack, unable to move freely, perhaps half smothered. "All right," she conceded. "I'll get rid of it. Wait here."

She went to the stall door and flung the sack outside. Some instinct told her that it would be of no use to try to coax the bear down from the post. She returned to the place where she had slept and sat against the wall. When she heard the bear scraping its way down the post, she did not stir. The bear wandered around the stable, sniffing. When it came to her, it raised itself up, pressing its paws against her shoulders. She felt its mouth fasten on her neck again. She grimaced.

The bear suckled for a few minutes and then subsided. It turned in slow circles and collapsed with its rump pressed against her thigh. Melisto put one hand on it. It seemed to her that she had never touched anything more real than the bear cub. She curled herself around it and slept until dawn.

6. The Seer at Oropos

Melisto began to smell of the bear. She washed in the spring every morning, but she had only one chiton, and it reeked of bear. Some of the other girls pinched their nostrils shut when she passed by. Melisto suspected that they were jealous. Insofar as the bear belonged to anyone, it belonged to her. None of the other children were allowed inside the stall.

Melisto did not like the stable smell — the bear's droppings had a pungency that stung her nose like vinegar — but the ripe aroma of the bear's body was now familiar. She spent hours with the cub each day, tending it faithfully and without complaint. On the nights when she waded into the bay and watched the moon, she was barely conscious of the fact that it was she who saw, and the moon that was being watched. In the same way, she did not measure how much she loved the bear. She was the bear. During the early days, she brooded over what might become of it, but weeks went by, and she heard no more about the impending sacrifice. She pushed the matter from her mind.

She visited the bear several times a day, passing back and forth between glaring sunlight and the odorous dim of the stall. The bear welcomed her, sniffing, rooting in her skirt, pawing her and mouthing her. It was eager for food and company, wrestling and play. It was fed regularly, and even with elegance. Twice a day, Agathe, the old woman in charge of the kitchens, provided a generous bowl of porridge mixed with honey. The bear slurped up the barley and licked the bronze bowl clean. When every grain had been ingested, the bear punished the bowl, flipping it over and over, and battering it with its paws. Sometimes it knocked the bowl across the stall and under the door so that it skidded out of sight. Then the cub bawled and squealed until Melisto brought it back.

It seemed to Melisto that porridge was not enough for the bear. She foraged, gathering dandelions, cow parsnips, and fennel. She investigated the roots of plants, digging up any that appeared moist or starchy. She stripped young leaves from trees and filled her skirt with acorns, mushrooms, berries, and wild grapes. The bear investigated her offerings with a delicacy that surprised her. It turned the plants over with its front claws, sniffing with mouth ajar. It was only after a prolonged sniff-and-paw that the bear poked out its long tongue and ate. Once the bear had made up its mind that a plant was edible, it attacked all future offerings with gusto.

The bear was growing. The rope harness that had once been snug was tight. Melisto was tempted to unchain the bear from the post and take it outside like a man leading a horse to pasture. Always she hung back: she knew she wasn't strong enough to hold the bear. Once the bear tore the chain out of her hands, it was lost to her forever. The cub would go free, but it would also be hampered — perhaps even strangled — by the dangling chain and the harness around its throat and trunk.

So the bear remained captive, and she tended it. She noticed that it backed up, as far from the post as possible, to defecate, and kicked its droppings behind it, as if the stall were a den that should not be fouled. From this, Melisto inferred that the bear wished to be clean. She borrowed the stable pitchfork and scraped the bear's droppings outside the stall door. Whenever she visited, she checked to see if its drinking water was clear. It seldom was, because the bear regarded water as a toy. It dabbled its paws in the bucket and combed through the water as if it hoped to discover a fish.

Melisto stole food from the storerooms. Once, finding the kitchen deserted, she split a warm loaf and piled it high with soft cheese. The bear greeted her with whimpers of delight and lay down on its belly to consume the treat. It clasped the loaf between its front paws with such ardor that the cheese squirted out the edges. The bear gnawed and gulped in ecstasy. It ate with intense concentration, stopping from time to time to lift its head and lick its chops. One bitten-off chunk of bread rolled toward Melisto. She reached for it, meaning to return it to the bear.

The bear misunderstood. It thought she was taking that piece for herself. It reacted with insane aggression, screaming with outrage and swiping at her. Melisto dropped the bread and scuttled backward. After that, she kept her distance while the bear was eating. She believed that the bear liked her, but there were limits to its patience. She had learned that its moods changed

301

swiftly and drastically; it could be combative one moment and sweetly drowsy the next. Whatever it felt, it felt with every cell in its body. There was no moderation and no fraud.

She did not name the bear. To her, it was the only bear in the world, and she called it simply αρκτος, Bear. She didn't know whether it was male or female. Often when they wrestled, the bear rolled over on its back, but Melisto was kept too busy dodging its claws to investigate its sex.

As the bear grew, it became more familiar with her person. It suckled her neck and her fingers, pawed her, nosed her, and gnawed on her. If a sudden noise frightened the bear, it ran to her, rose up on its hind legs, and flung its front paws around her. Once it tried to climb her like a tree. Melisto's skin was covered with teeth marks, scratches, and indentations, though her puncture wounds were miraculously few. When they wrestled, Melisto pitted her whole strength against the cub. She was largely unconscious of the injuries she received while playing. The moments when the bear hurt her were only chinks in the joy she felt. The joy was the real thing.

Afterward, when the bear burrowed next to her, or tumbled into her lap, she felt as if her heart would burst. She sat cross-legged, her hands buried in the bear's fur, while her legs ached and tingled and fell asleep.

She was down by the bridge late one afternoon, digging worms — the bear greatly relished worms — when a shadow fell over her. She glanced up and saw Korinna. Her face was in shadow, but brilliant sunlight lit the edges of her violet-colored dress.

Melisto rose and stood with her head bowed. Now that the bear had come, she devoted fewer thoughts to Korinna, but the priestess still inspired adoration.

"Are you digging worms for the bear?"

"Yes," Melisto answered, wondering if she was in trouble.

"You feed the bear often."

"It's always hungry," Melisto countered.

"It's growing." Korinna walked onto the bridge and sat down halfway across. She took off her sandals and placed them beside her. Drawing her peplos up to mid-thigh, she wiggled to the edge of the bridge, and lowered her feet into the water. She patted the stone, inviting Melisto to join her.

Melisto rinsed her dirty hands in the water and wiped them on her chiton. Then she sat down beside Korinna, copying the older girl's pose. With unwonted politeness, she waited for Korinna to speak.

"We feed the bear well," Korinna explained, "because it is sacred to Artemis. The other priestesses know you've been feeding it. It isn't forbidden. You must know, Melisto, that your visits to the stable have been observed."

Melisto had not known. She cupped her hands in her lap and kept her eyes lowered.

"I warned you that a bear cannot be tamed." Korinna's voice was neutral. She was reminding Melisto of what she had said, not rebuking her. "All the same, you have formed a friendship with it. I believe it's as tame with you as it will ever be."

"It likes me." Melisto spoke shyly. She was aware that it was a proud claim.

"Of course it does. You bring food, and you play with it. A cub needs to play, and in feeding it, you have forged a link with it. It is possible, with young animals, to create a bond. The bond might not last when the animal comes of age. It's one thing to play with a bear cub — and even now, you are black and blue —"

Melisto forgot herself and looked up into Korinna's face. "It doesn't hurt me," she said earnestly. For a moment her mind slipped back into the past. She recalled the bruises she had carried from her mother's pinches, and the sore patches on her scalp from Lysandra's hair-pulling. She remembered the loathing in her mother's face that struck terror into her soul. She had never been afraid of the bear like that.

"That isn't my point. The point is, even if the bear seems tame now, it won't be tame when it's full-grown. It will be strong enough to kill you, and the bond will be broken."

Melisto did not believe it.

Korinna swung her feet in the water. Her feet were pale and slender. Seen through the clear water, they appeared vaporous. "You know I tame the deer to drive my chariot."

"Yes," Melisto murmured respectfully. From the shelter of her favorite tree she had watched Korinna. The priestess fed the deer from her hands, and it was beautiful. She was patient, steadfast, uncanny in her rapport.

"I don't tame them —" Korinna stopped. She leaned back on her hands, scanning the blue sky. "I don't tame them the way I card wool. You can card wool and think of other things, and it doesn't matter how you feel when you do it; the wool will be combed. But when I tame the deer, I have to be clear in my mind, because the deer can sense what I'm feeling. I have to have a respect for them, an affection. Feeding them, that's part of it, and holding still, that's another part, but it isn't all. In the end, a wild animal doesn't trust you unless it senses something else. There is a bond between me and the deer I tame. But some of them are sacrificed."

Melisto felt a chill pass through her.

"If they are chosen to die, that's the will of the gods. I am a priestess of Artemis, and I must be glad. And because I have tamed them, I'm the one who leads them to the altar. I distract them while the priest readies the knife. Melisto, if the bear is sacrificed —"

"But the bear shouldn't be sacrificed!" Melisto's voice rose impetuously. She forgot that Korinna was Korinna. "I told you before — when the bear was sacrificed at Brauron, Artemis was angry! She doesn't want —"

Korinna's eyes flashed. "It's not for you to say what Artemis wants! How dare you interrupt me? I seek to do you a kindness —"

"What kindness?" Melisto's cheeks were red. She knew she was throwing caution to the winds, but she was too frightened to care. "You talk about sacrificing the bear —"

"Because I want to prepare you!" Korinna snapped. "The messenger from Oropos may return any day, and if the bear is to be sacrificed, you will be part of the ceremony! You —"

Melisto shook her head in confusion; she looked like the bear cub when a yellow jacket stung its nose. "What is Oropos?"

Korinna frowned at the fresh interruption. "There is an oracle at Oropos, with

307

a famous seer. When the hunters brought the bear, they gave it to us for sacrifice, but I wasn't sure what should be done." A faint flush rose in her cheeks. "You raised the question yourself — that Artemis might be angered, not pleased, by such a sacrifice. No cub has ever been sacrificed at Brauron. I spoke of my misgivings to the other priestesses, and they agreed to consult the oracle. The seer at Oropos is descended from Melampos of Pylos. He will know."

Melisto knew the story of Melampos of Pylos. He had lived hundreds of years ago and spoken the language of animals. "Then the bear might not be sacrificed!"

"It might not. But I think it will be."

"Can't you — ?" Melisto swallowed. She wished she had not spoken so rashly before. "You're the priestess of Artemis. If it's up to you —"

"It isn't! What power do I have? Are you fool enough to think I rule Brauron?"

It was exactly what Melisto had thought. "You're the priestess."

Korinna gave a short laugh. "Oh, Melisto! I am priestess — but only for a time. In due course, I'll go home and be married, like any other girl. The elders will choose another girl to personify the goddess. Perhaps Elpis, when she is older — she's of good family and graceful. But if she is chosen, she won't be in charge, any more than I am. It's the old women, and the old men who come for the banquets; they rule Brauron."

"The grandmothers?" Melisto used the nickname the girls had for the older women at the sanctuary. "The old women who welcomed us the first night?" She had scarcely noticed the oldest priestesses. They were as invisible as slaves, seeing to the domestic work at Brauron: overseeing the kitchens and the looms, greeting visitors, tending the shrines.

"The older priestesses; yes. They have more power. I'm the goddess's mask." Korinna tapped her cheekbones with her fingertips. "Her face, if you like. Artemis is a young goddess, so a girl must impersonate her. I always knew I might be chosen, because my grandmother served in her day, and my great-grandmother. I have a gift for animals. And of course, I am beautiful; that's necessary." She spoke of her beauty without conceit; it was as if she said, *And I'm right-handed.*

"I lead the processions, and I wear the fawn skin and carry the goddess's bow. I assist at the sacrifice, and I tame the stags. And the little girls fall in love with me, because they think I'm Artemis, but I am not holy; it is Artemis who is holy. The grandmothers tell me how to behave. They're the ones who make the decisions. They sent to consult the oracle, and they'll decide what's to become of the bear cub. Melisto, I tell you this out of kindness: I think the bear will be sacrificed, and it will be soon, perhaps the next full moon. You must prepare yourself to assist with the sacrifice, and not break your heart when the bear is given to Artemis."

"But what if Artemis doesn't want it?" Melisto's voice shook. At that moment, she saw that she didn't care whether Artemis wanted the bear or not. Artemis was less to her than the bear.

Korinna rose to her feet in one fluid movement. Her whole body spoke: she had tolerated Melisto's bad manners long enough. Swiftly she picked up her sandals and crossed the bridge barefoot. She was no longer a girl, but an offended goddess: haughty and sublime.

Melisto watched her go, but with blind eyes. She was thinking of the bear: of the harness embedded in the bear's fur, of the stout post and the heavy chain.

7. The Knife

"Melisto, are you awake?"

Melisto uttered a moan of protest. She wished Elpis would leave her alone. Now that the nights were warm, they no longer slept curled up together, but head to foot. Elpis's feet smelled like grass and sweat and dirty little girl; Melisto stank of bear. Often, they kicked each other in their sleep.

"I forgot to tell you. They're going to sacrifice the bear."

Melisto's eyes opened. She sat up in bed. "Who told you so?"

"You know how Tanis hasn't been here?"

"No." The handmaid Tanis taught hunting, and Melisto was not interested in hunting. She had no use for Tanis and hadn't noticed her absence.

"She left, but she came back. Today, when you were at the stable. Korinna met her at the bridge. Maia and I were wading,

311

so we heard. Tanis came back from a place called Oporos —"

"Oropos."

"That's what I said, almost. There's a seer there, and he told Tanis that the bear cub should be given to Artemis on one of her holy days. He said if Artemis didn't want it, the hunters wouldn't have been able to trap it. Korinna says you ought to be prepared, only she tried to prepare you and you wouldn't listen. I don't like it." Elpis spoke decisively. "I feel sorry for the bear, but I feel sorrier for you, because you like the bear so much."

"Did they say which holy day?"

"No. But Korinna said it had better be soon. She said the bear's getting stronger all the time, and it won't be easy to cut its throat. They might have to club it to death. Are you crying?" Elpis edged closer, peering through the dark.

"No." Melisto aimed a light kick at Elpis. She didn't want Elpis's sympathy, or her body heat. Incensed, Elpis kicked back. Melisto retreated to the foot of the bed, as far away from Elpis as she could get. She wrapped her arms around her knees, tying herself in a knot.

A white flash lit the room, and Melisto tensed, expecting thunder. There was none. The weather had been sultry: there had been heat lightning for six nights running, but no thunder and no rain.

Elpis gave an irritable sigh and stretched out to sleep. Melisto clutched her knees and tried to think what to do. Her mind flew to the bear, chained to its post in the barn. She had left her bed before to visit it at night, and Elpis had never told on her. If she went now, she might be able to untie the knot that connected the chain to the harness.

She slid sideways, moving stealthily so as not to wake Elpis. Her toes touched the cold floor before she remembered. Untying the knot would not be enough. She needed to free the bear from the harness. If she didn't, the rope around its neck would contract as the bear grew, tormenting it and dooming it to starvation.

What she needed was a knife. Perhaps it would be better to wait until morning, when she visited the kitchens. She would steal a knife from the kitchen: a strong knife, not too large, but sharp and stout enough to saw through rope —

She heard the sound of sandals against stone. Torchlight brought the shadows to life. One of the grandmothers spoke. Her voice was hoarse and commanding. "Girls. Get up. Go to the altar. It's time."

The girls swarmed from their beds. Those who slept naked found their chitons and tugged them over their heads. Breathless but staunch in their devotion to Artemis, they raced out of the dormitory and into the humid night.

Melisto's heart hammered. What if Elpis were mistaken, and the bear were to be sacrificed tonight? She had wasted time lying in bed, fretting and planning. Now, perhaps, she was too late.

A low growl of thunder: the girl ahead of Melisto jumped straight up into the air. A small child squealed. Heat lightning was one thing, but thunder presaged a storm. Always before, the night ceremonies had been held when the sky was clear and the moonlight was strong. Melisto raised her face to the sky. Gray clouds were billowing, casting migrant shadows on the earth. The ground looked watery and uneven.

The flock of girls reached the open space around the altar. Melisto forced herself to look in all directions. Tethered in front of the temple was a goat.

A goat. Melisto's knees sagged with relief. One of the priestesses began to play the double flute, and Melisto fumbled for the hands of the girls next to her. The children formed a ring around the altar. They looked to Korinna to see if they should dance. Korinna's hair was wind-tossed, and she wore a white himation. She stepped to one side, beginning a counterclockwise circle. Her voice rose in a song of praise, a hymn to Artemis.

The girls chimed in, taking up the melody one by one. Melisto felt her skin turn to gooseflesh. Under that troubled sky, the music was eerie as well as beautiful. The air was freshening. Melisto filled her lungs and sang louder. When the last phrase died away, Korinna nodded to one of the older children, who went to untie the nanny goat.

The girl led the goat toward the altar, tempting her by scooping out handfuls of grain from a basket. Suddenly the goat balked. Perhaps the wind made her skittish. She shook her horns and backed up, haunches shivering. Then she plunged

315

forward, horns lowered, butting the girl and knocking her basket to the ground.

At that moment, there was a white glare of lightning. The sky split open and the rain poured down.

It quenched the priestesses' torches and made the children shriek. The goat bleated and scampered away, rope dangling. One of the priestesses shouted, "Girls! Inside!" The sacrifice would have to be abandoned. The goat was unwilling: a bad omen.

The shivering girls did not wait to be told twice. They broke their circle and streamed toward the building. Only Melisto did not go. She dashed for the portico of the temple and hid behind a stone column. As soon as the others had gone, she ran toward the altar. The sacrificial knife was concealed in the basket of grain. She found the fallen basket, raked through the grain, and found it.

A thrill of fear ran through her. The knife was sacred. It was also the tool she needed. The blade was curved close to the handle, designed to cut through an animal's windpipe. The knife was so sharp that when she tested it with her forefinger, it sliced the outer layer of skin before she knew it. She

316

made a fist around the handle and began to run.

By the time she reached the stable, her chiton was sodden and her hair hung straight with water. She darted under the overhang and wiped her face with her wet hands. As soon as she climbed into the stall, the bear trotted up to her. It wrapped its paws around her waist and pressed its face against her, a child hiding in its mother's skirts. Melisto stroked it, grateful for its warmth. Loose hair and grit stuck to her hands.

When the bear loosened its grip, she sank down in the straw. The bear circled her and tramped into her lap. Still standing, it began to suckle her neck. Melisto tensed against the pain. She stuck a finger in the corner of its mouth to break the suction.

The bear made a sound of infant satisfaction. It was glad she had come through the storm. It hummed like a hive of bees and settled down close to her. The rain was falling more gently now. Melisto was tempted to let the bear suckle until it was sleepy. Then they could curl up together, and she would be warm. She wanted one more night with the bear.

But the risk was too great. Usually the girls put themselves to bed, but on a night like this one, the priestesses might take a head count. Korinna would guess where she was, if Elpis did not tell. Melisto steadied the knife in her hand. She gripped the harness and slid the knife under it, flat against the bear's fur.

The bear squirmed. It never liked being interrupted when it was suckling, and its skin under the harness was tender. It understood that Melisto was not playing, but trying to interfere with it. It twisted free with such force that the rope skinned Melisto's fingertips. She yelped and stuck her hand in her mouth. When she pursued the bear, it swiped at her with its left front paw, leaving a row of bleeding scratches on her leg.

The stable filled with white light. Melisto jumped when the thunder crackled. The bear ran and scurried up the post. Again the air glared white, and Melisto saw everything: the silver waterfall that rimmed the stable roof, the dark gleam of the iron chain, the bear's panic-stricken eyes.

She hunkered down next to the stable wall. She wished she had thought to bring food for the bear. She might have distracted it, as the sacrificial animals were distracted. She banked the straw around her naked legs and waited, shivering and listening to the storm.

Time passed. The sound of the rain on the roof was no longer deafening. When Melisto heard the bear scrape-sliding down the post, she made herself keep still. She whispered, "Artemis." Now that she was here, in the stable, she had no doubt what the goddess wanted. Patiently she waited for the bear to come.

It padded across the stable floor. First it checked its dish, flipping it with one paw and huffing with disappointment. Then it wandered over to sniff her. Melisto murmured love words and extended her arm, fingers drawn together. The bear licked her and fitted its mouth around her hand. She allowed it to suckle until it was almost asleep.

She meant to attack suddenly, taking the bear by surprise, but the bear sensed her decision even as it dozed. She attacked; it revolted; the two things happened simultaneously. She grabbed the harness and threw herself over the bear, straddling it, using her whole weight to hold it still. It screamed with outrage as she shoved the knife under the harness and sawed with all her might.

She could not hold the bear. It hauled itself out from under her, dragging her several feet across the stable floor. She could not hold the bear, but she kept her grip on the harness and the knife. She had gained an advantage: the bear was not only pulling against her, it was forcing the knife through the rope. As the bear writhed and fumed, the blade bit through the last strands.

The harness was cut, but the rope was still embedded in the bear's fur. Melisto snatched at it. There was a noise like cloth tearing as the bear scrambled to its feet and yanked free.

Melisto stood up. She felt as if her whole body had been skinned raw. She flung down the knife. It hadn't been an hour since she was afraid to touch it. Now she didn't care what happened to it.

She stumbled to the stall door. The rain was falling lightly: a steady patter. "Come on!" she urged the bear. She shoved the stall door open, dragging it over the muddy ground. She flew straight ahead, into the rain, and the bear followed — whether because it viewed her as a mother or because it tracked her as a fleeing quarry, she did not know. She only knew that it was close behind her. Now she must lead it away from Brauron, beyond the boundaries of the sanctuary.

She ran. She, who had never liked running, who had always hated her clumsy slowness, ran as if her feet were winged. Her limbs were as tireless as a god's; the blood rushed under her skin and she glowed. The bear, confined for months, ran alongside her. It bounced and curvetted, the hind paws overtaking the front paws with every stride. Melisto sketched a wide loop around the dormitories. When she crossed the bridge, she stopped and looked over her shoulder, not knowing if the bear could swim. The bear splashed into the spring and clambered up the bank. She shouted, "Bear!" and sprinted onward, leading it farther afield.

She dodged around trees and through the grassland. All at once she glimpsed the bay in the distance. Without thinking about it, she had brought the bear to her favorite place. She looked behind her and saw it was sniffing the roots of a tree. Soon it would begin a new life and find its own food. She called, "αρκτος!" and it raised itself up and looked for her.

An idea stirred within her. She dragged her chiton over her head and stood naked and tingling in the rain. She raised her hands as if they were paws adorned with needle-sharp claws. Tipping her head back, she let the rain wash her: arms and nipples, neck and belly and thigh. A tension gathered in her throat and emerged as a growl; she bared her teeth and felt the hair on her arms spring erect.

She pounded the wet ground with her muddy feet and shook her arms, swaying. She was dancing, and she was a Bear, one of the goddess's own. She had no need to stop and think what step came next. She could not make a mistake. She was aware that the bear was watching her, and the rain had intensified. The storm was strengthening around her.

Then the sky split, like a thin plate shattering: each fragment edged with white fire. The thunder that followed was earsplitting. Melisto sprang straight up in the air. She rushed downhill, heading for the strand, where the salt water seethed against the pebbles. She had a wild idea that the bay might shelter her; she would wade out and crouch down in the water, where the raindrops would not strike so hard against her skin.

She never reached the water. Another bolt of lightning cracked the sky, but she had no time to see it. Only the bear saw the strike, and it was terrified; the afterimage burned on its retina. Melisto felt a blazing and unnatural heat. Her last thought was rebellious: nothing should feel like that. She glowed, lit up like a shooting star, and like a star, she fell.

The Sphinx Speaks

What? Are you shocked?

A ten-year-old girl
    is struck by lightning. A moment of
      feeling wholly alive

      — and then her death. Did the gods
      take her?

        and if they did, why?

        Who had it in for her?

Did Zeus, mightiest of gods,

    decide he was weary

    of this harmless girl? All right: she
      was a brat,

        and a wild girl, but did Zeus,
        almighty Zeus,

      waste a thunderbolt on *her*?

Or was it Artemis?
>She's a terror, with her arrows —
>>was she craving the amber
>>sphinx?
>Was she mad enough for a trinket,
>>a glob of tree sap
>>and a few gold beads,
>>>to kill a girl she liked?

Are the gods *like* that? And if so —
>if the gods aren't good
>what good are the gods?
>>>>Or are there no
>>>>gods?
>>>>>does it all mean
>>>>>nothing?

Don't ask me. I'm the Sphinx.
>I ask riddles. I don't answer them.
>I can tell you this:
>>sooner or later
>>you'll find yourself here:
>>the place where nothing makes
>>sense,
>>the place where you ask *What
>>does life mean?*

You'll be shocked,
    or suffering,
    and you'll want to know *why*

. . . and then life will go on
      not answering,
    and the wheel will turn, till there
      comes a time
    when you look on the world
and feel such wonder,
such tenderness,
you'll want to cup the earth in your
    hands;
    so much mystery!
    such richness of life!
    such intricate patterns . . . Why,
      look at the scars
      on Melisto's skin! Exquisite . . .
      Lightning does that.
      Heat hotter than the sun
        surges through the body,
        leaving scars shaped like fern
        leaves
          fractals . . .
          beautiful . . .

but then there's death —
which brings us back to the Greeks.
There's death in the world,
and the Greeks never forgot it.

There is death in this story. Not just owl-
eyed Melisto,
but Lykos. Remember Lykos?
A few pages,
and you've forgotten him already!
Let's see, you say,
thumbing through the pages.
*Which one was he? Oh, Lykos. The
little boy.*
*Menon's little brother, Rhaskos's friend
— if he was a friend.*
He died of the plague, or something . . .
— That's right, that's the
one.
Lykos: a microbe, a fever, and a
tomb. Now Melisto,
dancing her Bear Dance,
is lit by fire from the gods.
Was her death a sign of favor?
*or was she just too stupid to come in
from the rain?*

Don't ask my opinion.
    I'm the Sphinx; I'm asking you. Go
      on,
        speculate!
    Was it random, this child's death?
    Was it better for her to die young
      than to have to go back
      to the weaving room, an early
        marriage,
      death, perhaps, by childbirth?
Is it true? "Whom the gods love die young"?
    Actually, that hasn't been said yet.
    That saying
    won't be around for another fifty
      years;
    but it's Greek, a Greek idea.
        Would *you* like to die young?
                — Ha!

I'll give you fair warning. There's a third
    death coming,
    one that still shocks the world.
I won't spoil the surprise. Almost twenty-
    five hundred years

the man's been dead. He fed the
    worms
        and is immortal. Immortal.
    Now, there's a concept.

I wonder what you think?
        O you who bend these pages,
            what do you think?
        Do you believe that to die is to be
    over?
Or, if something follows,
        what's it like? what comes after?
Don't ask me. I told you, I'm the Sphinx.
        I only make the riddles. I don't solve
    them.

If you want truth,
        consult a philosopher.
            (There's one in these pages. Keep
            reading.)

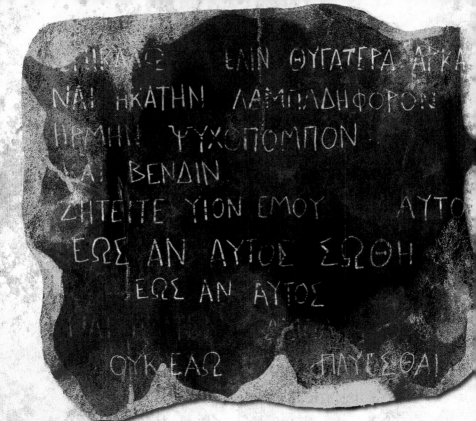

Translation

> I call…...elis... daughter of Arkadi
> by Hekate, the torchbearer…...........
>   Hermes, Guide of Souls,
>   and Bendis……………..
> …….search for my son……..him
> …..until he is found
>   until he is…..
>
> …………………………………………..
>   ...forbid…. to rest......

EXHIBIT 10

*Lead tablet with inscription ("curse" tab-
let); late classical period.*

This insignificant-looking slab of lead is in fact a magical object. For the ancient Greeks, there was no clear line separating religion and magic: they believed that spirits of the dead could be summoned and "bound" to perform acts for the living. The details of the binding ritual are not known, but tablets with writing on them played an important role. Thousands of these curse tablets, or binding spells, have been found in streams, wells, and burial grounds. Many were made of lead, which was cheap in Athens because it was a by-product of silver mining. Small pieces of lead often served as scratch paper. Wax tablets and papyrus may also have been used for binding spells, but would not have survived.

This early example of a curse tablet was found near the grave of a female child. In the minds of the ancient Greeks, a female's destiny was to bear children, and a girl who died before giving birth was unlikely to rest in peace. The ghosts of young girls were prime candidates for binding spells, because they either could not or would not enter the underworld.

This particular inscription is unusual. The dead spirit, presumably the daughter of Arkadi, is summoned by Hermes and Hekate, gods of the underworld, and commanded to locate a missing person. The creator of the spell also invokes Bendis, a Thracian moon goddess who was similar to Artemis.

THRATTA IN ATHENS

All day it had been hot, but now the wind was rising. Thratta halted in the street, adjusting her veil to make a canopy over her head. She made sure that every strand of her cropped hair was hidden. It was nearly sunset, the hour when the city gates would be locked. Anyone who knew her as the slave of Arkadios would expect her to be inside the walls by nightfall.

She reached into the basket she carried under her cloak. The knife was there, and so was the lead tablet. The four clay bottles were corked and unbroken. The silver coins she had stolen were sewn into the hem of her dress. She felt them bang against her shins as she walked.

333

The vast Dipylon gates loomed before her. She passed between them, her veil drawn over her face so that only her eyes showed. She considered slumping or stooping — her height was as distinctive as her red hair — but decided against it. Stooping was unnatural to her and might draw the guards' attention.

Outside the gates, there were graves on either side of the road. The tombs were crowded at odd angles, some marked with ceramic jars, others with marble posts that shone cream-color in the setting sun. Melisto's grave was unmarked, but Thratta found it easily. She had come there for the funeral and again three days after, to tend the grave.

The grave would not remain unmarked. Arkadios had ordered a marble slab from one of the finest craftsmen in Athens. He had spared no expense at his daughter's funeral, and he paid no heed to those who whispered that her death was a punishment from Zeus. Lysandra had beaten her breast and torn her hair, but she shirked her maternal duty: she could not, or would not, prepare Melisto's body for burial. It fell to Thratta to bathe the dead child and rub her skin with oil. Thratta had dressed Melisto in her white shroud, packing the cloth with sprigs of ivy and oregano.

She hadn't wept. It was a point of pride for Thratta to shed no tears, and her hands did not tremble as she touched the patterned scars. She felt as if someone had struck her heart with a fist. She had lost a second child. She told herself that Melisto had not been hers to lose. She had not been fool enough to love her master's child. But she had been forced to tend Melisto, to dodge her questions and try to drum some manners into her. She had come to respect the little girl's toughness and to value her affection.

Now Melisto was dead. She would ask no more questions and carry no more water. She would never marry or bear children. With that thought came another: it was the restless dead who could be bound to serve the living.

Now Thratta knelt down and unpacked the jars from the basket, sniffing each one to learn what was inside. Mouthing a prayer, she poured the contents on the grave. First milk and honey, then wine, then water. Grasping the knife, she slid back her veil and sawed a lock of hair from her head. She scattered the hair over the puddle of liquid offerings.

Last of all, she removed the lead tablet from the basket. It was palm-sized, but heavy and cold against her skin. The scratches on the surface were faint, and the darkening air made them hard to read — Thratta could not read in any case — but she ran her fingers over them. She had told a scribe in the marketplace what to write and paid him with a coin she'd stolen from her master. She hoped the scribe hadn't cheated her. It seemed to her that she'd spoken more words than the ones he wrote down.

She licked her lips, remembering the spell. "Hekate, torchbearer, mistress of the dead. And Hermes, Guide of Souls. I bring you milk and honey and water and wine. Find the child Melisto, daughter of Arkadios. Bind her to do my will. Bring her here to serve me."

The words sounded flat. Perhaps she ought to have sung them. She closed her eyes. "I call you, Melisto, daughter of Arkadios. By Hekate the torchbearer, mistress of the dead, and Hermes, Guide of

Souls. And Bendis, goddess of the moon and the hunt; gracious Bendis, remember how I worshipped you when I was a child. Remember the sacrifices my father gave you: the goats, the heifers. Find the girl Melisto and bring her here. Bind her to serve me and set my son free."

She scraped aside a little of the loose earth, making a hollow for the curse tablet. She spoke the spell a third time, crooning as she covered the lead. "Search for my son. Search for him and find a way to set him free."

There were no more steps to the ritual. Thratta opened her eyes, put the jars back in the basket, and got up. Now she must make her way to Piraeus, a journey of seven miles, and from there, if the gods favored her, to Thrace. Down in the harbor city, she would find a ship. All she needed was a ship captain who would take her money and ask no questions. There were many Thracians who worked in Piraeus, not all of them slaves. She might find someone who knew her kinfolk. Once she reached her own people, she could prove her rank. She had the tattoos on her arms, the marks of her clan.

She wondered whether Arkadios would hire a slave-catcher to pursue her. If she were recaptured, she would be beaten, perhaps branded and starved. She was gambling on the hope that Arkadios might not have the stomach for revenge. He was deep in grief; he would remember that Melisto had loved her. And she had been careful not to steal too much money. A man of Arkadios's fortune might not even notice the loss.

She looked her last on Melisto's grave, picturing the child who lay under the earth. She felt a pang. She remembered the day Melisto broke her arm. She thought of all the times she'd stood by, powerless, as Lysandra vented her spite against her daughter. Thratta picked up her basket and turned to go.

She had not taken three steps when a gust of cold air whirled around her, yanking the veil from between her fingers. Thratta's skin prickled. Against her will she turned to face the thing behind her.

The girl Melisto stood atop the newly dug grave. She was no longer dressed in her burial shroud, but in the yellow tunic of a Little Bear. The glowing tint of her dress

338

seemed to light up the dusk. Thratta could see every detail of the child's face. She had always heard that the shades of the dead were either black and decayed, or ghastly white, but Melisto looked like herself: compact, stocky, brown-skinned, with a flush of healthy rose on her cheeks. There were scratches on her arms and legs. The hair Thratta had braided so often was loose and windblown.

Thratta realized that she had never expected her spell to work. Horror and hope seized her in the same instant. If Melisto stood before her, the spell was cast. If the spell was cast, Rhaskos might be freed.

Thratta ran her tongue around the inside of her mouth. "Find my son. My son, Rhaskos. I told you about him long ago — do you remember? They took me from him. He had red hair — I marked him with blood and ashes — his left arm." She bared her arms, showing her own tattoos. "Find where he is. Set him free. I bind you to do this; by Hekate and Hermes, I command you. You will never rest until my son is free. By Hekate and Hermes and Bendis, by your own Artemis, I bind you."

Melisto's lips parted as if to ask a question. Then her face changed; it was no longer solid, but grainy; no longer grainy, but translucent. She vanished. Nothing was left but an orange glow where her tunic had been.

Thratta waited until her knees felt strong. Then she turned her back on the city and began her journey to Piraeus.

EXHIBIT 11

Kylix (drinking cup), mid-fifth century BCE.

This black-figure kylix was found at Kolonos. Though the outside of the cup has been damaged, enough painting remains to show that it was decorated with dancing satyrs, followers of the god of wine, Dionysus. A cup like this one was probably used at a symposium, or drinking party.

The interior of the cup is better preserved and depicts a ship surrounded by leaping dolphins. As the drinker held the cup by the handles and emptied it, the ship would appear to float on waves of wine. The symposium was often compared to an ocean voyage: the drinker was adrift in a sea of poetry, philosophy, and drunkenness.

The Greek historian Timaios tells the story of a symposium where the guests were so drunk and dizzy that they thought they were on a ship about to capsize. In an effort to avoid shipwreck, the drunkards gathered up all the furniture and flung it outdoors. They remained "seasick" for some time, and the house where the party took place was thereafter called the House of the Ship.

RHASKOS IN ATHENS

1. Piraeus

The winter after the Petraios festival,
    Menon went to Athens to recruit
      soldiers.
    Long ago his grandfather helped
      Athens fight the Persian Wars.
    Menon thought it was high time
    Athens returned the favor.
He shipped off to Athens, and he took
    me.

By then, I'd served him two or three
    years.
He took it for granted I looked up to him.
    He owned me,

so I wasn't about to tell him the truth.
   Truth was, after the Petraios festival
      we were enemies. We were like
         two curs,
            circling each other,
         hackles raised,
            sniffing out ways to thwart and hurt.
He was better at hurting.
I was better at hating.

He'd been made a general.
For weeks at a time, he'd go off to war,
      come back and greet me,
         punching my shoulder,
         knuckling my hair.
We both pretended that it didn't hurt.
      He hated me in ignorance.
      I hated him in secret.

He wanted the Athenians to see his wealth:
      his retinue of slaves. So off we went.
I'd never been on a ship before,
      and I was seasick. Menon was
         scornful

and pleased. By the time we reached
  the harbor at Piraeus,
    it was starting to sleet:
    a strange harbor, a foreign city —
    a five-mile walk to Athens,
    the wind finding holes in my
      cloak,
    my stomach uneasy,
    and Menon on horseback.

I'd never seen such crowds —
  men and donkeys and pigs,
    mud and sleet and miracles:
  gods and heroes cut from stone,
    cloud-white goddesses
    and slim boy-gods;
  patterned tunics painted
      turquoise —
      honey-color —
      terra-cotta pink —
    and every blue:
      sky or sea or Poseidon's
        beard.
  They were everywhere, those statues:
  measuring me with their eyes.

I don't know when I first looked up
but halfway to the sky,
there it was, the city's crown
encircled by purple mountains
steeper than any hill in Thessaly
— the Akropolis.
By then I'd found my land legs, and I
wanted to *see* —
My teeth were chattering,
my belly empty as a broken jar,
but there were wonders on every side,
and I wanted to stop and *see* —

but Menon was on horseback,
and I had to keep up.

2. Symposium

That night we went to a symposium.
I guess you've never been to one.
They're for grown men.
Free men.
Athenian men, if you hear them talk,
are the freest of the free,
and free men need entertainment.

At the beginning
    there's music,
    pretty slave girls;
        flute players and acrobat-dancers.
        Astonishing!
Girls are weak, everyone knows that,
        but I couldn't do the things they did:
    flip through the air backward
    or walk on my hands —
        I tried. I fell down.
They didn't wear too much, those girls,
        I liked watching them.
    I didn't know any girls, so I was
        curious.

The rooms where the symposia were held
    were always the best rooms. Paintings
        on the walls,
    patterned stone underfoot. At the
        beginning,
    the air was fragrant with garlands and
        incense
        and tempting food;
        sometimes — by the end —
    the stink of piss and vomit.

The point of the party is to drink.
And talk. How much you drink,
    and what you talk about,
    is up to the man in charge for the
      night: the symposiarch.
He decides
    how much water to mix with the wine
    and when the men should drain their
      cups.

There were couches lining the walls
    — so the men could lie down and
      drink.
    I wasn't supposed to stand in front of
      anyone,
      so I kept moving,
        trying not to take up space.
The men drank and argued —
    the things they argued about!
    Menon called *me* stupid,
      a thickhead Thracian, but even I
      knew
      better than those men.
They liked to ponder: what was first?
    the first chicken, or the first egg?

How could anybody find that out?
And what's more, who cares?
Here's another thing: they said it was
    impossible to cross the street,
        because before you walked the whole
            way across,
        you'd have to walk half the way across,
        and before you walked half the way
            across,
        you'd have to walk a quarter way
            across,
        and before that, half the quarter,
            half of that,
            and half of that. You could never
                get across,
            because of all those bits of street
                you'd have to cross
            before you could cross —
        but I've crossed hundreds of streets,
            and my legs make short work of it.

Then they'd ask, with puckered brows:
        does everything in the world change?
        or does everything stay the same?

Even I know

> it's not one way or the other.
> Some things change, like eggs,
> and others don't. Like rocks.

The talking was a contest. I saw that.
The man who talked best was the winner.
That first symposium, Menon was very
  quick

> and made the others laugh. Everyone
>   admired him —
> good-looking,
> only twenty years old
> and already a general.
> By the end of the night,
> he was reeling
> with wine and conceit.

I carried the torch and led him back

> to the house of Anytus, where we
>   were guests.
> I helped him into bed
> and set a water jar beside him.

In the morning he was still drunk.
He slept heavily

one knee up
one arm over his face. I knew he
 would sleep till noon.
  I knew *him*.
  Every slave knows his master.

3. Akropolis

It was my chance, and I took it —
 I shoved my feet in my sandals,
 hugged on my cloak. It was early;
  the sky was turning pink.
The streets were full of shadows:
 veiled women carrying water.

I rushed for the crown of the city,
  the steep slope, the overhanging
   glory
  of the temples on the rock.
The men at the symposium
 had boasted of those temples:
 pure Pentelic marble,
 even the roof tiles.
 Somewhere on that hill

was a giant statue: the Trojan Horse,
with life-sized men
crawling out of its belly!
That morning, with Menon asleep, was
my only chance to see it,
I ran till my chest ached.
Around me, up the hill
through the streets
distractions: shrines
festooned with ivy,
temples, tavern-keepers
bawling out the price of
wine,
shops and stench and smoke —
The wind was cold against my teeth.
I was gasping like a fish
stumbling, knocking into people,
but I couldn't lose my way. In
Athens,
the Akropolis is always *up*
halfway to the sky. I kept going
up
until the city was *down*. There was
so much to see —

the sunrise above
and the city below.

There's a ramp on one side of the mound
— the mound is steep as a waterfall
but the ramp zigzags —
so the heifers and goats
can walk up the hill,
to be sacrificed.
I could see the paint on the temples
scarlet and blue,
and the gold leaf
flashing
the great gates ahead.
The marble blushed in the morning sun;
the light seemed to pierce the stone,
or glow out of it, I don't know which.
Columns and spaces —
Stripes of white that stung my eyes —
And the spaces between
mysterious
dark and dazzle:
glaze and glare
shadow and softness.

Between the columns:
>   guards
>   at all five gates. I stopped.
If anyone was going to be turned away,
>   it would be me.

>   Foreigner.

>   Tattooed.

>   Red-haired
>   barbarian.
>   They'd know I
>   was a slave.

Where's your master, boy?
>   *He's home in bed. He's drunk.*
Why aren't you tending him, boy?

>   They'd treat me
>   like a runaway.

It was like biting into an olive gone bad,
>   only there was nothing I could spit out.
>   I took a step back
>   away from the crowd.
>   I saw my shadow waver across the stone.

There were still things to see: I could go back,
>   look at the shrines, the fountain house,

a bigger market than any in Thessaly —
    but everything had gone sour.
I had to get back.
If Menon woke up —
    and I wasn't there
    I'd be beaten for sure.

I made my way downward,
    lost the path
    ended up in a hollow,
    a circle of olive and willow trees
        where an old man was dancing.

I didn't know who he was.
He was naked, I saw that.
    And it wasn't a gymnasion, and he
        wasn't young.
    He was ugly. He was like an old
    satyr,
        the arms sinewy, but a belly like a
        full bowl,
        a swaying gut.
    His nose looked smashed,
        as if he'd been a boxer
        and fought too many rounds.

He wasn't too clean,
    he was humming,
      raising his ropy arms to the sun,
        the hair in his armpits
        like two birds' nests;
    his feet striking the ground
      in a strong rhythm.

Even I
    a slave
    a thickheaded Thracian
      could see how unseemly it was: an
      old man
      who had no beauty to display:
      dancing
      naked to the sky. He was worse
      than I was.
        At least I was young
          with no sag in my flesh;
        And I had more sense
          than to dance like that.

I thought of jeering at him —
Menon would have mocked him —
      but then: I wasn't Menon.

I didn't want to be like Menon.
That man was as happy as a child at play;
    he didn't even seem cold,
    that naked
  ugly man.

I ducked behind the willow
    so he wouldn't know I saw.
I found my way back,
    but I was sore inside. I'd missed my
      only chance
    to see the sights of Athens;
      that's what I thought
      that dawn
when I beheld first the wonder of wonders
                 Sokrates.

ALKIBIADES IN HADES

Sokrates!
>   what can a slave boy,
>   a clodhopper with a pitchfork,
>   know about Sokrates?

I've nothing against slaves. I owned dozens
   when I was alive;
>   no, I've nothing against slaves
>   — but a half-breed Thracian
>   who sneers at symposia,
>   what could he know of Sokrates?

>   Sokrates was *my* friend.

In fact, he once said
>   that he loved two things best of all:
>   philosophy

and Alkibiades. That's me.

Don't try to pronounce my name unless
you're Greek.

I am

I *was*

Αλκιβιαδης Κλεινιου
Σκαμβωνιδης.

All my life long, I was famous! Even now,
twenty-four centuries after my death
(I was murdered)
my name is mispronounced
by scholars all over the world!

But I'm not here to talk about myself.

Hermes offered me time off from Hades
if I told you about Sokrates.

I leapt at the chance. After twenty-four
centuries,
Hades is tedious. And to tell you the
truth,
my home down there
is not in the best neighborhood.

Plus I'm a restless sleeper. Murder —
that is, *being* murdered —
leads to insomnia.

Enough about me.

I'm here to tell you about my friend.
We'll start with his name. Σωκρατης. First
syllable, So. Not sock.
He never wore socks.
We had socks, we Greeks —
our second-best poet, Hesiod, sings of
socks —
but Sokrates never wore them. He seldom
wore sandals:
the soles of his feet were as thick as
hooves,
and his cloak . . . We used to tease him,
that hairy, hoary old cloak
that stank like a badger's den,
same cloak, season in, season out . . .

Now, I wore silk:
purple-dyed, fantastic,
tickling the grass around my feet.
I wore my hair long
and crowned myself with
violets —
a cure for drunkenness.
(It doesn't work, but it's becoming.)

361

My armor was gold and ivory. If I'd been
  less a man,
      I might have been mocked,
      but I was a paragon
      of strength and grace,
      and a virtuoso at war.
It was said: if the hero Akhilleus
      did not resemble me in every way
        he was not handsome. By the
          gods,
      I was beautiful!
    Not just in youth,
      but in every season of my life . . . !

Forgive me. We were speaking of
  Sokrates.

        His name: *So*, as in *so what?*
            Kra, as in *crop*.
    Tes, as in *tease. So-KRA-tes.* No socks,
                please.

        His father was a stonemason.
        His mother was a midwife.
        He used to say he was like her,

only instead of helping women bring
forth children,
he helped men bring forth ideas.
Unlike me, he was poor —

Oh, I was wealthy!
an aristocrat to my fingertips:
a spendthrift, a playboy,
charismatic, silver-tongued,
the offspring of Great Ajax who
fought at Troy!
I blazed and bedazzled!
Half the men in Athens
and all the women
— or the other way around —
caught fire from me!
I was Eros with a thunderbolt!
If Sokrates had been my lover —
(I tried to attract him) —
he would have been the only one I
ever had
who was worthy of me,
the better part of me,
the man I seldom was.

We shared a tent at the battle of Potidaea;
　　he treated me as if he were my father.
　　I was eighteen. He was pushing forty.
　　He bore the hardships of fighting better
　　　　　　　than I did.
Better than any man there! We were cut off
　　　　　　　from supplies
　　　　　and had nothing to eat,
and he didn't seem to care. But when the
　　　　　　　food came
he enjoyed it more than anybody. And as
　　　　　　　for drink,
　　　　　　he enjoys his drink,
but no man on earth ever saw Sokrates
　　　　　　　drunk.

　　That winter at Potidaea was shocking,
a hard frost. We wrapped ourselves up in
　　　　　　　old sheepskins,
　　　bits of felt, anything. But there was
　　　　　　　Sokrates,
　　　　　　　barefoot
　　　walking on the ice,
no fuss. One sunrise, he started thinking
　　　　　　over some idea —

it was summer by then — he stood there
all day,
lost in thought. At nightfall he was still
there;
some of us checked during the night.
still there . . .
all night
still there . . .
When the sun rose, he said his prayers
and walked away. I never found out what
he was thinking.

He saved my life at Potidaea,
single-handed.
I was wounded;
he wouldn't leave me,
stood over me
and got me out of the fray, armor and all.
Athens awarded me a suit of armor and a
crown —

—What?
You think they should have given *him* the
honors?

365

I thought so, too. I went to the
  committee to protest,
      but I was the one
      with the family connections
         (you know how these things go)
      and I was so much more
         the kind of person who wins
            awards . . .
Did I mention I was an Olympic
  champion?
      Chariot racing! Entered three teams.
      Came in first, second, and fourth!

            Now Sokrates —
Sokrates never cared for the trophies of
                war.
    He'd stride across the battlefield like a
             goose,
        his head in the clouds,
           unfrightened;
        his feet naked, and that
           god-awful cloak.
He was as brave as any man in Athens,
      and unlike me, he was faithful.
        He was loyal to the city . . .

To tell you the truth, *I* changed sides.
> More than once. Oh, I won victories
>> for Athens,
> but also . . . against Athens. Whatever
>> side I was on,
> that was the winning team!

On the battlefield I was —
> let's not mince words — a genius.
>> A fox for strategy, a whirlwind for
>>> speed —
>> Wherever I went, I made myself at
>>> home.
>> Among the Persians, I went mad for
>>> luxury;
>>> With the Thracians, I was always
>>>> drunk;
>>>> In Thessaly, I lived on horseback;
>>>> In Sparta, I ate pudding made
>>>>> from pig blood,
>>>>> cut off my flowing hair,
>>>>> and scorned all comforts. Even
>>>>>> the Spartans,
>>>>>>> who admire *no one*,
>>>>>>> honored me! Even the
>>>>>>>> Spartan king —
>>>>>>>>> till I ran off with his wife.

Ah. Enough about me.

When I was alive,
the potters of Athens
used to make these toys: clay statues of
sileni,
little figures of beefy old men,
bald and fat
with thick lips
and horse's ears. If you open them up,
inside there's a prize, a grab bag:
a tiny statue of a god. That's Sokrates.
He was ugly all his life,
impudent as a satyr. When you first hear
him, you think
his ideas are laughable. He talks about
pack mules
and shoemakers and blacksmiths:
ordinary people,
ordinary things. His arguments sound like
sheer nonsense,
but if you open them up
they're the only ideas in the world that
have any sense in them.
When most men talk,

nobody gives a damn what they say,
    but when Sokrates talked

I listened:
    staggered and bewitched. There were
    times
    when I was filled with holy rage.
My heart leapt into my mouth,
    and my eyes filled with tears —
    my soul was turned upside down.
He made me feel
    that there were things inside me
    crying for attention
        — I don't mean the usual kind of
        attention;
    I had plenty of that all my life,
        even now, in Hades,
I can't get enough of myself! . . . There's
    hell for you.

What I meant was this: I felt with him
    something I never felt with anyone else —
    a sense of shame.
There were times when I'd have been glad
    if he had died.

369

But he outlived me. A man like me makes
  enemies:
      the Thirty Tyrants,
      the Spartans.
They came at night and set fire to the
  house.
      I leapt through the flames
          sword in hand.
      They shot me full of arrows.

Enough about me. In my lifetime, I was
  famous
      and infamous. I am famous still
      largely because I knew *him*.
He's the thing I miss most about being
  alive —

              By the gods, he was magnificent!
                  So beautiful,
                  so rich in virtue,
                      so golden,
                      Σωκρατης . . .

a chariot race. Votive objects — that is,
offerings to the gods — were often valuable
in ancient Greece. The land
was rough and mountainous,
with few roads, so chariots
were not practical for travel
or trade. They were status
symbols serving the function
of a pampered sports car,
and were most often seen in
public processions or athletic

EXHIBIT 12

Miniature chariot wheel,
circa 525–500 BCE.

This bronze chariot wheel was found near a sanctuary of Apollo. It may have been given to Apollo in thanksgiving for victory during a chariot race. Votive objects — that is, offerings to the gods — were often symbolic in nature. This miniature wheel symbolizes the whole chariot.

Chariots were luxury items in ancient Greece. The land was rough and mountainous, with few roads, so chariots were not practical for travel or trade. They were status symbols, serving the function of a pampered sports car, and were most often seen in public processions or athletic contests.

Rhaskos, Menon, and Sokrates in Athens

ᚱᚢᚱᚱᚢᚱᚱᚢᚱᚱᚢᚱᚱᚢᚱ

1. The Square

Four days later, I saw him again. By then
　I'd heard of him.
　　Sokrates, I mean.
　　　I'd been to two more symposia
　　　　and heard, "*Sokrates*
　　　　　says —"
　　　　which led to raised voices
　　　　argument
　　　　and laughter.
　　The Oracle at Delphi
　　　said Sokrates was the wisest man
　　　　on earth.
　　Menon itched to meet him.

So Anytus took Menon to the gymnasion. It
  was called the White Dog,
            not the best place in town.
                  Foreigners and half-breeds,
                  metics, human mongrels
                  were allowed to work out there.
            And there *he* was,
      my dancing man, that grizzly old satyr;
      it turned out he was Sokrates.

I didn't stare;
      A slave is supposed to keep his head
            down.
      A glance was enough. It was the same
      man.

Once they'd been introduced, Menon
  began to ask questions.
His eyes gleamed: a cat who'd spotted a
  mouse.
            He was courteous. Even bashful.
He asked Sokrates if excellence could be
  taught.
The word he used was *ἀρετή,*
            which means goodness

375

or excellence. If something's good
   at being the thing it's meant to be,
   or doing the thing it was made to
   do,
      that's *ἀρετή*.

Menon spoke modestly,
   a young man consulting a sage.
It was a trap. He meant to trick Sokrates
   into saying something stupid.
Which he did. Or so I thought. Because
right away
      Sokrates said he didn't know.
         He didn't know if *ἀρετή* could be
         taught.
      Not only that, he wasn't sure what it
      was.
Not only *that*, he didn't know anyone who
did.

Menon started to tell him. He said *ἀρετή*
      was lots of things: a man ruling a city,
         helping his friends and harming
            his enemies;
      a woman obeying her husband.

Sokrates exclaimed, "I'm in luck!"
>and you could see
>he was set to have himself a good
>>time.
"I asked for one kind of excellence,
>and you give me a whole swarm.
But if I asked you, *What is a bee?*
>and you answered me,
>>*There's this kind of bee, and that kind
>>of bee . . .*
I'd have to say, *You haven't told me what a
bee is.*
>All bees have something in common,
>and that something is what makes a
>>bee a bee.
That's what I'm after.
What is virtue? What is excellence? What is
ἀρετή?"

They went on like that for a while.
They talked about courage and wisdom
and justice
>and a bucketful of things
>that have nothing to do with me.

I wasn't paying attention.
There's a lot to see at the White Dog:
    wrestlers struggling in the sand pits,
    a man throwing the javelin.
There were three flute players,
    playing different tunes.
Across the courtyard
    there were paintings on the wall.
      Herakles, I think:
      grappling with a lion,
        mobbed by swans.
    I strained to see.

Men left off watching the athletes —
    Sokrates could always draw a
      crowd —
    and came to listen. At one point — I
      don't know why —
Sokrates asked Menon what a shape
  was.
Menon said shapes were triangles and
  squares and circles —
    but Sokrates asked again, "What's the
    same about all of them?"

I pricked up my ears,
　　　　because I know about shapes —
　　　　not that I recall anyone teaching me.
　　　　　I know what a circle is,
　　　　　　and a square,
　　　　so it seemed like a simple question,
　　　　　　but I couldn't answer it.
Menon couldn't either. He'd thought this old man
　　　　　was going to be easy to trick,
　　　　　　but now that they were
　　　　　　　face-to-face,
　　　　he couldn't say what a shape was. He said:

　　　　　　　　"You tell me, Sokrates."

And Sokrates said, "If I tell you what a shape is,
　　　　will you tell me about excellence?"

　　　　　　　　　　　"I will."

"In that case, I must do my best. It's in a good cause."

By then, I was paying attention. Sokrates
   said
      a shape was the outside, or the limit,
      of something solid. Which I guess it is.
Then Menon wanted to know what color
   was —
      not just blue or green or black
      but what color *was*.
         He wasn't going to keep his
         promise about ἀρετή
      until Sokrates told him.

Sokrates said: "Anyone talking to you,
   even blindfolded,
      would know you were good-looking!
You lay down the law as a spoiled boy does.
      You'll be a tyrant
         as long as your good looks last.
Now, I can never resist good looks,
         so I'll give in
      and let you have your answer."

Menon was pleased. He tossed back his
   curls,
      shrugging and showing off
      at the same time. He hadn't noticed

380

that Sokrates had called him *spoiled*
and *tyrant*.
Sokrates was fool enough to dance naked
on the hillside of the Akropolis,
but he knew what Menon was.

There was sun in the courtyard,
but we were under the portico
and it was cold. I stood with my head
down,
braced against the chill.
I got to wondering if *I* knew what
ἀρετή was.
It came to me that, if I could draw
a horse
that really looked like a horse,
I'd call that ἀρετή. I started
thinking about horses.
If you ask me, just by being a
horse,
a horse is excellent. But some
are better than others —
the swift horses,
the ones with horse sense,
and the ones that are beautiful —

Menon was telling Sokrates that
  excellence
      was the ability to *get* things —
          gold and silver, and good health
              and honors —
      and Sokrates asked,
"Do you call it excellence if those things
  are acquired unjustly?"

                              "Certainly not."

Then Sokrates said Menon was making a
  fool of him.
      They'd agreed that justice was part of
          excellence,
              but *getting things* could be done
                  with justice
              or without justice,
          so *getting things* couldn't be the
              same thing as excellence.
"Let's go back to the beginning. Answer
  my question:
          What is ἀρετή?"

Menon complained that Sokrates was
  confusing him.

Sokrates was like a wizard
putting a spell on him,
numbing him
like a stingray,
making him forget
everything he knew.
Then Sokrates started quoting poetry
and saying that learning was like
remembering.
I stopped listening when he started with
the poetry.
My toes were numb —
I was rubbing one set of toes
against another
trying to warm them —

Then Menon said: "Come here."
And he meant me. Everyone was looking
at me.
The old men, and Anytus
and Menon, and the wrestlers,
who'd stopped wrestling.
Sokrates asked Menon: "He is Greek and
speaks our language?"

Menon said yes, I was,
  which surprised me,
  because he always made such a point
    of me being a Thracian barbarian.
    But then, my father —
Menon's father, or his uncle —
was Greek. It's the male that creates
  life,
    not the female,
      so —
  I was Greek.
  I'd never thought of that before.

"Listen carefully, and see whether he
  learns from me,"
    said Sokrates,
      "or whether he's just being
        reminded."

He led me from the portico into the
  sunlight, by the sand pits.
The others followed. He smoothed out the
  sand
    picked up a stick
    and drew a square.

384

I was in a panic.

Sokrates was doing some kind of show
  with me,
      and I was going to look stupid
      in front of everyone. I felt like a
        snared rabbit.
          A rabbit doesn't know about the
            knife
          or the cooking pot,
          but once it's caught,
          it knows that what happens
            next
          isn't going to be good.

"Now, boy, you know that a square is a
  thing like this?"

                              "Yes."

"It has all four sides equal?"

                              "Yes."

385

He drew a cross in the square.

"And the lines that go through the middle
are also equal?"

"Yes."

He asked me how many of the little
squares there were,

and he pointed with the stick, giving
me time.

I started to feel better. My mother taught
me numbers,

and I thought, maybe he was going to
stick to easy things,

like two and two making four. I
glanced up.

There wasn't any malice in his face.

"Now, could you draw a square double the
size of this,

with all sides equal?"

"Yes."

"If the first square has four small squares inside it,

> how many will the second square have?"

"Eight."

"How long will each side be?"

> "They'll be twice as long, Sokrates. Obviously."
>
> I used his name.
>
> It's polite for a slave to speak the master's name.

He handed me the stick. Here's the thing that scares me,

> that makes me laugh:
>
> *I almost drew a horse.* It was just for a moment
>
> when my hand closed around the stick,
>
> but I wanted to draw a horse. I felt a horse gallop down
>
> from my thoughts

to my arm
to my fingers
to the stick.

Instead, I drew the square:

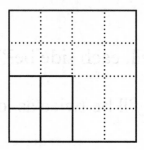

I saw I'd got it wrong.
If you make the lines twice as long,
you get something that's four
times bigger, not two.
And I didn't have eight little squares.
I had sixteen.

I was ashamed. I mumbled:
"It's not right."

I don't know if Sokrates heard me,
but he asked me to try again.

He asked how I could get a square that
was twice as big,

not four times. Already I had a new
idea —

I said yes, I thought I could.

He answered, "Right! Always answer what
you think."

I started over;
this time I made the lines only one
and a half times as long —

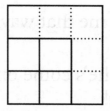

but it still wasn't right. I could see it.

I wanted eight small squares, but I had nine.

Sokrates asked me again: how could I
make a square

twice as big as the first one?

I stared at the marks in the dirt.
"It's no use, Sokrates. I honestly don't
know."

That's when I expected everyone to laugh,
but they didn't. I lifted my eyes, just a
minute,
and saw Sokrates beaming at me
as if I'd said something
astonishing
and good. It was as if he were
proud of me.
I couldn't remember anyone
ever
looking at me that way. He said to
Menon,
"Look how far he's come on the path of
remembering!
At the beginning, he didn't know how to
draw the square,
— and he still doesn't. But he
thought he knew,
and he answered boldly, as he should
have;
he felt no confusion.

Now he feels confusion!"

Menon said, "That's true."

"But isn't he better off? We've helped him!
    Before he thought he knew the
        answer,
            but he was wrong.
Now he *knows* he doesn't know, and he's
    eager to find out!
Now he will seek the truth in our
    company.
        Let's give him another try. I won't tell
            him the answer.
                If you catch me instructing him,
                    stop me.
                I will only ask him questions."

He showed me the square again,
        and this time he divided it
            corner to corner.

They were halves, but they were triangles.

He told me those slanty lines were called
  diagonals.

He was asking me questions,
      and I was answering them,
      but the fact is, once I saw them
      — those diagonals —
        the whole answer came in a rush.

I could imagine
      having four triangles
        and moving them around —
They'd spin like the fourths of a chariot
  wheel
        — a wheel isn't square —
        but at the hub of a wheel,
        where the four spokes meet . . . ?
        there are triangles, four
          triangles —

If I took half that square
    and made it somersault
        back
        to back
        to back
        to back
I'd have a square twice as big.
    Four halves make two!

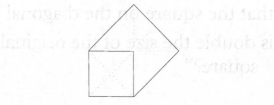

I reached for the stick.

Sokrates gave it to me right away.

    I drew another square, made of
      triangles,

    and counted the triangles,

      poking each one with a stick.

    I rubbed out the extra markings with
      my foot.

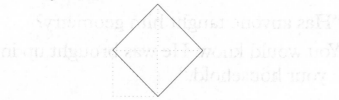

I looked up. Several of the men were
nodding,
  and one burly fellow —
    his name was Aristokles —
    raised his eyebrows
    as if to say *Well done!*

Sokrates was grinning. "Is it your personal
opinion
  that the square on the diagonal
  is double the size of the original
    square?"

          I couldn't keep from grinning
                            back.
                          "Yes."

Sokrates spoke to Menon. "What do you
think?
Only a few minutes ago, he didn't know!"

              Menon said, "True."

"Has anyone taught him geometry?
You would know. He was brought up in
  your household."

"No one ever taught him anything."

> It flashed through my head:
> *I was taught to pick up turds.*

"All the same, those opinions were inside
  him.
Because I questioned him, he was able to
  remember.
He found the answer by himself.

> He must have formed his ideas *before*
>   this life,
>
> > when he was not in human
> > shape.

He remembered like someone
  remembering a dream."

I stood there with the stick in my hand,
> my mind whirling
>
> > swift as a chariot wheel
> >
> > > in the course of a race.

Like the discus
> leaving the hand of the thrower
> my mind spun free —

I raised my eyes to the sky
    and saw an omen: a hawk
    scything the blue,
    a blessing from Apollo.
I almost interrupted. I almost shouted,
    I remembered the chariot wheel!
      — then for a moment I wondered
    if that was cheating: remembering
      one thing
    that reminds you of another.
But then I thought,
    my memory gave me the chariot wheel
    at just the right time.
Any way you worked it out,
    I wasn't stupid. And if learning was
      remembering,
    I could remember more things
      just by *thinking.*
    I wouldn't need anyone to teach me,
    and I wouldn't have to be stupid all
      my life.

Then Sokrates was saying
    that since nobody taught me
      geometry

(because that's what it's called,
    those problems with squares and
      lines: geometry)
I must have understood it in my soul
before I was born.
Before I was even human.

He said, "If the truth is always in our soul
    the soul must be immortal. One
      must take courage
    and try to discover —
that is, to remember —
    what one doesn't happen to
    know.
One thing I'm ready to fight for —
    that we shall be better, braver, and
      more active men
    if we try to find out what we don't
    know."

I was on fire, thinking about my soul.
I hadn't known I had one,
    because of being a slave. But Sokrates
    seemed to think I did:
    a wise part of me
from before I was born.

I was as good as other men, slave or not,
    because of my soul.

By now, Menon was bored with the
    question: *What is ἀρετή?*
        He wanted to skip ahead
            and talk about how virtue could
                be taught.
Sokrates wouldn't let him. He still wanted
to know what it *was*.

They asked Anytus
    and Anytus answered sullenly.
I thought he didn't like Sokrates —
    later I learned I was right.

Sokrates said if there ever were a man
    who had ἀρετή himself,
        and could teach it to others,
            he would be like a living man among
                ghosts.

That's not the end of the story.

When we left the gymnasion, I followed
  Menon.

     Athens is crowded
     and foot traffic is slow.

There was a narrow passage —
    a cluster of men, talking;
       we were caught behind them.
    I overheard:

"For once, the slave came off better than
  his master.
He was honest about what he didn't
  know."

    "Menon's not the first to make a fool of
                himself
   in front of Sokrates. And he won't be the
               last."

I stood behind Menon
    and watched his neck turn red.
I heard one man scoff: "Thessaly,"
    as if Thessaly were a pigsty. The
      others laughed.
I understood: we were foreigners in Athens.

And Menon had come with his hand out,
  asking for troops.
He was overconfident,
      and they didn't like him.

When I led Menon home from the
  banquet that night,
      there was no moon, and the streets
        were a maze;
      Menon was reeling, unsteady on his feet.
        We came to a blind alley —
I'd counted the streets, but I made a
  mistake.
Menon asked me what I meant
      by leading him all over town
        like a bull in a labyrinth. Did I take
          him for a fool?
I said *no* and he seized my arm
        — I thought he'd jerk it out of the
          socket —
      He slapped my face
and broke my nose. Again.
        I screamed. I heard a door open —
          and then shut: *Only a drunkard,
            beating his slave,*
              nothing to worry about.

400

He hurled me to the ground and kicked me.
I tried to get up. I know I fought back,
    but at the end
I curled up in a ball
    and gave Menon what he wanted;
      I begged him to stop.
He said he'd sell me
    the very next day.
We were enemies, Menon and me.
He'd finally caught on.

The next morning, he took me to the slave
  market
    and sold me for ninety-three drachmas.

I pleaded with him. It wasn't parting from
  him that I minded;
    it was my whole world.
    Thessaly, Georgios,
    the horses. For the last time
      I twisted my face
      to look like Lykos.
      I shamed myself
      trying to find the man
      who once loved his brother.

But he never looked back. Not once.

2. The Slave Market

No day was ever so long.
I was thirsty. My face felt puffy,
    and three of my teeth were loose.
    If anyone had offered me food
        — nobody did —
    I couldn't have kept it down.

For sale in the Agora:
    spices, weapons, wool,
    cuttlefish and pastries,
    tools and wine and ribbons and toys
        and me. There was a woman next
        to me,
    with a crying baby,
    sobbing herself:
        "Buy us both. Look, she's little.
        She doesn't eat much.
        And she's pretty, so pretty! In a
        few years
        she'll be worth more,
        you can sell her at a profit!

Just let me keep her now. I'll share
   my food with her.
     I'll work hard. I'll do anything.
      Almighty Zeus,
        who pities those who beg,
          hear my plea!"
She was shameless.
I wondered if my mother ever begged for
   me like that.
All that endless day, the woman carried on.
     Her baby was livid and snot-nosed;
       it grizzled and whined
         till I wanted to wring its neck.
I couldn't. My hands were shackled.
     My swollen face was a brand:
     This boy's no good. I beat him, and I'm
       getting rid of him.
     Let the buyer beware.

There's a place near Athens called Lavrion
     where they dig for lead and silver,
     narrow tunnels leading to Hades's
     realm,
     dark and close, the air foul
       poisonous.

No slave lives long at Lavrion. During the
  war,
      the Spartans promised the slaves
          they'd set them free
          if they'd turn traitor. Every slave
            at Lavrion
          agreed. They fought for the Spartans.
          Every single one.
          I would have, too.
          I tried to pray
          that I wouldn't be sent there,
          but I couldn't think of prayerful
            words.
My mind flopped and panicked, like a fish
  in air.
From time to time I raised my head
      to look for Menon. He might change
        his mind.
There was the marketplace
      crowded with strangers,
      booths and awnings,
      jars and baskets,
          donkeys and goats and chickens
          but few horses. There's no
            pastureland in Athens.

I was a stable boy
    in a land without stables.

One man looked at me,
    gripped my swollen face, tilting it up.
    "The swelling won't last, but the
        nose — "
He shook his head. "And the tattoos. Pity.
    Except for that, he's a good-looking boy."
He didn't buy me.

An old man asked how much I cost.
    He had a quiet voice, a mild manner;
        I hoped he would buy me,
        but he was losing his eyesight,
    and he wanted a slave who could read.

Another man came by. He was short,
    swarthy
    with powerful arms. His cloak was
        rough-woven.
        He moved briskly, head bent,
          as if he were used to waiting on
          people
        almost like a slave himself.

He wanted a Syrian boy, maybe an
Egyptian. "A sharp-witted boy,
around twelve years old. Old enough
to do a man's work,
but clever,
good with his hands."
The trader said, "No Syrians today.
I've got a Thracian, now. Thracians
are strong.
Barbaric, but you could tame him.
You'd better have him."

The man looked at me. "Someone used
his fists on you.
Your master?"

I hung my head.

"What d'you do to deserve it?"
I thought how yesterday
I'd stood at the White Dog, with
the stick in my hand,
joyful because I had a soul.

"Nothing."

"Then why'd your master beat you?"

"He was drunk."

He accepted that. Nodded.
"What work are you used to?"

"Back in Thessaly, I was a stable hand.
The master's son chose me to wait on
him.
I did what he told me to do."

"Ever work with your hands?"

"With a pitchfork and a bucket."

"Ever tend a donkey?"

"Yes."
(I forgot to tell you that.
My master had donkeys and teams of
mules.
I like horses better, but I've worked with
donkeys.)

"Let me ask you something. I've a donkey —

I sent my last boy out to haul clay.
There's a spot on the path
where the donkey balks, day after
day.
The boy beat that donkey sore,
but he couldn't get her past that spot.
What would you do, if it were your job to
dig clay
and you couldn't drive the donkey
down the path?"

I lifted my head and looked him full in the
face.
Disrespectful. What got into me? I think it
was that donkey
being beaten every day, on the same path,
by some stupid boy who didn't know
better.
Or maybe it was my soul.

"Your last boy was a fool.
Donkeys are smart. When they balk,
it's because they think something's wrong.
When a horse is afraid,
it shies and runs away. But a donkey's
different.

408

A donkey stops to take a look.
A donkey wants to see what's wrong.
Your boy beat her, and the donkey knew
what was wrong.
That path was a bad path,
a path where she was beaten every day.
No wonder she didn't want to go there."

He didn't like the way I spoke.
"You're right — the boy was a fool —
but it's not for you to say so.
You've a mouth on you, boy, and a savage
eye.
You're not for me."
He turned away, and the slave trader sang
out,
"A hundred and twenty drachmas!"
— but it was too late. The man was
walking away.

There was a girl in the marketplace —
when I thought about that later
it didn't make sense. Athenian girls
don't go to the market,
and she wasn't a slave, that girl.

Her hair wasn't cropped, and she walked
  erect,
Her tunic was short and bright as flame.
  I'd heard Spartan girls

    wear short tunics — thigh-flashers,
      they call them,

    so I thought she was a Spartan girl.

She crossed paths with the man who
  hadn't bought me.

    She laid her hand on his forearm
    and looked into his face. She seemed
      to speak.

I couldn't hear her. She was too far away.

The man stopped

    as if he'd lost his way. He changed
      direction,

    but she pursued him, matching his
      stride. She lifted her palms,

    touched him, made him look at her.

He came back to the slave trader.
"A hundred drachmas."

      "You'll beggar me," complained the
                    trader,

but they went on from there.

"One twenty."

"One hundred."

"One fifteen."

"One hundred."

"Forget it. He's strong and he's healthy,
this boy.
They pay more than that at the mines."

"I'll pay you one hundred."

"You're wasting my time."

"One hundred. I tell you, I won't pay
more."

"Are you deaf? I said no!
How can I live if I don't make a profit?
I've children to feed! One hundred and
five."

"One hundred drachmas."

The trader gave up. One hundred
drachmas.

The stranger led me away.

He was a potter and his name was
Phaistus.
He spoke in sharp jerks, warning me:
"There's a proverb. *To make pots is to
work hard.*

I'll teach you my trade. It takes
strength
and it takes skill.

If I tell you to do something and you
don't understand,

you *tell* me you don't understand;
d'you hear me?

Don't risk ruining a pot
because you're too scared to ask a
question.
You have to learn.
You'll treat me with respect. My last boy
was lazy,
a fool and a cheat.
I couldn't turn my back on him. If
you're idle

412

or you lie to me,
        I'll beat you,
            and I've a strong arm.
I'm not a rich man. I've worked for
    everything I own.
I've a shop and a wife and a slave. Two
    slaves, now.
As far as my wife goes,
            you'll treat her with respect, too.
    If she asks you to help in the kitchen
            or weed the garden,
            you'll do it. You'll tend the donkey,
        dig the clay,
        do what you're told, and show me
            respect.
Do you understand?"

                    "I understand."

He led me down a zigzag street
        and then another. We came to a shop
            with a striped awning,
        rows of pots on planks,
        and a door almost hidden. He took
            me into the courtyard:

413

two round pits for clay,

    a small house, only one story,

    a shed on one side for the donkey.

His wife appeared, a small woman,

    thick-waisted, but quick and light on
      her feet.

I didn't like her. She clapped her hands at
  the sight of me.

She smiled so broadly

    that one eye squinted and almost
      vanished.

She scurried forward, led me to the
  kitchen altar,

      and made me kneel down. "Oh,
        Phaistus, look at his hair!

      He'll be beautiful once he's healed.

      We'll call him Pyrrhos!" As if I were a
        dog.

Pyrrhos means *fiery*.

Half the red-haired slaves in Athens are
  called Pyrrhos.

I was a new member of the household,

    so they poured dried fruit and nuts
    over my head

and prayed to Hestia that I would prove
fruitful, hardworking, and loyal.

After the ceremony,
  the master's wife — she was called
    Zosima —
  went to the kitchen and tore off a
    chunk of bread.

She spread soft cheese on it. I felt a dull
  surprise
    that she should give me cheese. The
      crust was hard.

I was afraid to bite down —
  lest my teeth fall out. I asked for a
    cup of water
  and she gave me one. I was so thirsty
    my hand shook.

They had an old slave, Kranaos,
    a man so worn and silent and dry
    he was like a dead insect —
      he had cheese, too.
        She wasn't a good housewife,
          this Zosima;
        she was wasteful. Whatever she
          and her husband ate,

she gave the same thing to the
slaves.
I wasn't sorry, but it showed she had
no sense.

Kranaos slept in the house. When night
fell
I went to donkey's shed.
I made a bed of straw
and pulled my cloak over myself,
but I couldn't get warm. I was thirsty
again,
and everything hurt.
Then she came to the shed:
Zosima —
with another blanket, a cup,
and a jar of water. "There's a sponge
inside the jar.
If your face hurts, you can sponge cold
water on it.
There's wine in the cup to help you sleep."

I stared at her. I couldn't imagine
why she was trying to take care of me.
There was something pleading about her.

416

I didn't understand it. I took the
  blanket —
        it was heavy, thicker than my cloak.
With the straw, I would be warm enough.

                        "Thank you."

Her face lit up,
        and her eye crinkled shut;
        she reached out and patted my
          shoulder —
            as if she were patting a dog.

I gulped down the wine
        and felt my head spin.
I wrapped myself up and I slept.

HERMES SPEAKS:
ELEGY AND RIDDLE

Let him sleep. He thinks he's alone
    except for the donkey. There are mice
        in the shed,
    and a cat on the prowl.
Then there's you
        invisible
        following the story,
and me
        Hermes, bringer of dreams.
I flick my golden wand,
    and his bruised face softens.
        He dreams that he's close to his
            mother —
            but it's only a dream. She's far
            away
                dancing off the coast of Skyros.

418

I've been meaning to tell you about that.
   Now, while the boy sleeps,
      is as good a time as any.
You remember Thratta, don't you?
      She was called Meda when she was a girl.
I like to think of her as Meda. Last time
   you saw her
      she cast her spell, binding
         the girl she kept from loving
         to the boy she loved.
Then she hightailed it to the harbor,
      with a fistful of stolen money. As god
      of thieves,
      who am I to judge? She had a plan:
         board a ship to the Black Sea,
         bribe the captain,
         home to Thrace and freedom!
Unlucky Meda!
      A storm blew up and the ship went down;
         she was bound for a watery grave.

I was on call; I am Hermes
      who succors the dying. High on
         Olympus
      I tied on my sandals, adjusted my cloak;

419

Downward I plunged with my wand in my
  hand,
    dodging the lightning:
Thunderbolt, sea spittle, silvery froth on
  the wine-dark sea.
There she was: waterlogged, gulping down
  salt water, drowning.
I caught up her hand — and I yelped:
                                Yeeeowwww!

Gripping her hand was electric, like
  grabbing a stingray!
All of the wrongs she had suffered —
    tingling, crawling under my skin!
      What kind of life had she led,
        this ill-fated Thracian woman?
      Kidnapped, enslaved and dishonored,
        robbed of her five-year-old
          son? . . .

I knew my mission: to usher her down to
  the House of Hades.
    Show her the way
      and gentle her pain
      with the touch of my golden rod —

But I'd had a shock.
And I had an idea.

And I'm not a predictable god.

So —

Deftly I parted her fingers. Then fused
   them:
      tendon and knuckle,
      tissue and bone;
Magicked and molded the pliable flesh,
      like a pastry cook rolling out dough.
Fastened my palm to her face —
      strong as an octopus sucker;
Dragged her jaw forward, creating the
   beak —
      multiplying the teeth.
Stabbed with my thumbnail the crown of
   her head —
      air sac! and blowhole!
         and echolocation . . . !

All of this time she was watching me
      glassy-eyed
      fearless and wonderstruck.

Memory was drifting away from her:

>anger
>and anguish
>and loss.

Next: underwater. I sleeked my hands over
  her muscular sides

>(O gloss of obsidian!)

Fashioned her innards: adjustable rib
  cage,

>a three-chambered stomach,
>collapsible lungs.

I sculpted her belly —

>it shone like an opal,
>taut as a tooth, and pale as a cloud,
>gray/pink/iridescent —
>>Magnificent craftsmanship!
>>Even Hephaistos
>that gloomy perfectionist,
>>Even Praxiteles
>would have been proud!

Next was her back —

>the storm was receding.

I ran my hand over her salt-crusted skin,
    shifted the vertebrae,
      fashioned a flap out of cartilage,
   sculpted it
       — not like a sickle, but more like
     a sail —
   triangle, signal and fin.
After the fin, the peduncle; tapered and
  powerful,
     flattened her feet and spread them
      out wide
      w i d e
      like the sticks of a fan,
      bone into cartilage: fleshier
      flashier

              O, what a fluke!

Flicking her tail, she rose to the surface,
  seeking the sunlight.
Bowing and bobbing her head, an
  additional curve
    in the infinite sea.
Whistling and hooting, she went on her way:
    a free thing, seeking her playmates.

That's how she left me:
    arching and frolicking,
        thankless!
            finding her place in the pod;
No one but me would have thought of
    it —
        I am a genius as well as a god!

Rhaskos/Pyrrhos in Athens: Donkey

1. Phoibe

The only one I liked was the donkey.
She was the only one
>   I didn't have to *respect*. They called
>   her Grau,
>   which is what you call a slave woman
>   who's too old to call *girl*.
>   *Grau* means *hag*.
She wasn't such a hag. That first night in
     the shed,
I heard her shifting and snorting. Once she
     brayed
>   and I almost jumped out of my skin.
>   Once she pissed:
>   a sound like rain.

The whole shed stank. Old urine
   half-rotted manure
   and moldy straw.

A little before dawn, I thought I'd better
  get up
     before the master woke me
        with a kick, maybe.
I went to the donkey's head and spoke to
  her.
Her ears swiveled; she was listening.
I untied her halter
     and led her out into the dawn.

I'd feared the worst.
I feared she might be old or
  broken-down
    and it would be my job
     to flog the last years of work out of
     her.
She wasn't such a hag. She had supple
  knees,
    clean bones. She was dark gray,
     but the fur around her eyes was
     pale,

and the inner corner of her eyes
was black
as if she'd been weeping black
tears.
Her eyes were clear and patient.

She had sores all over her back —
mats of fur and dried clay.
Her feet weren't clean. There's a smell
when a horse's hooves are sickly.
If Georgios lifted a hoof and caught a
whiff of that smell,
it meant a good beating for someone
and I can't say I blame him.
You don't get that smell from a day's neglect,
but from filth underfoot all the time.
A horse is only as good as his hooves.
Even a donkey is worth something.

I plucked her grass from the courtyard
and she nuzzled my hands.
I plaited clean straw and rubbed her
down,
loosening those mats.

She was smart. Right away,
>   she knew I wasn't going to hurt her.
I told her I was in charge of her now,
>   and I was going to keep her clean
>   and get a good hard floor under her
>   feet at night.
Her clownish ears
>   flicked back and forth
>   catching every word I spoke.

There was a shovel leaning against the
>   shed,
>   so I got started on her stall.
I was at work
>   when my master came out in the
>   courtyard.

He stopped in mid-stride
>   and turned to look at me. It was light
>   by then
>   and he's an ugly man.
I heard the words come out of my mouth
>   before I could stop them.
"Her stall's too wet. A donkey's feet are
>   like sponges.

She's got to have better footing.
A donkey is only as good as its hooves."

                    He frowned. "Pyrrhos —"
he was silent for a moment, thinking —
      "You sound like you're accusing me.
   You're quick to speak up for yourself. I
                          don't like that.
   You have something to say, you watch
                                       me;
              wait till I'm ready to listen.
You don't speak up any time it suits you.
   You wait until I speak to you. Do you
                               understand?"

I stared at the ground.
When he said *Pyrrhos*
      I forgot that was me.

                         "Go on, then."

He walked away from me
      and started talking to Kranaos
      about the kiln.
      Which is something that you can talk

about for hours,
    but I didn't know that, the first
      day.
I didn't know how pots were made.
I couldn't imagine all the things I was
  going to learn,
    or the backbreaking work ahead. That
      first morning,
    when we were about to sit down to
      eat,
I heard Zosima whisper, "Don't be too
  hard on him, Phaistus!
    And don't try to teach him
      everything at once.
    He's only a child."

                "He's got to learn."

He was right about that. I had a lot to
  learn.
That first day, he taught me
    how to wedge clay,
    which is folding it
    and thumping it
    and rolling it

430

till you can cut it with a wire
and not see any air pockets inside.
I wedged clay until my wrists hurt
and my hands
and my back
and then he showed me
I could do it with my feet.
So I wedged clay with my feet
until my toes were frozen —
clay's cold —
and my legs ached
and even my bottom.
I was almost at the point of crying,
when he said I'd done enough, and
done it well.
He told me I could take Grau for water,
and where the troughs were in the Agora.

I led her there and let her graze
while I stole glances at the city.
I was glad to be away from my master,
alone with the donkey. I stroked her —
she liked my fingers
scratching up and down her spine.

She rocked back and forth on her heels,
saying in donkey-talk,
*I like that. Right there. More, more,
more!*

Animals know when things get better.
People might not know, but
animals do.
That very first day, Grau knew
I was going to be good to her
and I swear to you, she was glad.
I whispered: "I'm not calling you
Grau."
And I named her: Phoibe.
I never named anything before,
and I didn't know how naming
something
makes you feel
as if it belongs to you. *Phoibe*
means *shining*
— which didn't suit her then,
because her coat had been
neglected —
but it gave us something to hope for.

432

2. Kranaos

I didn't like Kranaos.

He was a slave himself; he was no better
  than I was;

> but Phaistus called him kiln-master,

> and it turned out

> he was someone else

>> I had to respect.

>>> "That man knows about the
>>> kiln.

>>> There's no man in Athens
>>> who knows more."

>> That's what Phaistus said. The
>> solemn way he said it —

>>> you'd have thought Kranaos
>>> was a god.

The room where Kranaos slept

> was on the other side of the shed wall,

> so every morning, I could hear him

>> coughing and wheezing

>> and hawking and spitting.

> It made me taste the phlegm in my
> throat.

Kranaos used to say
    he'd breathed in too many kiln-fires
    and the smoke had darkened him
       gullet to belly.
He was as black inside as an old bottle.

He was the oldest man I ever met. He was
  a slave,
    but half the time he sat idle,
      huddled in his cloak,
      like a tortoise in its shell.
    He was always cold,
      looking for patches of sunlight
      or hogging the space near the
        hearth.
        Zosima let him. She treated him
        like a father,
          mashed up his food in little
            pieces
          and coaxed him to eat.

I didn't like him. He watched me,
  spying out every fault
  so he could tattle to the master.
    "The boy knows nothing."

That was his favorite thing to say.
Sometimes, for a change,
  he said it *to* me. "There's a world of
  things you don't know, boy."
Then, to the master:
"The boy daydreams. Stops his work
  and stares into space."

I wasn't staring into space.
I was looking at a jar.
There was a wine jar with horses
  on it . . .

See, when I went to live with Phaistus,
  there were jars and pots and plates
    everywhere. I didn't want to
      knock one over
    and risk a beating. There were so
      many,
      rust red and bright black
      people in helmets
      spears sticking out in all
        directions
      all those patterns: crosshatches
        and leaves
      and meandering keys —

435

they were crowded, those jars:
pictures running in circles
like a dog chasing its tail —
I never looked at them.
It was too much work to
look at them.

But my eye caught this jar with horses
on it,

and the horses *weren't drawn from the
side.*
They were facing me. You could see the
muscles
of their noble chests
and their back hooves lined up
behind the front ones.
You could see their wide foreheads
and the life in both eyes.

I could never figure out how to draw a
horse like that.
I'd tried. But I couldn't figure out where
the lines should go.
Phaistus had figured it out.
That's why I was staring. It wasn't
daydreaming.

Anyway, Kranaos thumped me between
the shoulder blades
and dragged me off to show me the
kilns.
Phaistus had two: a round one and a
rectangle.
Kranaos could talk about those kilns
all day and all night.
His breath was like a rat that had
been dead a while,
and he leaned close to me
so he could mumble
all on one note. An
ever-flowing stream
of knowledge and foul breath:
He told me how you have to load the pots
so that none of them touch.
He said that some places inside the
kiln
were hotter than others, and you had
to place each pot
just where it wanted to be.
He showed me the air vents
and said that at first, you needed a
hot fire, with plenty of air,

and then a hotter fire, with no air,
>   and moisture — wet sawdust or
>   green wood.
The whole time the pots cooked
>   you had to give them the fuel they
>   wanted:
>   charcoal
>   brushwood
>   olive prunings
>   nutshells.
What I foresaw was,
>   whatever kind of fuel that was handy,
>   that would be the kind Kranaos
>   wouldn't want.

This turned out to be true.

I didn't foresee
>   how smoky it would be
>   or how we'd all be coughing,
>   Phaistus, Kranaos, and I.

The first time we fired the kiln,
>   Kranaos clawed a lump
>   from the jars where the clay was set
>   to age.

438

He rounded the lump and told me
      that clay was for the Kiln God,
      and I should always put some in
        for him.

I didn't believe in any Kiln God.
It makes sense that we should we pray to
  Athena,
      the goddess of the city,
      the goddess of craft.
I didn't know about Hephaistos —
      we didn't worship him in Thessaly —
      but once I found out about him, I
        believed in him.
It stands to reason you'd worship a god of
  fire
      — but a Kiln God?
Why would a god want to live in a kiln?
I didn't believe in the Kiln God
                             yet.

What I did grasp
      was that if Kranaos could sacrifice
        lumps of good clay
        to the Kiln God,

439

it would be just as easy for me to
   reach into those jars
when no one was looking
and dig out a ball for me.
You can draw on clay
   smooth it flat
   and cut in with a bone tool. You can
      make a horse
      and shape it
      draw it from the side
        or from the front. You can keep
         drawing
   and rub out your mistakes with
      water
      and roll up the clay
      to hide what you did.
If you keep that clay moist and supple
      and hidden,
      a single lump
      will hold all the horses you want
        to draw.

3. Phaistus

He could have been worse.

Weeks passed. The swollen moon shrank
and fattened. In all those days,
he never beat me. He *threatened* to
beat me.
He cuffed me:
smacked my arm
or swatted my shoulder, barking,
"Wake up!"
"I'm talking to you!"
"Look sharp, Pyrrhos!"
but he never struck hard enough
to leave a mark. He never picked up a
stick or a strap,
never aimed at my head
or kicked my feet out from
under me.
I kept waiting to find out
what his beatings were like
so I'd know how my life was going
to be.

He worked me, dawn to dark.
He kept me sweaty and aching. *To make
pots is to work hard.*
I hauled water. Broke up the dry clay

pounded it
submerged it in water
sieved out pebbles and roots and
   dead bugs. I wedged clay
   until the skin around my
      fingernails
   was cracked and bleeding.

He didn't starve me, though. When we
ate —
   Phaistus and Kranaos and Zosima
      and me —
Phaistus sat on the couch, because he was
the master,
   but we all ate the same.
Phaistus explained, "We all work. We all
get a square meal."
If it was all right with him,
   it was all right with me.

I didn't say so.
Phaistus didn't like my mouth.
   Just knowing that
      made me think of smart-ass
         things to say.

442

I kept them inside. I didn't want to push
  my luck.
Then I discovered
          if I kept my mouth shut
          he didn't like that, either.
I tried saying as little as possible:
      Yes, master. No, master.
          His eyes would narrow
              and he'd glare, suspicious.
                  It was perfect. I was safe
              and getting on his nerves
                  at the same time.

Every slave knows his master.

Phaistus was thin-skinned —
      that's why he needed all that *respect.*
When he waited on customers,
          he was slavish,
          busy and brisk as a flea.
          "You've chosen well, sir. You've an
              eye for quality.
          I never painted a better cup
              than the one you chose."

Then he'd shout for me to bring burlap
and straw
>to protect the cup. "Look sharp,
>Pyrrhos!"
Showing he was master, throwing his
weight around.

Against my will, I did respect him. Not all
the time;
>but when he took a brush
>>to an unbaked pot
>>he could draw
>>>>>anything.

Sometimes he drew the background first:
a swarthy sky
>that fit around red horses
>and red heroes. By painting the sky
>he shaped
>>warriors that really fought,
>>cranes that really flew,
>>maenads in a frenzy. And when he
>>threw a pot —
>>I was supposed to spin the wheel —
>the clay changed from rank mud

to something alive. It stretched and
  spun upward
    quivering; he hollowed it with his
    thumbs
    reached inside it
      made its belly curve
      pinched up the rim
      and raised a tower
        whirling
          swaying
        glistening

Then: *"Not like that!"*
  He'd start yelling
    because I hadn't spun the wheel
    right —
    I hadn't been fast enough
      or I'd spun it crooked —
    and he called me an idiot
      a stupid donkey. He smacked
      the ruined pot
    and thumped his feet against the
    ground
  having a tantrum.

He swore I'd never learn.

"He *can't* learn."
That was Zosima, standing in the
doorway.
"He's never seen anyone throw a pot
before,
and he can't take his eyes off the clay.
That's what's the matter with him."

She came forward
and put her hand on my shoulder —
I'd rather Phaistus cuffed me.

"Get up, Pyrrhos.
I'll show you how it's done. First watch
Phaistus.
Then watch me spin the wheel."

I got up, my knees aching;
Phaistus grunted, and she took my
place,
kneeling at his feet. He cupped his
hand,
scooped up water from a bucket,
wet the clay. *"Now!"*

She spun the wheel
>> perfectly. She seemed to know
>> exactly what he wanted,
>> the speed, the steadiness. His fingers
>> opened up
and the clay became
>> a breathing
>> swelling
>> changeable
>> animal.
I watched. She was skillful with the wheel,
>> but I didn't care about that.
I wanted to do what *he* did.
I wanted to make magic
>> and spin the clay to life.

4. Zosima

I didn't trust her.
Right from the start I knew
>> there was something she wanted
>> from me.
She watched me too closely. She smiled
>> too much.
She'd named me. Like a dog. *Pyrrhos.*

She fed me
    as if I were a dog. Slipped me tidbits:
      a handful of sticky figs
      a crust dipped in honey.
      "A growing boy is always hungry,"
      she'd say.

What did I know about women? Not much.
Georgios used to say that Woman was an
    evil thing:
      a meal-snatcher, a troublemaker,
        changeable as the sea.
I didn't know what the mistress wanted,
    but I made up my mind,
    I wasn't going to give it to her.
    I wasn't going to be anyone's
      dog-slave.

Zosima was the first up, before dawn.
I could hear her sandals — she wore them
    loose —
      smacking the soles of her feet:
    slap-flap
    slap-flap
    slap-flap

Her feet were quick and grubby
and looked too small to carry her.
I'd hear her in the courtyard. She'd
go out in the dark
to fetch water. She said it was her
chance
to see the other women
and the first streaks of dawn in
the sky.
She went out by daylight, too,
to bargain for food in the market. She
was sunburned,
the mark of a bad woman
or a poor man's wife.
She bartered with the neighbors:
a platter for a jug of wine
clay beads for dye
wool for dried apples.
At supper she'd boast to her husband
how much money she saved.

I pitied Phaistus. Here was this woman
who squinted when she smiled
and talked too much
and wouldn't stay in the house.

At least she was a worker.
> Her sandals flap-slapped through the
> house all day.
She kept the fire on the hearth
> and made bread and broth and
> porridge.
She dug the garden
> and tended the chickens
> and tamed the raw wool over her thigh
> and wove thread into cloth.

One day I came inside the house
> and saw her sitting,
> with a water jar in her lap. It hadn't
> been fired,
> > but it had dried leather-hard,
> and she was painting it. She had a
> tiny brush in one hand,
> and she was painting a pattern like
> this:

She lifted her head and smiled her
lopsided smile.

"My father was a potter.
He owned the shop before Phaistus,
and taught me to paint.
I painted borders when I was younger
than you.
It's not as easy as it looks —"

I took a step nearer. It didn't look that easy.

"— because you're always painting on a
curve.
Phaistus paints the stories, the figures,
but I'm better at borders. Even he
admits it.
I like keeping my hand in.
He'll teach you one of these days."

It was hypnotic: the small brush,
the even strokes: every line the same
thickness.
When she finished, she gave me the brush.

"Take that and wash it for me, will you?
And take the bowl of slip back to the shop

and seal it with wax.
Tell the others it's time for supper.
I traded a jar for duck eggs.
We'll have duck eggs, olives, and new
bread."

She was always excited about food,
and while the rest of us ate,
she talked. Her words splashed over us
like water from the fountain:
women's gossip, mostly:
how the chickens were laying
and who was getting married,
who might have seen a ghost.
I didn't understand why Phaistus
never told her to shut up.
I didn't understand why she seemed so
happy.

Except that sometimes, she wasn't.
Every now and then there'd come a day
when she'd be quiet. She'd stop
mid-task
and place her hand on her belly,
a strained joy in her face.

Then, the next day
    she'd be short-tempered
    and she'd smell: a powerful odor
      that I didn't like
    but one that reminded me of my
      mother;
    of burying my face in her skirt.

I saw her once in the courtyard, weaving —
    She dropped the shuttle,
      lost her temper.
She snatched the loom as if it were a slave
    and beat it against the house wall
      cracking the frame;
    the loom weights tangled and
    clanked —
      it was as if some god
      cursed her with madness.

I told Kranaos,

    and he said: "Boy, you know nothing.
    It's one of her woman-times. She's
          bleeding.
      Don't you know about that?

A woman's body is a sickly thing. Not like
a man's.
Every month, they have to bleed,"
and he flicked away from his crotch
as if shooing a mosquito;
so I knew where women bled.

I hadn't known before. How would I know?
With horses, it's different.
A mare comes into heat,
but only once a year.

"Every month, they bleed,
unless there's a baby on the way.
That's what galls her. She wants a child,
and every month, until the blood comes,
she thinks there'll *be* a child.
She's a fool. She's been married eight
years.
And not so much as a miscarriage.
The master could divorce her.
She's no good as a wife."

I said, "She's good to you,"
which surprised me.

454

It was almost as if I were taking up
   for her,
     which I wouldn't
      because I didn't like her.

After that, I could predict the
   pattern.
First the hoping
    then tears
    and the smell of blood. I saw
     what she wanted from me.
She wanted a child,
    and until she got one
    she wanted to pretend I was
     hers.

I didn't want a mother.
I'd had my own mother.
There was no one I'd loved more,
    and there never will be,
     but the last time I saw her
      she cut me with a knife.
Is it any wonder
    that I hardened my heart?

5. Sokrates

Twice a week I dug clay. Phaistus showed
  me how.
He took me to the banks of the Kefissos
  River
       and showed me scales and ridges
        in the earth.
He taught me to moisten the dirt,
       roll a tiny snake, and wrap it
       round my thumb.
     Clay needs to be sticky, but not too
     sticky;
     grainy, but not brittle.
I filled Phoibe's saddlebags with
  clay.
Sometimes it wasn't good enough.
     Kranaos said, "The boy knows
     nothing."
     Phaistus said, "He has to learn."
That was my master.
That was Kranaos.
That was my life.

To tell you the truth,
     I didn't mind digging clay.

456

If I wanted to take a few minutes
      to ride Phoibe by the river,
      or draw a horse,
      there was no one to tell on me.

It was getting to be spring;
      the willows were leafing out;
      the oak trees scabby with buds;
I was leading Phoibe back home,
      her saddlebags full.
Then: a curve in the riverbank
      a grove of willows
      an old man sitting on a rock
        barefoot
      a loaf in his hand.

I knew him at once.
      I called out "Sokrates!"
I can't believe I yelled like that.
        "Sokrates!"

        He looked up. I saw in his face
          the struggle to place me.
        "Why, you're Menon's boy!"

"Not anymore. I live in Athens now.
I work for a potter, Phaistus."

Sokrates nodded.
"I believe I know your master.
A good potter and a good painter.
But I don't know your name."

"It's Rhaskos. That's what my mother
named me,
but the potter calls me Pyrrhos.
I remember the day when you drew that
square
and asked me to double it.
Remember?
You talked about how my soul had
knowledge.
I've thought about that a lot. I like
thinking about it."
I sounded like a little boy
asking another boy to play with him.

"Then you have a taste for philosophy?
Strong meat for a young mind!"
He was grinning,

458

that grin I remembered that had no sneer
in it.
"Children are like puppy dogs. They'll rip
an idea to shreds
just to work their teeth!
But it's not always a bad thing,
to let puppies teethe —
I gave you a taste of meat and you liked it,
didn't you?"

"I did. I did!
I haven't forgotten what you said —
I mean, what I understood.
I didn't understand the whole thing.
But everyone says you're the wisest man in
Athens —"

Sokrates wagged his hand to shut me up.
"Then everyone is wrong.
They think they're quoting the Oracle at
Delphi,
but what the priestess said
is that there was no man in Athens wiser
than I am.
That's not the same thing.

The priestess might have meant
that Athens is the home
of other men just as foolish —
or, the gods forbid, *more* foolish, than I
am.
In which case Athens is in peril, don't you
think?"
I laughed out loud.

"Or perhaps the priestess meant to praise
me
for knowing I know nothing.
I'm wise enough to know that I'm not
wise.
Even small things confuse me.
One and one making two, for example!
Isn't that a strange thing, Rhaskos?
Which of the ones turns into a two?"
I thought he was teasing me, but
there was a funny knot in my mind,
because
when I thought about it,
I didn't *know* which one turned into
a two.

460

I didn't want him to think I was stupid.
"I never thought about that, Sokrates.
I think they both turn into two.
 I mean, there have to be *two* ones,
 or there can't be a two.
 Isn't that the point about numbers?
 You can't make two out of one."

 "Can't you?"
 He broke his loaf in half
 and held out half to me.
 "Join me on the riverbank, Rhaskos!
 I believe you want to be friends,
 and that's fine with me.
I tell myself I am a man who desires little,
 but I'm greedy for friendship.
 I'd rather have a new friend than a new
 horse. Eat!
 When I was your age, I was always
 hungry."

I sat down. I felt giddy.
The wisest man in Athens was saying we
 could be friends.
 Me. And Sokrates! Though it

461

occurred to me
   that if someone offered me a
     choice
  between a friend and a horse,
   I'd take the horse,
  because a horse can be a friend.
Then there was that loaf! Just by breaking
  it
   he turned it into two,
   which was a kind of joke,
    and proved me wrong.
I tethered Phoibe
   and went to sit with him in the shade.

Now, here's the strange thing —
   the spring sun was brilliant,
    and the shade under the willow leaves
     was darker
    so that my eyes were bewitched —
I got the idea there were three of us.
   Sokrates
   and me
   and under the willow boughs, this girl,
   her face leaf-dappled

and her dress mussed: a glow of
marigold . . .

I blinked, and she wasn't there. I had that
queer feeling —
as if everything that was happening
has happened before.

The loaf was in my hand. I bit into it.
It was coarse, so I had to chew hard.
Eating brought me back to myself.
I wanted to tell Sokrates how much I
wanted to be friends,
but I couldn't find the words.

"Here's a curious thing, Rhaskos.
I'm greedy for friendship, but I don't
know what a friend *is*.
What would you say it was?"

I kept chewing. I was stalling.
I didn't want to say anything stupid.
It was a long time since I'd had a friend.
Of course, Phoibe was my friend, but
I didn't want to say so.
People make fun of donkeys.

I wasn't friends with Phaistus. You can't be friends with your master.

I'd learned that. As for Kranaos,
not even close.

"Here's the truth, Sokrates.
I haven't had many friends. Back in Thessaly, there was this boy, Lykos.

He might have been my brother.
When we were little,
we fought all the time, and he always won.
He wasn't my friend then. He was my enemy. But later —

he wanted to go swimming with me,
and I thought we might be friends;
except he died.
If we'd gone swimming, I'd have counted him as a friend."

Sokrates listened. He suggested:
"So a friend is someone you go swimming with?"

"It doesn't have to be swimming. Talking with you,
that's enough for us to be friends."

"Then friends are made by talking
                together,
        or swimming together."

"That's right," I said,
    "or if they were women, they might
    weave together,
        or carry water. Except —"

                    "Except?"

"Except doing things together . . . that's
not the whole story.
Kranaos and I — he's the other slave at
the potter's —
    we spend hours side by side, wedging
    clay.
And we're not friends."

"So friends are friends if they swim together,
            but not if they wedge clay.
        Is there something about clay that's
            dangerous to friendship?"

I laughed again. Little bits of chewed bread
    flew out of my mouth. "You're
    making fun of me!

465

It isn't *doing things together* that makes friends. It's something else.

Even though Kranaos and I are both slaves —"

> "But there's a new idea, Rhaskos!
> You were about to say, *Even though we're*
> *both slaves,*
> *we're not friends*, weren't you?
> Is it being *alike* that brings forth
> friendship?"

"No. I mean, yes! Maybe. Sometimes.
Lykos and I were both boys, so we could have played together.
Kranaos and I are both slaves, but —
he's old and I'm young.
And I can't stand him."

> "But I am old, Rhaskos."
> He didn't say it as if he were sorry for himself.
> He was just making a point.

"It's different with you. You're wise —
and I'm not. Kranaos isn't wise."

466

"We seem to have a new idea, Rhaskos!
Perhaps it's being *unlike* that creates
friendships.
I'm old, and you're young, and we feel the
pull of friendship.
Perhaps it's *difference* that
makes friendship. Let's think
about that.
Does a sick man want to be friends
with another sick man
or with a doctor? Does a poor man want
to be friends
with another poor man
or with a rich man,
who might be able to help him?"

"No!"
I shook my head like a dog killing a rat.
"I know what you mean, but that's
not friendship!"

"Many men would say it is."

"Then many men are wrong! . . . A poor
man wanting money?
That's not friendship!

467

And the rich man won't get anything for
  helping him.
That so-called friendship is no good for
  him!
As for that sick man wanting a doctor —
            he doesn't want the *doctor*.
He wants to get better! He doesn't care a
  fig for the doctor!
The doctor's just a tool so he can get what
  he wants!"

            "Rhaskos, you astonish me.
    You see quite clearly what other men
                            don't see,
          that the sick man longs for *health*
                        and loves health,
      and the doctor is only a means to that
                                    end.
  Now I tell you; I've been cheating a little;
    I've put this question to other boys, boys
                who were older than you,
        but they haven't seen what you saw."

I felt my face get hot.
"I know these things because I'm a kind of
  tool.

Men use each other as tools all the time.
That's how the world works."
> I thought about Zosima, fawning on
> me,
>> because she wanted a child, any
>> child.
> I thought about Menon, wanting me
> to admire him
>> and root for him and wipe up his
>> vomit.

"That's how the world works, but it isn't
friendship."

> "Then what is friendship, my dear boy?"

I lowered my voice.
> I was afraid what I was going to say
> was womanish.
>> "If someone likes another person —"

>> "Aha! Then friendship is a sense of
>> congeniality?"

"What's that?"

"Of liking someone, of agreeing with them,
of being happy in their company."

"I think so. Maybe."

"If a mother sees her child playing
with fire
and punishes him,
is the mother a friend to the child?"

"No. Yes!
Because she's saved him from being
burned . . ."

"But the child has just been beaten. Is he
happy with her?
Are they friends at that moment?"

"No, they aren't friends *then* —
or maybe, the mother's a friend to the
child,
but the child isn't friends with the
mother."

"Can there be a friendship if only one
person loves?
When we say, *He's my friend*, do we mean
I like him or *he likes me*?
Or are friends like shoes?

Do there have to be two of them?"

"I don't know, Sokrates. I think so. But I
  don't know."

I thought about him turning one loaf into
  two,
       and I thought about Zosima giving
         me tidbits
       and me eating them
       and liking them, but not liking her.

I was confused. And anxious
       because I'd spent so much time
         talking under the trees.

"I should go back soon. My master will be
  angry if I'm late.
       It isn't that I don't like talking to you.

I like it, even if I don't know what I'm
  talking about.
       But I have to get back to work."

       "Why don't I come back with you?
         I often frequent the potters' quarter,
       and I'd like to pay my respects to your
                                master.
         I'll explain to him that if you're late

it's because I waylaid you,
with a search for the truth.
Shall we?"

I was proud to walk beside him. I was
thinking:
What Sokrates had done with me
was the same thing he'd done with
Menon.
He asked me a question that sounded
simple,
and I thought I knew the answer, but
I didn't.
It made Menon angry, but I wasn't angry.
I liked wondering. I felt as if my mind
were a toy,
full of riddles to solve.

We came to the spot on the path where
Phoibe always balks.
She stopped short. I gripped her halter.
Sometimes she tries to back up, but I
don't let her.
She's getting better.
She used to tremble when she came
to this part of the path.

472

Now she just stops, her head up,

     her breath coming in short puffs.

I explained to Sokrates: "Phoibe always
  balks here,

There's something about this place she
  doesn't like.

     The slave before me used to beat her,

     which made things worse. I don't
      beat her,

     but I don't let her back up, either. We
      have to wait here

     until she goes by herself."

                  "And will she?"

"Yes, but it takes time. We have to wait her
  out.

It's boring, but it's worth it."

Phoibe twisted her head inside her halter

     and screwed her donkey lips sideways

      to nibble my hand. She wanted to
       play.

I wouldn't play. She had two choices:

     stand still or go forward.

She knew what her choices were.

At last she took a step forward,
　　　and I praised her,
　　　　"Good girl, Phoibe, good girl!"
　　　coaxed her. Another step.
Once we got past the bad place
　　　I stroked her and scratched her
　　　and let her crop the grass.

　　"You may not know all things, Rhaskos,
　　　but it's clear that you know donkeys."

Once again, I felt the sheer joy
　　　of being with Sokrates; of not being
　　　stupid.
I pulled up Phoibe's head
　　　and we headed back to Athens.
I kept looking to make sure Sokrates was
　　still beside me.
I couldn't stop smiling.

　　　　"You know, Rhaskos,
　　　I think we're donkeys ourselves.
　　　Here we are, as happy as swallows,
　　because we've each made a new friend,
　yet neither of us can say what a friend is."

warrior is Akhilleus, and the woman is the
Amazon queen Penthesilea.

Penthesilea was the daughter of Ares, and
a powerful warrior. As the greatest of the
Amazons who fought for the Trojans, she
was the female counterpart to Akhilleus,
the greatest of the Greeks. When Akhilleus
dealt the death blow to the queen, their
eyes met, and he fell hopelessly in love . . .

The treatment of this dramatic scene is
so primitive that it is a matter of wonder
that the bowl was ever fired. Akhilleus's
arms are different lengths, and his buttocks
are improbably round. Penthesilea's pose
is even more awkward; she seems to be
attempting a split. At the same time, the
artist was able to convey some of the pathos
of the battle: the invisible line that connects
their eyes runs parallel to the warrior's
spear.

EXHIBIT 13

Black-figure bowl with Akhilleus killing Penthesilea, circa 400 BCE.

This naive drawing shows a battle scene: single combat between a male warrior and an Amazon. Inscriptions inform us that the warrior is Akhilleus, and the woman is the Amazon queen Penthesilea.

Penthesilea was the daughter of Ares, and a powerful warrior. As the greatest of the Amazons who fought for the Trojans, she was the female counterpart to Akhilleus, the greatest of the Greeks. When Akhilleus dealt the death blow to the queen, their eyes met, and he fell hopelessly in love.

The treatment of this dramatic scene is so primitive that it is a matter of wonder that the bowl was ever fired. Akhilleus's arms are different lengths, and his buttocks are improbably round. Penthesilea's pose is even more awkward; she seems to be attempting a split. At the same time, the artist was able to convey some of the pathos of the battle: the invisible line that connects their eyes runs parallel to the warrior's spear.

Rhaskos/Pyrrhos
in Athens

⌐⌐⌐⌐⌐⌐⌐⌐⌐⌐⌐⌐⌐⌐⌐

The summer after I came to Athens
    Zosima broke her sandal strap,
        and my secret was brought to
        light.

It was a bright afternoon.
Phaistus set up shop outside the
    courtyard.
Kranaos was napping in the sunlight. I
    was in the workroom,
        wedging clay on a plaster slab.
I rolled it out with a rolling pin
        and picked up a bone tool. I took a
        deep breath
        and started on a horse.

When I draw a horse,

> I'm in another world. There's only
> the two of us,

> and I can almost hear the horse
> whinnying, *Make me, make me!*

> *Show the arch of my neck,*

> *and the spring in my haunches!*

Loose the wind in my mane

> *and set me free!*

And I'm gentling him, saying, "Hold still,
my beautiful,

> let me double-check those slender legs.

> I want to capture every angle."

I was hunched over,

> the smell of the clay in my nostrils,

> when something made me raise my
> eyes

> > and there she was, so close I could
> > have touched her.

> > > She stood between me and
> > > the door.

> > > She ought to have blocked
> > > the light,

> > > > but the light streamed
> > > > through her.

Loose hair, sunburned
cheeks,
     her lips parted as if to
     speak —

The hair on my arms stood erect
  a prickle ran down my
  spine —
       I saw you, Melisto!

Then a voice behind me: "Phaistus!"
Zosima, barefoot, come from the
  house —
     there had been no flap-slap,
     slap-flap
     to warn me she was coming.
She was peering over my shoulder. My
  horse —!
I wedged one hand under the clay
     smacked it, flipped it over
     squished it
     pounded it —
"Phaistus! Come here,
     come and see what Pyrrhos did!"

Then there *he* was — Phaistus — (and the
girl was gone).
"What's all this?"

"Pyrrhos! Why did you have to ruin it? He
was *drawing*, Phaistus!
The most beautiful horse! Pyrrhos,
show him!"

The master was annoyed;
he'd been called in for nothing.
Already he was looking over his shoulder,
afraid of missing a customer.
"Is that all?"

"No. Stay a little, Phaistus. He can draw.
You have to see.
I'm sure I never saw a boy draw
as well."
She took the tool from the slab.
"With this. He carved into the clay."

"He was supposed to be working."

I saw a way out. I would play the slave,
humble myself, distract him.

481

"I was wasting time, *despotes*." I called
him *Master*.

I seldom called him that; I found a
way around it.

"I won't do it again."

"You will if I tell you to."
He took the lump of clay,
picked up the roller I'd used. Flattened it.
"Show me what you can do.
Draw the horse."

My heart jumped in my chest. My mouth
was dry.

I stared at the tool in my hand.
Like the wing of an insect in flight
it juddered. Like one of those
white butterflies
that never flies in a straight line.

"I don't have all day, boy.
Draw me a horse."

I cut into the clay. Too deep —
the clay rose up in ridges, both sides
of the blade.

I lifted my hand. Nip-slash for the horse's
  ear.
The curving descent down the neck.
The back. The rump. The complicated
  legs.
       The taut belly. Back up to the
         head —
     a straight line down the muzzle,
     the sharp angle of the jaw, the
       beautiful cheek;
I've groomed so many horses,
    passed my hands over their bodies,
      I know the shape of a horse under
        my hand.

"There, Phaistus! What did I tell you?"

       "Who taught you to draw, boy?"

"Nobody."

       "Nobody did a good job."

What did that mean? Was it a joke?
Clunk. He set a wine jar before me,
    peeled the clay off the plaster slab,
    and flipped it upside down.

"Copy that. Line for line.
Not the jar. Just the picture in the
middle."

It was a hard picture,
with no horses in it. There was my
old friend Akhilleus —
the greatest of warriors,
the one with no luck.
On the jar, he was fighting the Amazon
Queen —
a she-wolf, a warrior in her own right —
but she was no match for
Akhilleus.
He pierced her heart with his spear;
she gazed at him in her death
throes,
eye to eye,
and at that moment, as her life ebbed
away
he was shot by Eros, god of love,
and he loved her.
She loved him. But by then it was too late;
she was bound for the House of Hades,
and he couldn't undo what was done.

I told you he had no luck.

That was what I had to draw. I
   remembered Menon's javelin,
      the weight and threat of a spear.
I slashed the spear into the clay.
Then fierce Akhilleus, masked by his
   helmet,

         his broad shoulders, his narrow
            waist,
         meaty thighs and half-moon
            buttocks.
That part wasn't too bad. I started to
   enjoy myself.

         but the Amazon Queen —
      collapsing
         with her knees coming forward
         — I couldn't figure out those
            knees,
         or the love and grief in her face.
      "I can't, *despotes*."

   "No, you can't, yet. But it's not too bad."
               He opened a jar of slip,
found me a pot that had cracked in the kiln,
   and handed me a brush. "Try it again."

This time was the worst of all. I'd never
  used a brush.
    The hairs bent,
        and the slip oozed in falling beads.
The pot was curved,
      and my hand wouldn't obey me.
      "I can't, *despotes*."

"You will." Zosima set her hand on my
  shoulder;
      my flesh twitched, like a horse
      shuddering off a fly. "You just need
      practice.
      Phaistus, don't you agree? Some god
      has taught this boy,
        or given him a gift — ?
    Won't he be a help to you?
Aren't you glad you chose him?"

        Phaistus went to the doorway,
checking for customers. His back was to
                      me.
           "Someday, perhaps.
Right now, I don't need another painter.
    There's not much call for fancy work.

What I need is a second donkey:
a boy who hauls clay,
and gathers brushwood,
and does what he's told.
Still, you were right to tell me.
Now that I've seen what he can do, I'll
have to teach him."

He turned back to me, his brow knotted.
"You keep working. Copy that drawing.
Once you've got the hang of using the
brush,
I'll give you a bowl to paint. What's more,
I'll fire it.
It won't look like much,
but later on,
you'll be able to look back
at the first thing you did
and see how far you've come."

Zosima went and stood behind him.
She slipped her hand into his. He
squeezed her fingers,
and went back outside. Zosima
turned toward me,

487

her face glowing. It was as if she were
    proud of me,
    though what right she had to be
    proud, I don't know.

I scooped up another lump of clay
    and began to knead it.
Zosima stood by, watching.

I pretended she wasn't there until she
    wasn't.

MELISTO SPEAKS

Though I haunt him, I cannot make him
  see me.

What do I know of slaves? Not how to free
  them.

I would help if I could
    but I am helpless.

I'm a ghost. If our eyes meet for a moment
—

    He's afraid; he forgets me,
      like a nightmare.

I am mute,
    so there's no communication,
    and I have no idea of what to tell
      him.

I was young when I died. Forgive me,
  Thratta —

I can't do this. Your son is like a
  fortress.
Neither magic nor mother-love can reach
  him —
  I can set free a bear, but not a boy.

RHASKOS/PYRRHOS IN ATHENS

ᗏᖻᗏᖻᗏᖻᗏᖻᗏᖻᗏᖻ

After that day, I practiced.
Each day, Phaistus gave me a piece of
   broken pot
      and a jar to copy.
I worked to make my brushstrokes strong,
      decisive as a cast spear.
I never liked Phaistus better than when he
   taught me.
He didn't praise me,
      but he gave me his full attention.
If we skipped a day, I missed it.

Kranaos hung over us with a glint in his eye.
He didn't like me painting. I ignored him,
      which was stupid,
         because I know how it feels to be ignored.

491

There came a day —
    Kranaos and I were out in the
      courtyard —
    there was a pot the master had
      covered
    with a damp cloth.
Kranaos said, "Hand me that cloth." I
reached for it —
    and stopped. The cloth twitched.
    Something warned me. I lifted the
      edge:
      a scorpion
         bigger than the palm of my
           hand,
         the jointed tail clear yellow —
         ugly, deadly, and symmetrical.
        That was what Kranaos wanted —
    for me to grab the cloth
    and the scorpion to sting!

Rage rose in me.
    I seized the cloth
      and flicked the scorpion at
      Kranaos —
      at his bare feet.

492

He gave a yell
      and tottered to one side —
      even as he stumbled, I saw from
         his face
I'd made a mistake. He hadn't known.
The scorpion skittered under a bush.
Neither of us were stung.
      I had time to feel relief —
      but not to explain. Through the air
   whistling
      the old man's stick! I yelped —
he aimed;
      I leapt back,
         banged into two pots, shattering
            them both —
      he fisted my tunic,
      yanked me to my feet;
         I kicked —
      knocked over a jar of slip —

Slip. I have to tell you: slip
      is only clay and water,
      but skimmed and sieved
         and rinsed and strengthened;

it takes hours
and buckets and buckets of
water
to make one little jar of slip. So —
overturning a whole bowl —
I was in trouble.

Kranaos lost his mind. He pulled my hair,
smacked my back with his horny old
hands,
scratched and beat;
I put up my arms to shield my
head.
I hadn't been beaten since Menon.

Phaistus came from the shop. He bellowed
at us both,
and I tore myself away.

The rush of the wind
— the streets — people who
stared —
a goose honked and flapped aloft —
the dogs barked.
I leapt like Zeus's lightning. Like a stream
that zigzags

and dodges the rocks
I fled through the town. I didn't
know where I was going,
but I was as swift as the god of
thieves.
Away. That's where I went
and up. A spasm in my side —
and I slowed
— to catch my breath —
I'd come to that grove of trees
where I once saw Sokrates
dancing.

Green blurred around me. I dropped on
the grass,
panting,
my shoulder throbbing,
an oozing scrape on one cheek.
I wished he were there: Sokrates.

I stayed there
fuming. Kranaos: that old man,
that dried-up, rotten-tooth, vile
old man.
I wished I'd hit him back.

"There you are." Phaistus —
                    breathing hard.
"That red hair makes you easy to track.
                    So now you're a runaway.
                    I should beat you black and blue."

"I'm not a runaway! Kranaos went after
    me!
Maybe I was the one who broke the pots
        and knocked over the slip —
            but it wasn't my fault! Kranaos, he
                schemes against me!
There was this scorpion —"

I bit back my words, because what I'd
    almost said
            wasn't true. Kranaos never threw the
                scorpion at me.
            I threw it at him.
I wanted to say *Kranaos started it*,
            except it wasn't true.

                                    "Stand up."

I stood so he could beat me.

Between my teeth, I muttered,
"Go ahead. I don't care!"

He circled me, taking stock of my
wounds.
"You'll mend. A few scrapes and bruises,
that's all.
He's an old man. I'm surprised he could
hit so hard."

"He used his stick."

Phaistus lowered himself to
the grass.
He wasn't going to beat me after all.
He set his feet side by side,
knees bent,
arms resting on them.
"Kranaos is old, and his hands are shaky.
He can't paint anymore.
He was never as skilled as I am —
or as skilled as you'll be, one day.
He's jealous of you, Pyrrhos."

"He had no right to hit me!
He's not my master!"

"You show him no respect.
When he shows you how to load the kiln,
you roll your eyes.
He's an old man. You should remember
that.
If I, who am his master,
pay homage to his skill,
who are you?"

I started to speak. He wouldn't let me.

"I've been wanting to ask you that for
some time, Pyrrhos.
Who do you think you are?
I've treated you well.
I teach you, and I'm patient.
You have enough to eat, and my wife treats
you like a son,
but there's no gratitude in you.
No loyalty. Kindness is wasted on you.
Every time I send you to dig clay,
you linger a little longer
and come back a little later.
You sulk. You don't speak,
and your silence is pregnant

498

with disrespect.
That day you came home with
Sokrates,
you seemed like a different boy.
I thought, *Maybe Zosima's right.*
Maybe there's something in him.
If there is, you keep it hidden.
It's been six months since I bought you.
You're quick to learn, I give you that, but
for the rest —
Every day you draw a little better,
but every day you disappoint me."

I didn't know what to say.
Then some god spoke in me. I
looked up,
into his face. Not like a slave,
but eye to eye,
like Penthesilea gazing at Akhilleus.
"I'm not as bad as you think I am.
I'm not. I'm not!"

He heard me. He got up.
"Come!"

I followed. He didn't head back to the
  house.
I thought he was taking me to the slave
  market.
My stomach clenched. I saw myself back
  there:
        humiliated, shackled, for sale.
I thought of the silver mines at Lavrion.

He led me to the Temple of Hephaistos.
There's a wood fence to one side,
        covered with carvings and graffiti.
The master knelt down. He traced the
  carving with one hand.

                "Do you see this, Pyrrhos?"

"Yes. But I can't read."

                        "I should teach you.
A pot's worth more with an inscription."
        He touched the words again and read
                                        aloud:
                "Iason, son of Zenon, sells his slave
                        Phaistus, a Theban,
                        to the god Hephaistos

for the price of four hundred drachmas,
on these conditions:
that Phaistus shall serve Iason blamelessly
and perform the burial rites for Iason when
he dies.
Once his master is buried with honor,
Phaistus will inherit the property of Iason:
his tools and his stock in trade.
Markos, son of Linos, will serve as his
Protector
and guard him from insult, and from being
reenslaved."

His voice grew stronger.
"And Phaistus will be free and
untouchable."

"You see, Pyrrhos, I was a slave.
I saved money for years, and I gave it to
the god.
I bought and earned my
freedom.
I can never own land or a house —
I am not a citizen, and I'm bound to a
protector,
but I am no longer a slave."

"That day in the marketplace, when I
bought you,
you were all beat up. I asked why your
master beat you,
and you said, 'He was drunk.'
Only one man in ten would have
understood,
but I was that man. I watch you with the
donkey.
You don't beat her, because you know too
well
what it is to be beaten.
It's the same with me. I should beat you
for your own good;
I should take a stick to you —
but I have no stomach for it. Iason was a
hard master.
When I was your age, I had more stripes
than a tabby cat.
No matter how hot it gets,
I don't strip down;
I wear my tunic when I work.
I don't want anyone to see the marks.
Iason was a hard master, but
I treat you justly,
for all the good it does me."

502

We sat there in silence.

My knees ached. I thought he would say
   more,

    but he didn't.

He got to his feet, and I followed him
   home.

HERMES SPEAKS

Let's take a break. Allow me to kick off the
winged sandals,

    wiggle my toes,

    and put my feet up. It's Dullsville in
      Athens:

Kranaos is napping. Phaistus is worrying
about money.

Zosima, poor thing,

    is weaving ribbons for the shrine of
      Artemis,

    hoping that the goddess of childbirth

      will grant her a baby. She's not
        good at ribbons.

      She needs spectacles,

        but they won't be invented

for sixteen hundred years.
Melisto's doing

. . . whatever ghosts do, don't ask me,

and Meda's a dolphin.

Rhaskos is on his knees in the Temple of
Hephaistos.

He's begging the god for his freedom.

Someone ought to tell him about
manumission. Come to think of it,
someone ought to tell *you* about
manumission.

Pull up a chair. Get comfortable.
I'd offer you a cup of nectar,
but it's against the rules.

Manumission is what they call it

when you free a slave. *Manumitted*
is what they call you

once you're freed. Rhaskos can't
stop thinking about it:

*Phaistus used to be a slave, and
now he's not.*

Poor Rhaskos! He didn't really grasp what
Phaistus told him;

but he heard the name *Hephaistos*,
    so Hephaistos is his new favorite
        god. Oh, I'm not jealous!
He'll come back to me! Everyone
    does.
Sooner or later everyone needs to
    take a journey,
        get hold of a little money,
        enjoy a good night's sleep,
        come up with a watertight lie
            (not to mention going to hell
            with any kind of *style*).
Once they do, I'm their god.
    Hephaistos is good at crafts,
        but I'm crafty. All fish come to my
        nets.

What were we talking about? Ah, yes,
manumission. Let me ask you,
    Why would anyone free a slave? . . .
        What's that, you say?
            Because it's the right thing to
            do?
                Bless your
                    heart!
                Maybe. Or —

Let's say your slave is getting old and can't
work hard;
he's just another mouth to feed,
and you're tired of him: You set
him free.
(Kranaos worries himself sick over this.
If Phaistus sets him free, he'll starve.)

Here's another reason: Sometimes fathers
free their slave children,
if they have no other sons.
Neither of these scenarios will work for
Rhaskos.
His father had free-born sons. He
didn't need a spare.
Moreover, Rhaskos is strong and young
and bright;
there are years of work to be got out
of him.

Now, Phaistus —
Phaistus was set free *on condition*
that he perform the burial rites for his
master, Iason.
By now, I hope you've grasped

that funeral rites are important. It's a
ghoul-eat-ghoul world
in the House of Hades. If no one
looks after you —
no coins for the ferryman,
no cakes for the three-headed
dog,
no wine, no oil, no prayers —
things aren't going to go
well.
When you die, you need to make sure
there's someone left behind
who'll dot every *i* and cross every *t*.
Iason was childless. He knew he was
dying.
He put Phaistus in charge of his
funeral;
afterward, Phaistus was freed.
Worked out nicely. Freeing a slave is
pleasing to the gods,
who — you may have noticed this —
don't have slaves.
We Olympians are accused of behaving
badly;
our tempers are hasty;

508

we tend to hold a grudge;
we run pell-mell after other
    men's wives —
once in a while, we chop a few
    bits off each other —
but we don't keep slaves. That's
    where we draw the line.
If you, my mortal friend, are dying,
    and a teensy bit unsure
    about what might happen to you
    next,
    you might want to free your slave.
    Give the gods a thrill!
What have you got to lose?
You won't need slaves in the House
    of Hades!

Where was I? Ah, yes; manumission.
Few slaves are set free with no strings
    attached.
    Most slaves, like Phaistus, are freed
    on condition . . .
What kind of condition? I thought you'd
    never ask.
If you're the slave owner,
    you get to spell out the terms.

Suppose you tell your slave, "Here's
   the deal.
I'll set you free, but
      you have to live next door
      so you're handy to come and wait
        on me.
You have to do
      whatever I tell you,
      as long as I live.
I claim the right to punish you any way
   I choose,
      which means I can strike you,
        starve you,
      brand you with an iron,
        tie you to a tree and whip you
          senseless —
      anything short of death."

(It's against the law to kill a slave.)

"If you want to be free, you have to pay
   me for your freedom,
      or buy me a slave to replace you;
        you can give me one of your
          children —
        if I let you have children.

If at any time you fail to please me,

> the deal is off. I get to keep your
> money,

>> and you're back to being my
>> slave."

Who would *take* such a deal?

I'll tell you who: the man whose life is
worse.

A man would rather seize a
slender hope

> than have no hope at all.

If you're freed, even *on condition*, you can't
be sold to a new master,

> and you're safe from the mines at
> Lavrion.

You might be able to have a family,

> eat a little better,

> own a little property,

> make a little money,

> but be careful! If you earn more than
> your old master,

>> that's considered rude,

>> and you have to give the surplus
>> cash to him.

Luckily — or unluckily,
   depending on how you see it —
   Phaistus
   is not the kind of man to dangle freedom
   in front of Rhaskos's nose
   and yank it back.
He knows too much. But he's not going to free Rhaskos.
He can't afford it. What if he could?
What if Rhaskos were to go free
   without condition? What would that look like?

To begin with, it would cost money.
   Rhaskos
   would have to get permission
   to earn money
   and keep it for himself.
He'd need to save . . .
      . . . let me see . . .
        Phaistus bought him for a
        hundred drachmas,
        but he's worth more now;
        he's older

and learning a trade.
Still, Thracians are cheap . . . Let's
     say he's worth one twenty;
          he'd need two hundred and forty
               drachmas
          to buy his freedom. That's about
               the price
               of a cheap cavalry horse,
                    or six and a half months' salary
                         for a skilled worker,
          or one thousand four hundred and
               forty loaves of bread
          and enough wine to wash them all
               down.

Once he's saved the money,
          that's where Hephaistos comes in.
          It doesn't have to be Hephaistos;
          any god could help out.
          I could do it.
          You see, Rhaskos isn't a person —
               Ooh, don't pull that face with me!
               You know he's a person.
               I know he's a person!
               As Sokrates pointed out, he has a soul.

He's a person, all right. But
according to Athenian law,
he's someone's property:
like a pruning knife, or a
battle helmet.
You can't draw up a contract
between a person and a helmet!
Manumission is a contract,
and a piece of property cannot
set itself free.
It's against the law.

But there's a way around it. Here we go:
Rhaskos gives his savings
to the priest
at the Temple of Hephaistos;
the priest gives the money to the
god.
Now Hephaistos is rich,
and can buy himself a slave.
You *can* have a contract between a person
and a god:
The priest (a stand-in for the god) handles
the cash.
Phaistus gets the money.

Hephaistos gets the slave.
    Since the gods don't *have* slaves —
      Rhaskos is free.

If he's free without condition,
    he can go where he wants
      and do as he pleases.
    His new status will be announced at
      the theatre
      or carved in wood or stone.
    He'll never be a citizen
      or own land. He can't buy a house,
      and he'll need a protector.
    His status will be low,
      but he'll be free: a manumitted
      slave,
      not to be insulted,
      not to be seized and beaten.

That's why Rhaskos is praying in the
Temple of Hephaistos.
While we were talking, Melisto followed
him in:
    there are torches burning in the
    temple

and shadows moving. She's one
more shadow,

one more flame.

She stands at his elbow, listening to
his prayers.

She wishes he would turn his head to
see her —

but he won't. His mind is caught
up

with the thing he desires,

the thing she is bound to help him
find.

There they are:

the girl as electric as amber,

and the boy, indestructible as clay.

RHASKOS/PYRRHOS IN ATHENS

᠋᠋᠋᠋᠋

1. Scorpion

Six days after I learned about Phaistus,
    I was sweeping up.
    I found the scorpion behind a stack
      of pots.
    I poked it with the broom —
      it didn't stir. The tail was
      stretched out straight.
      I picked it up. Cautiously —
      I don't know why,
      but I wanted to draw it.

Later I scratched it on a broken pot. It was
    complicated,
      unexpected. The legs were thin near
      the body;

517

then they flared out, elbow-like and
    muscular:
easy to draw
        and impossible. So many segments —
        but I liked how the pincers
            hugged the curves of the pot;
        I curled the tail like a crescent
            moon;
    I pressed the dead scorpion into
        wet clay
        and examined the imprint.
I wanted to show my work to Phaistus,
        but I didn't want to remind him.

2. Silence

I kept thinking about Phaistus.
        He'd been a slave, like me,
            but now he was free.
I wanted to ask a hundred questions
        but my tongue was as still
        as the dead scorpion. I thought of
            him saying
        Kindness is wasted on you.
He'd stopped teaching me to draw.

When he first bought me, he tried to shut
  me up.
After a while, I shut myself up.
Something about the way I did it
      drove him crazy,
        so I shut up even more.
Now I wanted to talk, and I couldn't.
I was like a boy trying to play catch
    with his hands tied behind his back.

Then Sokrates came and my mouth was
  opened.

3. Sokrates

I saw him often,
    but mostly from a distance. Even at a
      distance:
      that same hairy cloak,
      the goose-like strut,
      and always, he was talking.
He'd talk to anyone. Women, even slaves.
He was friends with Simon,
    the cobbler who fixed Zosima's
    sandal.

He loved the Agora. He'd ask the potters
   how trade was
      and stoop to read the pictures on
         the jars.
Mostly he was surrounded by young men —
      aristocrats, and some of them were
         beautiful.
Fresh from the gymnasion, their skins
   gleamed with oil;
         graceful, taut-muscled,
            they strolled and lingered,
         showing off how they were free to
            waste time.

I tried to eavesdrop. I'd find some excuse
      to cross the market square and
         listen.
Once I heard him talking about a group of
   men
         who were chained up, prisoners in a
            dark cave —
         I wondered if they were slaves at
            Lavrion.
         I wanted to hear if they got free.
Before I could find out

Phaistus called me back to spin the
 wheel.

There came a day — I was gathering
 brushwood;
     it was scorching, the dog days of
      summer.
      I felt like a pot in the kiln,
       my skin blazing red, darkening —
      I was close to the river —
I heard someone humming. A glimpse
 through the trees:
     an old man wading.
My heart leapt. "Sokrates?"

      He tented his eyes with his hand,
       squinting against the sun.
       "Rhaskos! Is that you?
Come join me in the water! I want
      someone to talk to!
I've been remembering a wise man named
        Herakleitos —
He said that that no man ever wades twice
       in the same river.
       What do you think of that?"

That was Sokrates. That was the kind of
  thing he thought about.
I loved how he asked me what I thought.
I'd never heard of Herakleitos,
        and what he said didn't make sense.
You can wade in the same river any time
  you want.
I'd dipped into the Kefissos all summer.

I tethered Phoibe so she could graze
        and waded into the river by Sokrates.
          It was so cold
        it made me grit my teeth and grin.
Water brown and yellow with silt,
        foaming white around my knees;
        it came to me what Herakleitos
          meant:
          water changes.
The river keeps moving. You can step in
  the same river,
        but the water swooshes past you
          and runs into the sea.
"I think maybe he's right, Sokrates.
    Not about the river,
        but about the water."

"Do you think all things are like that,
Rhaskos?
Are all things moving and changing, all the
time?
Is there anything everlasting,
unchangeable,
any absolute beauty or goodness?
I wonder about this. I even dream
about it."

The water stung my legs with cold.
I squatted down to let it soak my tunic.
"I don't know, Sokrates.
I went to a drinking party once,
and they asked that same question:
does everything change?
Or does everything stay the same?
I have to tell you, I thought it was a stupid
question.
I thought: some things change, like eggs,
and others don't, like rocks.
But maybe that was a stupid answer."

Sokrates smiled. He bent over and
scooped up a rock
from the riverbed.

523

He handed it to me. It glistened.

It was a yellow rock,

bigger than a drachma, but smaller than
an egg.

I have it still.

"Is this rock unchangeable, Rhaskos?"

I turned the rock over in my hand.

One side was smooth, stroked by the
water;

the other side was rough.

"No. The water's changed it.

Though it can't change by itself. I could
pound it with another rock,

chip it, maybe break it. So rocks *can*
change . . .

The stars don't change, but they move in
circles . . .

I don't know if moving is the same thing
as changing . . .

Even the gods change. I mean, Zeus
changed himself into a bull,

and a swan. They can change into
anything they like!

Maybe your man was right. Everything
   changes.

The river and the gods and even
   rocks."

I looked to see if that was the right
   answer.

    Sokrates didn't say anything. He was
      watching me,
        watching me *think*.

    I had the idea he was waiting for
      something.

He waded to a shady spot on the
   riverbank

    and sat down, soaking his feet.

I could see his feet through the water.

They were wide and bony,

    brown-spotted,

      yellow as the rock in my hand,
      horny and warped.

I splashed over and sat beside him.

I tried to find my soul

    so I could remember the truth.

"I can think of one thing that can't be
  changed, Sokrates,

> but it doesn't have to do with
>   absolute goodness,

the past can't be changed.

> Maybe you meant me to think of
>   something beautiful,

>> like the gods or the stars.

> But they change. The only thing I can
>   think of

>> that doesn't change

>> is the past."

He nodded slowly. We sat and listened to
  the ripple of the water.

> The mud under my legs felt moist
>   and sticky.

You notice all kinds of mud if you dig
  clay.

This mud was rich with it. I pressed my
  knuckle into it

> and began to draw. Joints with spaces
>   in between:

>> the leg of a scorpion. I went on
>>   talking.

"The Spartans won the war.
I bet the Athenians wish they could
  change that,
      but they can't. My mother was
        kidnapped when she was a girl,
          so she became a slave,
            and I was born a slave. I can't
              change that.
Menon used to punish me for nothing,
      just because he felt like it. He
        broke my nose.
      Now it's crooked. I'd like to change
  all that,
          but the past can't be changed."

              Sokrates was listening.
            He cupped a handful of water
              and splashed his arms.
"What you're saying is that time moves
                in one direction only.
      But here's another question for you:
is time real? is there such a thing as time?
      I wonder if the gods have one kind of
                                time,
                which is everlasting,

and we have another,
which follows the path of the stars,
and works according to numbers . . .

"My friend?
It seems to me you're no longer listening.
What are you drawing?"

I muttered, "It's a scorpion,"
and stared down at the mud.
It was a good drawing;
I'd learned that shape by heart.

"Your master said you loved drawing
horses.
He told me he was teaching you."

"Not anymore."
I flattened my hand
and wiped out the scorpion. All of
the sudden
I was telling him the whole story:
how Kranaos was always tattling on
me,
how I'd thought he meant to trick me,

how I flicked the scorpion at him.
The strange thing was,
I told the whole truth. I wanted
him to blame Kranaos,
who was a sneak,
but I didn't slant the truth.
I spoke low, but he heard me.

"When you tossed the scorpion at
Kranaos,
did you know it was wrong?
Was it a mistake, or did you do it on
purpose?"

"I did it on purpose."

"Good. It's better to do wrong with
knowledge
than to act in ignorance.
I believe no man
would ever do wrong
if he were not ignorant.
You thought Kranaos meant to hurt you.
That was a mistake.
So you struck back.

You did wrong and you did it knowingly.
The next time, you might not make a
mistake.
You might not do wrong at all."

It seemed to me he was missing the point.
"Maybe. But Kranaos got me in trouble."
I traced the scraped place on my
shoulder,
the greenish bruise on my arm.
"He had no right to beat me. He's not my
master!
If he weren't a weak old man,
he'd have half killed me. And now
I'm being punished."

"Perhaps you're lucky, Rhaskos.
To do wrong is harmful to the soul.
The best thing is to do no harm,
but if you do wrong,
the next best thing is to be punished.
It was wrong to frighten an old man with a
scorpion.
Perhaps Kranaos used his stick as the
surgeon wields a knife;

530

there was a little tumor of injustice in your
soul,
and Kranaos cut it away. Now it won't grow,
and your soul will remain in good health."

It wasn't what I wanted him to say.
I felt my face get hot.
"What about when Menon beat me for
nothing?
What about the damage done to my soul?
What do you know about being beaten?
You're a citizen,
and a grown-up,
and nobody can touch you!"

"Listen to me, Rhaskos!
You say Menon treated you unjustly;
that he broke your nose and struck you
without cause.
I'm sure you speak the truth,
but he didn't touch your soul. Believe me.
There is nothing disgraceful in being
beaten without cause.
What is disgraceful is to be the man who
strikes unjustly.

If any man were to slap my face,

or steal my purse, or cut me with a knife,

or even put me to death some
shameful way —

I would not be ashamed. My soul would
be unharmed."

I got up. Here's what struck me: no matter
who beat me,

it was all right with Sokrates!

It was all right for Kranaos to beat
me,

because I deserved to be
punished;

and it was all right for Menon,

because he only hurt my body

and not my soul! Either way, it
was no skin off his back.

I said, "I have to go.

My master will be angry.

You've never had a master, so you don't
know about that."

I started up the bank. He came after,

but I ignored him. I untied Phoibe
and urged her forward —

only Phoibe's slow. You can't
hurry her. And Sokrates —
he caught up with me.

"Rhaskos, tell me! Can a man be a good
man and still suffer?"

I didn't answer.
I'd had enough of his wisdom for one day.
Everything was wrong.
Sokrates didn't understand me,
and now I hated him,
my only friend.
The sun was too hot. I was burning,
my skin and my temper;
I was burning alive.

"Let me ask the same question another
way:
Is there such a thing as an evil pleasure?"

I whirled around to face him,
Phoibe's rope in my hand.
I was still holding the yellow stone.
I hated him,
but I didn't want to lose the yellow stone

533

because it was all I was going to have
once we stopped being friends.
"Of course there are evil pleasures!"
No one who ever saw Menon drunk
was left in doubt about that.
Beating me and watching me cry —
that was one of Menon's pleasures.

"But don't you see, Rhaskos? If there are
evil pleasures,
then *pleasure* is not the same thing as
goodness.
Pain is different from *evil*.
Menon caused you pain, but he didn't
hurt your soul.
Your soul is pure, untouched by what he
did."

There was something about the way he
looked and spoke
that ate into me, sank in
like dye into cloth. That night, when I
couldn't sleep,
I remembered his words.
At the time, all I could say was
"Leave me alone!"

He sighed.

There was sadness in his smile.

"You told me your mother named you
Rhaskos,

but your master calls you Pyrrhos,

which means *fiery*. I think *Pyrrhos* is the
better name.

You are gripped by passion just now;

you would sting me like a scorpion.

A man who is mastered by passion

is an unlucky man. His feelings
flow forth

like wine from a leaky pot.

Some men take pride in losing their
tempers. But for my part,

I think it's better when pots don't leak.

You're young. You're thoughtful for your age,
so I forget how young you are.

You still have time to strive and learn.

Be your own master, Rhaskos."

With that he turned away.

I glared after him.

We'd been having a fight, and suddenly it
was over.

4. Rhaskos Listens

"Phaistus?"

"Zosima."

"Are you asleep?"

"I wish I were. It's so hot . . .
You think it's any cooler in the courtyard?
We could carry the mats outside."

"If we sleep outside, I'll have to be
modest
and lie under a blanket. I'd rather stay
here.
There's a breeze coming in the window . . ."

"I don't feel it. There's not a breath of air."

"Phaistus, what's the matter?"

"Nothing."

"You've been silent and grim all evening,
and Pyrrhos, too.
Both of you scowling

and picking at your food!
What's gone wrong between you?"

"It's nothing to do with the boy.
I saw Markos in the marketplace today."

"What did he want?"

"Nothing. We didn't speak.
He's lost weight. He's a sick old man.
When he dies, I'll need a new protector."

"Is that what's worrying you?
You've never liked him."

"No, but he doesn't rob me blind. He's a
  just man.
The rent he charges for the shop is fair.
If he dies, and I can't find another
  protector,
    I could be sued; I could lose
      everything.
If worse comes to worst, I could be sold.
I think I'd rather die than go through that."

"Phaistus. Stop.
That's not going to happen."

"How do you know it won't?
What does a woman know about the
  law?"

"If Markos dies, you'll find a new
                                protector.
You're respected. Any man of sense would
                          be proud to help you.
              You won't lose your freedom."

"I've come so far."

                                        "I know."

"It's not just me. If I lose the business,
    what becomes of you?
And Kranaos? Even the boy — "

      "Phaistus, what's happened to Pyrrhos?
              He's scarcely spoken for a week,
                              and tonight —
        I never saw him look so wretched."

"Don't know. He was hauling brushwood
  all day.
Ask the donkey what's wrong with him."

"You're not teaching him anymore."

"Listen, Zosima. Last week —
     I didn't want to tell you. I knew you'd
     take his side —
          the boy threw a scorpion at
          Kranaos,
               hoping it would sting him. An
               ugly thing.
A child should treat an old man with
     respect. Zosima!
It wasn't funny."

                    "Was Kranaos hurt?"

"No."

"Then it's a little bit funny. Oh, come on,
                              Phaistus!
               All boys are mischievous,
               and Kranaos is an old misery!"

"Listen, it wasn't a boyish prank.
And it wasn't mischief, it was malice.
A scorpion could kill an old man like
     Kranaos. He's not strong.

The boy broke two good pots
and knocked over a jar of slip.
Kranaos went after him, and Pyrrhos
deserved it."

"That's where he got those bruises!
Kranaos is always finding fault with
Pyrrhos.
He nags."

"He's trying to teach him. The boy should
pay attention.
He could learn something. There's no man
in Athens —"

" — who knows more about the kiln! I
know.
Blessed be the gods who gave us
Kranaos!
All the same, he hawks up phlegm every
morning
and spits on my clean-swept floor.
Can't he spit outside?
I stepped in it yesterday, in my bare feet!"

"I'll talk to him — Shhh!"

"Why are you hushing me?"

"I thought I heard something. Right
  outside the window —
He could be listening."

"Who, Kranaos? He's as deaf as any
  stone."

"No, the boy. I wouldn't put it past him."

"I wish you'd stop calling him *the boy*.
  He's our son. He has a name."

"He's not our son. I know you've grown
  attached to him;
I haven't. I'm doing my best.
I'm not going to sell him if I don't have to
  — "

"Phaistus, you can't sell him! We agreed!
  You promised me you'd buy a child,
  and that we'd raise him as our son!"

"I said, *if* we have no children of our own.
We may still have children."

541

"Don't."

"Older women than you — "

"Don't. It's been eight years.
Eight years married, and I'm still not a
woman.
I'm a freak, a failure, unfinished.
I wouldn't blame you if you
divorced me."

"Zosima, you were kind to me when I was
still a slave.
I remember our wedding night, when I
lifted your veil,
and looked into your eyes, and saw
you loved me.
I will never divorce you.
I just wish I'd waited before I bought the
boy.
I wanted a Syrian, or an
Egyptian boy.
A Thracian's trouble. It's the strangest
thing . . .
The day I bought him, I'd made up
my mind not to.

542

I'd turned my back on him. I was headed
    home
        and then — it was as if some god
        seized me by the arm and towed me
            back."

                "What if it were a god?"

"What?"

            "What if he's meant to be our son?
You said yourself: you've never known a
            boy who can draw like that.
        I wish you'd go back to teaching him
                He was happier when you
                    taught him."

"You're a fool about that boy, Zosima.
He doesn't care two figs for you. He's
ungrateful."

            "He's not. He doesn't show it,
            but he's aware of every kindness.
No matter what happens, you can't sell
                    him.
                I forbid it."

"What kind of wife says *I forbid* to her husband?"

> "You know what kind of wife I am.
> You knew when you married me."

"I suspected — "

> "A vixen! A she-wolf!
> With a squint, too! Don't forget the
> squint."

"You only squint when you smile,
  and I'm happy when you smile,
   Zosima.
     . . . your lips are sweet,
       but it's too hot to kiss.

> "Pyrrhos is our son.
> In time, he'll understand that.
> And so will you."

"He's a Thracian barbarian.
  And even if he were Greek —
I wish I felt like his father, but I don't."

"Phaistus, you need to sleep.
Change places with me. It's cooler near
the window.
You'll rest easier there. Just try to go to
sleep.
We have one another, and we have
enough.
I'll stop talking now. Sleep."

EXHIBIT 14

Clay figurines, terra-cotta, Athens, fourth and fifth century BCE.

These charming miniature figures were probably playthings. Though rattles were used for music and religious rituals, this pig was probably created to entertain an Athenian baby. Both horses have pierced legs, which suggest that they were mounted on wheels and used as pull-toys. Traces of pigment show that the figurines were once painted with bright colors.

RHASKOS/PYRRHOS IN ATHENS

That night I couldn't sleep. It was too hot:
    the grating of cicadas,
      the airless shed, and the smell of
      sweaty donkey.
I got up, left the shed,
    and went out in the courtyard.

Not much cooler there. Street noises,
    far-off laughter from drunken men,
      nighttime murmurs
      from Phaistus and Zosima.
I listened. On purpose. I strained to hear.
I seemed to see Sokrates
      standing at my elbow, questioning me.
      He thought it wasn't ἀρετή to
      listen.

Thinking about him made me clench
my fists.
What right had he to judge me? I
wanted to punch him.
I thought of things I wanted to say to
his face,
words that would shame him,
wound him,
make him burn
like me.
At last, they stopped talking. I stretched
out on the grass.
I itched and wiggled and twisted,
tightening myself. Something bit me.
I raked my sweaty skin.
At last I slept.

Long ago my mother told me
dreams don't mean anything,
but if someone comes and stands
over you
on your right side —
or maybe it's the left side —
I was young, I didn't know left
from right
— but if someone *stands over you*

it's a dream from the gods.

I saw the dream. Wavering, bright as a
   torch in fog:
      a girl my age. No, she was younger:
         immaterial
           the fluted folds of her tunic
              were restless and astir.
   Her hair was unbound,
      her eyes gleaming like an owl's.
   On her arm and shoulder, a
      spiderweb of scars,
         an intricate pattern,
           the lines changing course like
           rivers.
   She kept her hands behind her back,
      hiding something.
   I'd seen her before
      but that night
         my mind was made supple by sleep,
         and I could remember:

That first time: the slave market — I'd
                seen her there,
      her robe as bright as a bride's,

550

but too short; I'd thought she was a
Spartan girl.
I thought of Phaistus —
It was as if some god
seized me by the arm and towed me back.

Then Phaistus bought me,
and I forgot about her.

And the second time: she
was with Sokrates,
in broad daylight, under the willows,
swinging her feet,
kicking up splashes.

And the time I was drawing,
the day Zosima came in barefoot,
and caught me making a horse — !

There were other times, too. I'd be hauling
water
or digging clay. Phoibe would lift
her head,
sniffing, her ears swiveling;
I'd catch a glimpse:
a glow like amber,

a shadow like smoke in the air. But
   always
      there was something to distract
      me,
      and I'd forget.

So there you were, Melisto:
    the dream standing over me,
    and I couldn't pretend I didn't see
    you.
I saw you close at hand:
    I could see your burn scars, your
    lightning marks,
      the mosquito bites on your legs,
      the freckles on your cheeks
      as you brought forth the thing
      behind your back —

A terra-cotta horse. A toy.
    I seemed to feel the clay between my
    fingers
      cool, damp, tough; I imagined
      myself
      pinching the mane,
      making a crisscross in the belly,

drawing out the legs. I thought,
I could make that!
My mind flashed ahead,
   like a child leaping over a stream. I
      imagined the toy finished;
         I painted it:
            two oval black eyes,
               dug-in nostrils.
   I'd paint that horse with spirals and
      stars,
         with jags of Zeus's lightning —
I saw myself in the Agora,
   my hands full of coins:
      being praised by my master,
         buying my freedom.

I remembered you when I woke, Melisto,
   but my first waking thought was: the
      horse!

Turn, Counterturn, and Stance: Hephaistos and Rhaskos

TURN: **HEPHAISTOS**

The boy's first terra-cotta:
a toy. He thinks, because he's working on a
   toy,
it will be easy,
but he is one of my own,
and anything,
anything,
anything,
      he makes
will take everything he has:
all his cunning,
perseverance,
tenacity, and mother wit.

Look at him!
He is fighting for his freedom
— his fingers tighten like fists.

COUNTERTURN: **RHASKOS**

I thought it would be simple.
A toy: a horsie for a rich man's spoiled
son;
how hard could it be?
I took the clay in my hands,
but it fought me:
slippery,
obstinate,
stone-cold,
and my fingers were all thumbs.
I squeezed and clawed,
and plucked and pinched;
I was tying myself in knots,
doom-ridden —
while the clay snaked through
my fingers:
my thought-horse galloped away.

555

HEPHAISTOS

He hasn't learned to keep his mind on the
　　horse.
He's all nerves. He's scarcely breathing,
　　　trying to bully the horse in the clay.
He ought to know better;
　　　a horse cannot be broken like that;
　　　a toy is not made by brute force.

RHASKOS

　　　　I thought the horse would be the
　　　　　　straightforward part.
　　　The hard part: persuading Phaistus
　　to give me permission to sell my work.
　　　　　Plus earning the money:
　　hundreds of drachmas. It was hopeless.
　　　　I couldn't even make the horse!

HEPHAISTOS

How can I get him to see
　　　he's not the one who will make the
　　　　horse?

It's the passion he has for the
horse
that will summon the horse in the
clay —

RHASKOS

The clay held out against me.
No surrender. I started over.
Stupidly. The horse was lost, was trapped
in the maze of my thick Thracian skull.

HEPHAISTOS

Rhaskos, think of the child at play,
and the joy he will find in
the horse.
Play with the clay.
Just play. Imagine the horse . . .
Now, gallop away.
Think of rhythm and fire and force;
power, spirit, and grace;
the luminous eye and the
fragrant breath —

What in thunder is that?

RHASKOS

I was trying to find the horse —
I was trying to draw out the legs:
they were too short,
too thick. The body was wrong, round as a
bubble —
the belly too large —
Then . . . something got into my hands
and what was meant to be
a delicate head on a cresting neck
became bloated and stout —

BOTH
A pig!

HEPHAISTOS

I am a god,
but I didn't divine
the pig in the clay!

558

Where did that come from?

RHASKOS

I made a *pig*!
With the ball of my thumb,
I dug in the ears,
and hollowed the snout —

HEPHAISTOS

How did that pig get in there?

BOTH

Ha!

RHASKOS

How did that porker get out?

HEPHAISTOS

Look — he's bewitched by the work of his
hands —
irresistible piglet!

559

RHASKOS

I made a pig, and that pig makes me laugh
—

    It's *good*. And now for the horse!

STANCE: HEPHAISTOS

He struggles — and his work is not in
    vain,
persists — and I, the deathless god,
    applaud:
Rhaskos the slave becomes a child again,
and by his crafting hands becomes a god.

RHASKOS/PYRRHOS
IN ATHENS

1. The River

Sokrates. I didn't forget him.
    After the quarrel, I'd see him in the
        Agora,
            jabbering like a magpie.
    Once he saw me:
    His brow lifted, and his hand;
        his face split in a smile.

I was still mad at him,
    hoping he wasn't mad at me.
When he wasn't, it threw me off guard.
    I was relieved,
        but I was still angry.

I thought I should stick to it,
    like a man. My heart was torn in two.
I turned my back on purpose.

There came a day —
    weeks had gone by. Sycamore leaves
        were crisping,
        the olives dark as plums;
I was riding Phoibe,
        heading for the river to dig clay,

    and there he was.

Facing me. Alone. Motionless. His
    head up,
        his eyes open
            but unseeing. His arms hung at
                his sides;
        it sent a shiver down my spine.

I know there's a thing called a stroke.
    A man can be struck down by a god;
        afterward, he can't speak.
        He loses his voice and the use of
            his limbs.
        I thought Sokrates was struck
            down.

I didn't stop to think: What could
  I do against a god?
I jumped off Phoibe
  and ran to him. "Sokrates!
  Sokrates!"

He didn't hear me.
  A slave doesn't touch a
   free man
  unless he's given orders.
  I yanked his hairy cloak,
   tugged on his hand;
  I jiggled it;
  he went on staring
   at the Invisible;
  he was like a corpse on its feet.
I screamed, *"Sokrates!"*

I thought of the river.
  I'd scoop up water,
   splash him, sprinkle him, drizzle it
   down his throat —
  I darted forward,
   stubbed my toe,
   fell —

"Rhaskos!"

His voice: deep and calm,
    and peaceful. I raced back to him.
    "You were standing there —
        just standing there, Sokrates!
        I couldn't make you hear me!"
All my anger, nursed for weeks,
        blown away
        like smoke sifted by the wind.

    "Rhaskos, I'm afraid I startled you.
    You caught me when my daimon was
            upon me.
        I have a daimon, you see, a spirit,
            a kind of sign;
        it comes to me, and I have to pay
            attention.
The rest of the world falls away. I've had it
        since childhood."

I know what a daimon is. He didn't have
  to tell me.
    A daimon's like a mule,
        half god
        and half something else.

"I know about daimons," I started
to say,
"but I've never met anyone —"
Then I stopped.
My thoughts began to spin
and wobble
like a pot caving in on the wheel.
I blurted out, "Is it a girl?"

Sokrates gazed at me in wonder.

You probably think I'm boasting. I'm not.
That very first day, when I drew the
square
he looked at me like that,
as if I were something
he didn't know a slave could be.

"I've missed you, Rhaskos.
One of the things I enjoy about you:
you never ask the same question
everyone else asks.
People have asked if my daimon is bad, or
good,
or why I should have one

when other people don't.
But no one ever asked if my daimon was a
girl.
The truth is, I've never seen it.
It's like a voice I can't hear.
I seem to be listening. I am full of
expectation,
but it never tells me what to do.
It stops me in my tracks.
It's a kind of holy obstacle.
I don't understand it,
but I believe it comes from
the gods,
so I obey it. But tell me:
Why did you think it
was female?"

"*I've* got one,"
I said, and I don't know why,
but that was funny,
so we laughed.
Again, my tongue was freed:
he was listening. I could tell him
things, even crazy things
because he was a little crazy.

I told him about you, Melisto.
He followed me to the river
　　so I could dig clay.
　　He sat on a sun-warmed rock
　　　　and listened while I worked. He
　　　　asked me questions.
We wondered if you were a god. He made
me laugh, because he said,
　　when someone talks about a kettle,
　　that's easy,
　　because every man means the
　　　same thing
　　　　when he talks about a kettle.
But when a man talks about something
important —
　　like *courage*, or *justice*, or the *gods*,
　　half the time,
　　　he can't say what he's talking
　　　about.
The higher and finer a thing is,
　　the less men can say what it *is*.
So it stands to reason that the gods —
　　who are higher and finer than
　　anything else —
　　　are almost impossible to talk about.

But he thought we ought to try.
He thought we should ask questions.
    There wasn't anything so holy
        that he wouldn't ask questions.

        "The gods are said to be beautiful:
            is your daimon beautiful?"

I stopped with my spade in my hand. "She
  isn't grown up yet.
    Her hair is mussed up,
      and she has scratches all over her legs.
But I want to look at her. Her face has
  meaning . . .
If I saw her clearly, it would be like finding
  out a secret.
    That's as close as I can get."

"And you're quite sure she's someone you
               never saw before?
In Thessaly, perhaps, when you lived with
               Menon?"

"No. I never saw her there.
I've wondered if she might be a ghost,
    but she's got nothing to do with me."

"I wouldn't be so quick to say that,
        Rhaskos.
        You say she follows you,
and she visited you in a god-sent dream.
        Ghost or goddess or daimon,
she must have *something* to do with you.
Could she be one of your ancestors,
                perhaps
            a Thracian girl?"

I wedged my spade in the earth. "She's
    dark-haired.
I think she's Greek. Her skin is sunburnt,
    with mosquito bites.
The more I think about it,
        the less she seems like a god.
Why would a god put up with mosquito
    bites?"

        "A very good point, Rhaskos. Why,
                indeed?"

"They wouldn't.
Even a daimon wouldn't.
She's not like a ghost. She doesn't look
    dead.

Not pale or sickly or shriveled.
    Though she has scars —"

      "Scars like yours? Thracian tattoos?"

Trust Sokrates to have a sharp eye!
    I looked at my arm —
    crusty with dried clay —
    it was hard to see the marks that
      disfigured me.
"My mother made those scars.
I don't know why she cut me."

        "I do. They're clan symbols,
        the marks of your tribe.
    I fought with Thracians in the war.
      Many of the men had tattoos.
    They're a sign of noble birth among
        the men.
Another Thracian could read them, and
      know your lineage,
      and where your people
        come from.
I haven't the knowledge. But I've seen two
      Thracians meet,
    examine each other's tattoos,

and throw down their swords. A warlike
              people, the Thracians;
    fine musicians and good horsemen."

I shook my head from side to side.
My head felt like a beehive. There were too
  many thoughts
      buzzing and zigzagging —
Shadow flashes of that darkest night,
      the soot-black stall,
      the weight of my mother on top of me,
        pinning me down,
        cutting me,
          rubbing my wounds with ash,
    shock
    blood
    disfigurement.

Now Sokrates was saying I was of noble blood.
    My darkness became light:
      My mother knew she would be
        sold —
      she knew we would be parted —
      she wanted to give me a name. A
        clan,

a birthright, proof that my
forebears were noble;
I was too young to understand,
so she carved the truth on my
skin.

"Rhaskos?"

(You no longer seemed real to me,
Melisto.
Even Sokrates wasn't real,
but I knew he was asking me a
question.
A slave answers when he's spoken to.)

"Her scars aren't like mine. They're beautiful,
patterned
like the veins in a leaf. I've never seen scars
like that.
She showed me a horse, in my dream —
a toy horse. I've been practicing . . ."
but I couldn't keep my mind on all
that.
"Are you sure about what you said?
That my tattoos are a sign of noble
blood?

You said you'd fought with the
Thracians —
      but they're barbarians. They killed
        those boys at Mycalessus —
      they killed everyone, even little boys,
      even women and farm animals.
      I don't want to be like that."

He looked past me so long, I wondered if
      his daimon had come back,
        but then he spoke.

                "Rhaskos, I've been to war.
I've watched men fight, and I've fought
                myself.
      To be a soldier requires a fierce spirit.
A kind of passion comes to a man during
                battle.
      A man fights, his fierce spirit roused,
        panic and fear on all sides —
        The best soldiers are like dogs;
          the fierce spirit obeys reason
as a dog obeys his master. But sometimes
      a man tastes blood and becomes a wolf.
I've seen men kill brutally and needlessly,

Greeks as well as Thracians.
Until men learn the love of wisdom —"

He didn't finish. Or maybe he did;
I'd stopped listening. Looking back,
I hate to think of all the times
when Sokrates spoke and I didn't
listen.

Somehow I was standing in the river.
I cupped a hand of foaming water
and rubbed the dirt from my scars.
They gleamed under the wetness.

"Rhaskos. Be your own master."

He'd said that before, the day he made me
angry.
This time I wasn't angry. I looked at him.
I felt the air against my teeth;
I must have been grinning like an
idiot.
I was Thracian, but I could be a dog, not a
wolf;
my scars were not shameful,
and my soul was mine to master.

574

2. The Akropolis

Phaistus was in the courtyard when I went
  back.
He frowned at me as I passed.

> "You take your sweet time."

I didn't answer back. I unloaded Phoibe,
  brushed the dirt from her coat.
I went into the shed
  and took out three figures:
    the pig,
    an owl,
    and my best horse so far.
I held them behind my back.
I stood before Phaistus and waited.

> "What is it?"

"I made these," I said. My voice came out
  strong.
"I thought we could sell them. We've never
  sold toys,
  but other potters do.
They wouldn't do it if they didn't make
  money.

You're always saying times are hard;

> and the best pots, the ones made for
> banquets,

>> don't sell. Not because they're not
>> good,

>> but because they cost too
>> much.

I thought, if we had cheap things
to sell,

>> we could make money. I even
>> thought of selling beads.

Black beads, with red designs —

I never saw beads like that, but they'd be
handsome.

The mistress could paint them. She's good
at fine work.

And I could make toys.

When times are hard, men don't buy gold
or silver,

>> but they might buy clay beads for
>> their wives . . .

>> or those women who bare their
>> breasts in the Agora,

> *they've* got money. Some of them
> have children.

Even when times are hard, people buy trinkets,
  if the trinkets are cheap enough:
  trinkets for women, and toys for children."

I held out the toys. "I made these.
I know I'm no good at the wheel —
    but look at these."

                    He took them.
              The pig made him smile.
            He said under his breath,
      "We could make a mold from this . . ."

I almost said, *What's a mold?*
That's how ignorant I was.
I didn't know what a mold was.

          But then he looked at the horse
                and frowned. "Pyrrhos —
            the neck, the shape of the head —
        the horse is good. But it won't survive the
                                kiln.
          It's too delicate. The ears will break off.

The body's too thick. There's moisture
        and air trapped inside.
        It'll burst. Or crack.
All the same, the modeling's good —
        you must have practiced.
And you're thinking. You're thinking about
        the business."
    He spoke those words as if they were
        praise.

I made up my mind to defend myself.
"Before, what you said —
    I wasn't wasting time.
I saw Sokrates in the middle of the road;
    he was in a trance, and I stopped.
I thought he might be struck down, or
    dying. He's my friend.
We talked, but I worked the whole time."

      He was back to looking at the pig.
        He said, under his breath,
        "He needs friends."
I was curious about why Sokrates,
    the wisest man in Athens, should
    need friends.

578

But we were talking, Phaistus and me,
and so far, he wasn't angry.

"I've heard that's how he acts when his
daimon is with him.
Some god talks to him, I don't know
which one.
Half of Athens knows about it. Some
people think he's lying,
but he's an honest man.
Once Athens was proud of him."

He was still studying my figures,
stroking them with his thumbs:
"These are good. It's not true, what you
said,
that you can't throw a pot on the wheel.
The wheel's difficult. You haven't caught
on to it yet.
I haven't given you time.
. . . The way you've shaped this head,
I've never seen a nobler head on a toy
horse.
It reminds me of the horses on the
Parthenon,
the sun god's horse . . ."

"I've never seen the Parthenon."

He looked up then. He'd told me
again and again
not to speak unless I was questioned,
but his look was a question: his eyes
narrowed.

"I've never been up the Akropolis.
The guards would see my hair;
they'd know I wasn't Greek;
they'd guess I was a slave.
They wouldn't let me in."

He spoke to the sky. "Mighty
Hephaistos."
He shuffled the toys against his chest
and stabbed one finger at me. "Stay
here."
Into the house he strode, shouting for
Zosima.
He came back in an instant,
empty-handed,
Zosima flip-flapping behind him,
Kranaos hobbling after her. "Look after
the shop.

I'm taking the boy up the hill. He's never
seen the temples.
By the deathless gods, he's never seen
anything!"

He struck out a hand like an oar,
beckoning, drawing me along in his wake,
and I followed him: through the streets
taking the shortest path upward.
"You have to see this, Pyrrhos.
You like horses; I'll show you a bronze
horse —
gigantic, with life-sized men crawling out
of his belly —
I'll show you a statue of Hermes, carved
by your friend Sokrates —
his father was a stonemason.
I'll show you statues and pictures and
pulleys and cranes!
I'll show you the gods, boy!
It's a strange thing; I've often wondered:
the gods made men, but few of us worth
looking at;
most men are plain as rats.
When men make the gods, we do them
justice!"

I ran to keep up with him,
      he was so eager. He made me stop
    and pick wildflowers: an offering for
       Athena.
We zigzagged up the hill. He told me how
  the temples were built,
      how oxen hoisted the great stones
       up that mighty hill.
It wasn't as hard for them as you might
  think.
The oxen climbed the hill unburdened;
     the stone blocks were on ropes, at the
      bottom of the slope;
    when the oxen reached the top,
      they circled round a post
       and dragged up the stones as they
       went downhill.
Phaistus knew some of the stone-carvers;
      some were slaves,
    but they were paid good wages, same
     as free men.
He explained to me about levers and
  cranes,
    and the guards let us pass at
      the gate.

Through the crowd
          I glimpsed sun-glazed bronze
          greeny-gold
          golden-brown
          the goddess Athena, taller than
              six men,
              grave and fierce,
              about to hurl her spear.
Phaistus had his hand on my shoulder.
          He pulled me back
              into a room with marble walls:
          a whole room full of pictures
          gaudy and gorgeous with color,
          each picture telling a story:
              Perseus, Odysseus, Akhilleus —
I could have stood before each one
and stared all afternoon.
          But beyond that room, there was
              more —
          so Phaistus steered me on.

You must have seen what I saw that day —
          stone that glows like honey through
              cream,

the triumphant gods,
       centaurs and caryatids —
the deep, rich colors;
       the shrines:
       red-lipped goddesses tickling the
          air with ribbons,
       boyish gods crowned with flowers.
The march of shining columns
       toward the sky;
          a march of glistening white and
             glorious blue;
          the dark inside the temple, the
             flicker of torches,
          and another Athena, taller than
             the first,
             her ivory skin so lambent
             she seemed to have no edge:
             it was as if I gazed at her
                through tears.

Then back outside,
          the sharp light,
          the fragrant smoke of temple fires,
          borne by the ceaseless wind.

I could look down on the Agora —
   Phaistus pointed out our house:
     the size of my smallest fingernail.
He showed me the giant Trojan horse
   and told me the whole story;
     how far-off Troy was taken
     and how the bronze was cast.
I'd never heard him talk so much.
His hands were restless,
   pointing,
     outlining,
   stroking the stones that were too high
    up to touch.
It was as if he'd made those temples.
   He came from Thebes,
     but up here, on the Akropolis,
     he was an Athenian;
   He belonged to the world
     of men who made things. He
     made me feel
      that I belonged, too. There I was
    with my Thracian tattoos on my arms,
    but in that hour, I was Athenian, a
     maker.

The sky was red with sunset
> when we came down the hill. I
> kept looking back;
> the stones of the temples were
> bathed in gold.
I had been changed. Sokrates once talked
about how beauty
> draws forth the soul. The things I had
> seen
> astonished me,
> dazzled and humbled me —
but also, there was Phaistus:
> we climbed that hill together,
and when we came down, we were
changed.

EXHIBIT 15

Klepsydra, terra-cotta, fifth century BCE.

This vessel was part of an ancient Greek water clock, holding approximately 6.7 quarts of water. The klepsydra was made up of two containers, as shown here. The top basin was filled with water, and the wax spigot at the lower rim was plugged with wax. When the wax plug was removed, the water trickled from the upper basin into the lower one, measuring a unit of time.

In Athenian law courts, speakers were allowed to speak from the time the wax was removed until the upper basin was empty and the lower basin was full.

Hermes Speaks

Klepsydra: a Greek word coming from
   kleptein, "to steal,"
     and *hydor* — that is, "water."
The Greeks knew that water is life,
     and time is a thief. Now, I am God of
     Thieves,
        and when I want to play fast and
         loose with time
        I do. Let's go splashing in the river
         of time!

Last time we met, it was autumn.
Now it's spring, more than a year later.
    The sun-chariot
        careens round the earth, while the
        wandering planets

somersault in circles, panting to
keep pace —
What? You think the earth goes racing
round the sun?
So does Aristarchus (another Greek!) —
but he hasn't been born yet.
Give us another hundred years to sort out
the solar system.
Give us Time, that best of teachers!
Oh, Time will steal from *you*, my
mortal child,
will trickle away, liquidate your
precious hours —
a grave situation in more ways
than one.
Yet time brings the spring,
gilds the green apple and ripens
the grape.
It's not all bad.

Let's take a tour around the city. I'll bring
you up to speed.
Sweet spring in Athens, and not yet
dawn!
Windflower, clover, and violets!

591

Rhaskos is curled up in the shed, sleeping
like a cat.

If we were to brush a finger over his
jaw,

we'd find it softly bristled, like a
sage leaf.

He's entered his teens. He's not
much taller,

but his muscles are well formed.
Strong hands.

To make pots is to work hard.

Slumped against the wall is Melisto;

she's not looking well. Of course,
she's been dead a while,

which is unwholesome,

but even allowing for that,

her shade is sickly.

To Rhaskos, she's like a shadow on the
retina;

he's learned to see around her.

He's lost interest in why she's there to
haunt him.

It's hard on her. Haunting is taxing for a
ghost;

being ignored makes it worse. She's
not where she belongs;
I've offered to escort her
downstairs,
but she's obstinate. No, she's
cursed,
and she'll stay cursed
until she does what she's bound
to do.

Let's move on to something cheerful:
there's Phoibe,
and nuzzling at her flank
is a little hinny — half donkey,
half horse.
Phoibe escaped from the shed one night
to tryst with a rich man's stallion;
twelve months later: the hinny!
Phaistus is thrilled. Something he
can sell,
and he didn't have to work for it.
Phaistus is lying awake, poor man,
worrying. The city is poor;
the toys were too cheap to make a
profit.

The beads were a success, but a man
can't live off beads.
He's always in a lather,
fretting over money,
the fear of failing his wife,
the fear of losing his freedom.
He's a good man, Phaistus,
but not amusing.

Even less amusing is Kranaos,
who is snoring. Openmouthed, wet-
sounding snores,
with pauses in between,
as if he might
stop
breathing.   Wait!
Was that it? Is he gone?

No such luck. Oh well! It won't be long
before I lead him off to
the House of Hades.
Half of him's gone already:
that is, his mind.
He was struck down by a god
and has guzzled the waters of Lethe.

594

Weak and witless, he tries to tend the kiln.
his memory is riddled with holes.
The pots are dull and smoky.
He kept his secrets about the kiln. Now
they're lost to Time,
and the kiln god is disgruntled.
It's curious. Kranaos was a slave,
and — between you and me — a
pill,
neither good nor amusing,
yet he is sheltered, fed,
missed by the Kiln God,
respected by Phaistus,
fussed over by Zosima.
An unexpected ending to a long
hard life.

Enough about him. Let's follow Zosima,
who's on her way to the fountain house;
she stops to puke in the bushes. Ick.
She has morning sickness
but you think she minds?
Hardly.
Every time she loses her breakfast
she chants a hymn to the gods.

She gazes at the courtyard through a veil
of joy: There's the home
where she lives with her beloved;
there's the shed
where Rhaskos sleeps —
Rhaskos, whom she loves. And
she loves the little hinny;
she's silly over baby animals;
she's tempted to go inside
to fondle its ears. Instead, she
lifts her water jar
and makes her way through the streets,
stopping for a funeral procession.
(That's a Greek thing: you have
your weddings at night,
your funerals before dawn.)
She tries to feel sad, because someone is
dead;
she murmurs a prayer to wise
Persephone,
but her lips keep curving upward.

She reaches the fountain house
and greets the other women. She
finds her dearest friend

and whispers her happy news. The
friend whirls to face her;
they embrace,
rock
(women always rock when they
hug),
lean back, throw out their hands,
embrace again. Other
women encircle them,
lose their place in line:
whispering, squealing,
laughing.
It's a pretty sight:
the women in their pleated robes,
chattering, relaxed, their veils
slipping.
The water foams and chuckles;
the jars are overflowing.
Soon Dawn will daub the sky with finger
paints,
watercolor tints of saffron and
rose;
the women will sashay home,
balancing their jars.

I wouldn't mind following. I like
women. Love gossip;
but we have to get back.
I have to take old Markos down to hell.

Remember that funeral parade? Markos
was the man who died.
Who? you say, and there's life for you:
someone turns up his toes, and
someone else says, *Who?*
The death of Markos is key to our story.
Markos was a citizen, protector to
Phaistus.
An ex-slave must have a citizen to
protect him. That's the law.
Without a protector, the freedman is at
risk.

And while we're talking of matters
at risk . . .
let's pause a moment here,
in the Agora. This is the place where
a man we know,
a man I find both good and amusing,

will stand trial. He will be accused
    of corrupting the young
    and refusing to honor the gods.
Here he will defend himself
    while the klepsydra measures out his
      words;
    here his time will trickle away
      from one clay bowl to another.

ATHENA SPEAKS

Now is the trial of Sokrates: philosopher,
seeker of wisdom.
Twenty-four-hundred-odd years have gone by:
the jury's still out.
Was the man guilty?
or was it a blunder, a crime against justice?
I, Athena, the guardian of Athens, bore
witness that day.

First was the sacrifice,
brought to the table: a ram without blemish,
healthy, immaculate,
worthy to offer the unfading gods.
Here comes the magistrate, hiding the knife:
a slice to the windpipe:

600

Blood on the table. The magistrate washes his hands in the blood.

Raising his fingers, he calls on the gods of divine law and custom.

Five hundred jurors are sworn to uphold the law of the land.

RHASKOS AND PHAISTUS

"There's something I have to tell you — "

I stared at Phaistus —
I was making the ram's head
        — that's a way of wedging clay.
You rock the clay, lifting and folding;
        it coils into spirals, like a ram's horn.

Something I have to tell you.
Who says that to a slave?
When someone says, *I have to tell you*,
        it means there's bad news,
        and they don't want to tell it.
Who minds if a slave hears bad news?
I knew old Markos was dead and Phaistus
    was afraid.

602

Without a protector, he could be hauled off to court
     and stripped of his goods.
     He and Zosima spoke of leaving Athens,
     selling Phoibe and her foal,
       the tools and the stock —
They hadn't talked of selling me. Yet.
That didn't mean they wouldn't do it.

     "It's about your friend Sokrates."

My heart jerked
     like the leap of a toad:
Sokrates was old, but he couldn't be dead.

       "He's in the Agora.
He's been accused of crimes against the city.
     He'll stand trial this afternoon.
     I thought you ought to know."

"What crimes?" Who could accuse Sokrates?
He'd fought for Athens in the war.
He was poor, but he was a citizen —
He wasn't a slave, that can be punished for nothing.

ATHENA SPEAKS

ᓄᒥᓚᓄᒥᓚᓄᒥᓚᓄᒥᓚᓄᒥᓚ

Spectators gather. The water clock trickles.
Court is in session.
The plaintiffs speak first, accusing Sokrates .
. .
Three hours pass.
The men on the benches shift uneasily,
weighing the evidence.
The slave boy fills the klepsydra again:
Sokrates may speak.

SOKRATES DEFENDS HIMSELF

Gentlemen of Athens, these men who have accused me — I don't know what they've made you think. They were so persuasive, I almost forgot who I was. There's just one problem. Scarcely a word they said was true.

One of their worst lies was this: they said I was a terribly clever speaker, so I might be able to trick you. It's a shameless lie, because the minute I open my mouth, you'll find me out. I'm not clever with words at all, unless you call it clever when a man is able to speak the truth.

I will tell you the whole truth. But by Zeus, it won't be in flowery words. I'm seventy years old, and I've never appeared in a court of law. So pay no attention to how I speak. Pay attention to what I say: whether or not it's the truth.

605

RHASKOS AND PHAISTUS

Phaistus glowered at the doorway.

He was always on the lookout for a
customer,

    but not this time. He went and shut
    the door.

      "They say he doesn't believe in the
             gods —
      not the city's gods: not the Twelve.
          It's a serious charge."

"That's not true! He believes in the gods.

He just likes to ask questions about
them."

          "That's bad enough.

It's a citizen's duty to honor the gods,
   not gossip about them.
  And that's not the only charge.
They say he corrupts the young men of
      Athens."

"Corrupts?" I didn't know the word.
It hung in the air,
  a spider dangling from a hidden
   thread.

   "That he makes them worse, with his
      teaching.
   He leads his pupils into evil ways."

"That's not true! He teaches me, and I'm
  not corrupted!
He talks to me about ἀρετή, about my
  soul.
He taught me, just because I'm a slave,
  I don't have to be slavish!
He makes me ashamed to tell lies. How
  can that be corrupt?
He has ἀρετή! And he's the wisest man in
  Athens!"

SOKRATES DEFENDS HIMSELF

꧅꧅꧅꧅꧅꧅꧅꧅꧅꧅꧅

Now, hear me out! I have a reputation for being wise. What kind of wisdom? Human wisdom, I suppose. And here is my witness: the god Apollo and his Oracle at Delphi. But what the priestess at Delphi said was not that I am wise, but that there was no one wiser.

When I heard about this, I thought, *Why does the Oracle speak in riddles? How can there be no man wiser than Sokrates?* Because I am truly aware that I don't know anything, great or small.

608

Rhaskos and Phaistus

— I was almost yelling at Phaistus.
Menon would have slapped my face.

"Listen to me, Pyrrhos. I've nothing
against Sokrates.
I know he's been a friend to you; you love
him like a father —
but he's made fools of powerful men,
and they hate him."

"What powerful men? Who are they?"

"A man named Meletus, a second-rate
poet —
I've seen him; he's got a nose like a beak.
And Lycon, he's a skilled speaker. But
they're only tools.

It's Anytus who hates Sokrates most.
                    Sokrates taught his son,
and the boy rebelled against his father.
Anytus has hated him for years. It's not
                         just Anytus —
        The city remembers Alkibiades."

Anytus was Menon's friend.
I remembered the day I drew the
   square —
        he was there that day. He spoke to
          Sokrates —
        there was a threat in his voice.
He didn't like Sokrates, even then.

There was another name, one I hadn't
   heard.
"Who was Alkibiades?"

        "A rich man, and a general. He's
                    dead now,
     but Sokrates loved him. That's nothing;
        all Athens fawned over Alkibiades.
           Myself, I favor women,
       but I never saw a man so beautiful

or so false. Alkibiades betrayed this city,
joined forces with the Spartans,
fought with our enemies,
yes, and dishonored the gods!
He and Sokrates were as different as fire
and water,
but they were thick as thieves.
He was corrupt. I believe Sokrates
tried to teach him self-control,
but no one could teach wisdom to that
man.
Some people still blame Sokrates."

"That's not fair!"

"I never said it was.
But over the years he's become a nuisance.
Sokrates asks too many questions,
and he asks them of powerful men.
Only a fool pokes a hornet's nest."

SOKRATES DEFENDS HIMSELF

I've spent my whole life in search of wisdom. At first, I sought out statesmen and sages so that I could learn from them, but when I questioned them closely, I found that they didn't know what they were talking about. They seemed wise to other people — and they seemed wise to themselves! But they weren't. I came away from them thinking that in one way at least, I was better off than they were: I *knew* I knew nothing.

I realized with alarm that my questions were making me unpopular. But I had to persist in my search for truth. The lover must follow the beloved.

My hunt for wisdom next led me to question the poets: great poets such as

612

Homer are known to be wise. But when I questioned the poets, I discovered that their poems were given to them by the gods. They were like seers: when they were chanting and composing their verses, they were inspired. But once they stopped singing, the god left them, and they couldn't explain their own work. They didn't know anything. *But they thought they did!*

Then I went to the craftsmen. I don't know how to make a shoe, or glaze a pot, and these men did — and they understood the things they knew. When I pressed them, they could answer my questions! But when it came to larger matters — the most important things in life — they were as ignorant as I am, and they didn't know it. Because they understood shoes, or pots, or armor, they believed themselves wise, and in this they were mistaken.

So it seems to me that only the god is wise. And what the Oracle was saying is: *The wisest of you human beings is the one who, like Sokrates, has recognized that he is worthless when it comes to wisdom.*

RHASKOS AND PHAISTUS

"He's not a fool. He's interesting. He
   makes me laugh.
He doesn't brag about the things he knows
—
   he's always saying what he *doesn't* know!
Even though he has a daimon —"

      "That's another thing. A daimon.
      Other men don't have daimons.
   You pray to the gods, and you sacrifice;
         you go to the festivals;
      you bury your dead with honor;
         you obey the law;
  you believe what other men believe.
That's enough. If a man has a daimon,
   he ought to keep it to himself."

SOKRATES DEFENDS HIMSELF

ᛒᚢᚱᛊᚢᚱᛊᚢᚱᛊᚢᚱᛊᚢᚱᛊᚢᚱᛊᚢᚱᛊ

I also stand accused of not recognizing the gods of the city, but of believing in my own daimon instead. It is true I have a daimon, a spirit that guides me. But such spirits are born of the gods. To say I believe in my daimon, but don't believe in the gods, is like saying that a man believes in mules, but not in donkeys or horses.

Over the years, I've become the target of hostility, and hostility of a bitter and lasting kind. Even so, I try to find wisdom and to seek out ἀρετή. I believe the god commands me to seek these things — so I go all over the city, trying to find someone who is wise. If I find someone who thinks he knows something when he doesn't, I point it out.

Now, young men — especially rich young men, because they have time on their hands — like to follow me about and listen to me ask questions. They are delighted when I point out that someone is not as wise as he thinks he is, and they try to imitate me. This leads other people to say I corrupt the young.

RHASKOS AND PHAISTUS

"What will happen if the jury finds him
guilty?"

"They may not find him guilty."

"But what —"

"I won't lie to you. The charges are
serious.
They could put him to
death.
More likely, he'll have to pay a fine. They
might exile him,
strip him of his citizen's rights and make
him leave the city."

617

I sank my fist into the clay. Pounded it.
It was shameful for a man to lose his
    rights,
        and Sokrates had no money to pay a
            fine —
        he'd shared his bread with me, but he
            was poor.
As for his death —
        I shoved the table away from me.
        Made for the door —
Phaistus snatched me back.

        "I thought it might come to this —
            you wanting to rush off to the
                Agora
            and upset the trial! Forget it.
    You have to be called to testify in court,
        and nobody's called for you. Nobody
            wants your opinion,
            and you're lucky they don't.
    No court accepts the word of a slave
        unless he's been tortured first;
        that guarantees he'll tell the truth.
            You don't want that, do you?"

My heart was in my mouth. I *had* meant
    to run outside,
        push my way through the crowd until
        I found him.
I wanted to shout out his innocence,
        to deafen the jury, awaken the gods!
Now I was afraid. Sometimes, near the
    prison,
        they lashed men to planks, cruelly
        tight.
They tossed them in pits and left them
    to die.
I kept away from that place,
        but I heard them screaming.

                "Other men will help him, Pyrrhos.
                    Rich men. It's beyond you.
                        You're still a boy.
                    You and me, we're little people.
                If we keep our heads down, and our
                            mouths shut,
                we might make it through hard times.
                The glory days of Athens are over.
                The good times were forty, fifty
                            years ago —

619

Sokrates can remember those days.
People laughed at him,
but they liked hearing him ask his
questions;
even his enemies thought he was
harmless.
"Since then we've suffered nigh on thirty
years of war,
plague,
defeat.
We lost our democracy to tyrants. Twice.
We've lost the Long Walls that kept us
safe.
Even the rich have less, and the poor are
poorer.
Everyone's afraid,
and worn out,
and there's Sokrates, still asking
questions.
It no longer seems harmless. He ought to
shut up,
but he won't. He can't be silenced.
It doesn't matter whether the charges are
true or false.

If they want to get rid of him, they will."

I was back at the table.

I don't know whether Phaistus led me
 there,

> or shoved me, or tugged me,

> but there I was, with my belly against
> the table's edge,

> and there was the clay, with the deep
> hollows

>> where my knuckles had punched.

I slid one hand under the clay

> and flipped it, smothering the air
> bubbles.

>>> "Listen to me, Pyrrhos!
>>> Worse may not come to worst.
>> Sokrates has rich men on his side,
>>> aristocrats like Plato and Krito.
>> He's a good speaker. He'll defend
>>>> himself.
> If all else fails, they'll bring in the family:
> go for pity. A weeping wife to touch the
>>>> jury's heart,
> or children, pleading not to be orphaned.

That kind of thing goes over well.

The point is, you have to go back to work.
It's not your battle to fight."

SOKRATES DEFENDS HIMSELF

꧁ꤢꤢꤢꤢꤢꤢ꧂

I don't think a long speech is necessary to point out that I'm innocent of these charges. But it is true that over the years, many men have come to hate me. This kind of hatred has doomed other good men. If I'm convicted, I won't be the last.

So now perhaps someone will say, *Aren't you ashamed, Sokrates, to have devoted your life to asking questions that may get you killed?* And here's my answer: When someone takes a stand, he has to hold his ground and face the danger. When I fought in the battles of Potidaea and Amphipolis and Delion, I held my ground and obeyed my commanders. And when the god tells me to live a life in pursuit of wisdom, questioning myself and others, I cannot desert my post. Th

And when we fear death, gentlemen, once again we are thinking we know something we don't know. Death may be the greatest good we can imagine. I must not disobey the god — an act that I know to be disgraceful — in order to escape death, which might be something good.

Gentlemen of Athens, I salute you, and I am your friend. But as long as I draw breath, I will listen to the god rather than to you. If you release me, I will go on saying the things I say, and asking the questions I ask.

You are Athenian, and your city is the greatest and most famous in the world. But aren't you ashamed when you worry about having as much money as possible, and piling up glories and honors, instead of making your soul the best that it can be? This is what I say to anyone I meet: the god commands me to persuade you not to put the care of your bodies above the care for your soul.

Order please, gentlemen! I am about to say something that will raise a storm of protest! *If you kill me, you will harm yourselves more than you harm me.* Meletus and Anytus can't harm me. The law of the god doesn't permit a better man to be harmed by a worse one. They can kill me, of course, but what they are doing is damaging to their souls: they are trying to kill an innocent man.

I'm not speaking in my own defense. I'm defending you, so you won't make a mistake by killing me. Athens is like a large, noble horse — a horse that is lazy and needs to be awakened by a horsefly. I'm the fly. The god placed me in this city to wake you up and land on top of you all day long. But perhaps you find me irritating: you'll finish me off with a single swat and try to spend the rest of your lives asleep.

If you don't know whether I really am a gift to the city, here's how you can tell. I am always coming up to you, like a father or an older brother, and reminding you to concern yourself with ἀρετή. If I got something out of this — if I took money for it — this would make sense for me. But here is my witness: my poverty.

Why is it that some people enjoy spending time with me? They enjoy listening when people who think they're wise are proved to be no such thing. It has its amusing moments. But I've been commanded to ask these questions by the god, who has come to me in oracles and dreams.

Well, then, gentlemen, that's all I have to say. At this point, most men bring in their family to shed tears and produce as much pity as they can. I won't do this, even though I am in danger of being put to death. I was not born from oak or stone, as Homer says; I have sons: two young children, and a youth. But I won't have them come here to plead for me, and I won't beg you to change your votes.

Why not? Justice seems to me to demand not that I beg, but that I tell the truth. I leave it to you and to the god to judge my case.

Athena Speaks

Five hundred men with ballots in hands arise
from the benches.
Stretching and muttering, aching from
sitting and listening so long.
Forming a line, they pass between two
massive urns:
one wooden, one bronze,
dropping their ballots and casting their votes
sealing his fate.

Rhaskos and Phaistus

◲◱◲◱◲◱◲◱◲◱◲◱◲◱

"How long will it take?"

"Before they decide? Only the
gods know.
No trial lasts longer than a day,
I know that.
Simon the cobbler went to
watch the trial;
he's friends with Sokrates.
I asked him to come by afterward
and let us know."
He picked up a lump of clay
and stepped sideways, facing me,
each of us at opposite sides of the table.
He bent forward, starting a ram's head.

We worked together in the same rhythm,
> folding and kneading and rocking the
> clay.

It was slave's work, and beneath him,
> but he kept at it,
> finishing each cylinder,
> tapping the ram's nose against the
> table,
> setting the cylinders in rows.

I knew why he stayed, and I was grateful.

ATHENA SPEAKS

*Two hundred and eighty to two hundred
twenty —
he's guilty.
Now once again the philosopher speaks:
it is his right.
And also his risk: to suggest his own
punishment;
What shall it be?
Too harsh and he'll suffer, too light
and he's likely to madden the crowd —
Catcalls and boos. He raises his hands.
Hoarsely he speaks:*

Sokrates Suggests His Punishment

I am not angered, gentlemen of Athens, by what has happened: you have found me guilty. Actually, I'm amazed that the vote was so close. If just thirty votes had gone the other way, I would have been set free.

So what penalty do I deserve? Something good, gentlemen of Athens; a punishment that would fit the crime.

As you know, gentlemen, there is a banquet hall in the heart of the city, and famous Athenians — Olympic athletes and so on — are privileged to dine there for free. Most of these men are rich men, and don't need free meals, but I do. Why shouldn't I have my meals free, and sit in a place of honor? That would be justice: that's the punishment I propose for myself. I know I have done no injustice to any man. So I'm not going to treat myself unjustly and say I deserve some harmful penalty.

No doubt someone will say, *Sokrates, can't you please just shut up and mind your own business?* This is the hardest thing to make you understand. I can't shut up. It would be disobedient to the god to mind my own business. The greatest good for a human being is to talk about ἀρετή, to ask questions and examine. A life without examination is not worth living.

As far as fines go, I could perhaps afford a hundred drachmas. My friends here — Plato and Krito, Kritobolus and Apollodorus — are willing to spend thirty times as much to set me free. So I propose three thousand drachmas as a fine; they have promised to pay for my freedom.

ATHENA SPEAKS

Shameless!
a hiss from the crowd,
a ripple of indignation:
This time the old man's gone too far.
he'll pay for his crimes.
Arrogant! what kind of thinker can equal the
worth of an athlete?
Growing and swelling, the wrath of the mob:
Sokrates must die.

SOKRATES SPEAKS

So I am to die. You haven't gained much, gentlemen. I am seventy years old; I would soon have died without your help. On top of that, you will be found guilty of killing Sokrates, a wise man.

My daimon, who often stops me from doing what I mean to do, said nothing when I came here this morning. It didn't stop me from saying the things I've said. So I think that probably what has happened is a good thing, and death may be something good. Either death is like not existing at all, or it is a change, a migration of the soul.

Now if death is like sleep without dreaming, death will be an unspeakable gain. For eternity will be like a single night.

But if to die is to go somewhere else, and all the dead exist in that place, what greater good could there be than to join them? It would be amazing to meet with the heroes of old and talk to them. What would I give to question Agamemnon, who led his vast army into Troy? or Odysseus? or countless other men and women of fame? It would be almost too much happiness to meet them.

At any rate, in the House of Hades, they don't kill people for asking questions.

You, too, gentlemen, must look forward to death. Be of good hope. Fix your mind on this one belief: Nothing can harm a good man, whether living or dead. Nor are his affairs neglected by the god.

I bear no grudge against those who have condemned me. Only grant me one favor. When my sons are grown, if they put money or anything else before goodness, question them! Rebuke them and remind them of their souls!

But now it is time to depart, I to die, and you to live. Which is better, only the god knows.

EXHIBIT 16

Votive offering to Asklepios, terra-cotta, fourth century BCE, found on the southwest slope of the Akropolis.

Asklepios may have been a real person who lived around 1200 BCE and practiced medicine. By the time of Sokrates, Asklepios was considered the son of Apollo and had risen to the status of a god. He was able to heal the sick and even to bring the dead back to life.

The person who gave this clay brick to the temple evidently suffered from an eye ailment. Temples to Asklepios are full of clay representations of body parts: legs, hands, breasts, and internal organs. Many are carved with inscriptions that praise the god for his healing powers.

On his deathbed, the philosopher Sokrates instructed his friend Krito to sacrifice a white cockerel to Asklepios. The sacrifice of a rooster was often performed after an act of healing.

RHASKOS SPEAKS

꙰ᔕᒪᒥᕲᔕᒪᒥᕲᔕᒪᒥᕲᔕᒪᒥᕲᔕᒪᒥᕲ

They didn't kill him for a month.

Every year a ship is sent to Delos
    bearing seven youths and seven maidens,
      in memory of the fourteen
        Athenians
    who were sent to feed the
      cannibal Minotaur.
Theseus, Prince of Athens,
    threaded the maze and
    slaughtered the monster.
His ship is still docked in the harbor. It's
ancient,
    patched so often down the years,
    there's not a splinter of the old
    wood left.

But once a year, the ship is crowned with
   flowers
         and sets sail for Delos.
From the time the garlands of spring
   flowers
            are lashed to the mast
            to the day when the ship comes
               back,
            it's a holy time. The city has to be
               pure.
No bloodshed. No man, no matter how
   guilty, is put to death.

So Sokrates was in prison till the ship
   came back.
When the time came, he'd drink hemlock:
            a poison that turns a man to stone
            and stops his breath.
It was better than what might have been.
He could have been strapped to a plank,
      garroted, trapped in a pit.

Phaistus was good to me. He told me I
   could visit the prison.
         I didn't want to. I wished Phaistus

would forbid me to go —
though it wouldn't have stopped
me.
I'd have still gone. But I was afraid to
be with a man
who was doomed to die.
The idea made my heart race and my hair
rise up,
as if death might be catching.

Zosima gave me a new-baked loaf;
it wasn't very big, but it was hot.
The jailer let me in. I wasn't the only one
who'd come.
Sokrates sat among his friends —
he was sitting on a bed. Someone
must have brought it there
and set it up. His legs were shackled.
He sat with a lyre across his knees.
I didn't know he played the lyre.

I felt like a fool, standing there with
my loaf;
he didn't see me right away,
but when he did —

"Rhaskos! Come and serve as my judge;
　　　　I've been setting verses to music,
　　　　　　a fable of Aesop.
　　　　　　　See what you think!"

I didn't know what to think.
He seemed merry. He plucked the lyre,
　and I tried to listen.
The song was about the King of the
　Apes —
　　　　who tore a man to pieces for telling
　　　　　the truth.
Sokrates sang it lustily, though his voice
　was scratchy;
　　　　　the tune was one he'd made up
　　　　　himself.

　　　　　　"So, Rhaskos! what do you think
　　　　　　　of my music?
I've sometimes heard a voice inside me
　　　　　　　　whisper
　　　　that I ought to practice the arts.
　　　　　I've never worried about it,
　　　　because what art is greater than
　　　　　　　philosophy?
But now that I'm about to die, I see;

I ought to have spent more time
making music.
I must go on learning, even as I grow old —
Do you like my song?"

"I don't know, Sokrates.
I don't know much about music.
It sounds all right to me."

The men laughed. I felt myself get red.

"You're an honest fellow, Rhaskos,
not a flatterer. Stay that way.
I remember the first day we met,
you looked at me and said, 'Honestly,
Sokrates, I don't know.'
I knew right then I liked you."

He remembered —
but that was the last time he spoke to
me that day.
His grown-up friends were there, and
they'd brought wine.
They talked about music,
passed the lyre back and forth,
singing verses by Homer —

643

I edged over; left my loaf on the bed.

I muttered that I had to go to work.

I was luckier the second time.

He was alone, asleep.

Lying flat, he looked old and maybe sick,
clutching his cloak like a blanket;
his skin was blotched and purplish,
ribbed and damp.
He had crusts of yellow crud
in the corners of his mouth.
He shifted in his sleep, squirmed
against his shackles,
grumbled;
then his eyes opened
and they were clear.

"Rhaskos. My friend."

That was the best moment.

"Does your master know you're here?"

"He said I could come."

"Good."

He sat up and folded his cloak around his
shoulders;

> he looked more like himself then,

>> not like a sick man under a
>> blanket.

He eased his legs over the side of the bed,

> rubbed his thighs, and grunted a little.

His ankles had welts where the shackles
chafed.

I pointed. "Do they hurt?"

> "What? Oh, those. They're not too bad.

>> Remember what I told you,
>> Rhaskos —

> Men view pain as the greatest of evils,
> but they are mistaken. The body feels a

>> sharp pain,

> or an acute pleasure, and mistakes those

>> feelings for reality.

> Remember: pleasure is not the same as

>> goodness,

>> and the pain I suffer is no great evil."

I racked my brains for something to say.
"I don't have any food this time.
> No loaf."

645

"Just as well. My kind friends bring too
much —
savories and treats, things I can't
digest.
I'm not used to all that food,
it's charming of them, of course.
My wife comes every day.
She brings what I'm used to: plain
bread or porridge.
It's good of her to come.
All this" — he spread his hands,
wiggled his toes to show off his
shackles —
"upsets her.
She's fond of me in her own way."

He looked at me sideways, a glint in
his eye.
"Have you come to hear
me sing?"

"No." I said it too fast. I didn't want to
hear him sing.
All I could think of was that he was going
to die.

At last I said, "There's a story you used to
   tell —
        I heard part of it once, in the Agora.
            I couldn't stop to listen. I never
                heard the end.
It was about a cave.
        There were some men trapped inside
            a cave . . .
        What happened? Did they ever get out?"

            "Ah, Rhaskos! that wasn't a story.
        It's an idea I have, a metaphor:
            Imagine a group of men,
                shackled — as I am now —
            held captive, inside a cave —"

"Like the miners in the silver mines?"
That was how I'd imagined them:
        trapped men buried alive in the dark.
"Who caught them and chained them up?
Were they slaves?"

            "No, no, they weren't slaves!
        It isn't a true story. It isn't a story at all.
        I wonder what you'll make of it. Listen.

"Suppose there were a cave —
and the people inside spent their whole
lives there.
They'd never seen the sun or the sky;
They were shackled, held in place,
so they always faced the
back wall;
and behind them was a fire —"

"Close enough to burn them?"

"No. Behind them, but at a distance.
Sometimes animals and men
passed between the fire and the
people in the cave,
casting shadows on the wall.
Suppose you were there, Rhaskos —
Suppose you stared straight ahead and saw
the shadows move.
Suppose you saw the shadow of a horse,
for example.
What would you think?"

"I'd be thinking of how to get out.
I'd be worried about starving to death."

"No, no! Suppose you had plenty
of food;
suppose you were used to the cave.
Remember, you've spent your
whole life there;
you'd be used to the dark.
From time to time, you'd see those passing
shadows.
What would you think
of them?"

He opened his eyes very wide —
he often did that when he asked a
question.
I clasped my knees and tried to think.
It flashed through my mind: this might be
the last chance we had
to speak together. I wanted to
tell him
how much it meant, the way he
talked to me,
and didn't make me feel stupid.
There was so much I wanted to say,
I felt the pressure of those words
inside my throat.

At the same time, there was a picture in
   my mind:
      that dark cave
         and the restless shadows, fire-lit.

"I'd be curious. I'd want to know what
   made the shadows —"

                              "Would you?"

I thought harder, deeper. "No . . .
Maybe I *wouldn't* be!
      I'd just see shapes —
         they'd be like painted designs,
            coming and going.
      They wouldn't have anything to do
         with me.
      They wouldn't seem real. I might
         think they were spirits . . .
         If I'd spent my whole life
            underground —
         if I'd never seen the sun —
      I might not know what a shadow
         was —
      I wouldn't know a shadow was a
         shadow!"

He was nodding, smiling.
I felt the familiar excitement.
I wasn't stupid. He was pleased with me.
"And what if one day you were
unshackled
and dragged toward the light?
Past the fire, out into the blazing sun?"

"I'd like that."

"Would you? Or would your
eyes sting,
would you plunge and kick and try to get
back underground?"
He flapped his hands to mimic me
kicking.

I laughed. "I'd still want to get out!
Maybe the sun would blind me at first;
my eyes would water —
I might like moonlight better than
the sun,
nighttime better than day —
but in time, my eyes would
get strong.

I'd start to see real things. Maybe one day
   I'd see a horse —
      a *real* horse —
        and I'd think, I've seen that shape
          before.
That noble head, the mane flowing like
   water —"

    "But this time, you'd see more than the
                       shadow;
                you'd see strength
           and depth, and color,
              and power."

"I'd see a *real* horse! I'd be crazy with
   wonder!
      Maybe later, I could ride it —
You can't ride a shadow."

                   "No, you can't.
         You imagine my story well."

"Then it's a story? But where's the
   ending?
     A story is supposed to have an
      ending."

"Perhaps you'll find the ending one day.
Perhaps I will. Soon.
Perhaps I've been living in a
shadow-world,
and I'll come to see the real world.
Wisdom —
truth —
absolute beauty.
I've been waiting and searching
all my life."

I wanted to shake him.
"You sound like you're looking forward to
death!
Aren't you even angry?"

"What, because I have to die?
Rhaskos, I'm seventy years old.
I should be a fool, pitying myself
because at long last, I have to die.
They say hemlock's quick.
I won't go blind, or deaf,
or forgetful, as some old men do.
There isn't time."

There *wasn't* any more time, because just
  then, the jailer came in,

> with a woman and a boy. The boy
> was sturdy,

>> broad-nosed, older than me.

I thought he was one of Sokrates's pupils,

> but he stared at me, unsmiling;

>> I stared unsmiling back. He didn't
>> like me being there,

>>> the same way I didn't like him
>>> being there.

He didn't want to share his father.

That's how I knew who he was.

The woman kept her veil close;

> only her eyes showed: a glance like a
> hawk's.

She didn't come right out and say, *What
  are you doing here?*

> *He's no kin of yours! Get out!* She
> didn't have to.

I said, "I have to go," and I went.

The last time I saw him, I saw him die.

The sun was setting. It was crowded in the
  cell.

I stood with my heels against the wall.
I wasn't sure he knew I was there.

    Every minute that passed,
    I wanted more to leave;
    I clenched my hands and held my place.

He sent his wife home. She sobbed and
  clawed her face.
One of his friends,

    a beautiful young man named
      Apollodorus,

    knelt before him crying. He never
      stopped.

Sokrates reached down

    and gathered up the young man's
      hair,

    running his hand through the curls,

      the way you finger-comb a horse's
      mane.

He chided Apollodorus for weeping,

    but I don't think he minded.

He talked about the soul with his friends.
  He insisted

    that death was freedom for the soul.

He was sure he had nothing to fear. To die
is to come alive again.
He argued about it. He *proved* it.

Then the poison came.
The jailer who brought the cup was in
tears.
Sokrates was touched.

I didn't cry. I felt as if there were a bird
caught in my throat
something thrashed and flapped
and shrieked inside me
but it couldn't get out.

The jailer unlocked Sokrates's shackles, so
he could have a bath.
Sokrates wanted to save the women
the trouble of washing his corpse.
Or maybe he was ashamed. Here in
prison,
he didn't have the wind
to blow the stink off him. He was
gamier than usual.
Either way, it was lucky for the women.

He wasn't gone long. He came back clean,
    reached for the jailer's cup,
      and drained it. He'd had to pay for
      the poison himself;
        that's the law. It cost him ten
        drachmas.
Someone asked him how he wanted to be
  buried,
    and his face lit up with mischief.

              "Any way you like!
            if you can catch me!
            if I don't slip through
                your fingers!"

He did slip through our fingers —
That was how I felt. The poison was
  quick.
After he drank it,
    he circled the room — that's what the
    jailer told him to do.
    I backed up close to the wall —
His friends walked with him,
    around and around;
    he circumnavigated the room.

I thought our eyes met once
but his were glazed.
I knew he was in pain,
    private,
        all-absorbing.

Hemlock kills you from the bottom up,
We watched as his gait became stiff.
He no longer strode, but stumped;
    he was still asking questions as he
        lurched round the room.
The jailer told him to lie down.
    He lay in bed; his breathing was
        labored;
        he stiffened and seemed to
           quiver.
The hemlock mounted to his chest,
    and he yanked the cloak over his
        head.

Just before he died, he made a great
    effort,
    and dragged back the cloak,
    he said something, loud but garbled.
    I caught the word "Asklepios!"

the god of healing —
that's all I heard.
    That's the last thing he said.

He covered his face again,
    his breath coming in gasps and
      rattles. We held still,
    silent,
    except for weeping Apollodorus. We
      waited
      and waited
      and waited
      long past the last breath.

His friend Krito uncovered his face;
    his eyes were fixed,
    his head thrown back, teeth bared.

Krito closed his mouth and shut his eyes.
I took to my heels
    and plunged out into the dark.

RHASKOS: JOURNEY

1.

The moon was up. I walked the streets
  gasping
      blinking
      breath whistling
      in and out. I would honor Sokrates;
          no slavish tear would fall —
      but that bird in my throat
          was beating its wings
            thrashing
          trying to force itself out. I headed
          nowhere
          turning corners at random. I
            heard carousing —

the low laughter of shameless
women,
drunken aristocrats:
rich men guzzling wine
smacking their lips over their
precious ideas,
while the wise man lay dead.

A dog barked. My sandal slipped —
something rotten underfoot.
An owl shrieked: Athena,
keening for Sokrates.

My feet led me homeward
stop
I stood in the courtyard.
Zosima sobbing inside the house:
*Why should she care about
Sokrates?*
He was my friend.

Phaistus shouting: "It's not what I *want*!
By all the gods, Zosima,
I've no wish to part with the boy! I'll never
find another like him.

But we can't afford him, and we can't go
on like this.
I can't risk my freedom.
Every day I go on without a protector,
we're in danger.
Someone could find out. We have to
leave —"

"Then take him with us! He's our *son*!"

"No. He's not.
I wish he were. Listen —
Simon's promised:
If I sell him Pyrrhos, he'll take them
both;
he'll take Kranaos off our hands.
The old man will be cared for;
does that mean nothing to you?
After a lifetime of toil, he'll die in a bed
and have a proper burial.
Pyrrhos will learn to make shoes. That's
not a tragedy.
People need shoes, and the work's not
hard —
it's easier than making pots."

"What has that to do with anything?
Phaistus, you're not selling our son!
We can sell the donkey."

"By all the gods, woman! we *need* the
donkey!
We need a beast of burden. You're close to
your time.
I don't know how long we'll be on the
road,
or how I'll find work.
I won't have a kiln or a shop —
I'll have to work on a farm —
the donkey will be a big help."

I'd heard enough. I turned
and fled the courtyard
away from the house
anywhere. I couldn't escape from
my thoughts.
Phaistus was selling me to Simon the
cobbler,
along with Kranaos.
They'd be leaving the city:
Phaistus and Zosima,

663

and Phoibe, who was my friend
and worth more than I was.

I ran
    zigzagged around houses
    until I couldn't run,
    I clamped my hands to my knees
        and gulped air. My throat was dry.
    I'd come to a dead end,
        a narrow space between ugly
        houses.
    I had nowhere to go but home.
I pivoted. Followed my feet,
    found my way back;
    the courtyard was silent, the
        argument over.
Zosima must have given in.

I went in the shed. I wanted to sleep.
    To crouch in a dark corner
        and never wake up.
Clop. A hoof on the hard clay floor;
    the floor I'd shoveled and packed
        down: Phoibe sidled over
    sniffing my hands, hoping for a treat,

wanting a scratch along her spine.
  Through the dimness I saw
    her long-lashed eyes
    dark as violets,
      the pale soft fur around her muzzle.
      she nickered: a question.
My mouth twisted and I wept. The tears
  washed down
    my cheeks   my neck
      Phoibe. Her little hinny.
      Phaistus, Zosima,
      Sokrates.
        Everyone I cared for,
    everything: the moist clay
        breathing between my hands
        the toys I'd learned to make
        lost. gone.
      the things I'd learned: worthless.
    every scraping of joy or hope
      would be taken away
        and always would.
I dropped down in the straw
  choked and sobbed and blubbered;
    what was the use

of trying not to be slavish? I was a
slave.
I would always be a slave.

A hand on my arm. A shock of pain —
A spark in the darkness. Sparks
like rubbing wool on a cold day —
my hair on end
I looked —

and you were there, Melisto, kneeling
beside me: solid and clear as amber. I
saw you: the freckles on your cheeks, the
creases in your dress: jagged lines like
brushstrokes of darkest ink. I saw the scars
on your arm, fernlike and branching.

I snarled like a dog: "*Who are you?*
Why do you follow me?
What are you doing here?"

Your eyes widened. You were sitting cross-
legged, like a boy: you flipped up one knee
and swung your leg sideways, nesting your
ankles together. You spoke commandingly,
as if you were a god:

"I've worked it out —
how to set you free! It's like a triple knot.
We'll untie it together.
The first knot's worked loose by itself. You
can see me;
you spoke to me!
Now there are two knots left.

"When I lived, I was Melisto, daughter of
Arkadios.
My father's a citizen. He'll serve as your
master's protector:
Then Phaistus won't have to lose the shop
or leave the city.
You won't be sold

"— but we need to bargain for your
freedom,
and you'll have to convince my father, so

"— we'll go to Brauron, to the Sanctuary
of Artemis.
Together. You have to come, because I
can't carry things.
Your mother sent me;
your mother, Thratta;

she was my nurse.
She loved you more than all the world.
I'm meant to set you free."

I caught only a scattering of words. My mind was deadened by shock. I was aghast. You were a shade, but you flared like a torch: saffron, marigold, molten bronze. The straw around you glittered like gold. The scars on your skin were ruddy, like glazed Athenian clay: incised by the hand of a god.

I cast my mind back to the first time I saw you.
You were my age then.

"You kept growing and got older.
I stayed the same age."

I hadn't opened my lips. You answered my thoughts. The other times, when I saw you, the light shone through you: you shimmered like dust motes in the air. But that night, the night of Sokrates's death, you were as solid in your flesh as I was. I blinked. You didn't disappear. I put out my hand to touch your tunic. There was a crackling sound in the air. My hand jerked back.

"I was struck down by Zeus's lightning.
I don't think it was a punishment,
but of course, I couldn't survive.
I think you couldn't see me before
because you didn't want to. I was
impossible,
so I was invisible. And I was of no use to
you.
But tonight your heart is broken;
you long for the dead to come back;
you see beyond the world of the living:
you're at the end of your wits.
The time has come for me to set
you free.

"Your mother laid a curse on me,
binding us together —
She's gone now. I don't know where she is,
whether she's among the living or the
dead.
I only know she told me to free you.
It's been three years.
I couldn't make you pay attention
to me.

But now I see a way. My father will help
you,
only you'll have to persuade him.
You'll have to convince him that you've
seen me.
You'll need proof.
So we have to leave the city. Tomorrow, at
dawn.
It's a journey of two days:
Two days there, and two days back.
I can guide you."

You spoke like a god, but also like a spoiled
child of the ruling class. You were used to
giving orders and getting your way. It flicked
on the raw.

"I can't just leave because you say so!
A slave can't just go on a journey!
I'll be caught and beaten, branded as a
runaway.
—What do you know about my life?"

"I've watched you for three years.
If you need permission to go, ask Zosima.
She'll help you."

"What can she do? She can cry all she
likes;
she can't change anything!
Phaistus is the master of the house.
A woman has to obey her husband."

"They *have* to. But they don't.
Haven't you noticed that?
Zosima loves you.
Give her the thing she wants most in the
world,
and she won't deny you."

I scarcely remember the rest of that
night.
I know I made you repeat
repeat
repeat
the tale of how my mother bound
you,
how she looked when she knelt in
the graveyard;
I made you repeat everything she
ever told you about me.
I was hungry for stories about my
mother —

then I'd remember Sokrates,
    his body growing cold even as we
      spoke together,
and I'd gasp for breath, and swallow,
    fighting for control. You sat beside
      me,
      hugging your scratched knees to
      your chest.
I can't remember all I said,
    I remember at one point, I went off
      on a tirade
      about how I didn't want to make
      sandals,
      I wanted to make horses. I'd never
      told anybody that,
      not even Sokrates.
I'd pause for breath and I seemed to
    see Sokrates,
      wearing his hairy old cloak,
      wading across the river
      between the quick and the
      dead,
      bound for the House of Hades.

"I'm sorry about Sokrates. I know you

loved him.
I used to watch you together."

Then I was ashamed, because it struck
me that this girl, this highborn girl, had
followed me, watching me, for *three years*.
I'd thought I was alone, and she'd been
haunting me, staring at me, spying on me.

"It wasn't like that.
I didn't watch you every minute,
I didn't watch every time you blew your
nose
or scratched yourself
or slept. It's an uneasy thing, being a
shade.
I can't tell you.
I don't belong to this world anymore,
I'm half banished, and my attention drifts
away . . .
You know how when you dream, you're
interested?
— except then you wake up, and there are
only fragments,
just a few things you remember. It's like
that.

673

There's always something dragging me,
                like an undertow,
separating me from the world of the
                living.
         . . . I used to watch you work;
              I could follow that.
When you were with Sokrates,
      you were happy and wholly alive,
            so you held my attention.
I watched you on the Akropolis,
     when you were dizzy with wonder;
I was with you that day in the slave
              market.
I tried to make Phaistus take you. He
          smelled all right to me.
That's another thing. There's things I
          smell and see and hear,
things I *know* that I didn't know
              before;
but I'm never at home. I'm not right with
              myself.
               I'm afraid to die,
to go down to the House of Hades —
Even if your mother hadn't bound me
           with her curse —

I might still be here. I don't *want* to leave
this world.
I'm like a sailor clinging to a wreck,
I'm sure to go down in the end.

"But in the meantime, there's you,
and this blessed curse that knots us
together.
I'm meant to help you, and I w*ant* to.
You should sleep now. Tomorrow we leave
Athens."

I didn't believe her,
but I was never more tired in my life
so I slept.

2.

I overslept. Melisto was beside me,
urging me to open my eyes.

"Zosima's gone to the fountain house!
Hurry and wake up! She'll be back
soon!"

. . . There was Phoibe, nibbling her

bedding,
> the hinny beside her,
> and Melisto gleaming saffron gold
> > in the predawn air.

I rubbed my eyes,
> got up stiffly,
> and went out past the gate.

The city was stirring:
> shadowy women carrying jars,
> > the sky as dark as water.

She was half veiled. I knew her by her gait,
> which was slower than usual. She
> > balanced one jar on her head
> and cradled the other at her side.

I spoke her name. "Zosima?"

She stopped, swaying a little,
> balancing the water jar.

I couldn't see her face. I went to her,
> took the jars from her,
> and set them down carefully.

Then I dropped to the ground,
> taking the pose of a suppliant,

bowing my head and clasping her
    knees.

She caught her breath sharply;
    I'd never touched her, not on
        purpose.
I raised my head to speak
    and found myself talking to her belly.
I knew something then:
        I'd been jealous of the child inside
            her;
        in the back of my mind
        I'd grudged the life of that child.

                              "Pyrrhos?"

She was bewildered. She touched the
    crown of my hair.
My heart twisted in my chest.

                              "Pyrrhos?"

"I came to beg from you, Zosima,
        mistress, *despoina*.
I have to ask a favor,
        and you're not going to believe

677

me —"

She hunkered down beside me. She was
clumsy, these days,
because her belly kept surprising her,
throwing her off balance.
She pressed her palm on the ground.
"Is it about last night? Did you hear me
arguing with Phaistus?
Listen. Phaistus isn't going to sell you.
I'll make him change his mind.
In his heart, he doesn't want to. He cares
for you.
He's proud of you. He's just worried;
he's afraid of losing his freedom.
But you have nothing to fear,
and no reason to beg. I'm your *mother*.
The first day you came to this house, I
knew it;
It's my duty to take care of you, and I
will."

"It isn't that. No, it is that,
but —
I need you to believe me. I can save us:

all of us: you, me, Phaistus —
I can find him a protector.
We won't have to go away. We won't lose
 the shop,
 and someday, I'll be free. This is my
  chance;
I'll help Phaistus, and in turn he'll set me
 free!"

                                              "How?"

"I can't tell you. That's the trouble.
There isn't time, and I have to leave the city.
Except —
 Phaistus will think I'm running
  away —
  and if the guards see me leave
   through the city gates —
 at this hour — without taking the
  donkey —
   I'm not running away. I swear it.
I'll be gone less than a week. I'll come
 back.
You have to get me past the guards,
 so they won't think I'm a runaway,

and you have to tell Phaistus not to
   come after me.
I swear by Bendis, my mother's goddess,
   and by Hephaistos, who guides my
     hands —
I'm not lying. I'll come back —"

                She shook her head.
      "You have to tell me more than that!
        What should I say to Phaistus?"

"I don't know! But I'm doing this to help
   him.
I'll find him a protector and come back.
Tell him that. He trusts you —"

                   "I don't —"

"I can't explain. It doesn't sound true.
The one who guides my footsteps is a
   shade.
I've seen a ghost. I know it sounds crazy —"

She opened her mouth. Not a sound came
                     out.
      She laid her hand on her belly,

which was round as a full moon.
People look different in the darkness;
in that dark, she was beautiful,
the veil framing her face,
the gleam of her eyes, the gloss of her
skin.
She shook her head.
"I can't. Pyrrhos,
if I let you go, and you never come
back —"

"But I will come back! I promise!"
I thought of what Melisto said:

*Give her the thing she wants most in
the world,*

and she won't deny you.

It was as if a wave turned over in my
chest,
and the words spilled forth. "If you
let me go,
when I come back, I'll be your son:
Slave or free, I'll love you;
I'll love you as a son loves his
mother,
and be brother to your child."

681

Those last five words came hard,
but the others —
I was making a promise I wanted to keep,
That I'd already kept and kept hidden.

She sat very still,
her head tilted to one side,
a bird hearing birdsong. Then she shook
herself,
flattened her hand to the earth,
and shoved herself to her feet.

"You'll need a cloak."

3.

We parted at the Sacred Gate.
Zosima bade me farewell before the
guard
and gave me a bundle to carry:
a loaf for the journey,
a moist lump of cheese.
She said to come back as soon as I could.
Her voice shook. I promised her,
"I will come back."

I passed under the arch, wondering what
   she would tell Phaistus.

      Would he be angry? (He would.)

      Would he send slave-hunters after
        me? (He wouldn't.)

I passed the tombs on the road
      and thought of Sokrates,

        how he said we could bury him any
          way we liked —

           if you can catch me!
           if I don't slip through your fingers!

Then she was beside me: Melisto.

                        "Follow me!"

She was off. There were others on the
   path,

      farmers bringing their wares to the
        city,

      pilgrims heading for Eleusis —

        they couldn't see her.

She dodged past them, whirled around,
   dancing backward,

        frisking like a goat. Beckoning,

          prancing — I was reminded of

683

being a child,
      of tag, and Do-What-I-Do —
      but my goal was to go unnoticed.
I dragged the cloak over my head
      to cover my Thracian hair
      and plodded after her. I felt like a
      drunkard the morning after.
Dizzy and dry-mouthed,
      I walked with grief on one hand
      and hope on the other. It was too
      much —
      but there ahead of me was that
      hoyden girl,
            Melisto.

The sun rose, and the grass was wet with
   dew,
      the wind fresh and gusting;
The poppies were in bloom, scarlet and
   black-eyed.
Melisto stopped to tickle them. The petals
   passed through her skin.
She couldn't grasp them, but the color
   blazed out,
            staining her fingers.

Our path slanted upward. We were headed
  for the mountains.
Away from the city, the crowd thinned,
        until we were alone. Then she
          bounded forward,
            leaping like a dog let off its
            chain.
        I had to catch up. I couldn't risk
        losing her.

She ran with her fingers outstretched,
growling like a wild beast,
  giggling.
      I pursued her, my bundle clamped
        under my arm.
The ground smacked my feet. Pebbles
  skittered underfoot.
My muscles stretched
      air filled my lungs,
        and I outran my grief. The world
          opened up
        speed and wind and sunlight. I
          thought, *Freedom*,
      a thing without pictures,
        but this is what sticks in my
          mind:

the two of us
    rushing under the sky,
        sharp-edged meadow grass
        red streaks of poppies
    a wide blue world full of air.

Melisto dashed back
    breathless
    to point out a patch of hairy leaves.
    "These are cat's-ear. Good to eat!
    And here's wild garlic." She made me
      taste.
From time to time, she had me mark the trail,
    anchoring sticks under rocks. I pulled
      threads from my cloak
      and tied them to tree branches.

            "Here! You can see!
This is where the girls passed on their way
              to Brauron —"

Again she pointed
    and in my mind's eye, I seemed to
    see what she saw,
    a trail of molten silver, or shining

686

dew,
the marks of small maidens' feet.

She spoke of Brauron,
of how she served the goddess as a Little
Bear.
It was the happiest time of her life.
Until she went to Brauron, she was kept at
home,
weaving in a yellow room.
She wasn't allowed to go outdoors,
because she was a girl.

I was surprised to hear myself speak.
"I wasn't allowed *indoors*.
Because I was a slave."

"I used to sneak out."

"So did I! Back in Thessaly.
At night I taught myself to swim.
At night I used to sneak *into* the house!
My first master —
he might have been my father —"

"You don't know?"

687

"No, he never spoke to me.
Never owned me. I didn't care!
Except he had paintings in his house — I
    cared about *them*.
        I used to sneak inside at night and
            look."

We were night-wanderers, both of us,
        rebellious,
            refusing to stay put.

                    She told me about her Bear:
                how she defied the priestesses
                        and set the bear free.

"Weren't you afraid that Artemis would
    punish you?"

    "No! I love Artemis! She didn't want the
                        bear to die!"

She loved the bear the way I loved horses.
We were rebellious, but we worshipped the
    gods:
        she made garlands for Artemis
        and sang to her under the white

moon.
I went in secret to Hephaistos,
>hid my toys inside his temple;
>I prayed he would help me make
>good things.
I told her about the Kiln God —
>who was unpredictable,
>and burned my pots.

She listened.
She listened as if I weren't a slave.

>She told me about her father —
>>her faith was founded on him
>>>as flesh is hung on bone.
>She swore he would help me. She trusted
>>>>>>him.
>She pitied me because I had no father.
>"I think Sokrates was your real father.
>*He* spoke to you. He liked to talk to you!"

When she spoke of Sokrates
>my heart twisted in my chest.
I ran ahead, so she couldn't see my face.

"I'm hungry."

I chose a spot in the shade, sat down,
and tore off a chunk of bread.
Two silver obols fell out of the loaf:
Zosima must have slit the crust with
a knife
and tucked them inside.

Melisto flopped down beside me. She
fidgeted.
I offered her cheese;
it was warm and runny;
it wouldn't last. Might as well eat it up.

"I can't eat. In the stories, they say that
shades drink blood —
but I don't. I only like the smell of food,
the way the gods do, I suppose.
I still don't know much about the gods.
But I can see how that cheese —
how the strength of the goat
and her mother-love
made the milk . . .
Now you eat, and the goat-strength
flows into you. It brightens you up.

You feel better, don't you?
I don't think we should be sad today."

She pointed at the sky.
Against the clear blue, a bird in flight:
    the neck a double curve, the wings
     silver-blue.

               "See? that's a heron!
  and it's on our right side. That's a good
                  omen.
There are lots of waterbirds at Brauron;
      they're sacred to the goddess.
  I think Artemis will help us. She loves
               freedom."
      She reached for a stem of grass,
           as if to pluck it
    and nibble the sweet pale green —
but the blade never stirred. She frowned at
                 it.
          Then she laughed.

"I haven't talked to anyone in such a long
                 time.
        It's been lonely."

I was afraid to know, but I still asked.
"What's it like to die?"

She raised her eyes to the mountain,
as if words might come tumbling down the
slope.

"It wasn't how I thought it would be.
When I was little,
I'd lie in bed at night, and the dark would
scare me.
I thought there might be Spartans under
the bed,
and they'd kill me.
I heard stories about the House of
Hades —
everything dim and lifeless, hopeless.
It frightened me so I couldn't sleep.
I thought dying would be a great weight,
a grinding pain that went on forever.
But it happened so fast.
For me, I mean. It was raining so hard,
and I was dancing —
and I was soaking wet. My skin was icy;
rain streaming down, and then there was

this heat —"

She shuddered.

"And then I was looking down at myself,
and I thought,
I fell down,
and I couldn't understand why I couldn't
get up.
The bear was panic-stricken —
you know how they run,
like a ball bouncing, rocking up and
down;
I wanted to run after the bear —
but I couldn't. I slept,
and my dreams were curious, very clear
and bright —
You know how you can dip a pebble in
water,
and see colors in the stone you never
saw? . . .
My dreams were like that. I kept
remembering things,
things I'd forgotten, but now they made
sense.
I was deep in my dreams, and I didn't

want to wake;
I wanted to understand.

"The next day came, and the priestesses
found me
and wrapped my body in a cloak —
and I thought, *They'll tend me,*
and I'll be well again.
They did things to my body, washed it and
anointed it,
and I felt very tender toward my body,
because I thought I might need it later
on.
They loaded it on an oxcart —
and brought it back to Athens
so I could be buried.
"My mother was afraid to touch me.
There were burn marks on my skin
— see?
The marks terrified her.
She tore her cheeks with her nails. She
wept —
but she was afraid of Zeus's lightning.
Your mother was the one who prepared
me for burial.

694

She didn't cry, but I felt the love in her
hands.

"I was starting to understand: I wasn't
alive.
I had a strange feeling
as if there were somewhere I had to go.
I remembered stories about the
underworld,
I didn't want to go there.
I tried to stay awake, but I kept
dreaming —
I saw Hermes, Guide of Souls — oh, he
was beautiful!
He stretched out his hands like a juggler,
as if he wanted me to play with him! —
but your mother called me back.
She set her curse on me.
She wanted me to find you and set you
free;
that was the deepest wish of her heart.
Your mother was good to me.
I felt I owed her something.

"You know how it is when you have to

stay awake?

only you can't?

I've had to hold on; I've had to keep myself

from slipping away, like water soaking into the ground.

But I'm awake now. Something's happening.

I'm not a bystander anymore. I can help you.

I think if I can set you free, I'll be free, too.

"But I don't know where I'm going, or what it will be like.

I want to tell you the things I never told anyone,

in case this is my last chance.

When I was alive, I didn't talk much.

So much of what I felt was a secret.

I think that's what I loved about the bear.

Neither of us had any words."

I put the last lump of cheese in my mouth.

It was salty. I turned it with my tongue,

wishing I had a drink of water.

"I don't talk, either.

If you're a slave, no one listens.

No one asks questions. Except Sokrates.

But even Sokrates . . . I wanted him to
   think I wasn't stupid,

so I was always trying so hard —"

She nodded fervently.
"I know. I *know*."
Then she looked at me,
waiting for me to go on.

I held up my left arm. "I have scars, too.
   Tattoos.

My mother made them. They're a mark of
   honor,

a sign of my kinsmen back in
   Thrace.

My mother was wellborn. She wasn't
   always a slave."

I told her about my mother,

how she used to teach me and play
   with me.

I counted to ten in Thracian.

She spoke of her mother, Lysandra,
who was like Menon:
carrying hatred like a hidden knife.
"I always knew she hated me.
She knew it, and I knew it,
but no one else was meant to know. It was
a secret."

She told me. She was a citizen's daughter,
but she knew what it was to be
slapped and pinched
and yanked around. She'd had her
arm broken.
I pitied her because of her mother;
She envied me because of mine.

"But it isn't just parents who shape our
lives.
It's our children. They say a girl who dies
without giving birth
will never rest in peace, because she isn't
whole.
I don't *think* that's why I'm a shade,
but it might be. Here's what I think:
I died before my first woman's
bleeding,

698

so I'll never have a baby,
but I gave birth to the bear,
because I set the bear free.
And I'll set you free, Rhaskos,
and in time, you'll give birth,
so I'll have grandchildren:
clay animals
and pictures painted on clay, red and
black:
pictures of the gods that live forever.
Maybe one day you'll marry Zosima's
daughter,
and have children with her —
they'll be my children, too,
because I set you free."

"Zosima's *daughter*?
You think I'll marry Zosima's *daughter*?"

"No, I'm teasing you!
I don't know the future.
Even the gods can't tell what's to come.
I don't know who you'll marry, or even *if*
— if you'll really paint pots,
if you'll ever own a horse.

699

"All I know is, that baby smells like a girl.
          Phaistus will be disappointed.
                    Zosima won't."

She knew Phaistus and Zosima. Why
    wouldn't she?
She'd watched me for three years.
She didn't know about my life in
    Thessaly —
          that was before she died.

   She'd ask a question, and I'd answer it —
                    and when I ran out of breath —
                    because the path was steep —
          she'd talk, telling me about her life —

— and I'd interrupt her, and our voices
    overlapped.
We told our secrets, and they shifted
    shape,
          changing into stories. She led me to a
              stream,
          and I drank cold water till my
              stomach ached.
On the bank, I drew her a horse,
          and she breathed admiration and

700

said:

"Oh! That's *good*."

I turned my head to hide the grin on my
face.

We headed up the mountain track.
        The sun-horses raced across the sky.
I couldn't believe how easy it was, being
    with her.
She was a citizen's daughter,
        and she was a *girl*. I'd never talked to
        a girl in my life.
    I thought they were different,
But she was more like me than anyone I
    ever knew.

The sun-chariot blazed and plunged over
    the mountaintop.
We found another spring.
I gathered the plants she showed me,
        dandelions, asparagus, and wild
        onions.
I gnawed them till my jaws were sore.
She showed me how to strip pine boughs

701

from a tree
    and make myself a bed.

She sat close to me as I slept,
    a torch in the night.

4.

She woke me in the middle of the night.

                "Rhaskos?"
"What?"

        "Get up! Come with me!"

I wanted to *sleep*,
    but she stuck out her hand;
    that touch that sent sparks flying,
      crisped the hair on my arms,
    and set my teeth on edge.
"What is it?"

    "The sky!" She leapt up and pointed:
      the heavens aglitter:
      stars singing and trembling

like bees near a hive.
"See? The Great Bear! Get up!
I have to teach you the Bear Dance!"

She was after me then,
tracing patterns in the sky.
The Great Bear, the Little Bear, and
Ariadne's crown.
I rubbed my eyes. I had no idea
which stars she was pointing out.
Who teaches constellations to a slave?
I wanted to *sleep*. I yawned and
grumbled,
but she was adamant,
stretching upward, fingers
splayed
as if she meant to scoop down the
stars,
stab them with her forefinger,
and pin them to the earth.
She made me see the patterns.
Then, all at once, she was dancing —

"Your hands. Like this. Like claws.
Stamp your heel on the ground,

703

heavy. Curl your toes!
Lift your hands to the sky!"

By the gods, she made no sense,
but I obeyed her. It was as if some god
made her teach me that dance,
It was as if some god
made me learn it.

I danced as a Bear,
hruffing and snorting and clacking
my teeth;
my knees drawn inward,
my claws held high,
the stars caught between them.

So Melisto danced on the night she died;
so Melisto danced with the bear she
loved;
so Melisto danced when the god struck
her down.

I danced till my body was slick with sweat,
salty and ripe.
I stank like a bear — I know that —

but at last she dropped her arms
and sighed
and let me go to sleep.

5.

Morning came. I ate the last of the loaf,
    wiped dew off the grass, and licked
        my palm.
I was still hungry,
    but the sky was stippled with saffron
        and milk,
    and the wind was fresh. Again we
        walked
    and talked. I never talked to anyone
        like that.
    No one ever talked like that to me.

I talk to you still, Melisto.
I've been talking to you ever since.

We spoke and we were silent;
    the path was steep,
        robbing me of breath.
    She pointed out caves in the

mountain —
    narrow entrances I might have
      missed.
"On the way back, if it rains —"
Looking back,
I see both of us knew
I would come back alone.

She was less giddy that second day,
    more thoughtful,
    gnawing her upper lip.
The caves reminded me of Sokrates,
    and I told her what he said,
      that maybe we were like people
        who lived underground,
        who'd never seen the sun, just
        shadows.

I told her how Sokrates died hoping
    to see another world:
    a country of health and truth
    and absolute beauty. "See, if
      Sokrates is right —
    and he was the wisest man in
      Athens, the Oracle said so —

maybe the House of Hades isn't what
we think.
Maybe it *isn't* sorrow and nothingness.
Maybe it's full of power
and color
and animals!
Maybe when you go there, you'll see a *real*
horse!
— or a bear as big as the Bear in
the sky
all stars and claws!"

She grinned. "I'd like that."
Then she stopped and gazed all
around
turning slowly:
the wind herding the clouds over the blue
sky,
rock and root underfoot;
each pebble, each stalk of grass
haloed with piercing light.
I knew what she was thinking.

There was nothing I could say, so I said
nothing.

We journeyed on, and the countryside changed,

It was a female land: secretive, soft and wild,

> The path was less steep, and I was grateful.

The reeds murmured ceaselessly. I saw pelicans,

> a kingfisher,

> a nest of quail.

We stopped beside a river, and I waded in to drink.

She told me to bathe my sore feet

> while she looked for the willow tree

> where once she camped with a girl named Elpis.

She had only a few friends, when she was alive.

She was like me that way.

Almost at once, she cried out,

> beckoning with both arms.

> "It's here! in the grass!"

The grass was lush and green:

a tangle, a hiding place,
but gold, pure gold, doesn't darken,
    and I tore apart the tussock:
a sphinx head of reddish amber,
    carved by a master —
the cut of the nostrils,
the austere curve of the cheek,
        a spear-point crown,
            and the gold:
twelve palmettes on a leather string;
        so much,
            so heavy.
I'd been afraid the necklace would be too
    light a thing
        to buy a boy's freedom. Now I held it
        in my palm,
    weighed it, admired it, almost feared it.
Each gold palmette
    was thicker than a drachma, solid
        gold —
            and there were twelve,
                each worth fourteen times as
                much as silver.

"Are you sure I can have it? Won't Artemis

be angry?"

"No." She was fearless, that girl.
        In that way, we weren't alike.
    She made up her mind and stuck with it.

I thought more than she did;
    worried more,
    wondered more.
I was more wary of the gods.

    "Artemis is the protector of youth —
            she'll want you to be free.
        Besides, you're going to give it back."

She sounded as if nothing could go wrong.
I knotted the necklace in my cloak
        and prayed she was right.

6.

In the middle of the night,
    her absence tugged me from sleep.
I got up and searched for her.
She stood by the river

like a deer listening for danger.
She knew I was there but didn't turn her
head.

                              "It's time for me to go."

"Go where?"

                              Her shoulders lifted.
                                   "I don't know."
                              She spread her hands.
                              She let me draw close.

I thought you were crying, Melisto,
        but I never saw you cry.
Your owl eyes blazed in the dark.
We stood face-to-face:
Akhilleus.
Penthesilea.

                              "Listen, Rhaskos.
                    You don't have to come with me.
                         I don't know where I'm going.
                         I only know I have to go *now*."

711

I forgot I couldn't touch her. I reached
out.

There was an instant when her fingers
were warm

gripping mine, a strong hand —

then her fingers stung, sparked —
I yanked my hand free.

"You see?"

You turned your back and started off. I
followed. You never looked back.

We followed the river to a bridge of
white stones. I crossed behind you. I saw
the gleam of pale columns: temples and
walkways. We'd come to the Sanctuary of
Artemis.

I felt both awe and fear. It was holy
ground, and I didn't belong: I was a slave,
and male.

We skirted the buildings and went
onward. The wind freshened and I smelled
the salt of the sea. I remembered what you'd
told me, Melisto: you were struck down at
the water's edge. We were going to the place
of your death. I looked at the sky, which was

clear. The moon was down. There was no lightning, no storm, only the Great Bear and the Milky Way.

On a low bluff overlooking the sea, you stopped. The water was dark, except for a curl of froth at the edge. I thought I saw a pod of dolphins plowing the waves, but they were far away; I might have imagined them. Standing behind you, I longed for a brush. I itched to draw you, Melisto: the dark confusion of your hair, the line that meandered from temple to cheekbone to jaw.

I grieved for you as I grieved for Sokrates, because I couldn't keep you.

You gazed out to sea. There was a moment when I saw through the starlight, and I saw things that weren't there. I saw the gleam of Sokrates's bald forehead: I saw the Guide of Souls, dark and golden at the same time. I saw him tuck his wand under one arm and extend his hands.

For the last time, you glanced at me, Melisto. You were breathing hard. You lowered your head like a bull about to charge. Your eyes narrowed, and you said *"Now!"*

Out in the dark was the thing that you feared, and you braced yourself, tensing —

Then you plunged forward and ran to
the shore. You stumbled on entering the
water; you kicked and splashed — and I
must have blinked, because then you were
gone.

And I've missed you, Melisto, I've
wanted you back. But at that time, my heart
was light, borne aloft by your ἀρετή.

7.

The next day of the journey, I was too
   hungry to go on —
     or so I thought. When I came to a
     farmhouse,
     I hid my cloak under a bush,
       went to the door,
       held out an obol,
       and begged for bread.
An old woman gave me a loaf and a
   watery cup of wine.
She wouldn't take my money.
     "Travelers and strangers come from
     Zeus.
     Zeus will reward me."

I went back to retrieve my cloak.

My mind was dull with hunger and
  fatigue,
     but it struck me funny: Here
      I was,
     carrying gold, pure gold, in my
      ragged cloak,
     and begging for bread. I glanced at
      the sky;
        the crescent moon had risen. I felt
        better after the loaf
     and picked up my pace;
        the knot in my cloak swung from
        side to side.

Once or twice I panicked,
     because I thought I'd lost it.

Melisto had shown me food plants,
     and I gathered them along
      the way:
     sharp herbs that left their tang in my
      mouth
     but did little to satisfy my hunger.
Still I was grateful.

The fourth day I had little food.
I hoped to reach Athens before the sun set.
    I thought of Zosima,
        of the trouble I'd caused her;
        four days I'd been gone, and
           Phaistus rebuking her;
        four days, and she'd think I was
           gone for good.
    I imagined her face at the sight of
    me:
        relief and joy,
        her squinty smile, and her flappy
           sandals;
        I knew she'd rush to get me
           something to eat.
I wanted to show Phaistus the amber
    sphinx;
        he'd see its beauty; he'd know its
           worth.
I wanted to tell him we could stay in Athens —

But the sun went down before I reached
    the city.
The gates would be locked.
I'd have to wait another hungry night.

I kept away from the road.

I didn't want to sleep too near the tombs.

Once again, I stripped limbs from a pine
  tree
    and made myself a bed.

I tied the necklace around my neck.
  Tightly.
    unknotted my cloak and covered
      myself.

I slept. But I was awakened,
    a sound in the night, a presence, an
      odor,
    a trace of music, the singing of the
      stars,
      the voice of the god.

I got up, every hair on end. A noise from
  the brush.

Then I saw her: more solid than the darkness,
    an opaque shadow
      larger than a dog,
      smaller than a horse,
      a lustrous eye,
      a savage death.

Melisto's bear was watching me. I stood
　　unweaponed
　　　I heard the huff of her breathing;
　　　　she was drawing my scent into her
　　　　　nostrils;
　　　　I was a warm smell
　　　　flesh
　　　　food —
I sympathized. I was hungry myself.

I didn't move a muscle
　　　breathless

　　　　danger
　　　　　— then my laugh came out as a snort.
　　　　Melisto had foreseen this hour
　　　and taught me what to do. I lifted my
　　　　hands,
　　　　　stamped one heel in the dirt,
　　　　　　and began to dance.

It was no dream.
　　　I danced, and the bear watched me,
　　　　and the music came from the stars,
　　　　　the Great Bear overhead:
　　　　perhaps the goddess herself was there,

armed with her silver bow,
ready to shoot me for one false
step.
but I didn't misstep. I danced.

I danced. I growled and pivoted,
huffed and clawed the air,
shifted my weight,
circled and swayed.
I danced till I'd sweated out my fear,
and the bear grew bored and padded
away;
I danced till I was dizzy and faint,

and the goddess was appeased.

8.

There was one last knot to untie:
the final gamble. The sun was rising
as I entered the city.
I longed to go home,
but I had to see Arkadios.
He was a citizen and a busy man,
away from home all day —

719

I couldn't wait till nightfall.

Melisto had told me how to find the
  house:
She'd described the carved gatepost
      and told me the name of the slave at
        the gate.
"Are you Sosias?"

  "I am. Who told you my name, and what
                    do you want?"
                  He was sizing me up.
          I was ragged, and not very clean,
                a red-haired nobody.
          He was in charge of the household,
  a trusted servant, with other slaves under
                          him.

I tried not to sound too meek.
I tried not to sound too bold.
"I came to see Arkadios. He'll want to see
  me."

        "Will he, now? Who's your master?"

"I work for Phaistus, a potter in the Agora.

I knew your master's daughter, Melisto."

"The master's daughter's dead.
Struck down by Zeus three years ago.
You'd know that, if you knew the family."

"She's the one who told me your name."
I dragged my cloak around my neck,
holding the knot at arm's length.
I clamped my fist around it,
squeezing, so he could see.
"I have something for your master, here,

but it's for his eyes alone."

He was curious,
but he shrugged as if he weren't.
"I'll ask if he'll see you. My guess is, he
won't.
He'll tell you to leave your gift with me."

I tightened my grip on the knot
and shifted my weight to the balls of
my feet.
If he came at me, I was ready to run.

Instead, he opened the gate.
"You can wait in the courtyard,
but don't think you can come in the house.
There are women in the kitchen, working.
What's your name again?"

"Rhaskos. I mean, Pyrrhos.
My master calls me Pyrrhos.
Arkadios won't recognize my name."

He nodded.
He understood how it was with
names.
I wondered what his real name was.

I followed him into the courtyard.
I could smell bread baking.
My stomach gaped open, like a yawn.
There was a rosemary hedge,
fragrant,
and a bench, which I knew better
than to sit on.
The house was well built, modestly large,
the roof tiles unbroken, the altar
scrubbed clean.

722

I saw a tortoise,
> crawling steadily, intent on some
> tortoise errand.
Melisto had told me about the
tortoise.

As I stood waiting, a door slammed,
> and a little boy scampered into the
> courtyard.
At the sight of me, he stopped, jamming
his fingers in his mouth.
He looked like his sister: broad-
shouldered, sturdy,
> bushy-haired, owl eyes.
A man came after him. He was like the
boy,
> like Melisto,
> barrel-chested, battle-scarred.
The little boy whirled round,
> raced over the grass,
> and hurled himself at his father.
>> Arkadios caught him up,
>> tossed him in the air,
>>> flipped him and juggled him from
>>> hand to hand.

He grabbed the boy's wrists and swung
  him around,
      horizontal. The child screamed for
      joy.
Arkadios tossed him again,

      higher
      higher

      caught him under the armpits,
      and set him back on his feet.
I wondered if he ever tossed Melisto like
  that.

            "Off you go, Takis!
            Your papa has work to do!"

The boy circled the courtyard,
    running full tilt and barking like a
    dog.
He made a beeline for the tortoise.
He squatted down, plucked a handful of
  grass,
      and tickled the animal's mouth.

The tortoise drew in its head.

       Arkadios would have passed me;
         he was headed for the gate.

I blocked his path.
He frowned.

  "Oh, you! Sosias said there was someone.
    Who are you and why have you come?"

I gabbled,
"I'm Pyrrhos, slave to Phaistus, a potter.
His shop is near the shrine of Hermes the
   Trader,
      inside the city wall. I come on my
        master's behalf.
He's a freeman, an honest man and a good
   potter.
His protector, Markos, is dead.
      He needs a new protector."

      Arkadios's eyes were deep-set,
        not wide, like Melisto's;
sharp but not cruel. He wanted to be off.
          "No doubt.

But I don't know the man.
If your master wants a favor, he should
come himself.
Tell him that."
He started toward the gate.

"He wouldn't dare.
He doesn't know I'm here.
He wasn't the one who sent me. Melisto
told me to come."

He stopped. His body stiffened.
"My daughter Melisto is dead.
If someone told you to use
her name,
that was a mistake. Take yourself off.
You'll get nothing from me."

I started to go;
he was used to being obeyed;
I was used to following orders.
Then I planted my feet.
"I know your daughter's dead,
but she spoke to me. You won't
believe me,

726

but I saw her shade. She told me to
   come to you.

She wanted me to show you this." I
   unknotted my cloak:

   against the rough wool, the gleam of
      gold,

      the twelve palmettes,

      the riddling smile of the amber sphinx.

I held the necklace out to him.

I watched his face.

                              Astonishment.

                                    Fear.

                                 Suspicion.

                                    Rage.

            "Where did you get that?"

"From a meadow near Brauron.

Melisto took me there and showed me
   where she left it.

It's proof. Her mother told her to give it to
   Artemis,

      but she lost it on the journey.

Now it's found. She bade me bring it back
   to you.

It's proof that I saw her,
     proof that she spoke to me."

                    Three strides.
      He stood over me, blotting out the
                 morning sun.
He snatched the necklace. It was in his
                 hands,
        and so was my fate:
he could have seized me then and there.

There was time to imagine myself in a pit
     close to the cell where Sokrates died.
I saw myself lashed to a plank, begging for
  water.

             "Where did you get this?"

"I told you. From Brauron. Your daughter,
  Melisto —
    she wants you to give it to Artemis.
She said you would help me, for her sake.
I know you don't believe me, but I saw her.
    She has freckles,
      and one of her bottom teeth is
      crooked —

so it overlaps the tooth beside it;
when she was puzzled —
she used to stick out her bottom
jaw
and chew her upper lip.
She has two cowlicks on the back of her
head,
so her hair always looks mussed.
I saw her. I *saw* her."

"You saw her when she was alive.
Or someone told you what she was like."

"No. No one told me.
Don't you believe in ghosts?"

He did. Everyone does.
But no one expects to see one, or wants
to.
He was too swarthy to turn pale,
but there was a gray cast to his face,
as if his blood had turned to lead.
"My daughter's dead and buried.
There's no reason why she should appear
to you.

She was buried with honor. My wife tends
                                    her grave.
                    Everything has been done —"

I saw the pain in his face.
        He'd believed his daughter was at
        peace,
                    not one of the restless dead.
I hadn't foreseen that. I hadn't thought.
I'd been rash —

                        "You're a liar and a thief."

I felt my face get red,
        but I steadied myself.
        Be your own master, Rhaskos!
"If I were a thief, would I come to you? No.
If I were a thief, I'd sell the gold in the
    marketplace,
            piece by piece.
Instead I've brought it back to you. It's
    yours."

        He turned the sphinx head in his palm,
                        stroking the carved face.
            I couldn't tell what he was thinking.

I pressed him. "I'm telling you the truth.
What I'm asking won't cost you any
    money.

> My master needs a protector. It was
>   Melisto's will

>> that I should be set free. It was
>>   her idea.

Tell Phaistus that you'll serve as his
    protector

> *if he sets me free.*

It doesn't cost anything, being a
    protector.

All Phaistus needs is the shelter of your
    name.

> I'll work for him, but as a servant, or
>   a son —

He'll teach me how to make beautiful
    things."

I had thought to assume the pose of a
    suppliant —

> to kneel before him and clasp his
>   knees —

> but my knees had turned to water,

> and my words rushed fast, and
>   faltered.

I could see the rancor in his eyes,
and the confusion:
my freedom? Phaistus?
none of that had any meaning for
him.
All he cared about was Melisto,
and her death was an unclean
wound.

"Even if my daughter haunts this earth,
why would she appear to you, a stranger?"

I took a deep breath.
"We were linked together by the gods."

He snorted with disbelief;
His eyes raked me from head to foot;
they lingered on my arms. His skin
darkened,
the blood rushing to his head.
"I know who you are!
There was a Thracian woman who used to
work here —
a runaway! She told you about my
daughter!

She was tattooed, the same way you are!
You're her son!"

I stood confounded. I'd never
thought —
neither had Melisto
— he'd see the resemblance to my
mother.

"I'm her son. But I haven't seen her for
years."

"Do you expect me to believe that?
I don't know what kind of swindle you
have in mind,
but I remember *her* —
Hardworking and silent, like a decent
woman —
but what slave was ever loyal to her
master?
She slunk away under cover of night
after my child was buried. She stole from
me.
The household was in grief, and she chose
that time to run,
the shameless bitch!"

At that word *bitch* my blood boiled;
    a red mist rose before my eyes.
I lifted my head, like a free man,
    and stepped forward. "My mother
      was no bitch!
She was kidnapped when she was a girl,
    dishonored, and sold into slavery.
If you were a slave, and saw your chance to
  be free,
    wouldn't you take it? You tell me she
      stole —
What about what was stolen from her?
She was robbed of her freedom and
  her son!"

His fists were clenched. So were mine.
I knew he wanted to hit me. I wouldn't
  step back.
I scowled at him to show I wasn't scared.

"My mother was wellborn.
The scars on my arms are the marks of
  our clan.
She made them with a knife.
I think she cut me

734

so she would know me,
        if she ever saw me again.
It never happened. I lost her. You bought her.
She was your slave, and Melisto's nurse.
She prepared your daughter's body for the
    grave.
        Your wife was afraid to do it."

        He was the one who stepped back;
                        the color of his
                        skin was ghastly.
                "No one knows that.
        Only the members of this household.
        Your mother must have told you."

"No! Melisto told me!
She loved my mother,
        but not her own.
She told me everything —
        how my mother took care of her
        the time she was knocked down and
            broke her arm —
She loved my mother, and she loved you —
        but not your wife. If it weren't for my
        mother —"

"Get out, or I'll have you whipped."

I'd said too much. Gambled too much,
　　told too many truths. Lost my
　　　　temper. Lost.

I was at the gate, and I turned.
He stood like a statue, not weeping.
I know what it is not to cry.

"She had ἀρετή, your daughter.
She was brave, and she loved freedom.
She was happy at Brauron. The night she
　　died,
　　　　she set a bear cub free.
　　　　That's what she loved: the bear cub,
　　　　　　my mother, freedom,
　　　　　　and you. She told me about you.

"The night she was born, you had a
　　headache;
　　　　your wife shrieked with pain because
　　　　the child wouldn't come.
You felt as if your head would split in
　　two —

736

like Zeus, when his skull was hewn in
    half
        and Athena sprang forth.
Then Melisto was born, and you held her
    by the window —
        it was a moonlit night.
        And your pain went away. You
            remembered the story of Zeus,
        and you said to yourself,
            This child will be my Athena.
That's how you loved her.
That's what she told me.
It was her favorite story,
        a secret between you two."

He raised his head and I met his eyes.
                We remembered Melisto.
                He unclenched his fist
        and stared at the sphinx in his hand.

                        "Come back!"

737

EXHIBIT 17

Fragment of marble with manumission inscription, circa 400 BCE.

Stone-carved manumission inscriptions, detailing the terms under which an enslaved person was set free, are abundant in Delphi and Thessaly, but rare in Athens. This does not mean that enslaved people in Athens were never set free, only that physical evidence is lacking. It may be that most Athenian slaves were freed orally, through public announcements at the theatre. The terms of the freedom contract would have been widely known, as the Theatre of Dionysus can seat an audience of seventeen thousand people.

Inscriptions may also have been painted or carved on wooden boards, which have not survived. This unique example of an Athenian inscription was found on a piece of stone (perhaps a stele) that was used to construct an early Christian church.

Translation

Phaistus, the Theban, sells his slave ....ros,

.....god Hephaistos for the price......................

on these conditions: that................opted son

...Pyrrhos....be free....untouchable

....no one...........right to bind him

And Pyrrhos.....be free to go wherever............

and will be in....own power

.....live wherever.....

and do.........he wishes to do.

EXHIBIT 18

Red-figure pyxis (type A), circa 400–375 BCE;
attributed to the Horse Painter.
Height with lid: 17.2 cm (6¾ inches)

Art historians are generally agreed that this pyxis is the earliest known work of the anonymous artist known as the Horse Painter. The liveliness of the figures, the sharply incised lines, and the dramatic vigor of the scene are typical of this artist, who is best known for his paintings of horses. If this pyxis is indeed his, it is the only surviving example of his work that does not include a horse.

The subject matter of the pyxis poses a riddle. It is highly unusual to see a picture of a boy and girl walking together on a Greek vase. Athenian boys and girls occupied separate spheres and had very little contact with

each other. Moreover, the girl child is winged and wears a short chiton. The winged goddess of dawn, Eos, is often figured on Greek vases, but she is drawn as an adult and robed in a long tunic. Scholars have argued at length as to whether the winged girl is Eos, a Nike, a daimon, a harpy, or even a ghost.

The bear is also surprising. Bears are uncommon in Greek art and are seldom portrayed with accuracy. This bear is admirably lifelike: the size, stance, and anatomy suggest that the Horse Painter may have actually seen a living bear. Because of the circular nature of the pyxis, it is not clear whether the children are tracking the bear, or the bear is stalking the children.

Author's Notes

When I first began researching this novel, I was shocked by the hardships of Greek life, by the oppression of women and enslaved people. Greek genius has inspired much of Western culture. Why couldn't those brilliant philosophers and playwrights, sculptors and scientists, have created a more humane society?

Many characters in *Amber and Clay* voice opinions that are offensive from a twenty-first-century point of view. I let these characters have their say, not because I share their opinions, but because their beliefs and actions are an important part of the story.

Greek Words

I tried not to use too many Greek words in this book, because it's irksome to have to look things up. However, there were a few Greek words that I couldn't manage without.

AGORA: The Agora was a large public space in the city. Most of the time I refer to it simply as "the market" or "the marketplace," but the Agora also included government buildings, temples, and shrines.

AKROPOLIS: The akropolis was the high place in a city, frequently protected by a wall. Often when people talk about the akropolis, they're referring to the Akropolis in Athens, where the Parthenon was built. However, most Greek cities had an akropolis, a high and fortified place that could be defended against enemies.

ANDRON: This was the space where the males of the household

entertained their guests. It was the best-decorated room in the house and located on the ground floor. Often the walls were lined with couches for banquets. Greek males banqueted half lying down, leaning on one elbow.

ἀρετή: This word is also written *arete*, and is pronounced *ah-reh-TEE* (Greek) or *AH-reh-teh* (Greek leaning toward English). It is translated as *excellence*, *virtue*, or *goodness*. Sokrates was very interested in trying to define what ἀρετή was. In our modern Judeo-Christian world, we tend to think of goodness as being nice: kind or merciful to others. For the Greeks, being nice was less central. The idea of human ἀρετή encompassed courage, justice, truthfulness, and self-control.

HIMATION: A himation is an outer garment, often translated as "cloak." I sometimes refer to himations as cloaks in this story. However, a cloak is often circular or semicircular, hanging from the shoulders. A himation is a rectangular piece of cloth and much longer. It was draped or wrapped around the body in a number of different ways. Greek women sometimes wore himations so that their bodies were completely hidden and their faces were veiled.

I used Greek spellings in this book, because it's a Greek book. In many cases, the Latin spellings — such as *Socrates* and *Achilles* — are more familiar. However, I wanted readers to get as close to the Greek as they could, and the Greek *Akhilleus* (Ak-hill-ee-us) is easier to decode than Achilles — which might have only two syllables, and begins with a sneeze!

Greek Verse

I never intended to write *Amber and Clay* in verse. My first drafts were all in prose, and they were bleak and stiff. One day, in an effort to shake the cobwebs from my brain, I tried writing a piece in blank verse. It was Hermes's first speech, and it came out fluently — neither bleak nor stiff.

746

I next tried using verse to tell Rhaskos's story. Verse, even blank verse, can do things that prose can't, and the narrative gained momentum and vitality. At that time, I was steeping myself in Greek literature. I found myself intrigued by a technique used in Greek plays called strophe-antistrophe. I decided to use the English words *turn-counterturn* for this technique.

Strophe means "turn," and Greek plays featured a chorus of dancers and singers who circled the stage, singing their point of view about what was taking place. This turn, or strophe, was followed by the counterturn, or antistrophe — a repeat of the same tune with the chorus circling in the opposite direction, often voicing a contrasting opinion. There might also be an epode, which I renamed *stance*. As the chorus sang the epode, they stood still in the middle of the stage.

Because the strophe and antistrophe were sung to the same tune, the verses had to mirror each other. When I wrote my turn-counterturn pieces, I tried to achieve this effect with syllabics: for example, if character number one speaks twelve syllables in line 14, line 14 for character number two will also be twelve syllables long. The syllabic lines made the turn-counterturn pieces finicky to write, but also fascinating. Because the lines mirrored each other, the two characters tend to reach dramatic peaks at the same time.

Homer's two great epics, *The Iliad* and *The Odyssey*, were written in dactylic hexameter. The American poet Henry Wadsworth Longfellow was inspired by Homer when he wrote his long poem *Evangeline*. His dactylic hexameter sounds like this:

THIS is the FOR-est pri-ME-val the MUR-mur-ing PINES and the HEM-LOCKS

ONE two three, ONE two three, ONE two three, ONE two three, ONE two three, ONE TWO

It's an interesting rhythm, but very chanty in English. If you listen to someone reciting Homer in Greek, it's sonorous rather than chanty. All the same, I wanted to use a little dactylic hexameter, even in faulty English. So there are lines of dactylic hexameter inserted here and there, especially in places where the reader's view opens to a panorama, or the action quickens.

I used elegiac couplets (dactylic hexameter followed by dactylic pentameter) for the transformation of Thratta into a dolphin. I also used elegiac couplets when Athena narrates part of Sokrates's trial. Unlike Rhaskos and the gods, Melisto resisted being put into verse, and so her story is told in prose. She does, however, speak in hendecasyllables when she complains about being a ghost (eleven syllables to the line and a strict pattern of strong and weak beats. For some reason, the rhythm seemed appropriate for a ghost).

History: Real People

Amber and Clay is a historical novel: that is, a combination of story and history. Whenever I read a historical novel, I'm often curious about what is historic and what was made up.

The smallest seed of *Amber and Clay* was planted when I read a brief play, or dialogue, called the *Meno*, which was written by Sokrates's pupil Plato. The *Meno* features the characters Menon, Sokrates, and an enslaved boy, whom I named Rhaskos.

Sokrates was a real person. Though he was one of the most famous thinkers who ever lived, he never wrote anything down. All the same, we know what he thought because three people who knew him well wrote about him. First and foremost was the philosopher and poet known as Plato. The Greek general Xenophon also wrote Socratic dialogues, and the playwright Aristophanes mocked Sokrates in his play *The Clouds*. (It is said that when Sokrates saw himself ridiculed on stage, he stood up in the audience and took a bow.) Though the three accounts of him differ, they fit together to show one man: a person who was endlessly curious, talkative, and eccentric. Sokrates had a playful mind, but he was deeply serious about his search for truth. I tried to make Sokrates's imaginary dialogues with Rhaskos a showcase for his ideas.

The enslaved boy in the *Meno* is never named. He may not have been a child at all, because in ancient Greece, enslaved men were called *boy* as long as they lived.

On the other hand, he could have been a child. Sokrates was trying to prove a point about learning and memory, and he chose to question someone who had never been taught geometry. A child might have suited his dramatic purpose better than an adult. Whoever he was, he comes off well in the dialogue. He was honest about what he didn't know and intelligent enough to solve the problem.

Other real people in *Amber and Clay* are Alkibiades, Anytus, and Menon himself. (Sokrates's friend Xenophon knew Menon well. He detested him.) Sokrates had a wife named Xanthippe and three sons, one of whom appears near the end of the book. I gave Plato a cameo appearance on page 394, but I used his real name, Aristokles. In the Menon household, Alexidemus and Thucydides (not the Greek historian) were real people. Galene, Tycho, Timaeus, Lykos, and all the enslaved household members except for Rhaskos are imaginary.

The characters Melisto (and her entire household) and Phaistus (and his whole household) are made up. Simon the cobbler, however, was real, and archeologists have found the site of his shop.

History: The Death of Sokrates

I worry that a reader of *Amber and Clay* may feel cheated and confused, because the death of Sokrates doesn't seem to make sense. Why was he put to death? Though Sokrates was associated with the corrupt and charismatic Alkibiades, he was known for his virtuous life.

The truth is that there was no single or clear reason why he should have been killed — nothing that makes sense to people of the twenty-first century. Historians are still arguing about whether there was a "real reason" why Sokrates was killed, and what that reason might have been.

It is said that within a week of his death, the Athenians experienced remorse for executing Sokrates. They realized that they had killed a good and wise man and planned to erect a statue of him in the marketplace. The statue was never built.

History: On Greek Slavery

Ancient Greece was a slave society. There is a particular meaning to that phrase *slave society*; most ancient civilizations practiced slavery, and most ancient cities contained enslaved people. A slave society, however, is one where a large percentage of the population is enslaved, in which the economy relies on unpaid labor, and in which laws and social relationships are based on the belief that some men are masters and others are slaves.

Today we use the term *enslaved people* rather than *slaves*, because it reminds us that the unlucky victims of a slave society were people. Being enslaved was something that *happened* to them. But the Greeks didn't think of enslaved people that way. They believed slaves were "slavish" — lazy, dishonest, cowardly, and unable to control themselves. The very condition of being enslaved degraded them. As the poet Homer said, "Whatever day makes man a slave, takes half his worth away."

Ancient Greek slavery was never based on skin color. People were born into slavery (that is, their parents were enslaved), sold into slavery, or captured in war. It was against the law for an Athenian to enslave another Athenian, so most Athenian slaves were foreigners. Greek citizens often saw their slaves in terms of ethnic stereotypes. Thracians like Rhaskos and other people from the north were believed to be tough and hardy, but brutal and thickheaded. Persians and Syrians, born in a warmer climate, were considered skillful at handiwork, but timid and frail. The Greeks saw themselves as balanced between barbarian extremes: they were strong *and* intelligent *and* skillful and brave.

Nobody knows how many enslaved people lived in Athens during the fourth and fifth centuries BCE. Most of my reference books estimate that at least one-third of the population was enslaved. These enslaved people did almost every kind of work there was to do. A company of Skythian slaves was armed with whips and instructed to keep order in the city. Enslaved people were bankers and teachers, farmers and craftsmen, cooks, wet nurses, entertainers, sex workers, and miners. The only thing that enslaved people did not do was run the government. Only male citizens could be part of the democracy. Slaves, like women and foreigners, had no vote.

I would love to say that Sokrates criticized slavery and wished to abolish it. He didn't. Neither did his contemporaries. Sokrates liked arguing philosophy so much that he spent time talking to enslaved people, and even to women. But for Sokrates, slavery, like war, was not so much an evil to be uprooted, but a fact of life.

History: On Animal Sacrifice

The Greeks were a religious people: almost every day was the birthday of a god, and that meant there had to be a sacrifice. Before every performance of the theatre, and every meeting of the government, an animal was sacrificed.

The animals that were killed were almost always domesticated animals, though stags were sometimes sacrificed to Artemis. Before the sacrifice, the victims were groomed, fed, petted, and distracted. It was considered unlucky for the animal to struggle or suffer, so they were killed as quickly as possible. When the death blow was given, the women present cried out in mourning.

The blood from the animal was splashed on the altar, and the meat was divided among the people who had witnessed the sacrifice. Meat was precious in ancient Greece. Because it was shared as part of a religious ritual, the poor got a few mouthfuls, as well as the rich.

History: About Brauron and the Little Bears

As Hermes tells the reader, there is almost nothing known about the little girls who "played the bear" at Brauron. The playwright Aristophanes wrote one line about them: one. There are three later manuscripts that tell us more about that single line; they give us the story of the slain bear and the angry goddess. The three manuscripts are similar, but the details vary.

I visited Greece and traveled to Brauron when I researched this story. Brauron is hauntingly beautiful, and there's a museum full of the artifacts that archaeologists have found there: statues of children, pottery, loom weights, and jewelry. Many tiny cups — the *krateriskoi* — have been unearthed, but only a small percentage of them have been photographed or catalogued. (As archaeologists remind us, we can't jump to the conclusion that the pictures on the cups are snapshots of daily life at Brauron.)

So Brauron is full of question marks. Nobody knows how many girls went to Brauron to serve as bears, or what they did, or how long they stayed. Nobody is sure how old the Little Bears were. On the cups I was able to see, they looked young, so I decided to agree with the majority of the scholars, who think the girls were five to ten years old. A few of the cups show girls running with torches, which granted me permission to set some of the scenes at night.

There is no evidence, written or archaeological, that shows how the girls traveled from Athens to Brauron — a journey of twenty-four miles. As a storyteller, I had to work out the details. I thought the girls would need adults to show the way, something to eat, and donkeys to carry the food. I decided that the yellow robes mentioned by Aristophanes would be himations, large and warm enough to serve as blankets at night. I tried to think logically, as well as dramatically: How does Artemis behave in Greek myths? What kinds of behaviors might please her? How could girls "playing the bears" serve the city of Athens? What bear behaviors might they imitate?

I am indebted to Thomas Scanlon, in his *Eros and Greek Athletics*, for pointing out the splayed fingers of the little girls running on the *krateriskoi*. Since the pots are so small, it took trouble to draw those tiny fingers: they must have been important. The splayed fingers suggested bear claws to Scanlon, and from this I decided that when the girls were running, they were impersonating bears. I am also indebted to Susan Guettel Cole's *Landscapes, Gender, and Ritual Space* for pointing out that Brauron was the frontier of Athens, and that the rituals performed there might have been devised to guard the central city. Neither Ms. Cole nor Mr. Scanlon is to blame for the imaginative leaps I took after I encountered their ideas.

A historical novel, like a daimon, is a kind of mule: half history, half story. Every author has to make up her mind how to handle the two halves. I tried to be as accurate as I could with the history — I did not, for example, create a Sokrates who wanted to abolish slavery. But when the facts are unknown, I felt quite comfortable using my imagination. In the case of Brauron, the facts are few, and the chapters are almost entirely my invention.

BIBLIOGRAPHY

Blundell, Sue, and Margaret Williamson, eds. *The Sacred and the Feminine in Ancient Greece.* Digital ed. London: Routledge, 2005.

Burkert, Walter. *Greek Religion.* Translated by John Raffan. Cambridge, MA: Harvard University Press, 2001.

Clark, Andrew J., Maya Elston, and Mary Louise Hart. *Understanding Greek Vases: A Guide to Terms, Styles, and Techniques.* Los Angeles: Getty Publications, 2002.

Cole, Susan Guettel. *Landscapes, Gender, and Ritual Space: The Ancient Greek Experience.* Berkeley: University of California Press, 2004.

Connelly, Joan Breton. *Portrait of a Priestess: Women and Ritual in Ancient Greece.*

Princeton, NJ: Princeton University Press, 2010.

Connolly, Peter, and Hazel Dodge. *The Ancient City: Life in Classical Athens and Rome.* Oxford: Oxford University Press, 2001.

Dowden, Ken. *Death and the Maiden: Girls' Initiation Rites in Greek Mythology.* London: Routledge, 1989.

—————. "Myth: Brauron & Beyond." *Dialogues d'histoire ancienne* 16, no. 2 (1990): 29–43.

Faraone, Christopher A. "Ancient Greek Curse Tablets." Fathom Archive, University of Chicago Library Digital Collections, 2001, http://fathom.lib.uchicago.edu/1/777777122300/.

Findlay, Ronald. "Slavery, Incentives, and Manumission: A Theoretical Model." *Journal of Political Economy* 83, no. 5 (October 1975): 923–934.

Fisher, N. R. E. *Slavery in Classical Greece.* 2nd ed. London: Bristol Classical, 2003.

Forsdyke, Sara. *Slaves Tell Tales: And Other Episodes in the Politics of Popular Culture in Ancient Greece.* Princeton, NJ: Princeton University Press, 2012.

Garland, Robert. *Ancient Greece: Everyday Life in the Birthplace of Western Civilization.* New York: Sterling, 2013.

The Greeks: Agamemnon to Alexander the Great. Washington, DC: National Geographic Museum, 2016. This exhibition allowed me to use a strigil, touch newly minted bronze, and examine maps, statues, weapons, vases, coins, and an installation of a Greek burial with grave goods.

Hanson, Victor Davis. *A War Like No Other: How the Athenians and Spartans Fought the Peloponnesian War.* New York: Random House, 2006.

Homer. *The Iliad.* Translated by Robert Fagles. Revised ed. New York: Penguin Books, 2001.

———. *The Odyssey.* Translated by Robert Fagles. Read by Ian McKellen. New York: Penguin Audiobooks, 2008.

Hughes, Bettany. *The Hemlock Cup: Socrates, Athens and the Search for the Good Life.* New York: Vintage Books, 2012.

Johnson, David M. *Socrates and Athens.* Cambridge: Cambridge University Press, 2011.

Johnston, Sarah Iles. *Restless Dead: Encounters between the Living and the Dead in Ancient Greece.* Berkeley: University of California Press, 2007.

Klein, Jacob. *A Commentary on Plato's Meno.* Chapel Hill: University of North Carolina Press, 1965.

Lefkowitz, Mary R., and James S. Romm, eds. *The Greek Plays: Sixteen Plays by Aeschylus, Sophocles, and Euripides.* New York: Modern Library, 2016.

Marinatos, Nanno. "The Arkteia and the Gradual Transformation of the Maiden into a Woman." In *Le orse di Brauron: Un rituale di iniziazione femminile nel santuario di Artemide,* edited by Bruno Gentili and Franca Perusino, 29–42. Pisa: ETS, 2002.

Matyszak, Philip. *Ancient Athens on Five Drachmas a Day: Where to Eat, Drink and Meet a Philosopher — Your Guide to the Cradle of Western Culture.* London: Thames and Hudson, 2008.

Mili, Maria. *Religion and Society in Ancient Thessaly.* Oxford: Oxford University Press, 2015.

Neils, Jenifer, and John H. Oakley. *Coming of Age in Ancient Greece: Images of Childhood from the Classical Past.* New Haven, CT: Yale University Press, 2003.

Oakley, John H. *The Greek Vase: The Art of the Storyteller.* London: British Museum Press, 2013.

Plato. *The Collected Dialogues of Plato, Including the Letters.* Edited by Edith Hamilton and Huntington Cairns. Translated by Lane Cooper. Princeton, NJ: Princeton University Press, 1961.

——————. *Plato's Meno.* Edited by R. S. Bluck. Cambridge: Cambridge University Press, 2010.

Reilly, Linda Collins. *Slaves in Ancient Greece: Slaves from Greek Manumission Inscriptions.* Chicago: Ares, 1978.

Roberts, J. W. *City of Sokrates: An Introduction to Classical Athens.* London: Routledge & Kegan Paul, 1984.

Scanlon, Thomas F. *Eros and Greek Athletics.* New York: Oxford University Press, 2002.

Schreiber, Toby. *Athenian Vase Construction: A Potter's Analysis.* Malibu, CA: J. Paul Getty Museum, 1999.

Sears, Matthew A. *Athens, Thrace, and the Shaping of Athenian Leadership*. Cambridge: Cambridge University Press, 2013.

Seus, Doug. Telephone interview by the author. October 14, 2017.

Sosin, Joshua D. "Manumission with *Paramone*: Conditional Freedom?" *TAPA* 145, no. 2 (2015): 325–381, https://muse.jhu.edu/article/596191.

Sourvinou-Inwood, Christiane. "Ancient Rites and Modern Constructs: On the Brauronian Bears Again." *Bulletin of the Institute of Classical Studies* 37 (1990): 1–14.

——————. *Studies in Girls' Transitions: Aspects of the Arkteia and Age Representation in Attic Iconography*. Athens: Kardamitsa, 1988.

The Theoi Project, https://www.theoi.com.

Vlassopoulos, Kostas. "Athenian Slave Names and Athenian Social History." *Zeitschrift für Papyrologie und Epigraphik* 175 (2010): 113–144.

Wrenhaven, Kelly L. *Reconstructing the Slave: The Image of the Slave in Ancient Greece*. London: Bloomsbury, 2013.

Xenophon. *Conversations of Socrates.* Translated by Hugh Tredennick and Robin Waterfield. London: Penguin, 2004.

Zelnick-Abramovitz, Rachel. *Not Wholly Free: The Concept of Manumission and the Status of Manumitted Slaves in the Ancient Greek World.* Leiden: Brill, 2005.

COPYRIGHT ACKNOWLEDGMENTS

I am also indebted to the Andante archaeological tour "Greece Uncovered" that I took back in October 2015. I met the archaeologists Aristotle Koskinas and Ioannis Georganas during that tour, and they were generous with their knowledge, answering every question.

About the Author

~~~~~~~~~~~~~~~~~~

Laura Amy Schlitz is the author of the Newbery Medal–winning *Good Masters! Sweet Ladies! Voices from a Medieval Village;* the Newbery Honor Book and New York Times bestseller *Splendors & Glooms; The Hired Girl,* recipient of the Scott O'Dell Award for Historical Fiction and the National Jewish Book Award; and several other books for young readers. A teacher as well as a writer, Laura Amy Schlitz lives in Maryland.

Julia Iredale is an artist who works as a freelance illustrator for clients around the world. Her work is informed by her love of mythology, dark fantasy, and human psychology, weaving these together to create beautiful, mysterious characters and worlds. She lives in Victoria, British Columbia.

The employees of Thorndike Press hope you have enjoyed this Large Print book. All our Thorndike, Wheeler, and Kennebec Large Print titles are designed for easy reading, and all our books are made to last. Other Thorndike Press Large Print books are available at your library, through selected bookstores, or directly from us.

For information about titles, please call:
(800) 223-1244

or visit our website at:
http://gale.cengage.com/thorndike

To share your comments, please write:
Publisher
Thorndike Press
10 Water St., Suite 310
Waterville, ME 04901